This is a work of fiction. Names, characters, places, and incidents either are the product of the author's imagination or are used fictitiously. Any resemblance to actual persons, living or dead, events, or locales is entirely coincidental.

Copyright © 2025 by Andrew Jones

All rights reserved. No part of this book may be reproduced or used in any manner without written permission of the copyright owner except for the use of quotations in a book review.

First paperback edition May 2025

Cover Photo by Ahmed Kurt

ISBN 9798316006441 (paperback)

No generative artificial intelligence (AI) was used in the writing of this work.

The author expressly prohibits any entity from using this publication for purposes of training AI technologies to generate text, including without limitation technologies that are capable of generating works in the same style or genre as this publication.

The author reserves all rights to license use of this work for generative AI training and development of machine learning language

For Dylan & Ryan

Brothers True

THE FERRYMAN UPON THE PLAINS

ONE

 THE LAST STRANGLE-WISPS of his grey-white hair danced in the light breeze of the summer evening, a wind far warmer than would quench need in the dried land surrounding him. Even the roaring river beyond gasped for something akin to rain, a little respite from this long and heavy season. Samwell sat on his pristine wooden stool, wishing for more cover atop his balding head, or if not such a miracle maybe the bushel of back-head hair that stubbornly grew only among itself would stop sweating him so. He felt comfortable atop his stool, it'd been with him through the seasons some thirty years now and done him no end of good on the long rests between visits. A good piece of handiwork, something worth passing down through the ages.

 A little morsel of ham, infused delightfully with chopped apple, insisted on sticking to Samwell's upper mouth, no matter how much he licked around the area. All that effort would achieve was further flavors falling upon his taste buds. Anna's cooking, even these many hours since her work was done, remained delectable. More delights were expected on his plate when night fully took the land. Samwell wasn't one for imagining what may or may not be, but in that moment the thought of perhaps a freshly cooked chicken and some potatoes bought from

Andrew Jones

Herman's farm just the other day. Or whatever was left on the pig, a nice juicy stew going, that'd suit Samwell and Anna for a good few days quite fittingly. Samwell was lost in food for thought. The river screamed for air.

    Samwell glanced over to the great mistress, how she yearned as ever for attention, for any soul to dare fight her fast-flowing nature. Many, Samwell believed, had been sucked under before his time, called to her, impossible to deny her beauty, only to befall fate's unfaltering hand. She was deep. Deceptively. A body as wide as her, in a place this far beyond civilization - could be shallow save a few sneaky ravines, but not this river. She held secrets so vast that Samwell himself, a man of many ages gone now, had discovered not much more than what served purpose for existing.

    O'er the distance before him, Samwell watched the other side of the river, scanning the horizon eternal, the heat waving land into mirage. He wiped beads of sweat from his forehead, the wisps of hair dampened down in one heavy movement, and looked back over his side of the river. Dust clouds rising from beyond, and the trundle of oxen and wagon breaking the tranquillity of the summer's late day, a little more work before rest. Samwell made his way to his feet, grabbing on to the ferry-wire's bankside post for aid, and licked a little more ham and apple, he'd be having dinner a little later tonight.

The Ferryman Upon The Plains

The four black oxen pulled up close to the riverbank and snorted, sweating same as Samwell, but sharing very little else. Sitting at the helm of the first of two wagons, a gruff voice behind a beard, hat and the rifle strap broke through nature's screams.

May we ferry?

Aye.

What'll it be?

Six a soul, plus ten per beast.

And their yolk?

Beast and its carryin' come as one, fittin' it's only as fair as can be.

Load up an ox, same as ridin' a steed?

Horse riders come and go, make money as they do, travellers kitted out such as yourselves, one destination in mind, many costs along the way. I'm not to take it all from ya, give yer a li'l chance to reach the west.

The west. That where we headin'?

Safe a guess as any, lest you're lost and thinkin' the sun's setting the wrong way today.

The trail-leader counted coins from his pouch and stepped off the wagon, handing the silver to the ferryman. Samwell stared into the eye of the ox closest. In the deep blackness of its orb Samwell caught a reflection, his wrinkles, his wisps, his sun-beaten skin, in a void beyond. The ox snorted and Samwell returned to the moment. He pocketed the coins and walked to the river's edge and onto a strong, flat wooden platform stretching out several feet onto the river. Samwell's ferry, docked and moored, attached by ropes to stringy wire above stretching across

Andrew Jones

the vast body, unto the other side, and by nifty knotting at the river's bank. A muscle memory by now, by rote, Samwell grabbed his pole, a rowing oar, and led the oxen onto the platform, the travellers hopping off the vehicle and following their wagons. The ferry bounced up and down, the river's chop making short work of the land-living stomachs. Before even unmooring, most of those ready to make ferry had paled out, the redness of a sunbeaten day lost on the river's anger.

  Samwell unhooked the mooring rope and raised the lip of the ferry, and began to push the ferry forward, width-wise over the river. The oxen grunted, the travellers bobbed, the sun beat, the river screamed, Samwell steadily paddled. Above, the wire bore the brunt of the river's flow, keeping the ferry from running with the tide, and Samwell was forever thankful on days like this to no-longer fight the water himself. Many years now his forearms ached before making it half-way wide, whilst he'd never show weakness, he slowed his pace as the seasons progressed. A passage some ten, maybe even five, years back would take fifteen minutes less than these days. But for all the tools and help, Samwell wouldn't let nature take its course, on his work or his body, he was the most stubborn beast atop the ferry platform.

  A traveller felt compelled to unburden their stomach into the river, then dove their hand in and scooped some water to recover. The trail-leader led the rifle strap around his front until the rifle-proper came from his back to his shoulder and grabbed the metal. He blew on the barrel and opened the magazine, taking out the bullets, inspecting them and putting it all back together again. An ox shook its head, sweat flew up into the evening haze. Samwell slowly rowed. He stared to the riverbank beyond as it waded closer and closer, up and down, ever closer. A deer walked to the riverbank and began lapping up water. The trail-leader looked over and raised his rifle. The deer kept drinking, growing larger as the ferry crossed near. The trail-leader placed the rifle on his shoulder and aimed, putting the deer dead-to-rights in his line of fire. Samwell placed hand on the weapon and pushed the rifle down. The trail-leader looked over.

 That's our dinner for five days there.
 You shoot that thing now, we're all going down.
 These ox'n'rnt scared o' no gunfire.
 Maybe on dry land. Kickback here's rougher than sandpaper. Your people don't look too good, not ready for a sudden swim fer sure.

 The deer looked over to the ferry, lapped at its nose then darted off into the distance. The ferry landed at the bank and Samwell quickly moored up. The lip on the ferry's edge was let down and the oxen were led off, followed by the pale travellers. The sun was making camp at the edge of the sky now, and Samwell took out his pouch of water, guzzling some and pouring more on his head. Those wisps falling over his nose. Samwell shook off the moisture and saw his customers setting back up, prepping to make haste beyond.

Andrew Jones

Lo, be well on the road. Find happiness wherever it can be.
The trail-leader looked back over to Samwell.
Yer somethin' else, ferryman. Next deer I see, I'll picture you when I shoot.
Samwell pointed right between his eyes.
Best'en you don't miss then, right here. Good luck out there.
Samwell waved them off and stood on his ferry, the river began to settle under him. Samwell leaned down and dove his pouch under the river's skin, collecting more sustenance, before unmooring and starting the journey back over.

Taking slower strokes with his long oar, Samwell rode the tide-beaten ferry across the river as the sun itself set, and darkness overtook the landscape. Samwell watched as a magpie landed on the rope-wire above, perching ahead of the ferry, in the middle of the raging river, looking around for last snacks. The bird's tail, almost as long as its body, shook in the breeze created by the river's eternal screams, and the magpie looked across the river, over to the westlands, and then back to the east. Samwell slowed the ferry down, letting the magpie perch a little longer before it took off, swooping across the sky and becoming one with the deep blue-black above. The stars began to flicker and break through the shroud of day.

Samwell landed back across the river as darkness fully encroached the entire world, and moored up through touch and many years of routine. He lit up a lantern on the dock and a cigarette for himself whilst he had flame. Samwell took the rowing oar out of the river and placed it by his stool to dry, taking the seat for himself, inhaling a little tobacco and rubbing on his forearms. Another long day's strain upon them. Samwell took the coins from his pocket and placed them in a satchel hidden in a dry bush next to the stool, clinking each one as it fell in. A suitable value for all his toils.

As the smoke cleared, Samwell caught glimpse of a figure moving in the dark. The silhouette waved over towards Samwell, lit to the side by lantern and to the front by cigarette.

I have news, father.

Bartholomew lit barely by excess luminosity from the lantern, revealed a smile across his face. His hat covered his hair and hid his eyes from light, but mustache and stubble seemed well-trimmed until five o'clock rolled around.

Well tarry no further, what of it?

We had a visit from Doc Augustine.

Bartholomew removed his hat, the brim no longer casting shadow upon his eyes. His hair, ill-kempt and knotted in clumps, danced in the air like Samwell's wisps. Samwell let out a long puff of smoke and stared at Bartholomew, his wrinkles forming an expression of worry.

Who's ailed? It's not sweet Jenny?

Andrew Jones

    Bartholomew chuckled as he stood before his father, taller now than Samwell ever could be.
    No sir, nothing of the sort. In point of fact, father, it seems you are to be a grandfather.
    Samwell let the last of his cigarette burn in his hand and dropped it to the floor, he rose up and stubbed the butt, not quite meeting eye-level with his child. The wrinkles now formed a smile.
    You are aware I detest tomfoolery.
    I shan't jest, father. It is truth.
    Then we must to celebrate. Perhaps Noah can accompany the ferry for the eve.
    Samwell gripped onto Bartholomew's arms and nodded, wisps flying in the evening air, lineage connected in the desolate landscape.
    Don't be foolish, tis my night and I shall to see it through as ever. The morrow, however, we can unite and make merry.
    Very well, you are a good son Bartholomew. And you'll make a great father indeed.
    I learned from the best.
    Samwell let go of Bartholomew and stepped back. Bartholomew placed his hat back atop his head, now half in shadow. He sat on his father's stool.
    Tis a lie, but a kind one nonetheless.
    Head home, father, and rest.
    Samwell reached down and took the satchel of coins, then made way into the darkness beyond. He turned back to look at Bartholomew, bathed in

lantern light, half a face to be seen, covered in wide smile.
 Shall I inform mother?
 Can you keep a secret for the night?
 Samwell shook his head, light reaching him only made out little fragments of movement but Bartholomew chuckled and acknowledged his parents' honesty.
 Well, I'm sure she can feign surprise tomorrow.
 Samwell chuckled back and nodded. He entered total darkness and walked still further.

 The roar of the river stayed to Samwell's left as he wandered in complete blackness, the stars above offering no shine on the land around, only in the inches of sky up there. A little ways down, a hitching post lit by another lantern found its way closer and brighter, with two grand, beautiful mares reined up to it. Samwell brushed his hand on the side of a brown-white-spotted horse and pressed his head against hers. He reached inside a pocket and took out some seeds, holding them up to Clover's mouth, letting her lick up the little specks of food.
 Ok lovely, to home, we carry weight tonight indeed.
 Samwell unhitched the mare and hopped easily onto her saddle. They backed away from the post, as the horses neighed and spluttered towards one-another.
 Stay safe, Sally.
 Samwell offered a caring glance to the hitched horse, before settling off into darkness once again atop his own beast.
 The cantor cautiously turned into a gallop as the stars stayed seemingly in place, yet the noise of the river

faded into the distance. The hoofs colliding with dirt below, rhythmically and with great frequency, overtaking all other noises around, and for a short while. The homestead's lights started flickering on the horizon. Clover slowed a little at Samwell's request and the two trotted as they approached the little estate Samwell built many years back. Three little houses close by one-another, all with lanterns outside to welcome weary, connected by a formed wooden pathway. Clover made her way to Samwell's abode and he hopped off, patting her gently as he alighted with wooden ground. Samwell took Clover's reins and walked her to the stable near, they took the boarded path with clumps of foot and hoof stomping as they went. No reason to be anything less than noisy, this was home, this was the one place safe indeed.

  In the stable, Clover walked to the water trough and slurped up many mouthfuls as Samwell filled another trough with oats. He checked on the other horses, resting up and calm, before hugging Clover one last time.

  Goodnight my sweet, see to yours as I shall to mine.

  Samwell closed the stable up for the night and walked back up the wooden path, to the house lit up welcoming, beckoning him home. The stars above were nothing compared to the brightness flowing out of his world tonight.

Anna Wright stood over a hot stove, the summer evening clamming her forehead with sweat. When the door opened, Anna let out a sigh of relief and gave the boiling pot of vegetables another stir, before putting the spoon down on the wooden counter and turning around. When she caught her first glimpse of Samwell since the morning, Anna's heart fluttered a little. There was never a time since they first met that either one wanted to be apart. There was never a first sight back after any day that either felt anything less than righting the world's wrongs by being there, in that instance, once more. Samwell hung up his hat and jacket as Anna walked through the house to greet her husband. A soft peck upon his craggly cheek united them forever once again, and as Samwell inhaled the ham stew boiling across the way, Anna took him in with her eyes.

Welcome home my sweet, little later than often. How fares you?

Samwell nodded silently as he walked past Anna, and sat at the dining table, slinking one boot off with his left foot, then the other boot with his right.

Father, what has brought upon this disposition?

Samwell turned away as Anna got closer to his chair, he shrugged away any answer to her question.

I saw Doc Augustine leaving Bartholomew's this afternoon, be it that?

Samwell's silence seemed to grow louder, his face tried to stay stoney and still. Anna edged a little nearer.

Oh no, is there sickness?

There is a condition.

Andrew Jones

Samwell barely contained his joy as he uttered those four words, he was not going to keep a secret long with interrogation like this and Samwell knew it was but seconds until they would both know they were future grandparents. His wording, however, shook Anna, and she steadied herself by the wall, looking over at Samwell, worried.

No. It's not dire, not terminal?

Tis lifelong.

Well, at sunrise we shall head to church and pray like there's no tomorrow.

The pot began to boil over, Anna slowly walked over and blew out the flame under.

Church, a fine place to send out to God for thanks.

Thanks? Father, not thanks, help.

Anna turned to Samwell, the back of his head stayed still, as he turned to look at his wife. Samwell's face beamed with a smile that lit up the home.

My dear, in a few months you will be Grandmother Wright.

What?

Samwell hopped out of the chair and skipped to his wife, holding her hands in his large, calloused ones.

Dear Jenny is…

They are with child? We must celebrate. Wait, why are we not celebrating?

Bartholomew insisted keeping his routine.

Anna's face dropped.

And you let him?

Anna hit at Samwell's arm a couple of times, playfully but with more strength than perhaps she meant. Samwell laughed at his wife's outburst.

He's surely done enough work already, a night of mirth is earned.

Samwell nodded, Anna was always right.

We shall tomorrow, of that I'm certain.

You're a naughty trickster, Samwell Wright. I should to the fort with you, they'll cut that out but quick.

Aye perhaps, but then'ed you'd miss me too much.

I'm certain a dog could replace you after a fashion.

Not completely replace.

Samwell began to sway Anna in the middle of their kitchen, a little two-step and holding close. Samwell brought his face close to Anna's, and they kissed softly.

You hath woo-ed me once again, into your arms I fall. Dinner is ready.

Anna gently stroked Samwell's cheek, they stared into one-another's' eyes, entire universes bloomed in Anna's green gems and the understanding of everything was made clear within Samwell's hazel beads. In the kitchen of this house in the middle of nowhere on this planet among many galaxies in the universe, here it was, and here ever it shall be.

*

Andrew Jones

    Bartholomew took a long drag on a cigarette as the breeze rattled on the dock's lantern, the river's tide going in and out of darkness, reaching up and falling back away every wave. Even with the dregs of the summer heat lasting on the dirt below, the air itself had chilled, the wind a little colder than comfort dictates, and with added water droplets from beyond, the hairs on Bartholomew's neck stood on end. Bartholomew found himself hypnotised by the water's movement, its constant noise, taking him out of the slight summer chill he was feeling externally.

    Baby boy, this land is a stable in the constant shift of everything, and you're gonna know so much we can't even begin to fathom, and you're gonna hear so much of what has once been yet no longer will. Like your papa, you will honor and love those that offer you same, you will grow with the world and live for the people that inhabit it. We have many seasons before you're here, and yet I feel no time will pass before I welcome you and hold you as near to me as you are to mama right now. My sweetest, the gift you give us with your life, oh how can I even state what it means? We're only hours since knowing you existed and yet all I can think upon, all I want to think about, talk about, live for is you my precious one. Like these waters, our name shall flow on indefinitely, with you is the spirit of eternal ancestors, with you is the strength of generations, the legacy that gifts us all with import on this strange orb in the midst of pure darkness. I'm sitting here, thinking of you, and it is truly the happiest feeling I have ever known possible. Each day until you arrive it will only grow, and when we first finally meet in true you will never disappoint, you will only ever be exactly as I wish you to be. Truly your own self, my baby boy.

  Footsteps broke through as Bartholomew finished his cigarette, the ashes dropping to the ground below, the smoke flying into the sky above. Bartholomew looked out into the darkness.

  Hello?

  Silence. He reached down to his holster.

  I have armament.

  Two hands appeared from the darkness, holding nothing.

  Fire not, brother.

  The raspier, slurring drawl of Noah reached across the land, carrying hot breath. Bartholomew relented towards his holster and let out a sigh of relief as Noah revealed himself and walked towards the dock. His was a weedy visage, unshaven and then some, sweaty, swaying and sauced. The bags under his eyes could carry a tune.

  Noah, you'll find yourself undone one day.

  I shall see many a winter before then.

  Noah rolled out some tobacco and licked the cigarette together before offering the pouch to Bartholomew, receiving a dignified rejection as Bartholomew discarding his own cigarette butt onto the ground below.

  Are you not intending to sleep this night?

Andrew Jones

    Noah patted around his jacket and pants for anything to light, then reached towards the lantern and began puffing away.

    How could I when we have much to rejoice? To find you're not home with your sweet Jenny, though, is quite queer.

    Who informed you?

    Noah gave Bartholomew a slight tilt of the head.

    Doc Augustine runs quite a mouth when quenched of his thirst. A healthy tab may be created, but not one I'm unhappy paying.

    Noah sucked in a deep breath and stared at his elder sibling, resting on the stool by the water.

    Look at you, dearest brother.

    I'm as I've always been.

    No! You're a creator, you shall give Father the legacy he's been wanting these long years.

    Noah reached down and clutched his spindley fingers around the back of Bartholomew's neck, those hairs now caught under the skin of Noah. Bartholomew was pulled up a little as Noah crouched, the brothers meeting in the middle and locking hazel-green eyes.

    I couldn't bare to let this moment succumb without merriment.

    Noah revealed a silver flask in his jacket pocket, his eyes darted down then back to Bartholomew, dashing a little daring flare.

    To yourself and Jenny, and the legacy of the Wrights!

Noah took the flask out and took a hit from the flask, thrusting the container into Bartholomew's hand. Noah's throat well-prepared accepting the libations with gusto, Bartholomew a little less-so, sipped and spluttered, given a kindly back pat by his little brother.

That is some very rough material hidden in your pocket.

It's exactly what's required for the job.

What job is that exactly?

Celebrating only the good, and forgetting any of the bad.

Bartholomew's smile fell a little as he watched Noah take a further sip of whiskey, wiping his mouth from any dribble.

We should have done this before.

What for? We've not had your child to celebrate up to now.

Not my child.

Noah glanced at Bartholomew, a silence even the river's roar couldn't cut through. Noah swigged again and turned away, handing the flask over to Bartholomew.

The way Doc Augustine's been flappin' his mouth, you think anyone in this country won't know come morn?

Noah looked back at Bartholomew, smile fighting back on his face. Bartholomew chuckled.

The lord help any poor soul seeing him about a fiery below-self.

Noah laughed heartily, and held Bartholomew close. The two brothers laughed against the darkness.

Andrew Jones

*

    It was blue to the east, a calling from before, harkening back beyond the journey of the Wrights, the journey of Cranham, the journey of man, the journey incarnate. A deep blue, barely to be considered beyond black save for a touch of light slipping into the faintest of edges on the horizon. Pre-chorus, this dawn would not awakening the lightest sleeper, even as the night's chill once again began to subside, the first signs of sun's sweat upon the air felt. As it was, Anna and Samwell Wright left their abode dressed up formally, hair cleaned and brushed, stubble sliced to the skin, a faint scent of rose and cinnamon wading through the atmosphere, permeating a world lacking in noise and life.
    The old couple locked arms and walked in step down the pathway leading their house to the estate built when Samwell were a more able body, and beyond. A road to nowhere laid out before them.
    Cranham Village sat still as the couple wandered through, the tavern doors not swung for hours, the tailors unsuited for the time, nary a wagon stocking up yet at the trading post. The only candle burning was at the Sheriff's, but neither Samwell nor Anna figured Hoxley was actually awake right now, likely more to be resting, feet on the desk, hat over his eyes, manning the building as little as he could. They walked through whilst

The Ferryman Upon The Plains

the blue lightened up beyond, and the spire of the stone church came into view. With it, Father Langston's silhouette wandering the grounds, witnessing souls coming to him, welcoming them in, open arms, open doors, open hearts.

The church was smoky inside, candles burning around the chapel, the altar afire with wax and wick. Father Langston made his rounds, keeping eye on both flames and the couple as congregation, Samwell and Anna found themselves kneeling before the pews, silent together in thought and feeling, connecting to the universe beyond side-by-side. More folk began to amass at the doorway and fell in line with the Wrights, before and behind, closing eyes and making contact to the man beyond. One soul chose to sit right next to Samwell, throwing off the old man, almost annoyed as he opened eyes to spy on who would disturb in this intimate moment. Doc Augustine sat in all his sixty years of life, a thick mustache, long hair and particularly buggy left eye, offering a smile and nod to the pastoral patriarch. With hushed voice avoiding echo in the chamber, his sound reached Samwell's ear.

Mornin' Samwell, Mrs. Wright.

Anna stayed closed eyed and closer to God than thee. Samwell welcomed a conversation with someone who responded.

I heard word of your visit y'day.

Nothing untoward, of course.

We appreciate your interference. A blessing to soar all souls.

Not one of you can keep much a secret I see.

Secrets are for sinners, Doc.

I shall pray you are blessed a healthy grandchild.

Anna's right eye opened and she leaned into the conversation, hands still clasped together.

Thank you kindly, but I fear God'll be sick of hearing about this child fore noon.

Anna returned to God, Samwell and Augustine stared at one another, an awkward smile apiece, the naughty kids in class. Samwell clasped his hands once again and took to talking to the beyond, Doc Augustine looked around the chapel, as Father Langston headed up to the pulpit and cleared his throat. What was to come would be a sermon of hope and love, of connection and community, of thankfulness and mindfulness, ending on a hymn of humanity and happiness. The collection plate weighed about the same at beginning and end.

Yellow like candle was the sky when the congregation made exit and wandered back to their posts among the village, the church's heat making the world feel colder even as the sun began its daily baking. Father Langston thanked them as they left, a hand held and a head nodded as every soul exited the building and began their day in earnest. Anna barely contained herself with the Father, eyes hiding the smile screaming to break across her face. Samwell gruffed to the Father, acknowledgment without words, as would be the way for most at this hour. Doc Augustine patted the Father on the shoulder and made mention of a little lunch meeting down the tavern - call it a check-up - test your constitution. Samwell and Anna waited to politely walk the Doc back to his place, still the main fairthrough quiet and sleepy before working hours.

    Care for an egg?

    The Doc shook his head and tipped his hat and made exit to his shop, his home, opposite the sheriff's, Samwell waved him off and Anna watched.

    More for you then.

    Samwell smiled.

    I'm fair to share with thee.

    Nonsense, I can but barely devour a single, have hearty and you'll do well all day.

    Ah mother, is this your kindest telling that I'm of no lunch today?

    With that you should have thought more whilst demolishing an entire plateful in the evening.

    Alas my stomach is always louder than my brain.

    Come father, perhaps if you're inclined to good fortune I might rustle a little boned stew in the pot whilst you ingest your morning's.

    The old couple left the village to wake up on its own terms, they would fill up suitably and spend pleasant hours in each-other's company before Samwell would have to set off for the day. Neither would much remember what they discussed or how they felt, but not being notable didn't mean this morning was of little importance to either of them.

Andrew Jones

*

It was something closer to ten than nine, judging by the sun's desire to rise so high, when Samwell hitched Clover up to the post and filled the trough for all three horses hanging around. Samwell clocked the black stallion half-asleep and sweating from the sun and shook his head.

The river's roaring could never be louder than the two harmonious snores emanating from Bartholomew and Noah as they lay on the dirt by the bankside. Samwell took in the sight of the two brothers as they were as adults, as they were as babes, always comfortable together, best when rested and couldn't talk back. Samwell's shadow surrounded the men and he took in a deep breath.
We have customers!
Samwell boomed out, the sons eyes burst open and they were both on their feet within an instant.
Well, we might have if you were attending your station but correctly.
Samwell stood shorter than his two sons, but still seemed the tallest man in the world in this moment.
I...
You are going to have to get used to been woken up all manner of times.

The Ferryman Upon The Plains

Bartholomew nodded and shook away some dirt and sleep. Samwell turned to his youngest.

And you, half a day early. Hope you'll be rested for tonight.

Noah's eyes shifted to his feet, Samwell's eyes shifted to the metal flask shimmering in the sun.

I'm figuring out what fixed up here.

Sorry pa, I overstayed my welcome.

Samwell looked back to his eldest, a little break in his stern stance.

He knows?

Yessir.

Samwell's face launched a smile the size of the sea. He stepped forward and took both boys into his arms.

What a day. What a day!

The three Wright men joyously embraced togetherness, before Bartholomew exited the grasp and picked up his materials.

I best be off, see to my Jenny.

You do her right, boy.

Of course, father.

Bartholomew walked off, a spring in his step, his shadow slipping away as his visage became obscured by the beating sun above. Noah slowly reached down to grab his flask. Samwell turned to him and reached out for the flask.

Son.

Pa?

Maybe it's best I hold onto this for the time. You've had more than plenty of late.

Andrew Jones

    Noah's grip remained as Samwell pulled the flask closer. Noah's arm outstretched.
    Not now pa, this moment I, perhaps most of all, may need some.
    Another yank closer and Noah found himself chest-to-chest with his maker. Samwell reached his free arm around Noah's thin, sweaty neck and pulled him in, Samwell's mouth directly on Noah's ear.
    This is not the path you need. Family, family over this.
    Noah stared into his father's eyes, even in his adult age he was still just a kid to this man. Noah let go of the metal container, Samwell kissed Noah's stubbly cheek and pocketed the flask.
    Get you some rest, then perhaps the parish.
    Noah let out a sigh and nodded. The river screamed between father and son, before Noah kicked a foot out and began walking away. Samwell gazed into the brightness to see his son return to the world, and once more found himself alone in the noise, the light, the heat. Samwell took his money satchel out of the jacket pocket and hid it by the bush near his stool, he blew out the lanterns and sat on the stool, looking over the horizon, looking at the roaring river, looking across the land beyond. T'was as it was as it will be as it ever shall be once and always again.

TWO

  A SLIVER OF SUN SEARED THROUGH the wooden slats and onto his right eye. A flickering of his eyelid before he himself returned to life. The shack was dark beyond the morning's flare through the gap in wood, and his head made a racket inside, but he was alive, he was awake, and he was alone.
  No, he wasn't.
  A finger came to light in the slow move of the yellow heat strip. He stepped out of the light and followed the finger to its arm, its torso, its face. The man's eyes still open, but he was no longer there. The hole in his temple had seen to that. He picked up the revolver. Nothing left in the chamber. Useless. Just weight now. He threw it onto the ground. Check the man, he thought. Maybe something will provide. He sunk his slender, tentacle fingers into the man's pockets and pulled out lint and a mint and thank goodness some coins. He threw the mint into his pocket, a man can get a long way with fresh breath even looking as rough as he. The coins. Two pennies. Barely anything. Couldn't get you a decent tug or something to throw back.
  But money's money.
  He burst out of the shack and ran, back to the sun, following his shadow, never looking back. Through trees and plants, passing hare and doe, he wasn't going to stop for as long as his legs would let him. Just keep going. Keep at it. A dog barked as he passed a rancher's hut, smoke

from the chimney mocking the sun with cloud. He took a breather and sipped at a cow's trough, he wasn't proud. The dog came to see him, he patted the dog, his fingers barely thicker than its fur. The dog stopped barking.

    The day wore on hard, and he swore he heard hooves galloping by him when he came upon a dirt road. Nothing across the way down, and not a soul all the way up. He stared into the eyeless hole of a half-picked coyote, wherever its brains once were, they weren't anymore. He found himself for a moment a vulture on the decaying creature, a little tuft of fur and muscle and fat, he picked the little bones out of his mouth and held them in his hand. The yellow sun and the blue sky and the red bone. He was sure he heard those hooves again. He made haste, outrunning his shadow now, feet scuffing on dirt, drowning out any horseplay.

    He avoided what looked like a town ahead, the sounds of life carried beyond its street. He had made it so far before night was to come, miles in his day now dust. The moon was high in the sky and the sun that once woke him to his fortune was making its own escape. He heard the siren sound of the river. He was close. He put it to his right and followed it. Sweaty, exhausted, thin and frail, but he had a few pennies to his person. He picked his pockets and threw the coyote bones onto the ground and looked at the reddened mint in the

The Ferryman Upon The Plains

palm of his hand. A man can get a long way with a fresh breath.

*

  The river seemed calm, the wind a little forgiving today, Samwell sat on his stool and sweated a lot less than other days this season. He stared at his boot, the dirt claiming ownership of the color of its sole, the tracks worn over years. He could just wash it in the river right now, Samwell considered, it wouldn't take his foot with the tide, but then he'd have a wet boot. Wouldn't look good if the ferryman had wet feet, maybe safer to ford their own way across than go with the man on solid ground dripping wet. He chuckled to himself. All these years manning the river, that'd be the moment something would come at him, he thought, of course only then. Samwell maintained his everyday instead, and sat there, and rested, and waited, and listened, and looked, and was.

  The wind twanged on the wire above, sturdy as the taut rope was, it could just decide one day to give instead of take, cutting through the breeze for so long it might just snap or collapse. It wouldn't, Samwell knew it wouldn't, it was built to last, it was all built to last, but man's plans are in God's hands. The old man listened to the twanging and felt the vibrations on the pole from the wind's battle with wire, it grounded him as much as it let him soar like a kite in that moment. To be a bird briefly perched, to open wings and let gust give graceful flight. Not that there was anywhere Samwell much wished to go beyond the here

Andrew Jones

and beyond the now. Samwell took a sip of water from his pouch and felt calm.

    Their figures struck the hazy horizon, two tall men atop stallions, ten gallon hats big even that far away, and making a decent time from there to here. Samwell hopped to his feet and touched his brim as the lawmen stopped by the bankside.
    One lawman offered a howdy as he hopped off his saddle, the other stayed silent, peering far beyond the river, always on lookout.
    What can I for you today officers?
    Wellsir, perhaps'n you've seen somethin' of a rogueish gang about these parts?
    Samwell removed his hat, forehead glistened off the sun's attack, and scratched at the wisps behind him. He shook his head and put the hat back on.
    I've seen many a sort these last weeks, but can't say any that didn't pass courteousness.
    The lawman swallowed a little saliva as he examined the aging soul in his natural habitat.
    Well, if you see any, head up your sheriff.
    Of course.
    Can we make crossing?
    If your man unmounts his steed.
    The saddled lawman dismounted without taking eyes off the distance. Samwell grabbed his oar and headed towards the ferry, the talking

lawman threw a hand in front of the old man and presented coins.

 This should ferry.

 Samwell examined the coins, rolled them in his hand for a moment, then put a few back into the lawman's palm.

 A discount for those that protect.

 Thanking you.

 Samwell stepped onto the ferry and made space for the lawmen to walk their horses onto the wooden structure before pulling up barrier and unmooring. The ferry's rope didn't pull hard on the wire above, the tide still calm and kind. Samwell began to punt across the width.

 Coming from afar?

 Few states over.

 Marshals then?

 Just lawmen lost in the hunt.

 These people, must be something fierce to ride so far west.

 Following a trail on the trail.

 Trail of what?

 Blood.

 Samwell paled, he shook his head, but it wouldn't let the shivers escape his body. The three men kept silent on the platform as it gently bobbed up and down. Samwell pushed on until his oar could no longer reach bottom and held the pole as the tide did the work transporting the ferry further across. He gently rowed a little when the ferry felt slowing, his arms baring the brunt of the push.

Andrew Jones

The talking lawman examined the rope leading to the wire above, and the structures in place on both sides of the river.

    Fine ferry ya got here. How long you worked on it?

    Goin' on thirty four years. Forded and built it all myself.

    Yeself? Ain't no governin' on this?

    Samwell shook his head once again.

    When we, Mrs. Wright and I, journeyed west in those days, wasn't much of anything in these parts. We figured, why'n keep goin' to find even less of anything if we could make a life here and now. So we did. And still do. Harshest, widest, deepest river I ever did come across, we did ever find ourselves facin', fordin' it was a trick and then some, don't know how our caravan continued on beyond, and whatever became of them, but I know I'm safe and happy and alive here, and this river, this darned miracle of God has kept me like that, kept us all like that.

    The ferry planted itself in the dock on the other side, Samwell moored and dropped the lip and the lawmen walked their horses off onto steady land.

    Well, thank you for the assistance and good fortune in your future. Keep your eyes and ears out, someone'll always be there to aid.

    The lawmen returned to their saddles, the silent one finally high enough to look onto the horizon once more.

Hope you find your men, officers, and with haste. Thanking you.

In unison the lawmen tipped hats to Samwell and clicked tongues at their mounts, heading off beyond. Samwell watched as they returned to figures in the distance, he rubbed his aching forearms and laid the pole on the ground for a moment. Samwell dipped his arms into the tranquil tide and soaked up some much needed moisture. A deep sigh as he stood back up and clung back to the oar. He looked to see if there was any movement on this side of the river, then turned back and set off across once again.

The river overflowed, its banks dripping out, the sky stormy and rearing up to attack the ground below, Samwell and Anna sat atop their wagon, their ox licking up river juice after the longest of hauls. They were young then. Samwell's hair thicker, full of colour, his wrinkles barely indented in his face. Anna's eyes sparkled with ideas and hopes and dreams and opportunities. She rested her head on Samwell's shoulder as they gazed at the water beyond. The wagon behind them holding precious memories of life on the coast, their back to the Atlantic that they, along with many others, found no reason to anchor by port. The West was calling, an entire continent unknown, open, the world anew, a chance to be the first, to make history. Those other wagons either settled up on the trail or moved on in the night. And then there was Samwell and Anna, barely married a year, nine of those months yolked to their ox, facing nature's scream. In Samwell's eyes, Anna saw herself, tired, dirty, clammy, but alive. In Anna's eyes, Samwell saw himself, a storm cloud behind, red-faced and sun-beaten, but yes, alive. They placed mouths together as thunder crashed, and once again felt the power of beyond consecrating their union.

    He was strong and stubborn at times, a scourge to anyone on the offense but it worked out well for folk found by his side or to whom he had their back. Samwell tested the river many times before diving in, toes, fingers, an arm, both legs, the water was cold but clean, no hidden predators below the surface, no dangers taking a swig of the stuff. It was an autumn's dawn when Samwell finally made his first full plunge. The sky was barely breaking out of its grey musk but the tide gave way, its banks dry for now, the waves lower than they'd been for the last month the Wright couple had made camp in the area, and he felt something call out from across the way. It was time, and it was going to go swimmingly. He took off shirt and shoe, sock and vest, his longjohns buttoned up but extremities now were one with the world.

    Samwell hammered a peg through some rope in the ground and tied the other end around his waist, the hammer and pegs clinging to his underwear, and pulled the rope to test for strength. It was hard to the dirt, no give in a few pulls, safe enough Samwell figured for the time and tide. The chills as he pushed body against body blew out his lungs for a moment, and Samwell took a little time fighting the flow to catch his breath before he waded out. His forearms forcing through the morning run of water, propelling him out and out and out as the water hit and splashed and began to run over him. Samwell's light brown hair, that in the sun would shimmer blonde, looked closer to black as the river wetted each strand with sudden impact. He was but a quarter of the way across the river when the first wave crashed hard.

 Submerged, Samwell's cheeks expanded, and his eyes took in the world under. The little light from above couldn't scour the depths the bed would sink to. The rope began to untie from his waist, the wetness slipping the knots from his grasp. Samwell clutched onto the rope and span underwater, a ballet of man and thread, until the rope circled his body several times over, and he swam to the surface for air. Gasping, he paddled and shivered and pushed on across, spinning every now and then to keep the rope around him.

 It was mid-morning come his arrival across the water, and he rolled onto the dry earth as the sun broke free of clouds, offering a little help from the chill and the wetness. He looked back at the land he once knew, from this distance it seemed so far gone, it looked new again. He couldn't wait to get back over there, where everything he knew was, where everyone he loved sat under wagoncover still, starting to feel a little more life than she'd ever known, than he'd ever known. Samwell pulled the rope tight and hammered pegs into the rope and ground, then prepared for the journey back. He held onto the new guide and began his journey across to the world he knew. All was Wright with this land now.

Andrew Jones

    Samwell stood atop his ferry, oaring slowly back over, his forearms aching, his back cracking, his skin breaking in the sun, his hair dancing in the air. A small man stood by the dock back on dry land, staring at the wood structure, the poles in place around the area, he leaned in and gave a deep stare at Samwell's stool as Samwell slowly made his way. Much as the man stared at his stool, Samwell stared at the man, examining him and thinking on intentions. The man looked over to Samwell as his ferry closed in to dock, the man waved showing his hands both empty.
    Good noon sir.
    He pushed his round spectacles up to the brim to see the entire world clearer.
    Hello. May I assist you?
    Perhaps.
    Samwell landed on dock, dropped lip and moored, the stranger not calculating into his routine.
    You seek transport?
    Not that kind of assistance.
    The man took in the entire river with his double-lensed eyes.
    How far'd you say this crossing runs?
    Samwell stood up next to the man, himself some foot and a half taller than the bespectacled being. Samwell turned to look back over the water he just crossed.
    'Bout three hundred foot.

The Ferryman Upon The Plains

    The man nodded then opened his tweed jacket, a hand diving into a pocket and removed a piece of paper, unfolding it from small to rather large size. The wind flicking at the paper, a light noise of air rippling. He held the paper out to Samwell.
    Would you mind, for a moment?
    Samwell clutched the paper. The man dove his other hand into the other side of his jacket and pulled out a pen and an inkwell. He opened the well and dipped the pen in, putting the lid back on and pocketing the well in routine like Samwell docked his ferry.
    Thank you kindly.
    The man took the paper back and jotted ink upon it.
    And the bed, how far down?
    What's this'll regarding?
    Just a survey, sir.
    Samwell surveyed the man, and held the rowing pole up.
    This, and then some. Ain't ever seen all the ways down. Ain't nobody did that seen all the way up again after.
    The man pushed his spectacles back up after a gravitational pull and put the paper in his mouth. He opened his jacket once again and pulled some measuring tape out, holding it against the oar from bottom to where it was dry, then took the paper from his mouth and juggled all items until more notes were made on the sheet.
    All very expected.

Andrew Jones

    You surveying a lot of crossings? Don't seem ya much the outdoorsman.
    The man rolled the measuring tape back in one hand, his other holding the paper and pen, slowly dripping ink onto the ground. He looked up at Samwell as he put the tape back in his pocket.
    You're not sizing me up too, is ya?
    The smaller man smiled politely and held his hand out, Samwell placed his in return and shook, looking down unto the weaselly figure.
    The state appreciates your many years of hard service to this here crossing point Mr. Wright.
    Samwell removed his hand from the courtesy shake.
    Ah, you're from that lot?
    Quite, and we're looking to compensate you kindly for all the efforts. The discovery, the founding, the upkeep.
    I've had many of you come by over time, and I'm still here. What's that tell ya?
    That you don't see the future, perhaps.
    The man looked away from Samwell, pulled out a satchel of water and gulped down. Samwell watched the small man squirm in the sun.
    I see it true as it is, sir. And in all these years it's never come as those enterprisin' fellas proclaimed.
    Maybe not, but this here ain't about simply off-loadin' your design. We're paving a path into the next age Mr. Wright, the state wants a permanence on this spot.

The Ferryman Upon The Plains

They want something they can control, you mean?

Not my say, my business is the crafting, not the designation.

With that, the little fella handed his water to Samwell. He gladly grabbed the satchel and replenished his hydration.

Sooner than you think, this land'll be built in ways you can't even contemplate. None of this make-shift work, this craft, production... sturdiness.

Samwell pushed the satchel back to the little figure and sat on his sturdy stool, dropping coins into his collection. He massaged his forearms and lay his oar pole in front of him.

I'm perfectly capable makin' my own way around here, been steady these many years on my own.

And yet you, as good as any of us, aren't built to continue into the hundreds. Time'll be your stick won't be movin' the speeds people desire and at the frequency they'll require.

I have boys, strong, hardy. They'll keep it up.

And you'll build more ferries? Down the whole river, fifty grandkids wadin' up and down all manner of day and night?

If that's what it takes.

The man shook his head and took his glasses off and rubbed his eyes, the sweat from sun to skin ran down his brow.

A nice thought but you best look to accepting what we offer here, for all that's good.

Is there menace in that intent?

Andrew Jones

The man put his glasses back on and stared at Samwell, now eye-level.

No sir, person to person, eye to eye, lest you lose everything and then some, these folks... They want what they want, and they get it however they can.

The man shook his pen until the last blots of ink dropped onto the dirt, waved his paper in the air then folded it up and pocketed both pieces.

It'll come, sometime and somehow, and I'd hope sir you're ready to move on 'fore you drown in it.

Samwell lit a cigarette and blew smoke towards the man, he coughed and waved off the puff.

Think on, Mr. Wright. No man ever stood on service forever. A legacy isn't something you live to see.

The man walked off, hopping on a small horse in the distance and disappeared over the world. Samwell spat water back to the dirt, next to drops of black ink. The sun made the liquid hiss into the atmosphere.

*

Many towns over you would hear bells ringing at sun's highest peak, but Cranham remained in silent awe of the sky's brightness. Folk about their days not stopping to observe the middle of it all, just getting on as hard as it felt against the heaviness of the heat dropped from above. The saloon still slept, for the most part, inside cleansed of another hearty night, only the saddest figures found casting shadow in the walls of the alehouse. In the deepest, dankest corner of the building, Noah sat with half a stein of ale already deep in his gut, the other half waiting on the table before him. He glanced at the brightness and turned away, swaying as he did, a man still at sea.

    The doors swung in and out, and the good doctor entered the place, greeted by the sparse patrons nearer the light with jovial glass-raising and general gruff howd-ya-do's. He eyed the landlord with previous knowing as he scanned the darkness and found hint of life from Noah's eyes reflected back. Augustine felt the embrace of darkness, sweat still on his brow from the half-minute tread across the street, and sat opposite the youngest Wright. The landlord placed a glass of ale on the table by the Doc and patted him on the back. Silence was where kindness seemed loudest.

    I say this with all the authority of a learned man, you're lookin' a little roughshod today.

    Doc Augustine had barely adjusted to the blackness but Noah's face was not one of sleep and ease.

    A healthy night of celebratories were had, Doc.

    Of course, only good things to come, right?

    Augustine quenched the summer thirst as Noah lifted his glass and sunk some more yellow into his pale complexion.

Andrew Jones

I tell ya, travelin' distances on the Lord's day, fixin' bones and bruises, folk surely let Saturdays run rampant lately.

The drink gone, Noah planted his glass back on the table and held his hand up. The landlord clocked him immediately and began fixing his customer a further offer.

So at least you played it somewhat sensible yesterday, right?

Noah nodded, or swayed, the actions were hard to differentiate in the dark, in the drunk.

I'm gonna be an uncle, what better news could there be?

The landlord landed the fresh glass before Uncle Noah and took away evidence of previous indulgence. Augustine raised his glass up.

To Bartholomew, Jenny, and their future childing.

Noah grabbed his fresh one and reciprocated.

A blessin' true.

They clinked cups and cemented faith in drink. Doc had already put his glass down when Noah finally stopped his sip, another quarter cup quelled.

No animosity?

Course not. Why would there be?

Everything alright?

Everything's all Wright.

Noah chuckled at his own play, Augustine wasn't so enthralled with laughter in the moment.

What's eating you, sawbones, wanna make more merry with the others over there?

You been to see them lately?

Doc?

Augustine sat silent, Noah knew what he was talking about, he didn't want to think about what was being talked about, he wanted to move on to any other topic possible. Augustine sat silent.

I cain't.

They worry about you.

They ain't talked to you about me. They ain't talked for an age.

Bartholomew, Jenny, they worry.

Oh, those they. Need not to worry, why'd they do that, they got themselves to look to, to fret over.

Jenny said you ain't even talked together for some while now.

Do what? Discuss threadin' needle, or flapjackin'?

She's family.

In law.

Law of man, law on high.

This is what they've always wanted. This is all we ever wanted. This is good, doc. This is everything father dreamed of. Finally.

Doc Augustine's arm made way to check up on Noah, patting him kindly. Noah shuddered at the touch but Augustine remained.

Andrew Jones

Perhaps make this your last for a spell, take a break. You're on tonight, right?

Noah turned his eyes from Doc's and felt drawn to looking upon the floorboards, the wall, the ceiling, anything but.

I'm fine and able, Doc. In body and spirit. Don't you fret.

But that's as much my business as yours.

Augustine removed his arm from Noah's and picked out some coins from his pocket, placing them on the table. Noah cleansed his mouth with the final drops of libation and planted the glass onto the table.

Alright then.

Noah made his way to his feet, the sealegs swaying and his boots creaking on the boards below, he took his hat and coat in his hands, over his arm, rather than wear them in the terrible heat bracing the village, and made for the light and the exit. Each step horribly close to the end, but something inside him settled balance with orientation. Doc Augustine saw him off and moved on to other sorts in the saloon, everyone was a potential customer anytime.

In the light and heat, Noah stood in the village street as people passed, offering kindness and manners. He looked around him, the Doc's building opposite. The church down the way. He stumbled and put his hat on, covering his face in shadow, and made his way out of Cranham village, and up to his house, near Samwell and Anna's, near

The Ferryman Upon The Plains

Bartholomew and Jenny's, Noah's house, alone and removed, nobody waiting to ease him in for the day's sleep. He took his time exiting from the world.

Bartholomew let the sun bask upon him as he lay eyes closed, the biggest smile breaking across all over. Jenny sat opposite, giggling at his visage as she splashed water over his naked chest. Her fiery hair soaked and dripping off the side of the bath's rim, she slumped a little in the hot water and put her feet upon Bartholomew's shoulders and grabbed at his cheeks with her toes.

You play with my joy too much I'll gobble upon each and every digit of your foot.

Bartholomew placed teeth on Jenny's big right toe and softly acted like a mangy dog finally found scraps. Jenny's giggle erupted into a belly laugh, and water splashed onto the floor below.

No, no, stop, you beast. I'll seek my husband onto you.

Bartholomew opened his eyes and stared upon his betrothed, her slight and pale frame caught in fits on the far side of the tub, and clutched her wrists in his hands. He brought her up and close and laid her atop him, their breathing growing intense and in harmony. Jenny stroked Bartholomew's face, his bristles pricking upon her soft fingers, as Bartholomew's large hands made journeys down the side and back of Jenny's slender body. Shivers shot through her, instinctive flicks of foot and elbow out and splashing water all over, Bartholomew smiled at the power he harnessed within his true love. He kissed upon

Andrew Jones

her cheek with hungry desire and closed his lips onto her ear.

Sit yourself right, I wish to pay lip service to our child.

Jenny's eyes bulged out with surprise and excitement, she clambered off her husband's strong body and sat on the rim of the bath. Bartholomew paddled his way out of the small body of water and placed hands on Jenny's milkywhite thighs and dove in, kissing deeply and plentifully. Jenny closed her eyes and found light stronger than the sun outside.

A harsh knock upon the front door put pause to the passion, and mother's voice rang through.

Good afternoon Jennydear, would you wish to accompany me on a wander?

Bartholomew laid his head on Jenny's leg and looked up at her, taking in her youthful excitement, her lustful eyes and reddening cheeks of pleasure meeting embarrassment, and she looked down at Bartholomew, mouth wet in ways she always loved, and cradled his head in her arms.

You as well, son, would be most welcome.

Bartholomew nipped at Jenny's thigh playfully then stood up, he helped his wife out of the bath and they cleaned up for mother.

Out a distance from the homestead, Bartholomew towered over the women, standing in his shadow arm-in-arm and looking at the patches of wild grass that dared to grow tall in the harsh and shadeless soil. Anna and Jenny shared comfort in the world and their place, Bartholomew taking in the two most important women in the world, basking in the light around and above him. A mare and her foal fed on some wild grass, the light-brown mother chomping down on the tallest, allowing her offspring to take the low-hanging feast. Bartholomew clicked his tongue and the horses looked over at the humans, the mare walked over, her foal slightly behind, seeming unsure of getting too close. Bartholomew reached out and gently stroked the grand dame, Anna felt natural urge to put her head on the mare's and meet eyes. They shared something so magic, a connection that Bartholomew, with all his years of rearing these beings, would never have. The foal walked into the shadow of her mother, near enough for Jenny to crouch a little and place hands upon. The mare glanced over and whinnied, the foal leaned into Jenny's care and nestled into her comforting grace. Anna and the mare took in the occurrence, and at once felt everything was to be right with the world. Bartholomew walked away for a moment and returned with a half-filled bucket of water, he poured some onto the mother's back and head, then let the foal feel replenished in the baking landscape. They shook water around, splashing the humans, before Bartholomew laid the bucket down and aided them drinking from the container.

  Bartholomew and Jenny held hands as they walked back, Anna took to walking behind, witnessing her first-born in all his beautiful joy.

Andrew Jones

We'll meet up outside after sun, father and I'll be well fed for sure, so make for eating before we head out tonight.
Bartholomew looked upon his wife.
We'll definitely be eating soon enough mother.

*

The night was encroaching on sun's station once again. Samwell was on his stool, another day closing up, a quieter day all in all. Truly a day of rest. His hat on, covering the back of his head from the last of the day's light, Samwell watched the East and the land's little brightness reflecting into his eyes, as his youngest stumbled into view. Noah had not spent the afternoon as promised, and quite openly wore his inebriation upon his face. The drunk struggled to keep his eyes open when faced with his father, standing to greet offspring and make shift trade-off, between the liquid in his brains and the light casting off one last flare in the sky before him, Noah squinted and shifted, and struggled to stand firm at land's end. Samwell insisted upon eye contact, fiercely, deeply.
Well rested I see.
I am as God made me.
God was but a part of the team there son, don't you forget it.

Noah pushed onwards and settled onto the stool, a little straighter once weight shifted from feet to rump.

I'm fine, you go home, see about yer son.

Should I concern about my other at this moment?

Noah inhaled the atmosphere, his mouth dry and lapping at all the moisture the river gifted the air. He raised his head to take in Samwell, serious and stern and bathed in orange.

I've been through worse pa, your care is kind but unneeded tonight.

Have you been to see Father Langston this day?

Noah shook his head not just at the question but the notion, the thoughts conjured thrust out with great fervor.

The only father I require spending time with is here, pa.

Samwell squinted as he took in his man child, shadowed by the world. The river's serenity matched the land beyond, and with it the old man took an agreeable disconnection to his situation, in silhouette Noah was but an adult figure in the landscape.

Very well, be safe, have a nice night.

Samwell threw out words without finding anything connecting himself or the bearer to them. He turned and left sight. Noah sat alone, on the stool, as darkness took hold of the world. He never noticed how black it had gotten until he lit a cigarette and it seemed to be a flare in the void. Noah made noises to himself in the emptiness, humming a tune he heard time and again in his days, one passed down, passed on, passing through the land now.

Andrew Jones

Samwell took a moment with Clover to hold her tightly, a hug he couldn't offer any human in this land, and felt an eternal and requited connection returned through her. He refilled the water and gave a little kindness to Noah's saddle, whilst patting around the pockets and holds, finding nothing secreted away. It was a brief moment of sadness Samwell found himself hit by, to think so low of his child, to act so backhanded unto his own, he apologized to Midnight in place of his son and rode off into darkness. There was too much good to partake in tonight, to spend wallowing in such bad would be a great offense.

*

Cranham on any Sunday night was quiet and respectable, a little life in the saloon but most souls settled down early before another week of work, yet this special occasion changed the town as a whole. The tavern harbored joviality that poured out into the atmosphere, almost to the river the noise and feeling carried. The community together in celebration inside the building, the beloved widow Madame Westington making the piano sing its heart out, whilst stableman Colin Maclaine bowed his fiddle with glee, Samwell tapped his foot on the wooden boards, keeping the beat as he felt compelled to reach into his jacket pocket and bring out a harmonica, the universe puppeting love and mirth through these figures.

    Samwell had managed to dive into a quick bath since he left his station by the river, and Anna had made damn sure his hair was looking respectable, any strays sliced, his beard trimmed a touch. Anna herself was sitting at a table in the middle of the saloon, next to dear Jenny and Bartholomew, clapping along to the music. Anna once again adorning the Sunday Best that had only had an outing half a day before. A few glasses of sherry on the table, half-empty, made Jenny and Bartholomew's desire to get on their feet and parade one-another about the floor to the rhythms of the sound impossible to deny. They were soon joined by many denizens of the region, all matching joy and love with the couple.

    The first to offer congratulations was the landlord Christian Olsen, dropping offer further glasses of sherry to the Wright's table and watching the elder man playing on his instrument. Olsen's jawline rarely made move for a smile, his emotions were hunkered within a big burly shell made to handle any and all situations that came his way, but this night saw fit to twinkle a little life in his eye. He kissed Anna on the hand and returned to his post by the bar as custom increased.

    Doc Augustine stopped by and sat in Samwell's seat by Anna to watch the fun, himself drinking a whiskey, clinking Anna's sherry glass. He was as close to a brother and an uncle that the Wrights had, and they welcomed his presence, moreso during moments as wondrous and hopeful as this than those times the doctor was called upon in fear and tragedy. He handed his spot back to

Andrew Jones

Samwell after a while, the old man necking his half-full glass and beginning on the fresh batch Christian kindly poured out a few songs prior.

    The young couple still desired the floor and one-another wrapped in arms and music, all eyes upon them. They weren't entirely alone there, with the musicians, as the sheriff Hoxley and his wife held one-another next to the youth. Hoxley the sheriff was a man in his forties - if you could believe that - whose eyes jumped to everything that moved around, without ever moving his tall, thin head. The wrinkles craggled around his face, time and life soaked into his facade, covered by a thick mustache and sideburns flavored salt and pepper. His wife a plump and cute woman still in the throws of her thirties let her blonde hair shine in the candlelight and her floral dress draped upon her revealing curves that delighted her husband, no matter how many times he took sight of her. It was a pure and full love between these two, and even next to the young couple sharing their wondrous news, they remained the most important part of one-another's life. They managed to take time out of their bubble to warmly smile upon Jenny and Bartholomew, shake hands, hug, kiss and discuss a good time to share a meal that the each one knew would never occur, but it did pleasantries to lie a little.

    An accordion joined the lively affair, swiftly followed by a bassline, the twins Thomas and Maxwell Mann had arrived, the double bass dominating the three-minute-younger brother whilst Thomas was able to dance and play and sing to the happy couple all at once. Both men could be dressed for the occasion, but it was their nature as the local tailors to be so suave at every opportunity. Thomas in blue, Maxwell in red, both allowing their light brown hair and thin, pointed faces to frame their bodies with a particular style and elegance that many others in town perhaps only dreamt of achieving, if they had time away from manual labor of course. A gorgeous patterned texture tailored for Lars Skellig, the young and handsome Swedish transplant, would be wasted within five minutes of his daily routine, hauling goods and tack about the place, through the dust and dirt and amid livestock.

    Lars was tapping away sitting on a chair nearer the saloon doors, able to overlook the street outside in case someone suddenly was in need of aid. He drank slowly of his ale, nursing the liquid, and found himself often drawn to the woman a table away, sitting on her lonesome for the time, dressed in plaid with a scarf of silk defining a neckline and hiding a little of her welcoming bosom. Hazel Worthing, textile weaver, was enjoying seeing her frequent partners the Manns performing so passionately, although suddenly finding herself alone in the saloon had her a little disconcerted. She looked around, saw Lars glance over and quickly avert his eyes, and decided to take her drink and sit by Anna. The mother had just finished tender conversation with Lauren Harding, covered in fineries and new husband Kelso in hand, the heiress was detailing to Anna possibilities of infrastructure investment in the area, a time Anna was glad to have music drown out other noise. Kelso Harding-Grant stopped Hazel in their walks to and from the Wright table and mentioned an expected delivery of wool and dye at his post in the morrow, something Hazel passed on kindly by, trying to sell on a Sunday night wasn't in her interest, and it still felt like neither Lauren nor Kelso were really interested in the Cranham community, rather the funds inherent to the people living there. The richest people in town headed to the very edge of the saloon, and would spend the night looking at the rest of town, distant and removed.

    The last arrival was Herman Ganz, the farmer, who had spent the last few hours dealing with some henhouse issues and had to wash various stains from his skin before returning to humanity. In his over-half-a-century of experience working with creatures and the land, today was not even close to the most exhausting of days, but Ganz still felt the strain as his age wore on. He made sure to shake firm hands with Samwell, their lives majestically woven together like a pattern from Ms. Worthing, and offered to purchase drinks, a gesture appreciated but not required as Christian once more replenished the Wrights with bountiful liquids. Ganz went to the bar for a whiskey and sat alongside Lars, they shared a look of understanding, they'd work together in the morning when the animals need a few more hands on deck.

The Ferryman Upon The Plains

  The night wore on and the music caused all but the eldest to partake in the joy. Even Father Langston felt a power flow into his body when he wandered the street that night, not that he'd find himself in the saloon, heaven forefend, but he certainly took the music back to church with him. Outside the saloon, Samwell, Bartholomew and the Doc were handed cigars by Kelso, he proclaimed of their superior quality, high demand back in the easterly cities and seemed more satisfied by his own words than the first puffs of his smoke.

  Jenny was beckoned by Madame Westington to sit beside the widow and played same notes on a higher octave alongside, Jenny felt comfortable next to the old lady, she even threw in some flourishes as they played, and the widow played back similar notes. Cranham was almost built exclusively by the Wrights, they were founders unlike any others, but Jenny was always on the outside of things. Being married in never pushed her into being as noted as the family born and bred, this though, this night, this Sunday night in the height of summer was when Jenny Wright truly became one of Cranham's founding Wrights.

  They drank and danced and smoked and talked late into the night, it was Monday by any clock's belief when the piano strings ceased vibration, everyone attending to their beds once again and Cranham awaited the dawn and whatever gifts it could bring with it.

*

Andrew Jones

    His hum had continued all the hours of the night, not a soul to ferry, not an animal to disturb. Noah was no longer completely pissed yet not wholly sober, in the limbo of the liver. He had lit the lanterns some time ago, after dwelling on the darkness for too long, and seeing thoughts he had quelled years before suddenly rush out onto the top of his mind, become seemingly real in the blackness. The light removed shred of memory and fear, only the truth found among the candles and their reach. Footsteps scuffed the dirt beyond as Noah lessened the volume of his hum and looked out. Icriss came into the light, dirty and sweaty, it looked like he'd been running through the world for years, but as he uttered his first words to the young ferryman his hot, minty breath waylaid any frets.

    Mighty fine voice ya got there.

    You need passage?

    That'd be swell. Horse ran off on me some ways back, what's the toll?

    Noah stood for business as Icriss took a breath by the warm lantern, the young man splashed water onto his face and slurped some river up before looking back at Noah, waiting for any answer. He took in the ferry, the man, and noticed Noah's revolver holstered by his hip, the pearl-white grip shining in the dark.

    Six for a soul.

    Icriss picked out the two pennies in his pocket.

The Ferryman Upon The Plains

Don't come cheap now, do it? This is all I've got to my name.

Noah looked at the coins in the man's wet hands and examined the frail figure.

You got someplace to rest across the way? Someone to alleviate, perhaps?

Icriss shook his head and scratched an itch at the back of his neck, at least Noah could tell the man wasn't hiding any potential weapons, for all his fluster he wasn't an immediate danger.

Can't say I do, just headin' forth, ya know?

At night, alone, without a beast?

Stranger things happen e'ry day.

Well, there's a place not far back you can find shelter for the night, perhaps enough to carry you across to the next day.

Please, it's pittance but it's all my worldly right in my hands. Just this once?

Noah shook his head solemnly, he felt the weight of his father upon him, how much kindness could be offered if not for a profit?

If I break the rules few ya, then I am to bend for the next one, and the next, until I no longer resemble the shape I'm in.

Icriss examined the path he had just ran through, then took Noah in.

How far back are we talkin'?

Ten or take, I'd venture eleven hundred yards. Take you a spell but there's somethin' at the end of it all.

Andrew Jones

And you can see Sheriff about yer horse, not like he's got much law to be upholdin' of late.
    Sheriff? Round here?
    Icriss seemed a little jumpy.
    Is this river swimmable?
    You're welcome to try, but it's wide enough, and deep. Tis reason we run a service, yasee?
    Okay.
    Icriss' resignment as he pushed his pennies into Noah's hands could be felt across the land, he put feet into the river, waves began to flow faster, the water once rested was waking up for the night.
    You've been mighty helpful sir, see you in this or the next.
    Hold yerself.
    Noah watched as Icriss began wading into the water further, wave after wave decided to hit on the exhausted soul as he pushed himself on, sinking into the liquid as the surface under deepened.
    Don't go fording ahead! Foolish choice.
    I must continue.
    Noah sighed as the man seemed resilient to intelligent thought, destined only to continue dangerously against nature itself. Noah picked up the oar and stood at land's end.
    Get out of there, come on. I cain't in good faith let a man attempt to end hisself.
    Really?

The Ferryman Upon The Plains

    Noah nodded and held the oar out, Icriss grabbed the wood as he turned, the water hitting up on his knees. Icriss made his way back to dry and Noah walked him onto the ferry, prepping the wooden platform.
    You're a crazed fool.
    Icriss hung his head low and shook off water from his legs.
    I know.
    But better keep you safe whilst I can.
    Noah set the ferry off and punted into the darkness beyond, the waves speeding the platform up. They were across the way within minutes and moored up.
    Blessings to you and yours, good night.
    Icriss hopped onto land and began to make his way out into the unknown. Noah watched, he shook his head and sighed.
    Wait.
    He handed the pennies back to Icriss.
    If you're intent to proceed ain't been impeded, I won't be takin' all you have. Give it to the next.
    Icriss pocketed the pennies once again and smiled.
    You're an eternal kindness in such a land, farewell sir.
    Noah nodded at the young man and began to ferry himself back across the river. Icriss walked off, Noah watched for as long as possible, until no sign was to be found. He stood on the ferry, feeling the river getting angrier below him, the light by his face rocking back and forth, he was dark, then light, then dark, it was sickening and impossible to settle. Noah rode on to the world he'd

Andrew Jones

lived on his whole life, once again entirely alone, removed from his family, any purpose, he was just Noah Wright. He had barely sat back on his father's seat when he picked his flask out of his pocket and, for the first time this shift, sipped the nectar of the metal container.

THREE

 THEY CAME FROM ALL OVER, THE FOUR, but they all came for the same reason. Down in Louisiana and Mississippi, across in Arkansas and Kentucky, they'd each saddled up on bloody trail across their fair states and made off further than thought, letters sent to loved ones over time never knowing if they'd settle home before the cold returns, this wasn't going to stop anytime soon, its increase in frequency and fervency only haunted them as they laid to rest in the night. The darkness overwhelming everything. They didn't to a person explore their innermost over the embers of the camp, hats over eyes, snakerope encircling each singular soul, it wasn't to be a group of growing acquaintance. They had jobs to do, the same job answering to different people. Federally appointed, state-situated, they held complete jurisdiction but found anchor in points of the populated land and led lives hunting horrors and delivering justice. This wasn't open and shut, there wasn't such simple motives. Or there was only one motive, and it was so very removed of logic and sentience, pure animalistic rampage that wouldn't rest when they did, wouldn't suffice from one person's neck ensnared by human snakerope, it would grow and create more as it went on destroying.

 Abraham had finished off a coffee in a cafe somewhere off Jonesville when a little furore arose on the

Andrew Jones

streets and he found himself ushering crowds away from a well, looking down the hole he could make out little after a point, but with the help of a rope pulled the body of a young woman out of the water, her tongue sticking out in jest to the marshal, her eyes rolled back and her body bloating. She'd passed long enough ago for the first maggots to find purchase within her chest, where her breasts once sat. The town would be checking every cup of water they sipped at for a good month before being comfortable gulping upon liquid unsullied by the recently departed. Abraham found no potentials in the town, nor in his expanded search and hearsay of the usual ilk. He rode on, hearing word upriver.

  Ezekiel was with wife for a pleasant evening of hash and beans and coffee, a meal suitable for starting a day and one that was more apt than he'd know then and there. They shared a walk around town when witness ran through, babbling on about horrors seen that not a single citizen could process. He kissed goodbye his betrothed and saddled and rode out, to the south of the state, the great Mississip spouting dampness and humidity into the world. Beyond the dirt paths, Ezekiel hopped off his horse and followed the odor of desecration, leaving earthly sight, wading into overgrowth and heavy grass, green and yellow and brown, and then red. And then redder. And then pink brown red, a link of gut, a rope of human leading on further. Ten feet worth, leading up to an open cavity. A young man with mouth agape, his last thoughts of surprise, agony, fear, hanging from a tree by further intestine. He followed the second gut link around the trunk, to find a half-naked woman, from waist up, tongue out, breasts removed, impaled on a branch. Abraham stood opposite the woman, staring beyond. Ezekiel looked at the fellow marshal, recognising aura, and walked over, seeing what the other was already taking in. The other half of the woman, split in many ways, rocks smashed up her crotch. The two marshals took one-another in and attempted to understand the scene. Ezekiel wouldn't want to eat hash for a long time after.

 Jedediah was fast asleep. They had put to justice a rustler courting cows around the farmland and he personally saw to it the task at hand. The night was shorter again, months until it'd turn the tide, but Jedediah was adamant to get the good night after many months of bad ones, long ones, hunting ones. A gunshot rocked through the land, and he knew that was for him. Awake in the blackness, he heard a second and knew the direction. Dressed, saddled, off east and toward the water, he heard the third and came across the gunman standing in a field alone, waving him down. The words were meaningless, they were more syllable and noun strung together than sentences of competence. It was spawning from a brain unable to process what has been seen, what has been done, and couldn't parse through and pass on the information. Jedediah was pointed in the direction and nodded brim to the gunman, riding off to discover whatever was so distressing. The creek misted and

Andrew Jones

hissed, his horse spooked by vibrations of water and snake simultaneously and he hopped off and led her away, Jedediah would go this part alone. Waving off atmosphere with his hat, he couldn't see much, but the splash of an alligator still chomping its dinner guided him off the immediate danger. A crunch below his boot could have been a twig, or a bug, or please God a snake's shedded skin, but as he crouched to get a look through the haze it was aiming square at him, an arm torn from its socket, and a finger in particular forced up from the hand, directed at the lawman. The scene beyond obscured, never taken in in its entirety, perhaps the creator saw to hide the horrors himself, sickened by the evil risen and playing out on his precious planet. Strewn about, parts and parcels of meat, limbs without a torso, never a torso without limbs though. Organs bitten and chomped upon, until Jedediah found himself wading through the water, coming face-to-face with skin ripped from skull, staring at him with lidless, eyeless sockets. Silhouetted in the mist, Abraham and Ezekiel rode up and discovered the scene from the south, there torsos stuffed with turtles and skulls surrounded by snakes couldn't paint an image of how this all begun. It was abstract agony into an orgy of gore. The three men didn't speak about what was in front of them, words were never found that could explain or explore the horror. They rode the river, asking ferrymen and local lawmen of any word lately about strangers and nightmares and abductions and destructions, but nobody saw or heard or knew much more until the next massacre broke out.

Zachariah tacked his horse and fed some oats, the week was quiet and they had time to just breathe between hermits in the hollers gearing up for local feuds and the expected inspection of land by an infrastructure organization intent on building some tracks through the state to connect their freight with their customers. He was happy in his station, it was everything he could want, a life, a love, a purpose, a presence, people knew him, people respected him, people would bow and nod and sometimes back down in his path and he liked that, he wouldn't be messed with. When Nile from the O'Leary clan and Venger from the Stelligs appeared together at Zachariah's land to call upon him and see him to a scene, it sent a shiver, nothing good could cause such sudden union and he was right. He rode up a hill until his horse struggled in the steep and got off and walked the rest, climbing near vertical before he would see clearly anything that signified destruction. A stag limped around the clifftop, its back legs hobbled and scraping on the ground, bleeding as it bounded. Its antlers pikes for two heads, tongues out, eyes squished. Zachariah stared at the animal until it finally slipped and rolled onto to the floor, unable to return standing. The heads scraping on the ground and flesh ripped, peeled from the skulls as the stag buckled and moaned and wailed its legs in the air. Zachariah removed his knife and slit the animal's throat, watching the blood spurt over the land and off the cliff, down to the muddy canal below. There was no sign of the bodies the heads had come from, he stood at cliff's edge

Andrew Jones

and scanned the land, it was quieter than ever before, something had ripped out the heart of the country. A shack's chimney plume burst from silence to black smoke in a moment, its walls began to flame, Zachariah watched and knew. He reached the building in its final gasps before collapse, the inside now as outside as the rest of the land, he could see what was being burned forever. Bodies, entwined, limbs in crevices, in orifices, in headless holes, whoever or whatever caused this welcomed the carnage long after anyone could scream, and played with the pieces as toys, experiments, and left the remnants to be discovered only by those unlucky enough to never understand humanity's depths of depravity ever again. Zachariah followed eyes and tongues and ears and teeth on a trail across the state and onto the river. He would meet up with the other three within a week, and all would just know that this journey had barely begun. Maybe it might never end. But they set out, and like those they followed, hoped to hunt, it would carry on without meaning or logic or precision. They just had to follow, and hope they'd one day catch up to the carnage in progress. They knew it had to be the way, not one of them wanted to bare witness to those in their time, but better than the aftermath. They'd only ever been for the aftermath. Nobody deserved to suffer like that. They'd see to it that nobody else would. They hoped. Hope. It was all they could count on.

The Ferryman Upon The Plains

*

    Jenny carefully opened the stable door, light flooded in and the horses began to shriek and yell, morning broken all over. She shushed them sweetly and grabbed some oats, letting a few lick up out of her hand. Jenny checked on the foals and gave them a little extra food and attention, muscling out the adults who came up to her first and foolhardy, and turned to Sally, today she would be Jenny's ride before Bartholomew needed her in the evening. Jenny pressed her head on Sally's and hummed gently, vibrating through their skulls and hearts, and started saddling the mare before noticing Clover among the horses in the building.
    Nudged awake in his bed, Bartholomew let out a groan that could quake the planet's core. His eyes slowly welcomed in the bright morning light of another Monday, and his sweet wife leaning over him.
    Pa's horse is still here. It's quite past the earliest morn, should he not be stationed?
    Perhaps Father took a long walk out today.
    Yes, maybe so, and Mr. Ganz's fields are empty since all his pigs took flight.
    Bartholomew's lids couldn't hold on much longer and he was dead to the world again for a sweet second before Jenny shook once more.
    I'm going to Fort Oak to get supplies for the week, just thought it best you know, maybe go see Pa about things.

Andrew Jones

Yes'm ma'am, I may just do that. In fifty or eighty winks time. Cain ya fetch me a nice bottle of wine fer my troubles? Had a hankering fer a deep red sploshing round my lips of late.

You promise to get yourself up and out and see to things maybe you'll find a nice drop of grape waiting for you come the morrow.

Bartholomew sat up and held Jenny in his arms, nuzzling her neck and cheek, sniffing in her sweet aroma, tasting her lips, feeling her back and hair around his fingers, it could have been seconds but felt like hours just the two of them in the world, before Jenny kissed Bartholomew and removed herself from his embrace. She smiled kindly and left the house, Sally's hoofsteps broke Bartholomew out of further slumber and got him awake but proper for the day. He splashed his face with some cold water and ate a bit of bread left from days back, hard now but still fine dipped in butter melted by Monday's sun rays.

He walked the estate, squinting at the brightness, his head still rattling through the demons of the drink from such great festivities, as he breathed in the dry broken dirt clumps that horseshoe kicked up, and that strange odor of melted wax and burnt out wick that sat for hours unattended. He rapped upon his parents' door and waited. A further knock for good measure before opening up and calling out. He was met with Mother responding from the bedroom, ushered in by her words, where Anna and Samwell lay calm

The Ferryman Upon The Plains

and under blanket despite the summer temperatures. Samwell sound asleep, Anna's eyes closed but her ears attentive.

Father?

Samwell's eyes opened and he moved to look at his eldest, suddenly yelping.

Oh. What time is it?

Time for Noah to rest.

Samwell nodded and began to lean, his feet popping out of the covers, when an almighty crack broke the world. He gasped and clasped hand onto back.

Oh my.

Are you alright?

Bartholomew leaned into the room, towards his papa, but Samwell raised hand to stop. Anna's eyes opened, she looked towards the other side of the bed, the twisted husband of hers trying to contort his son's stay and his own sudden stopping.

Not... completely.

Perhaps rest is required, twas a hearty night.

Anna reached out to her husband and rubbed his outstretched arm, making her way towards his side, testing for any place to offer love and aid without making things worse. Samwell shook his head.

Can't, someone must man the station.

You have two sons.

I don't mind, father. Jenny can cope the day alone. Rest up.

Anna looked at Bartholomew.

Andrew Jones

    I'll see to Jenny again today, we may again take a walk, or dote upon this old broken fool.
    I'll be ok.
    Samwell stubbornly persisted in moving, he let out a yelp and a gasp before a foot could bend to the floor and laid in silence again, finding pockets of pain-avoiding in pretzelling his body just so.
    Very well, one day. But we shan't make this a habit.
    Samwell rolled back into bed and laid there. Anna held his hand and rubbed his side.
    Jenny took Sally to Fort Oak, she'll be gone for some hours, would it be acceptable to saddle Clover for the day?
    Clover's a good horse, treat her right.
    Samwell yelped out his words before succumbing to sleep once more, Anna nodded and smiled at her son.
    You need never ask, this all is as much yours as ours. When you see your youngest, see that he's sent home certainly, not seen hide nor hair of him lately and find myself fearing for him in all this frivolity.
    Bartholomew understood the request of a mother for her kin, he kissed his parents on the forehead each and let them rest, closing the house up and seeing to Clover and the other horses in the stable. He opened the doors and let them run into the field behind, atop Clover, watching her fellow beasts roam free in the fenced, sunny world before

trotting off from the estate and listening out for sounds of running water.

*

The stubble had become wild on his thin cheeks, shading the gaunt crevasses that made the lower half of his face. His eyes struggled to stay open yet his lower lids were eternally dragged down by overpacked bags. Noah had lasted the night, he hadn't failed his post even with his imbibement long into the previous day and no real rest for years now. Each time he tried to succumb to the exhaustion and close off from the world something would weigh too heavy, break his breathing, sit on his chest, hurt his heart. He'd shiver and shake and sweat and cough and yell and scream and cry and was thankful to not live within earshot of his brother or father so they wouldn't know how painful everything was at all moments of the day. Noah was just continuing, that's all he could do now, continue manning the ferry, continue drinking with the Doc, continue joking about with his brother, continue living for his father, nothing for Noah though, nothing was ever for Noah, he only ever seemed to exist to make everyone else feel less alone. Here on the river's side, where nobody had stopped by since the poor, thin man last night, just himself and his thoughts, only drowned out sometimes by the water's crashing waves and tidal stream, he hated it the most. The sun now pouring light and heat all around him, inescapable light, inescapable heat, things were easier hours ago. Noah found himself staring at the ground, focusing on the dirt, the dry little

Andrew Jones

pieces of dirt above the ground, the cracks in the earth that housed insects and bugs and creatures able to live only in darkness if they so chose. It was almost meditative, projecting his consciousness into the nothing around him.

    Something began to move in the wildgrass a little away from Noah, his focus shifted entirely and he seemed to wake up fully, he reached for his revolver, clutching the pearl grip and pulling it out of his holster. He stayed seated on the stool and raised the gun up, thumb on the hammer just in case, eye in line with the barrel. The grass rustled and moved, he prepped himself, you can kill, Noah, it's you or them, you can kill. The wild grass parted and stopped moving. Two tall ears appeared behind the tall strands. A little hare, listening to the river, hopped on the hot dirt, chewing on a little grass, its cheeks dancing and teeth chattering, a little stalk sticking out of its mouth, feeding into it with a slow frequence. Noah followed the animal with his weapon, it bounded about, then off towards the distant land, but he never let it out of sight, thumb resting on the hammer, no chance of hurting the innocent being. The hare stopped and its ears began to twitch, both listening away from Noah, and then it started jumping away at a faster rate. Bartholomew came into view down the barrel, Noah saw his brother wave and pointed his gun at the ground.

    Where is papa? Is he alright?

The Ferryman Upon The Plains

    Bartholomew made it to the river's edge and splashed water over his face, gargling some before spitting it back into the body.
    Worn out from the night, it seems.
    I wish I were there.
    You were in spirit, I assure you brother.
    Bartholomew looked at Noah's gun, he felt his own still in its holster.
    You found anything worth wasting a bullet on?
    Just a rabbit caught my eye.
    That why they look a little red?
    Noah looked away as Bartholomew chuckled.
    You ever even fired yours?
    Bartholomew nodded.
    Of course, plenty of times.
    At anything alive?
    I killed some snakes. Them or me, not proud but not ashamed.
    Ever thought of aiming it at something bigger, maybe someone?
    Heck no brother, the time you find yourself pointing a weapon at your fellow man's the time you should find yourself pointing it at your own head, and I'm not in the way to let myself out of this existence, so why should I deem myself God to another's?
    What if it's them or you?
    Bartholomew thought for a moment.
    What if it's them or Jenny?
    Bartholomew sighed and shook his head.

Andrew Jones

These questions hold no merit, they are based entirely on scenarios invented just for asking, I wish not to consider them much longer.

I'm sorry, brother. I just find myself with a lot of time to think, and these days the thoughts have weighed heavy towards some specific ingredients.

You're not ok, are you brother?

I'm ok, Bartholomew, I'll be ok.

Father's already bedridden for the day, do I need to worry on you as well?

I'll be fine, brother, I swear. Some nights, maybe some nights spent alone, knowing the world's having such mirth and I'm - Well, brother, I maybe need to leave my post.

Noah left the stool and stood alongside his brother, he holstered his gun and examined his now-dripping-wet sibling, the night still wore on him, no water could wash that off.

So who's taking tonight's shift then?

Are you busy on another crossing?

Noah chuckled and patted his brother on the shoulder, his hand now moist to the touch.

Time was always going to turn.

A brief alteration, brother, nothing more.

For now.

Noah took his brother in with his eyes, then quickly stepped away before Bartholomew saw the wear of the many years of struggle in his.

Stay safe today.

And you yourself.

Noah nodded, a little hurt he couldn't fully hide what he feared to show most from his closest connection to the world. He took leave of the post and walked the way of the hare. Bartholomew took in the river's sights and its sounds, he closed his eyes and got a sense deep down of how this water would treat him today. A ferryman must flow with the water's tide, he knew that, he felt that, dripping wet, breathing the air, hearing the scream, he was one with the river.

*

Cranham was awake, a little later in step than most Mondays, but before sun's highest peak, the village had opened trade and doors and walked the dirt paths and wooden boards and rode in to get a bit of food and sustenance and a little help from the Doc for that aching in the head that wasn't there during last night's long party. Sheriff Hoxley was on his third cup of java and still found his head weighing down on the desk, half a plate of grits and hash losing heat and flavor by his side. Cranham's accomplished deputies Ransom and Kent were keeping the jail proper shiny and clean, its lack of use for most of the year thus far would seem great to any civilian, but it made every day for these three endlessly tedious, not that hunting for action was at the front of anyone's mind but a little bit of purpose can turn a man's soul from empty to rich in moments. Kent was brushing sawdust around the floor and out the door, onto the dirt streets, as Ransom polished the iron bars to a shine welcoming the

Andrew Jones

light from day bursting through the little windows in the cells. The deputies shared a cup of coffee as they chored, and Hoxley's snores were covered by more work lest the townsfolk consider sudden re-election of station.

    Footsteps dashed up the wood boards outside and Hoxley lifted his head, his wrinkles danced a contortion of surprise, fear, excitement and settled on grizzled and angry as he gulped some coffee, half of it ended on the thick broom above his lip. A young boy ran into the building and took his small cap off, showing the tangled, uncombed, overgrown hair adorning his scalp, and he took a moment to breathe whilst rummaging through his pockets and revealing a scrap of paper. Kent and Ransom stopped their work and gazed at the lad, Hoxley put his cup down and stared into the boy's eyes.

    What's all the ruckus fer?

    I was told this had to go to the local sheriff, man told me to run like there were no tomorrows.

    Hoxley leaned over and tried to grab the paper, the boy pulled the scrap just out of reach and shook his cap.

    He said you'd pay a nickel.

    Who told yer that fat load?

    The boy shook again and stood silent. Hoxley sighed and put his hand in his pocket, grabbing some coins and tossing them into the cap.

    Big guy, red face, he'd run some way hisself, like playin' tag with this, whatever it is.

The Ferryman Upon The Plains

The boy put the paper on Hoxley's desk, took the coins from his cap and pocketed them and placed the cap back atop his head, he nodded at the deputies then walked out of the building. Hoxley grabbed the paper and began unfolding it, the crispness of the paper as it grew in size double each time churned the stomach of the hungover Hoxley. He read the words written and placed the paper on his desk, Kent and Ransom stared and waited for any kind of word. The Sheriff brushed on his tache and calmed his brain.

You ever hear of them Marshals?

The deputies nodded.

They's tellin' us to be on the look out fer things, listen out fer things. Ya heard anything? Seen anything?

The deputies shook their heads.

Keep up the good work, boys.

Hoxley scooped a few grits into his mouth and chewed then closed his eyes and lay his head on the desk again. The deputies returned to cleaning the cells.

The boy jangled his pockets as he walked past the Mann twins' tailors, the two men hard at work stitching a blue-striped jacket of medium size, Thomas on waist and Maxwell handling the right arm and cuff, somehow able to handle things together without uttering a single word, which was how Cranham wanted things this day. A little quiet, a little calm, as little activity as humanly possible.

The kindly Madame Westington waved at the boy as he walked beyond the village, she sat on her porch and sipped at some freshly brewed and nearly-already-hot iced tea, her daily life of leisure looking after the large house that once sat prominently overlooking Cranham and now found itself in the shadow of the Harding/Harding-Grant estate built up behind and beyond would be interrupted by the kindly cleaning of the bedrooms shared by Lars Stellig and Colin Maclaine, who invariably tracted in more mud and sweat on average than a hot and horny swine. She embraced the domesticating giving purpose to her existence after years of grief and emptiness, but in her old age it began to feel harder and harder to wipe a surface for supper so she found herself idling on the exterior more often than staying in.

    A wagon came past heading into Cranham, welcomed into a large wooden station by Kelso Harding-Grant, he closed doors personally and away from the public. The driver began to take goods off the wagon as Kelso and he exchanged pleasantries and had a nice bottle of sarsaparilla together. Kelso took significant focus on some textiles being unloaded, he ran his fingers through some fabric that felt like heaven on the tip of his extremities, and shook hands with the driver before loading up wheat and meat and potatoes and pelts. Kelso carefully carried some finely made suits and dresses from the back of the station, folded them neatly and placed them at the front of the wagon, away from the food and animal products, and handed the driver another bottle of drink before helping the wagon exit the station and move on to its next destination. There wouldn't be another delivery on the books for a week, Kelso's hands would be rested from any further labor and by then the world would have changed entirely.

    A herd of horses were paraded through the streets, led by Colin Maclaine riding his beautiful, black stallion. He tipped his hat to the trade wagon as it exited the Harding-Grant station and let the horses pass by first, the driver raised his fresh bottle of sarsaparilla to Colin and appreciated the sight of eight well-groomed beasts tethered to one-another, walking seemingly in synchronization with one-another. His own horses exclaimed at the passing breeds, getting little response thanks to the muzzles being tied tight by rope. The wagon rolled on as Colin took the horses to his grand stable north of Cranham proper, the sound of horses told Lars it was time to open the doors and gates on the lot and help take the animals in. Colin hopped off his animal and walked each animal to its house, with Lars watching and silently taking note before hauling a bale of hay to each horse for the day. They'd check each animal out fully together, throwing crude jokes across the building, and then go back to Madame Westington's for an early supper of beans, potato and chunky, fatty lamb. For them, the day began barely after the saloon closed, and they were happier in company of one-another than any putting on airs.

    Jenny rode back into town atop Sally, a small wagon behind full of materials and rattling bottles. She was alongside Hazel Worthing, whose horse had a padded backside of wool and cotton, and they were chuckling over a punchline to a joke made on the way in regarding a

Andrew Jones

man who made a wish, bawdy as it was it felt nice for the two young women to make exit from the small community and embrace Fort Oak's many streets and bustling community and superior supplies, where they could be anonymous for a moment, without being ignored. The two women said their goodbyes and Jenny rode Sally on through the village and towards the Wright estate, Hazel hitched her saddle by the tailors and took the materials off her horse and entered the shop, waving to the Manns as they finished their work on the jacket. Hazel placed the fabrics on the floor by a collection of dresses waiting for owners and poured three cups of water out from a jug. The twins came and sipped with her and they admired the fabrics bought that morning, contemplating what could be made from the raw materials.

*

    Anna finished filling the tub up with boiled water and wiped her brow before seeing to Samwell, still laying down and moaning a little with every movement. She wasn't going to be able to lift her husband up on her own, he'd need to ambulate accordingly with her. By the time she'd walk him to the bath it'd be cool enough to sit in, but sometimes she wouldn't mind tossing the man in the hot pot for a moment just to give him a little jolt. Never in nefarious mind, of course, it would just relieve her own stresses, and perhaps make

The Ferryman Upon The Plains

Samwell think twice before succumbing to old age like this again. Anna knew neither of them were to be aging backward, this was going to be a more frequent situation in the coming years, the two of them aching and paining and shuffling and breaking and eventually decrepit and stationary and ended. But please, not today, not now, not when so much life is about to start, cruel irony of this would be lost on these kind and simple folk. Anna wrapped Samwell's arm around her neck and lifted him off the bed, they hobbled together through the world they had built with one-another and towards the water, always towards the water. The yelps as Samwell's toe first dipped into the water did not belong to the same old man who had laughed and danced the night before, and they sat by tub's edge and waited a little for the heat to die down, Samwell looking out the window to the fields beyond, Anna look at her husband, seeing his wrinkles crease as he took in the landscape. Anna held Samwell's hand as he submerged into the bath and soaked up its warming aid. A knock upon the door broke them apart, and Anna went to see about visitors as Samwell reconvened his eyelids and committed to a further hour's sleep.

    Jenny stood at the door holding a bundt cake slathered in apricot jam and a bottle of gin, her smile when Anna opened for her seemed a little forced but she thrust the gifts into her mother-in-law's hands and offered good day to the household. The women took space at the table and sliced the cake for two, the gin would stay in its bottle though, they'd agreed that last night was enough to last the week, and so a little water would quench them. Samwell loudly snored from the other room

Andrew Jones

as Anna filled Jenny in on the whole sorry state of their Monday morning. The morsels of sweetness the women suckled upon in their cheeks as they casually picked and bit at the cake kept mouths awake and alive as they let the day run away from them. Jenny found herself looking at marks in the wood around the house, scuffs and slices and notches.

 That over there, I see you eyeing upon, was when dear Noah, bless the boy, was but three and insisted he was man sized. We measured him there and Father, the silly goose, got right onto his stomach and made himself smaller. Of course now Noah is several notches taller than his pa, so it all worked out for him.

 Those, well, if I recall that would be the time your Bartholomew were reading a book of some kind, men out in the way with their hats and their guns and their silver badges and the like, and Noah always couldn't be left out and tried to read the book too, but Bartholomew weren't one to have something snatched from his hand like that. They pushed theyselves about and they grabbed and they shoved and they clutched and yeah they definitely woulda smashed against these walls a sorry num'er times to get what they want, or to get away from whatever ever'one else wan'ed. That Noah, boy if he wan'ed sommin he wouldn't let that go for all the sun in summer, so they'da fought for days if Bartholomew there didn't give in. He's such a good kid, well I guess man now, ain't he a man, what he's gone and done, and you there, what you both gone and done, but he's so good, always seein' to the bigger picture I guess. He'd give away his chance to cease the fight, to make Noah happy, to make things better all round, he'd give up what he'd want for the rest. Takes after his mother.

    Anna chuckled and bit more cake, Jenny sloshed some water around her mouth and swallowed. She was staring at three divots in the wooden floor. Anna smiled as she looked at those near-holes.

    The years Father would work night and day on the ferry hisself, it were just us three in this place for the days, I taught em as much as I knew before Madame Westington took over fer the whole place, what a fortune such a bright and open soul offering all she knew and all she ever taught to our offspring, but there were times when it were just the three of us and we were having to fill the days however. I figured they'd need to learn how t' dance something like good to appease the fortunate ladies that might one day waltz into their lives, so you're very welcome for that, and lemme tell you neither them boys had the graces passed down from my side of the family, they came out as heavy-footed as Father over there, darn near squashed my toes plenty times trying two step, think the most I got them down to were five or six step with scuffing between. Whatever you did to Bartholomew to make him as talented as he were last night, you could open a school and make plenty folk around here go from bull poke to ballroom in days. Sight to see, I say, imagine them hands up on Ganz's way all shuffling in time those big bodies moving like wind across the land. You done

Andrew Jones

good with my boy, we all try to make the best of our lives, of our world, not gonna lie letting him off to you gave me bedridden for weeks, evenin' if you were only down the walk from us, but you are a miracle, you bringing him up beyond what I ever dreamt he could be. And he certainly found a keeper with you, dear Jenny. What a soul you are. This cake's really lovely, make sure you keep some for yourself and Bartholomew later, he'll be tired when he comes home this eve. He's taken Father's shift today, as you hear the man's not quite up for work right now. Nothing a slice of this and a sip of that gin over there won't fix tonight, I'm sure. Bless ya, sweet daughter.

 Jenny and Anna held hands and ate and drank and talked for a while longer. The door closing woke Samwell up and Anna walked in to see her husband, she held a small glass of gin for him to drink but gasped as she looked upon the visage of her husband. He was more prune than human.

*

 The noon was hanging harsh upon Cranham, folk finally found ways through their hangovers and were once more awake, alert and around. Noah had barely slept a wink before heading up to the street, folk passing by looking at his exhaustion, at his jittery hands and squinting eyebags and his shuffling boots and his worrying thinness, the man who wasn't there the night before was returning and looking like death had ravaged him time ago. He reached the saloon as Christian Olsen himself planted hands on the doors and stopped entry.

    Best be on your way, you shouldn't return today. Doctor's orders.

    Christian nodded towards the Doc's clinic opposite, where Augustine leaned on his doorframe and nodded back to the landlord, and towards the young man ready to plea for a drop of elixir. Noah clicked his tongue at the large man blocking his path and scuffed the dirt on his boots on the boards at the entrance, then walked away and continued up the street. Doc Augustine followed on the other side, shadowing him.

    Y'should go get some rest.

    I don't wanna be home right now, Doc.

    Come over here then, lemme give you a seat at least.

    Ya got anything I can drink there?

    Kid, don't be foolish, look at yerself.

    I'm done with reflections, Doc, lemme see something good for once. Lemme close my eyes and see something worth waking up fer.

    Doc stopped at the corner of his side of the street, a horse huffed in his face and he wiped his spackled lens with a little cloth. Noah passed the Sheriff's and the three men inside looked at his gaunt figure barely blocking any sun as he moved across. Noah took in the smokey air from outside the Tailor's where the Mann twins stood inhaling their cigarettes, they nodded at Noah but said nothing, just watching him carry on. Noah found himself at the far end of Cranham quickly, with nowhere to go and nothing to do. Except ahead of him, where Father Langston had opened the door to listen to the hubbub and was beckoning the young man to come, Noah looked back over the village, all eyes upon him, no doors open, and scuffed more dirt from his boot before walking towards the church.

Father Langston embraced Noah in a deep hug, Noah couldn't move his arms to wrap around, but the warmth and love filled him with something he hadn't known for far too long. He rested his head on Father Langston's shoulder.

I cain't.

I know. But you must. I'm here with you.

You got any wine or somethin'?

My son, we don't do that here. But I have some personal stashed away I could offer if you really need strength.

Father Langston let go of Noah. Noah looked at the Father and considered, he fought, he tried, and Father Langston saw the war within him. He touched Noah's arm and gently walked him around the church.

Come. We can do this together. You, me and He.

Out back of the church small crosses in the dirt laid out a fair number of people who, over the many decades of existence, Cranham had seen and lost. Mr. Westington, the Mann parents, Doc's eldest, the first landlord of the saloon, and a few folk who just walked in half dead and saw about their final days or weeks in the bosom of Cranham. It was a little far away from the church, down the hill a step, with flowers blooming nearly fresh from laying, where Noah felt his feet buckle under him. Father Langston watched from a distance as Noah's heart tore from inside out and his face seemed to scream silently, two crosses sticking from the ground that pulled him towards them harder than he could fight, and grabbed his soul, wrenching and tossing and twisting and crushing it. He fell to his knees and placed hands on the dirt by each cross and his red, baggy eyes began to fill with water.

*

    Bartholomew sat on his father's immaculately crafted stool on the bank of the river as sun began to seek sanctuary on the other side for the late afternoon, his hours covering for Samwell lacking in much activity short of a couple of traders passing over and a couple on their way to make it rich in the booming gold hills many states still beyond. He was thinking of that rich bottle of red wine sitting on the counter at home, and the cups he and Jenny would share that night and the next few, a little indulgence to celebrate everything, to remind them of the wonders the world produces, and how they too have produced something so very wonderful indeed. He thought of his father, laying bedridden and aching, a night of good times having its consequences, but also knowing that it would not be the last time he'd see his father in that state, time has always had a knack for moving on without care for who it hurts as it does, and that the very seat he found himself atop will be one of the few things that'll be connected to his father when time finally takes its weighty toll on him. He remembered his brother, how he felt bad not talking more to him, how he'd struggled to do much more than friendly chat since everything fell apart for him. He wasn't doing his duty as big brother, but it was too hard on everybody, their hearts all broke and yet they had to carry on. Noah couldn't do that the same way, and Bartholomew wished so much to push the world aside and sit down with his younger brother and hug him and hold him and protect him and take his pain and his horror, but that was not his path, nor could he lead Noah from the path chosen until Noah was ready to see the way. It was a long time to wait, but he had to, grief being so destructive to those who lose, moreso than those who are lost, those will only know pain for such a short moment in time. Time will take you, but it wishes to make you remember all it has taken first, the knife that will twist before it fully slices.

      There was a rumbling from the other side of the river and Bartholomew looked over to see dirt flying in the air, a duststorm coming closer. He prepped the ferry and began punting over, anticipating whoever might perchance require transport. Samwell had hammered into his brood that whilst haste might make waste, convenience was a kindness the land rarely provided, and this ferry could offer not just help but ease of mind, it could lift spirits, it has every opportunity to change the lives of many. Bartholomew's heart would lift after every width traveled that those who came across would live on because of him, that he in some small part had changed the world. He docked on the far side as the sun began its setting, the light's last orange glow in his eyeline, and his squinting unable to clear his view as riders came over the hills.

Hello! Are you for crossing?

Bartholomew's words echoed, a yell that even the river couldn't drown. The riders pulled up by the ferry, finally blocking the light and clearing vision for Bartholomew to truly take in the figures before him. A gang upon horses, all staring at the man waiting on the wooden platform.

This ain't the man what helped me.

Icriss sat atop a mule, the smallest of the group, he had his hair greased up and seemed a little better fed than the night prior, but his breath's mintiness was fading fast.

Perchance you couldn't make much clear in the dark?

I seen what I seen.

The other fella that sparked conversation went by the name Winters on account of his albino nature, amplified by the light colors of his wardrobe and the pale horse he rode upon. He had unsightly fingernails that seemed clawlike in their end points, bitten or chewed or sharpened or broken into shape, but his left hand lacked a few digits, a wooden thumb piece wrapped around his wrist by leather strap had a hole right in the middle of it big enough for maybe a worm to crawl through.

Andrew Jones

    Howdy there, where's the other fella what travels this river?
    You seek my brother?
    Scrawny, kind, a little worse for wear?
    Bartholomew nodded at Icriss, a fair description.
    That be he.
    You've got yourself a fine family there, should be proud.
    Bartholomew couldn't quite take in the large gathering, his eyes refused to adjust to the dim night's fighting the bright final sun.
    I am sir. Indeed. Need travel?
    I know, six a soul.
    And ten per horse.
    Why, that's daylight robbery.
    A small man with strawlike hair and jagged teeth, torn clothing and sharp eyes piped in, Prip was what he was known as in the circles that deigned to know him. The others laughed at his addition, but Bartholomew didn't seem in on any joke.
    An old fella riding bitch to a native man spoke up, his voice quivering in age and many years of smoke and drink.
    Travellin' a river ain't so difficult. Many moons ago we'd do it all the time. What gives you such power? Authority and the like?

The Ferryman Upon The Plains

A few others egged on the question as Bartholomew felt smaller and smaller, stepping back a little from the gang.

Wellsir, I reckon our bein' here all these many years is why we can, and we do, offer such a service.

Must be purty borin' e'ry day, back and forth.

It's a hard life, sir, you betcha, but I help people get to where they're goin', and that means something.

And where d'you wanna go, son?

Bartholomew tapped the dirt with his foot, standing in place before the river and the ferry.

This is just as fine as any place, I'd say.

Teeth less than white shined brightly back with smiles not so friendly.

The figure riding the biggest horse dominated the sky, trotting a little closer, blocking the sun out. He looked to be feasting upon a particularly juicy tomato, the red running down his gurning mouth and onto the floor. The native man saddled ahead of the old fella leaned down to Bartholomew, two different rifles strapped around his back danced for place as he moved.

How many trips'll it take?

Bartholomew seemed overwhelmed as he tried to count the men and their beasts, but he struggled to tear his eyes from the largest figure and the fruit he was suckling upon.

With the stream being like it is today, three'd be safe. Three trips.

The big horse snarled as a strange man sporting two different sets of glasses that made his eyes somehow bigger and smaller at the same time popped his head up.

Andrew Jones

    And without you? Two?
    No crossin' without me.
    Is that so?
    This ferry don't go less I'm aboard.
    Icriss looked down at his busted boots.
    Oh man.
    If you insist.
    The native rifleman landed the final words, and with that the towering figure's horse reared up, Bartholomew stepped back and tripped over, landing on the dirt just by the ferry's lip. Winters leapt at the chance and scratched his one full hand at Bartholomew and tore the skin off his cheek in three places. Winters licked his sharp nails and it was clearer that maybe it was not tomato in the large man's mouth. The small Prip and his companion, an oversized bulk of muscle called Spitzer, hopped off their horses and stood either side of Bartholomew, he was surrounded, back to the water, nowhere to run. In an instant, the three men off their saddles picked the bleeding ferryman up and, despite his kicking out and wriggling, threw him onto the ferry's platform as the rifleman and the old fella rode their horse on board as casually as a Tuesday. The old fella took it upon himself to unmoor and row the ferry, with aid from the silent muscleman. Bartholomew kicked and tried to get up, but Prip put his sharpened teeth to use, biting into his ankle and tearing out flesh, muscle, nerve, tendon in horrendously slow fashion. The yells of agony Bartholomew let out

were washed away as the ferry created loud laps of water. Prip chomped upon the meat of the man as Winters clasped Bartholomew's neck, nails clawing into his skin, keeping him down. The screams ceased but they let him breathe, and he breathed plenty in fear and agony. It was a quick journey across for everyone except Bartholomew, for him every second seemed to take a year, and as he looked at these men taking over, taking him down, he thought on Jenny and he thought on the child, and he thought on his father and his mother and how they just last night were so much in love and happy, and he thought of Noah and he thought of the times Noah was so in love and happy, and with these thoughts he kept breathing and he kept still. The muscle man and the rifleman dragged Bartholomew off the ferry and pinned him to the ground, the old man began setting sail across for the rest of them. Prip stared into Bartholomew's eyes and smiled as he chewed on the man's flesh. He could see himself caught between the jagged edges and being churned up into mush in the bastard's mouth.

I didn't see your faces. I don't know your names. Let me get home, I'll never say a word.

The albino lit up a cigarette and smoked, putting the cylinder into the hole in his wooden thumb to hold, and offered it to Bartholomew. He took a slow hit from the cigarette and puffed smoke in the men's faces, they laughed and took in the exhale. The ferry was already embarking on the next journey, the smaller folk on board, the big blood-mouthed man atop the giant horse waited across the water, watching. Bartholomew struggled through and reached into his jacket, he pulled out his pearl-gripped revolver and pulled the hammer back. The gunshot would ring out across the land. It missed everybody around him. Not even a horse reacted to the noise. The big muscle man grabbed Bartholomew's arm and squeezed it, his hand released the revolver and it fell to the ground, but the man kept squeezing. Bartholomew yelped in agony as his elbow popped from socket and the skin in his upper hand released blood by the bucketload, a sudden balloon of skin exploding around everyone, and his arm went limp and lifeless. Prip spat the ankle mush into Bartholomew's face and the muscleman and the rifleman picked him up. Prip tore into Bartholomew's belly with the ravenous speed of an eager beaver, tearing through flesh and muscle to get to the sweet organs inside. Bartholomew opened his mouth to yell but Winters clawed onto the side of his jaw and slowly pressed his nails deeper and deeper into his skin, keeping his mouth from closing again. The rifleman let go of Bartholomew and sat on the stool and watched. Bartholomew fell to his knees and shook violently, Prip ripped into his guts and feasted, the muscle man grabbed hold of his head to keep him upright, as Winters began to pull his claw down, opening the jaw wider and wider, the sides of his mouth tearing. Blood streaming out. The muscleman grabbed his head tighter and Bartholomew's skull began to cave in, his jaw ripped off and in a moment the muscle man's fingers slipped and squashed Bartholomew's eyeballs, blood and liquid oozed from the holes. There was no more man. There were pieces of humanity, but nothing of the soul. The ferry docked again and the muscle man handed the old fella the top of Bartholomew's head that had stayed in his hands. The old fella dunked it in the river and washed the blood off, a half-decent skull with bits of brain and hair attached, he put it on his head and wore Bartholomew like a hat. The men looked over to the large man atop the large horse on the other side and waved as they left. Icriss lay two pennies on the bloody remains that was once Bartholomew Josiah Wright. Dead to the world.

 For the crossing
Icriss rode his ass off into the land yonder.

 For the first time in decades the crossing stood unmanned.

FOUR

  THE BLADE FIRMLY JABBED into the bark of the tree's thick trunk and etched a circle with aid of a hirsute hand, hair up to the knuckles, where callouses and blisters took over detailing. Two x's made eyes in the middle of the new shape. Samwell Wright was full of life and power in his mid-40s, a sight of neck-length wavy brown hair ready to curl at the hit of humidity, late summer every year living out near the river proved that hypothesis. His face lacked many of the deep wrinkles that would come to define his emotions in later life. He was a canvass only starting to be drawn upon, and in the spring of this year he had taken it upon himself to help homeschool his two offspring, not as his dear Anna had chosen to do in giving lessons on mathematics and literature and grace and manners and religion but in one of the things he knew he could actually impart to them. He presented this new circular face to the boys, Bartholomew at six was as cute as the day would be long, whilst little Noah barely managed to take in the activity presented before him before being distracted by the wonders of the world around them. The horses grazing a few feet over, on the recently hydrated long-grass that later in the year would live up to the name, but for now presented itself as more of a middle-grass variety, and the five formatted fliers above in the grey-blue sky as April jumped between sun and showers once again. The two young boys held their pearl-gripped revolvers in their hands, weighing them down something fierce and oversized for another decade of hormones and vitamins and plenty of meat and potatoes, but Samwell wanted to impart the import of handling oneself in any situation, especially the ones unspoken and unthoughtof. If you in your mind could handle that then every situation would be blissful by comparison.

Right between the eyes. Put an end before things find themselves out of control. Like Mr. Ganz does his cattle, fast and effective, no mess, no mayhem, get the job done and save everyone a whole hill of trouble. Bartholomew?

The eldest picked the gun up and aimed and pulled his hammer back and squeezed and in a powerfully loud instant shot off a round right into the bark, inches above the face's left eye. Samwell slapped his knee with giddy thrill. Bartholomew smiled and tried again, another hit to the face, this time the trunk took it on the chin. Samwell clapped his hands nearly as loudly as the bullets had fired. The horses whinnied and spooked off down the field. Bartholomew took his victory all the way down the chambers, four more shots, each hitting the face or just outside the circle. Father was most certainly proud.

Noah had watched and after the second round decided it was about time he had his go, struggling to pick up his nickel weight and keep it steady with both of his

Andrew Jones

tiny arms and all the muscles hiding in them. He popped his face onto the grip and closed left eye, his right aiming down the sight and making everything so perfectly in line with his barrel. Bartholomew's shots had shaken him with suddenness and volume, he was still struggling to hold the gun up and now he was trembling more and more as the treeface seemed to be shaking its head pleading 'no no no more!'. He tried to get his thumb up to the hammer but it was too far from his tiny digit, and every time he moved his whole hand to pull the hammer back he'd lose strength holding the revolver up, it'd fall to the floor and him with it. Noah could never quite get all the beats in motion to shoot the treeface, whilst Bartholomew was welcomed into Samwell's arms for a manly loving hug and hair-tussle. He watched as the other male members of the Wright clan walked away from him, distanced in every way. It would not be the last time Noah failed to shoot his gun and change his fate.

*

The boys were nearing age of manhood, Bartholomew's upper lip sprouting pockets of dark fluff that in some light could make folk take him for something closer to enlisting than he was, whilst Noah still had a little time before he'd spring up tall and thin and attract darkness on his body and soul, he the boy eternal of the two it seemed to be.

The Ferryman Upon The Plains

Just another one of those afternoons out of purview from Mother or Madame Westington or the newly built society of Cranham, and the lads were aimlessly wandering downriver, watching the water lap up to the land, they had time still before the sun'd tell them Mother's fire had turned beast to plate for their supper.

Noah watched a small branch wading in the river, bobbing up and down submitting to tide's demands, he reached out and grabbed the wood and shook the water off, the stick drying fast in the sun. He scuffed the ground with the edge of the branch and prodded at the dirt, making no mark. Noah dabbed the wood into water and with wetness marked the earth easier, writing 'NOAH' in the ground below him. He moistened the stick and added 'SAMWELL' and 'WRIGHT' below the first word. Bartholomew watched and asked for the branch, Noah was hesitant to hand over this possession for nothing. Bartholomew put his foot near Noah's name and threatened to scuff the words out with his boot, which made Noah start to cry and in the emotional furore give up grip of the branch. Bartholomew saw to the opportunity and began to write his own name in the ground as Noah sat sad nearby, but Bartholomew saw the consequences of his actions and stopped writing his own name. He dipped the branch in the river and began to draw a circle around Noah, telling him he's on his own planet now, Planet Noah, and he's king and ruler of that. Noah smiled a little through tears and began acting like a ruler, walking in his little circle as if he owned the place. Bartholomew handed the branch back to Noah and asked to make him a planet too, Noah re-hydrated the stick

Andrew Jones

again and began to draw around his older brother, but half-way through the wood snapped and Planet Bartholomew was gone before it was even made. Bartholomew looked a little sad but walked out of his circle and stood at the river trying to find another stick. Noah saw his brother and his desperate search for something unlikely to occur anytime soon, he had been brought back from sadness by the one who put him there in the first place, it was a wild minute for the young lad. He looked at Planet Noah and the half-formed Planet Bartholomew and casually scuffed the ground around his own circle, turning Planet Noah into an oversized C in the dirt. Bartholomew turned hearing the noises and watched his brother destroy his own world for their sake, he smiled and hugged his younger brother, C to Ɔ.

    They were further downriver than they'd usually wander and the sun was calling them in amber glow, the boys began to make haste back, crossing through the land, back to the water and the fire in the sky, and they found themselves in the wide open plain with not a single living thing in sight. The river's noise ran out, the sun began to kiss the horizon and they were still out and walking in the nowhere side-by-side.

    Dare you to pick that up.

    Noah pointed to a small scorpion scrabbling across the ground, its pincers bigger than its body, Bartholomew picked it up by the stinger and waved it towards Noah, he dodged and let out a shriek and began again to cry. Bartholomew put the scorpion down and held his brother's hand, gently offering love to his sibling, but Noah tried to tear himself from the companionship, angry at his brother for the little scare. Moments later a second shriek took focus a little away from the boys. Its pitch a tiny bit lower than Noah's. Footsteps scuppering on soil clarified that this was happening a little to their right and a little up the land from them, and a tiny vegetation growth looked like the prime candidate for hiding anything they couldn't in that moment ascertain visual upon. The boys looked at one another and back to the leafy tallgrass and bushes, both landing dominant hands upon the pearl grips of their holstered revolvers, around their waists, and slowly etched forward, nervous and confused and silent as can be. The bushes shook and hisses emerged first, the boys stumbled to cease stepping and clutched hard on grips, still holstered but raring to release.

    When her blonde curly locks first launched out of the green grass the boys didn't quite understand what their eyes were informing their brains, she in her mid-40s and skin leathered by sun and stress standing in the evening's orange kiss still removed from many of the garments many walked around in of this hour. She hadn't even noticed the two young bucks nearby taking her in with their eyes as she pulled the straps of her dress back over her shoulders and with that covered from sight her healthy and sagging bosom, which Bartholomew and Noah would recall deeply for years. In doing so, however, the material pulled above her waist and made sure the boys could understand the mysteries of the opposite sex in sudden detail. Before she adjusted and amended herself, she turned to the image in the corner of her eye and saw two young lads gaping at her figure. She winked and blew a kiss, then asked if they'd seen anything they liked, taking their stunned silence and stares for compliments and laughed and put herself together properly and made exit of the hiding place nature gave her for her proclivities. The boys let her walk on first before setting back off on their way to dinner. Neither Bartholomew nor Noah fired their guns that day, but Brady White two towns over would tell them both some weeks later in vulgar detail his experience firing his gun only minutes ago, which kept the boys out of trouble for several years at least.

*

He was a handsome young man indeed, the calm and sweet demeanor of Mother and the rugged yet strong build of Father formed something quite special in Bartholomew, and whilst he wasn't one for wooing any damsel found walking in his path, he'd give a gander to gal between merriment and learning the ropes upon the river. But here he was in his mid-twenties having settled into the house Father and Noah helped build for him and thinking his life was mapped out perfectly when lashings of Strawberry And Cream appeared seemingly out of nowhere. A few nights before, nestled in the warm embrace of the saloon with old friends and older drinkers, Bartholomew laughed and talked and drank and felt his life leading perfectly from the river to the watering hole to home and then again every day. It was almost the universe's sense of humor to time that moment for the doors to swing open and reveal a visage in red and white dots, freckled in face and dress and at just seventeen, Jenny Ayers was looking for a place to rest, her long ride over for the night. No place for a youngster, Landlord Olsen took a gander over the girl as she slumped on a chair far from the activity, a leer turned ogle as he assessed her age and decided to let things go, nobody'd do harm round these parts and she seemed to know what those doors signified before entry anyway. But his was not the only gaze caught in Jenny's pull, Bartholomew seemed immediately transfixed, he was no longer part of a group sitting and drinking and laughing and talking, he was sitting yes, he was drinking for certain, but whatever was said fell upon deaf ears, only his eyes were working at that moment, and they took in every single fiber of Jenny's being as she sat upon a wobbly wooden chair, hiding behind a table of planks hammered together haphazardly and waiting to splinter any poor soul deciding to rest skin directly upon it, trying to adjust to the candle-lit room from the external blackness of night and find a little heat in the strange anomaly of the cold desert.

  He was atop Sally, riding through the plains, heading for the saloon once again after a long day at the river, handed off duties to Father, himself happy to handle the nightshifts whatever may come, something that'd

Andrew Jones

slowly stop over the next years, and Bartholomew was hoping he'd see Jenny once again. He had the confidence to make acquaintance that night, bought her a warm coffee for her ails and wrapped her in his jacket to fend off the shivers, her clothing was fine when she set off but she never realised she'd find herself alone and off the beaten path, the last of her family, of her world. Jenny, she told Bartholomew, was sent out that morning in a rush, her pa had been sick for some time and was making noises that muted the dawn chorus with worry and she had this sinking feeling in her stomach as she hopped astride the family saddle to the doctor's, some three towns over. She waited outside, cautioned by the medicine man that perhaps whatever was happening could be caught, so she waited, and the coughs abated, but her pa never showed his face. The doctor looked pale when she next saw him, exiting the house hours later, having just seen to giving a comfortable end to her pa's last day. Not able to go in and say farewell, nowhere to go, nothing but her horse, Jenny just rode off, following the sun, chasing off her heartache. It was so very late now and she just sought comfort, and here was a sweet, kind, handsome young man with a hot drink and clothes and compassion and no ill intentions. The universe taketh away, but leaves the path to something new, something more.

Jenny was staying at Madame Westington's, the widow would make damn sure no funny business went on with any of the young men and this girl under her roof, not that Cranham was a breeding ground for anything beyond pure and kind souls, but it felt good for everybody to know just how safe this suffering young woman was to be, held in the bosom of love and strength, an outsider waiting to be welcomed in. Bartholomew hoped she was going to be around again tonight, where else would she go, anyway, it's not like Cranham housed multiple activity venues, and whilst she wouldn't be drinking, the saloon would welcome her socially. He seemed lost in thoughts of seeing her again, of maybe reaching out and holding her hand, or just looking upon her eyes and feeling the universe threaded between their souls. Sally walked with haste across the land, letting the weighty adult daydream at night, but in the silence a sudden shaking broke through and Sally's hooves began to double back, thrusting Bartholomew once more into the land of the living.

 A rattling sound from the darkness spooked Sally and Bartholomew held onto the reins, gripping them tight to not fall from her saddle. He stroked Sally's mane and neck as she whinnied and moved from left to right, backed up, seemingly at random moments of movement, as the rattling continued.

 Bartholomew lit a match and threw it to the ground, the snake hissed and slid away from the light, further from the horse and the man. Bartholomew hopped off Sally and lit another match, throwing it further, the snake spotted again and silking into further darkness. Bartholomew patted Sally as she sputtered and moved with distress, and with his right hand he reached for the revolver, pulling it from holster and aiming in the direction the snake fled. Another series of rattles to his left made Bartholomew turn aim from the burning matchheads and into the darkness fully. A little reflection of light in two small beads of black showed movement, the snake was coiling and raising, it hissed and suddenly its white fangs appeared from the inky blackness. The fangs launched forward and Bartholomew's thumb pulled back, in a blazing instant the matchheads sputtered out of light, the fangs fell black and Bartholomew's fingers squeezed.

      Bright flash. Thunderous crash. Red spots splattered upon Sally's legs and warmed Bartholomew's arm. The headless body of the snake crashed to the ground by their feet, the rattle gave a last whimper and Sally let out a loud cry. Bartholomew gripped the reins and brought Sally near, he put his head to her body and listened to the horse's heartbeat, it began to slow as he caressed her and shared warmth. Sally quieted and they both listened for any further hissing, any rattles, any soil sliding. After a minute, Bartholomew holstered his weapon and picked up the scaly snakeskin, he shook the tail and the rattle spooked Sally, but Bartholomew showed her he was in control, she settled again. They headed off to the saloon, both needing a drink after this. Bartholomew thought of showing Jenny the snake, maybe it'd be a good conversation, maybe the story of survival would make him seem manly to her, he wouldn't mention it in the end, the snakeskin would be found in a field by animals and the meat used to sustain life for many smaller creatures. Sally loved the saltlick Colin Maclaine offered her at the stable that night, Bartholomew told him of their survival and swapped Sally's luxurious pampering for a few glasses of ale with which Colin firmly enjoyed.

    This would be the only time Bartholomew fired his gun at a living creature.

*

    Noah wasn't a handsome man, he never had his brother's good looks and wide smile and genial nature and strong muscles and hopeful outlook and easy connection to others and love. Well, he had love, but it wasn't from the many that Bartholomew received on a daily basis. His entry into the saloon wasn't met with pats on the back and handshakes and cheers and maybe a shot of whiskey planted under his chin immediately. Noah'd enter the place and get a few looks and turns before activity returned to how it was, and he'd sink into a chair maybe at a table with someone or maybe, mostly, on his lonesome, to drink the night away and see to the sun's rising on the morrow, giving it a little company as he'd stumble back to the homestead that he and his superior elder sibling helped raise with Father nearly a decade ago when he was let from the house he'd known and turned to an adult in his own place.

    But by some miracle there was one who sought his company, lovely Dolly Hammond from two towns over

Andrew Jones

was enchanted by Noah's quiet compassion and dark sense of humor, to her he was much more like the men of wit and thought in her well-read books than the folk who'd ask for her hand on Saturday night dances that wanted a little hand in their big arms and maybe a little more as the night would wear on. To Dolly, Noah was sweet and earnest and, yeah ok he wasn't going to be the big prize at the state fair but a warm body and a kind heart all to herself was everything she could want in life. And when the two fell deeply in love and she made the house a home and the two families united as one in their passion and adoration and humanity it seemed like he had one up on his single brother, yes Bartholomew had all the village by his side, but who was there laying in bed making it worth waking up from the land of dreams every morning? Noah won the battle for love, and what a victory Dolly was. With a skip in his step, Noah seemed to closely resemble the outlook and the outgoing of his elder brother, love helped his soul soar, he was found and he sought out to give the world a little of the exuberance he was gifted through Dolly. Cranham rallied around them, this young man coming out of his shell, this young woman whose family had made good in bringing livestock across the country and turning so much dry land into green vistas. The news of their firstborn sent celebrations throughout the state, it was a magical time to be alive and little Raleigh's first gurgles broke Noah forever. He sat next to his exhausted betrothed, Doc Augustine handing him their tiny baby girl, and her coos and gasps and making sounds in their house, filling the home with the noise of The Family Wright for the first time caused Noah to let out a tear. He held Dolly's hand, the three connected, one asleep, one breathing, one crying. It was a perfect moment.

    The consumption swept across the land, some came away with a cough they'd keep until they perished, others were not so lucky. The walls echoed throaty sludge unable to be removed, until the house fell silent. Noah was sat looking out the window, his brother's place across the way, they suddenly once again shared the same number of residents. It was the kitchen, a place Noah knew little about, but where he stored what he needed most. He sat looking across, feeling so far apart, as he gulped another mouthful of whiskey straight from the bottle and took his revolver from its holster. He spun the chamber around and around, watching the bullets in their little holes move fast, and raised the gun up towards God. The spinning kept the bullets in their place for a bit and as the spinning slowed they each started slipping from place, falling onto the wooden floorboards with reverberating clinks. Noah slammed the chamber back into the revolver after a beat and clicked the hammer back, he squeezed the trigger and a small click told God that He was safe for another day. Noah took the gun away from Him above and as water fell from his ducts and the silence of the house encroached his ears he placed the warm barrel on his shirt, feeling the heat in his chest as he took aim at his heart. He pulled the hammer back again, a click in place, and looked around the house beyond, where it had

Andrew Jones

become a home for one wonderful year, a place where memories made had quickly been erased by nature's evil. He held the gun to his heart for a while and closed his eyes and saw Raleigh's little eyes and hands and tiny nose and gurgling toothless mouth and little wisps of hair atop her strange-shaped skull starting to look a little human, and he saw Dolly's wide smile and big blue eyes and heard her laugh and whisper I Love You in his ear and felt the electric touch of her hand on the back of his neck as she would pull him closer to kiss, passionately and intimately, in a world just for themselves to know and explore. And Noah wanted to go there, to be there, this was everything, this was the world he had lucked out in living within, and something had seen fit to rid him of it all, left him with nothing around, nothing ahead, nothing at all. Except the gun in his hand. Noah opened his eyes and looked at Bartholomew's house, his brother was out at the river, Father was resting up, Mother was cooking some meal to coax Noah out of his house again, she'd tried and failed to bring him back to them since everything crumbled. Noah wanted to stop being a burden, he wanted to go back to happiness, and to leave all this. But he couldn't do it. He put the hammer back on the revolver and threw the gun on the table nearby. If he did that, would he be reunited or would his exit cause his soul only further torment now and forever? He didn't want to even think on that any longer, he reached for the bottle and drowned out his brain. Noah wouldn't pull the trigger, likely, ever. It just wasn't in his nature.

*

  For Rowan Martin life had been endlessly untethered, his mother died giving birth to him and his father resented him for his original sin, spending the first years of life under the unwatching eye of his papa amid a sea of tents nearby the hills, nobody expecting to live long here, grabbing whatever riches they could before hightailing it to the growing metropolitans on the coast. Here, Rowan would learn to walk and talk and dig and mine, two of those skills he practiced beyond toddling age, as his father absconded in the night and left him to the mercy of a group of miners hearing late about bigger finds a state or two west. By the time the last tent packed up, Rowan was handed off to an aging couple happy to live serenely in the woods and hills away from the world, and they cared for the boy as his arms and legs formed joints and muscles and grew out for inches at a time, each spurt suddenly finding him less blobular and more akin to human form. A campfire unattended saw to a blaze that scorched an entire region in his ninth fall, the elderly man got his wife and adopted child out of the smoke before it engulfed everything, but his lungs and his heart couldn't handle the atmosphere and activity and he was gone by winter, leaving nothing for the two to survive on. They headed deeper in country, huddled for warmth and sleeping in stables and sties and coops. By the next spring Rowan was looking at ten years on this planet and only knew of tents, woods and the comforting snore of a

Andrew Jones

woman on her last legs. They made their way down to Mississippi, the balmy warmth of the spring embracing them both with clammy air and upon the delta's flat once-flooded soil they planted flag, finding favor in a small community of travelers that spent their winter among Florida's flora and fauna, with the skins and meat to provide for the season. There Rowan spent time fixing food and hunting whatever was around, with the help of a few seasoned folk he found himself taking down a gator that made the mistake of crawling onto land and sniffing around the encampment. Out of season, the poachers and hunters and their kin sought out a different prey, living close to the river had the ace up its sleeve of the riverboats designed for newly minted men and obscenely comfortable lineage to engage in various games of chance, luck and skill, and all it took to gain the upper hand for the lower class was time and observation, waiting for the ripest richman to be vulnerable in luck and location, and the hunters could strike it rich. A game of patience. Being but a child, Rowan could scamper around and beg for money, marking potentials with little tears in their fabric, and would see to distracting as the menfolk laid their traps down the alleys and tributaries of the docks with innocent songs from the hymnals, and some bawdier material that averted attention and assuaged any paranoia in the liquored up and freshly-coined winners of the night's games. A little look at a child singing about The Ladies Of Dover who for a few bob Would Bend Over and the chuckles of the victor would bleed into a walk down the nearest exit, who could be worried listening to an angel's raunch aria? Before Doctor Richter went and Licked Her it would be game over, and the hunters coffers would be lined with gold.

    Rowan's voice lasted a few years living out with the hunters, learning of the Floridian landscape by the fall, never having as much success killing as he did distracting, but by his thirteenth year adulthood croaked his siren song and the games were crapping out. They buried his adoptive nana on the delta two weeks before a flood swept them off the lands for the entire season, Rowan learnt to swim, fast, and landed upriver. The grasslands fertile and moist welcomed him and other lost souls, white, black and native alike. The name of the game was bison, and Rowan found his strength carrying corpses and learning to ride a horse, wagon in tow. They'd been rounded up by a man with grand smiles and verbose vocabulary who offered food, shelter, drink and most importantly women for their time and effort taking the big beasts and bringing them in-tact to him. He was sending them out of state, making money for the nitrogen in their skeleton through the Northwestern Bone Syndicate of North Dakota, the funds didn't trickle down much, he wasn't letting great young workers explore options and leave the life most valuable to him. Rowan's time let him learn several languages, and crass jokes from other cultures, as the railroad took shape on the land around them. He was nearly twenty when he watched his first train pass by, people waving at the men covered in blood carrying giant beasts. He saw what humanity could be, and for a moment imagined what it must be like aboard that roaring creature screeching across at speed. No longer did hooch and whores appease him, he felt an unlocking in himself. A desire. A destination.

    He stocked up over weeks and at night rode his horse away, following the tracks as they ventured further across the world, humming songs from his youth that gamblers feared most to hear.

    The railroad took him through small towns and empty shells to be built later, and over the next days he saw more trains pass, to and from the beyond, more waves going out than coming back. On a hot summer's eve he stopped at a cliffside, the train's rails supported on iron bridge like a miraculous metal monster that soared above the river below, but he and his horse could not find footing on its triangular links and wooden slats. He began to follow the river up, hoping for bridge or ferry to continue its journey. It was an hour later he came across the bloody remnants of Bartholomew Wright.

    Samwell was upright and nearly his old self at the dinner table, Anna sitting to his left, both scraping the last remnants of meat and juice from their plates, silence besides the cutlery's crowing. A gunshot rang out followed by fast hoofsteps galloping past the house and towards Cranham village. The old couple looked at one another for a moment, whatever conversation needed saying happened entirely wordlessly, and Samwell rose to his feet, grabbed his holster and hat and hobbled out of the house. Sally rode out of the stable with Samwell atop the mare.

    Rowan found the village after a brief ride, hoping to see the semblance of society capable of understanding what he found and praying the stranger riding in blasting warning shots wouldn't be fingered as the culprit. It wasn't worth worrying about that possibility at that moment, Rowan figured, and hell look at this quiet little place, he could probably make escape if tide turned on him without much fuss, certainly without putting anyone in harm's way. He rode on the dirt road laid out before him and into the street rich with lit buildings, a final warning shot took attention from any mirth and merriment made in the saloon and beyond, and quickly townsfolk and the Sheriff stepped in front of Rowan and his horse and heard him scream bloody murder.

    Samwell rode up after Rowan and saw familiar faces turning to him, jaws dropped and paling in the lamplight. He knew, without a single utterance he seemed aware, and the world silenced around him. His stomach dropped, no sickness in his life hit like this moment, the world seemed to simply stop.

    The doors of the church crashed open, and people hushed in tone talked about Noah as he made his way from God's house and into the bosom of Cranham. Hats removed from heads, people seemed to look at Noah with immense sadness and silence, unable to offer information that would wreck what little world the poor man had left to hold. Noah saw his father atop his brother's saddle in the middle of the village at night, a sight never seen before. Hoxley gave nod to his deputies and Ransom and Kent unhitched their horses and went straight out of the village, towards the river. Hoxley stared at Samwell, then turned to face Noah as the younger man, completely devastated from his sobering hours of grief.

    Sheriff?

    Hoxley cleared his throat and walked to Noah, standing with the young man, by his side.

    Saddle up, we best be off. Us all.

    Hoxley directed a finger at Rowan.

    You especially, we have questions.

    Rowan knew right now wasn't a time to look for an escape, questions weren't at least accusations, any help he could be to the good and innocent he would at least attend to.

    Noah looked at his father high above the villagefolk, he could see anguish in his pa's face, his day of broken body making weak the old man's ability to hide feelings from his exterior. Noah sensed everything was amiss, but still nobody aloud spoke what Rowan informed only moments prior. Hoxley unhitched his horse and rode up to Noah, but in his daze Noah didn't respond. Doc Augustine got atop his steed and rode to Noah's side, holding his hand out. A snap of the fingers and Noah noticed what was being asked of him. Silently he clasped Doc's wrist and was pulled up to ride along his pseudo-uncle. Hoxley led the civilian posse comprised of Samwell on Sally, Colin MacLaine and Lars Skellig, Thomas and Maxwell Mann, Christian Olsen and following a little slower Doc Augustine with Noah out back. They rode fast and loud for a while, hoofstomps crushing the deathly silence of the determined men sure as hell they were about to find themselves before a sight not a one ever wished to witness on their worst day.

    Night had worn on and the ferry was pitched in full darkness, the gallops turned to trots before finally ceasing and each man made contact with the ground, Noah and Samwell found one-another in the melee as Hoxley stepped up ahead and lit the ferry's lantern and made light all around. Flies were already buzzing about the bloody patch of person left lying on the ground before the world. Ransom and Kent stayed on their mounts and gazed across the world, each taking a periphery, looking over all horizons, neither of them much wanted to look upon the remains and what it meant beyond the mess.
    There tis.
    Rowan couldn't offer much emotion, only empathy and honesty, but it came out cold and empty. Samwell began walking towards but Doc put his arm in front and barred the old man from continuing. Samwell pushed Augustine's arm away and kept on, Noah stood looking into the darkness, away from the light that only held truth and finality. Samwell stared at the faceless mush.
    It could be anyone.
    In those clothes?

Andrew Jones

    Doc wished he could heal the pain, but Samwell was going through something no medicine could cure. Hoxley stepped towards Samwell, holding his hand up to push the man back and leave him from this waking nightmare, as he walked near Bartholomew's buzzing body he scuffed the dirt and kicked the pearl-gripped revolver from under garment and into sight. Samwell fell to his knees noticing the gun he gave his child many decades before. Noah turned at the noise and saw. He began rushing to the body, taking out his own revolver.
    Where are these cowards?
    Colin and Lars and Christian reached out to hold Noah back, Thomas and Maxwell Mann tried to help as well.
    Easy son.
    You don't wanna see this.
    Ain't worth what it'll cost ya.
    None of this should be. Let's step away.
    But Noah wouldn't, he pushed on, the might of half of Cranham barely repressed the young man in this most horrible day. Hoxley gave focus to the messenger, standing away from the group.
    You see anything more?
    Rowan shook his head, Hoxley nodded at him.
    You best get to gettin' then.
    Yessir.
    Rowan Martin made his exit slowly, bowing his head to the old man on his knees and the young

man restrained by a gang, he had many adventures and knew he'd have many more left in his life, but this was not one he needed to spend any further time in, this was not something that'd push him or the world forward, only turning back and crushing all included. He hopped atop his horse and rode out, following the river up more. He'd not find swift crossing over the river and never sought out the railroad again, his next detour saw the young man make a little connection with a couple of compassionate gals on a farm, much to their father's chagrin.

    Samwell was stuck to the ground, gravity seemed to pull him down and tear everything apart, he could utter not a sound. He just stared at the flickering image of his son's final form in front of him, the deep reds burnt into the ground from the heat of the day meeting the final gasps of sunlight, he could not find a face to give rest to, to offer wishes of peace in the next life. He just examined the lumps and the blood and the clothes and the gun. Doc bowed his head and put a hand on Samwell's back, attempting to offer love and kindness and strength and energy, to no avail. The other men let go of Noah and stood silent, taking their hats off and bowing to Bartholomew and Samwell. Ransom and Kent trotted towards the ferry and began following tracks barely noticeable on the ground. They lit torches and set off. For a short moment, Bartholomew was bathed in bright amber and white, before shadows crept back over his body.

Andrew Jones

    Samwell and Noah were silent and looking without seeing as the posse rode back, Doc Augustine carrying the body of Bartholomew. Noah had taken to riding Sally, Samwell found his dear Clover and checked her after all this time alone, before saddling. Nothing uttered in the long somber trot from the river to Cranham and walking down the street. People came out and lined the street and watched the procession and bowed heads and gasped and cried and shrieked as Father Langston opened doors to the second Wright child of the day. Samwell and Noah split off and went home, they saddled the mares and in the stable stood silently staring at one-another, if they could speak they would never be able to truly explore what was in their hearts and their stomach and their heads and their souls, but in complete wordless stance they simply understood they'd have to stay strong as they informed a mother she had lost half her brood and a wife that death had parted them.

    Jenny fell to the floor before words could even be processed, Noah tried to catch her but his weak condition offered limited aid. He picked her up and carried her home. The scream Anna let out parted the river in pain and anguish. Nothing like that was ever heard before, it was pure and sickening and destroyed the spirit of all who heard it. The guttural wail of pain no person should know. Samwell's eyes welled up and he held her tight. They stood in the middle of their estate together and torn asunder.

    His big forearms popped the tops of two bottles at the same time, and Christian began pouring whiskey into pint glasses, the many folk of Cranham sat around patiently, quietly waiting to commiserate. He began passing around sustenance to the weary souls and slowly everyone found themselves gulping the amber brown glory and staring at their shoes as the liquid slid slowly up the glass and found purchase on their lips. The landlord raised a glass to the heavens above, his voice rattled every board, booming into the dead of night that encroached the exterior of the saloon.
    To Bartholomew Wright, one of the finest fellas to ever walk this Earth. Loved by all, missed already.
    Glasses began rising to the roof table by table, people saluting their fallen friend, saying quietly and loudly and mouthing their farewells and tributes before ingesting the rest of their drinks. Christian walked the room refilling every glass. Looking over his establishment, he could see the entire village in one room, save the Doc, the Father, the Family and the Deputies. They spent the night nursing their drinks, in silence and contemplation.

    The twinkles of sun on the horizon sparked dawn's first break and Samwell and Anna exited their homestead wearing their finery. Noah stood outside his house dressed in black, his eyes riddled with water. They made no talk, Anna gripped her husband tightly, he took all her

Andrew Jones

pain in him, he couldn't look at his youngest son, his now only son. Anna and Samwell struggled to walk the few steps to Bartholomew's house and when they opened the door, Jenny was on the floor in a puddle of tears, her most formal clothing patterned with roses and most unsuited to the occasion. It was not in the plans. Anna reached her free hand out to Jenny and they gripped hands. Jenny was pulled up from the ground and walked arm in arm with Anna, still linked with Samwell. Noah walked behind the three as they slowly made their way towards Cranham high street.

The Doc came into the saloon and pointed at the Mann twins, Lars and Colin and Kelso and the men stood and solemnly left the building.

We need to build somethin'. Size ain't right, barely anythin' to bury, but we gotta make it look good, for the family. For Bartholomew. And time ain't seein' much kindness to help us.

Kelso had wood to spare kindly from, the Manns coulda been carpenters if textiles didn't fit them so well, and the youthful handyman cobbled together tools fast, carrying equipment swiftly in the dark. By dawn they returned to the saloon for a quick sip before changing into appropriate clothing. The entire village looked mournful and stood on the sides of the street as Jenny-Anna-Samwell and Noah made their way towards the church.

Father Langston had spent the night preparing a few words but he didn't make much of the way through before emotion rid sense from his lips. The village stood behind the Wrights in front of a freshly dug hole, Lars and Colin and Mr. Ganz, a little worse for wear, stood to the side by the pile of soil ready to lower their friend as Anna wailed and Jenny sobbed and Noah stared at his feet and Samwell looked at the emptiness his son was about to fall into. The coffin was made of fine pine, its freshly varnished odor made the inebriated village dizzy, being up so long certainly played into that as well, but it was a fine final resting place, fit for the best of souls. Bartholomew was lowered slowly by his many friends and everyone in turn poured a little soil onto him, until he was below the ground. The three men grabbed shovels and returned to the Earth what was taken only an hour ago. Bartholomew lay rested nearby his sister-in-law and his little niece.

    The sun was once more glaring its orange halfcrest on the horizon, dawn turning to day, as the Wrights filed from Cranham and returned to their private land in mourning. Anna walked Jenny back to Bartholomew's house as Samwell and Noah stood, looking opposite directions, in the middle of the estate.
    What happens, Pa?
    How?
    When they find, what d'we do?
    Samwell finds Noah in his eyeline, the young man looking away from the sun, into the last gasps of the night that took everything.
    Nothin. Law does what it does.
    A hangin?

Andrew Jones

    Samwell nodded.
    If it be.
    By someone else's hand?
    Better them than me.
    Noah's mouth seemed to froth.
    They take from you, you don't return favor?
    Samwell averted his eyes as his son seemed to pitch ideas so horrendous, insidious that the old man wouldn't dare witness.
    Not my place. To interfere.
    To end what you didn't start.
    Samwell considered the day and the location and the weeping widow and mourning mother only hidden through wooden wall, and lowered his voice.
    What you're thinkin over, proposin, that ain't an end. Tis the start of summin worse.
    Is just.
    To some, and to others is means.
    Noah began to speak through gritted teeth, he couldn't turn to his father in this conversation, his mind singular.
    Pa, you caint tell me - you saw as clear as I, ain't no service to allow them air.
    You go out lookin for what yer lookin fer, y'all find somethin just fittin, whether tis or not. Do no good.
    Noah spat some dry phlegmy glop out of his bile-ridden mouth.
    Better than doin not a thing.

The Ferryman Upon The Plains

Not in this instance, son.

Noah turned to his father, he stepped up, he was taller, if not as broad, as his Papa. He blocked the sun with his head.

Well, maybe not fer you, but is I could...

Samwell looked up at his son, his anguish crawling across his face, his wrinkles creasing in pain and sadness and anger.

I see your pathway here, Noah, don't find me a foolish creature. One hand does not wash another clean.

You think often of before and after, what if there is no after?

Then we at least lived good before.

Us and who else? Those rip from you, steal somethin, and you watch them escape?

Samwell grabbed his son around the shoulder and held tight, he brought the young man close to his face, to lock eyes.

When you steal, it can be returned. It still is. We're not talkin of that no more. This is breakin.

Perhaps it is, but some of us ain't ever gonna be fixed anyhow.

Samwell gently kissed his son on the cheek and held him close.

Perhaps if you attended more and shattered less yerself.

Noah pushed his pa away, the proximity, the devastating words, he couldn't be in this embrace. He began to walk towards the river, the last darkness in the sky.

Andrew Jones

    Before you turn, think upon who t'was that were to be upon that station, pa, lest Bartholomew.
    Noah left Samwell, the old man thought of himself standing at the river, by the ferry, in place of his eldest son, sacrificing instead of suffering now. He looked at the three houses he and his two sons built together, the world they made for themselves. Two now dormant. Samwell walked towards his own house and when inside poured a big glass of whiskey and sat in silence sipping, to his children he thought, one underground, one falling into darkness.

    Anna popped open the bottle of wine that sat dormant on Jenny and Bartholomew's kitchen counter since the day prior, placed in perfect view of the door for when Bartholomew would arrive home, to bare witness to the meaningful adoration the couple had for one-another. Rather than let it vinegar through sadness, Anna figured they'd both earned more than a little tipple to quench the hole ripped into their hearts. She poured out two glasses and placed one before Jenny who sat silent and motionless, staring at the floorboards, and sat opposite and sipped. The moment the red juice fell beyond her lips and kicked her tastebuds, she let out a gasp, a sigh, a confounding noise that could be heard as contentment were it not stemming from someone so horrendously wounded so recently. Anna looked at Jenny and followed her gaze to the pristine floorboards. Anna looked to the doorframes, the kitchen counter, no nicks, no breaks, no marks. Hermetic, it seemed, just waiting for the chaos of children, a child that now would not know their father, the founder of the house, half the reason they would exist. She took a bigger sip, there was no second sigh.

This was his favorite.

Four words that seemed to break through the house's stillness. Anna looked through reddened eyes at Jenny as she took her own first sip of wine.

We couldn't afford it often, but, when thing's are worth celebratin', you indulge.

Jenny fell silent again and put the glass on the table by her.

We had some wine once, when the boys were - - When they were boys, I guess. Some folk had no coin to trade but gave Samwell a few bottles for the ferry instead. And some deer, only dead a night. It was like we fell upon a feast, for days. It felt right, to go back to tradin' for goods, like it mattered. What we did, what we offered, its value weighed against things that we could use, that we all needed, or wanted. Wine's the taste of importance, of connection to the world, to the people, to what matters. We never had deer again though. Huntin' something as beautiful as that for its meat? Somethin' off about that. Somethin' rotten, good as it tastes, when you see a family boundin' on the plains, you never wanna see one on your dinner table again.

Anna finished her glass and got up and kissed Jenny on the forehead and held her close to her bosom. They stayed embraced for a while in silence, until Jenny reached for another sip of wine. She tasted the world, all that came before, and all that was no longer there. She held Anna's body close again, something was always better than nothing.

*

    It was night almost already, those long days of summer never felt shorter and colder, and Anna found herself laying in bed, still in her fineries, eyes red raw and dripping with agony. She couldn't escape the confines of the furniture, unable to even change position, she was entirely at the mercy of gravity's crushing pull towards the ground and the bed the only cushion between it and herself.
    Samwell sat at the dining room table, a candle nearby offering light in the emptiness of night. He looked out the kitchen window, there was nothing out there. The pane of glass offered a reflection of his broken self, the elder statesman at a complete loss of life, amid a land of inky blackness. He locked eyes with himself and stared deeply, falling into his own emptiness, the void created by some stranger that didn't care of the harm a swift action had upon an entire world. He sighed and the candle danced on his breeze. The Samwell in the glass flickered in and out of existence, his wispy hair first to go, his wrinkled brow fluttering into nothingness, his bloodshot eyes and eternal gritting mouth the few details that stayed longest in the flicker. He blew the

candle out and saw himself disappear into the blackness of the world. He sat in the dark all alone, his wife's sniffling across the house all to suggest he wasn't already lost to some plane beyond the living land.

*

    Lars Skellig sat his young and muscular frame atop Samwell's finely crafted stool, listening to the sounds of the water splashing around the moored ferry platform, the rope connecting ferry to land loosening slowly over time, not a knot of infinite grip it seemed. He sipped at a metal flask and sucked his teeth with a wince of the strength of drink offered from the receptacle. He'd been taking shift for a while now and the sun had said its goodbye a while back, but Lars was happy to be of use in this moment, doing something good for the community that had welcomed him so fully. He passed the flask into the darkness, a hand gripped at it and began to drink. If one squinted Doc Augustine could just about be made out on the ground, laying by the bushes near the river, offering silent community to his fellow man on this horrible day. The red soil had been washed thoroughly by river water already, a little elbow grease and the unforgivable final acts against Bartholomew had been wiped from the world. The two men sat around waiting to be of use to strangers who'd not know anything untoward had occurred only a day prior.
    Their eyes often focused towards hoof and footprints still embedded in the ground by the ferry and

leading upriver, where Ransom and Kent had already made their start before dawn broke.

    Is something?

    Lars' original language still struggled to parse intermediaries, the folk of Cranham wouldn't be caught suggesting sentence structure, who were they to talk, as long as everyone knew what they meant, the words were just window dressing.

    Blasted if there's a lick of a shred around no more. Hopin' them lawmen catch a hint on the pathway yonder. A scent, or a scuff, or praise be one of the bastards themself, all nustled up for a nap and left unawares. Nab em, talk em out and hang em right in front of the saloon. Drink and a show.

    In the darkness beyond, the lantern captured image of a lanky, swaying figure shuffling slowly and scuffing feet across the ground towards them.

    Hark.

    Lars leapt out of the stool on Doc's word and looked towards the oncoming. He burst out a singular loud Hallo! mixing born and residing accents into a soup of uncertainty. The figure threw open their jacket a little and drew their gun. Lars and the Doc looked at one another, the old man on the ground seemed a little confused, the young man hit a nervousness he'd never known.

    Hey, you watch where you're pointin', fella!

    Doc's words seemed to reach the man as the lantern's rays shone onto his face. Noah had been trudging around the land since dawn, he was sunburnt and red raw and his stubble had become a fluff of beard patch, his eyes hung sour like his nose was Atlas trying desperately to keep them both on his face. He pointed his gun at Doc.

 I ain't wantin' no trouble, no foolin, just hand over that gofersaken elixir.

 Doc held his hands up in surrender, clutching the canteen in his right hand.

 My good sweet lord Noah Wright, you are some forgin a strange path with that there weapon.

 Doc reached his right hand over to Noah, he sat up and even leaned over extra hard to give imbibement to Noah, to stop Noah making any sudden movements or stumble into a dreadful accident of exhaustion and mania. Noah grabbed the flask and sipped of it deeply. He holstered his pearl-gripped revolver as he drank. Lars sat back down on the stool.

 We ok now?

 Noah looked to Lars as he finished sipping, spills of whiskey falling down his sunken cheeks and he wiped them from his chin, suckling upon his finger's newly liquored taste, and he nodded to Lars.

 Are we ever to be set right again?

 He threw the flask towards the Doc, it landed by the older man's lap, in the dirt. He shuffled beyond them and to the bush by the stool, reaching in and picking up the hidden money satchel.

 You takin treasury now?

 Fixin to settle up if you must be so inquirin.

Andrew Jones

Doc picked some coins from his pocket and handed them out to Noah.
Then take these. Your brother's final fare. Hope it sees you better.
Doc dropped the two coins into Noah's hand. Noah felt each one land on his palm with a burning unlike any he ever knew. He stared at them for a moment before gripping them tightly. His heart sank, he knew more than he'd dare open about. Noah left the satchel be and set off following the tracks sitting in the soil.
So now you're the deputies' deputy?
No sir, I ain't about to let these monsters find justice in the remit of the law.
And I s'pose we aren't to be stoppin ya?
Perhaps your time is better spent on those you can hope to save Doc.
Doc shook his head and sipped at the nectar in the flask, handing it back to Lars. Noah waded into the darkness, following those tracks, he was resolute, he was unstoppable. If he couldn't be his brother's keeper, he would be his vengeance.

FIVE

 HE TOOK A DEEP INHALE and the end lit up, an orange ember broke out in the darkness and dark white smoke puffed from the end into the night sky. He let the tobacco seep into his core before releasing a breath up towards the stars. Samwell found himself between the three houses, standing in the dead of night cricking his neck so he could take in the worlds and possibilities of the heavens beyond. He tried to make out shapes and characters from the lights above but failed to connect the twinkling orbs to any other, every little light in the dark was alone and dying its own separate way. He took another puff and became lit up again.

 A scuff of foot on soil broke the distraction of Samwell and his ears took in the world down here once again, and with it the soft wailing of his sweet loving wife inside carried a dagger to his core. Samwell turned to see the faintest of glimmers of eye and teeth, and a hit of whiskey breath emanating as the Doc said a simple Hi to the old man. Samwell went to light a match but Augustine touched his wrist and shook his head, in the shroud his twinkling whites blurred and darkened. Anna cried out again.

 I have ether, carry the stuff should some poor sumbitch require it, not that your Anna's a- -

Andrew Jones

    This is healthy, this is natural. In the most unnatural damn thing to happen, this is how things is meant to play out.
    They stood in silence again and Anna's crying stopped.
    Thank you for what you've been done, you and the men up at the river.
    Course. It's as much important to us as it is you. Wouldn't stand to let you down.
    You come to see if we're alright?
    I know you're all far from alright, ain't here doin' some rounds, just thought it best to let you know your youngest has some sour intentions.
    I know it.
    He was something of a mess making his appearance at the ferry a short time back. I'm sorry to say I helped him on his path to imbibin'. Not for lookin' at easy excuses but he did hold a gun out, figured a drop of rye wasn't to lose life over.
    Kid ain't ever much been for firin' that thing, you know he weren't gonna blast you or whoever else was there for a nip.
    Maybe so, but only maybe. Grief can do a hazard to the head. He's gone on followin' them deputies and that faint hint of a trail, mind's on somethin' not good. Probably shouldn't be out there alone right now. I'd offer my service but I'm hardly useful out there. And this place, ya know, the one day I'm out off somewhere some poor bastard gets a crate collapsed atop them or a horse

kicks out and bucks them hard and god knows what anyone else'll do. Liquor em up and put em down, I reckon. Which is what the ether's fer, in truth, just makes me seem like I know what I'm doin', rather than makin' someone neck half a bottle of Olsen's cheapest swill.

The Doc tried a smile, Samwell could see his bare teeth but didn't respond to the drunken rambles. He turned away, his back to the Doc.

One son in the ground, another out in the night, I got these two gals absolutely wrecked. Cain't one man hold it all together.

E'ryone'll understand if you sought out blood for blood. If you and your youngest went out to get something in return fer what's happened. They'll take pity on your Anna and poor Jenny, but they'll take care too. Y'let Noah go out alone though, you'll look old. Broken. Unfit.

And I go by what e'ryone else thinks and says?

Maybe, maybe ya don't, I'm just thinkin' it's pertinent for you to think upon. Maybe you don't lose both your sons in one day.

Another silence as Samwell chewed his cheek a little.

Don't sit right, Doc. Huntin'.

I know it. I'm never one to stomach it mahself, the screams from the cows when Ganz takes his fattest to the slaughter make my hairs stand somethin' like a winter's night.

Not even that, Doc, it's the evil of it. Takin' anything God put here for us away, just wrong. He's the

Andrew Jones

one chooses when to give and when to go, what right we got to upend that? Just rotten.

You ain't talkin' bout huntin' to kill, just bringin' to justice.

What's justice, Doc? These men sittin' in four walls all day and night until they rightly leave of old age? We've seen what the law do to folk, back East wasn't humane and certainly out here it's only lost more humanity every passing season. Can I go help capture folk and watch em strung up before the whole world? Before God? And still see light come my time?

Those who refuse to obey the law are refusin' to obey God, Samwell. Punishment will follow.

Am I so bold as to think I could be God's punishment to these men?

Look to Job, all He did to that man. Mayhap you just fell into His vision and He chose you, and maybe He chose Noah, and saw to it to test your faith, to test your love, to test your dedication.

I don't wanna believe God's responsible for this.

If you want Him only to bring good, you're not believin' in Him correct Samwell.

I never wanted no part in takin life from a soul.

I know it.

If I do this, it's with heavy burden.

That's alright. Ain't nobody expectin' you to go out there gleeful like and singin' songs.

Make sure the girls is looked after. Damn that boy. He might be foolish and hotheaded but he ain't wrong.

Doc backed into the darkness and his footsteps fell away. Anna's sobbing returned. Samwell stubbed out his cigarette, the last embers flared into the air and he exhaled smoke towards the sky, blotting out the stars for a second.

In the stable the horses were laying on hay and enjoying the cold night air. Samwell quietly opened a door and closed it behind him, not letting the world enter the barn. He lit a lantern and watched as the horses puffed and spat and turned heads from the sudden brightness invading their rest. Samwell walked to Clover and patted her back gently, she rose to greet the old man and huffed into his face. Samwell rested his head against hers and closed his eyes.

Sorry girl, you've had quite a time aintya. No rest against the wicked I'm afraid. Get you some oats and some water and say your goodbyes to yer sisters, we got a long way to go fore we see any sign of return.

Samwell looked at Sally resting up nearby and looked away quickly. He let out a sigh and rubbed his forearms before picking up a bag of grain and pouring some in a trough by the water. A few of the mares came over and snacked up the food. Samwell scanned the stable and in the back wall could see Noah's black stallion standing tall and away from the females. Samwell walked slowly towards the horse and touched his front leg with gentle pat.

Andrew Jones

    Come on Midnight, we gotta get you to Noah kiddo. He needs you more than he'll ever say.
    Samwell bent down and picked up a handful of grain and held it out to Midnight. The horse's tongue lapped at the food and tickled Samwell's hands until he was clean of all oat. Samwell patted the horse and walked to the saddles piled atop one another, and began to prep the two horses, his back screaming in ache but his head drowning pain out with determination. He blew the lantern out and the light of stars seemed suddenly brighter than ever before as he led Clover and Midnight into the world.

    Noah was deep into the emptiness of the land and starting to shiver from the night's sudden chill, his breath escaping his mouth with puffs of vapor before him. The river still wrestled against the bank to his left and without sight all he could do was maintain based on the noise. His feet hit dirt and dragged along before picking up again each step, it was an exhaustion deep within him that was not finding a second wind in the journey through the land but Noah dragged each scuffing boot on the ground and stomped the next, further and further, ever onward, sure in his heart that he was following still something akin to a trail.
    A burst of hoofstomp nearby gave Noah pause, he stood still and popped his shoulders broader to pad any stampede that might hit him, and as he felt the wind from near wild animals

clopping past and away he followed his eyes onto the darkness where their sounds called out and pictured a family of horses gayly playing in the night, together, happy and united.

A light in the distance behind him brought Noah out of his head and he squinted to gain focus, failing from such a far proximity. Noah could see the light bouncing a little and getting bigger, maybe closer, but the river and the horseplay passing by made it hard to gauge with his clearest sense. Noah grabbed hold of his revolver and removed it from his holster and fell to one knee and steadied himself to aim down the sight, following the light as it grew.

Samwell's face started to reveal from the blackness, the lantern outstretched and above Clover's head as he rode helped show neither hand was holding weapon to any passers by. Noah watched as his father slowed Clover down, and Midnight behind reined up to the mare came to a stop alongside them. Noah holstered as Samwell slowly stepped off his saddle.

What are ya doin' pa?

Doc came my way, tellin' of yer plans.

And what did he know of them?

You aren't coy or subtle or anything inbetwixt boy.

Samwell brushed some dust off Noah's coat, holding Midnight's rein and the only light in the land in his other hand. He offered Noah help standing, but Noah stayed stubborn on his spot.

Consarnit, look at ya. A mess'd be disgusted to be around this.

Andrew Jones

I ain't in any kind of delegation for composure, not since childhood.

You're far more a boy these times than when you last played with toys.

Noah brought himself up to his aching feet, slightly taller now than his father but not wiser or stronger.

So you've dragged your ownself and two poor horses this way to talk me down and bring me on home?

I know my children more than anyone in the world. You aint fer turnin back whence you set your mind.

Darn right pa, best head away now.

That's not how this is.

Samwell held his hand out to his son, the one holding Midnight's reins. Noah couldn't see much from the lantern's brightness. Samwell put the lantern on the ground and in the silhouette of light Noah could clearer make the reach of rein to his black stallion standing, saddled, waiting patiently to be ridden.

Pa?

You ain't the only one what lost somethin.

Yeah, but you still got Mother. She's at home right now waitin' on you.

Samwell dropped the reins and grabbed Noah and pulled him close, pulled him a little down, so that father and son were eye to eye.

The Ferryman Upon The Plains

You think you don't have more to lose? Then why am I standin' here son? Or am I too just a shadow castin out of time and place?

What I intend to do Pa, it aint somethin to return from, even if I make it unscathed.

I'm wildly assured of that, but you think I'm lettin mah seed go alone?

Samwell relinquished his kin a little, still holding on a little but now with breathing room from the alcoholic musk.

You have no comprehension the destruction of the world. You think you do, I know, but there's layers upon layers that you never even sunk to.

Samwell fully let Noah go, the younger man stumbled on his aching limbs watching his father speak.

And as it stands, I aint here to give you a talkin to or turnin your head. We do this the Wright way. Together.

Samwell picked up the lantern and made his way atop Clover again. He waited as Noah found the reins to Midnight and hopped on the magnificent stallion. Samwell led with light as they rode on through the darkness, the river calling their place in the world, knowing somewhere further out they would come across something to guide them on, to lead them in their first hunt as father and son. Dawn was starting up again, and the two Wright men found purpose after losing so much.

The men rode their horses as summer's sun began to crest, in the morning glow the dirt and crud below showed no signs of life, no strains of weed or flower, so close to the screaming water still not a deer or a coyote or a lizard or a spider crawled or slept or nested around.

Andrew Jones

They sipped from the river every hour and continued down, never seeing more hint of others that may have passed in the melee of their aberrance and mayhem. Noah slept atop Midnight for a spell, Samwell never noticed, he was silent and staring in the distance and never took in the world nearby. He had chilled to a singular focus.

*

The morning glare wore Cranham well and life found itself moving on swiftly, already the middle of another week with little good to show on the ground, but the sky above kept moving and circling and lighting and darkening without care for the small figures below. Hoxley sat with Mrs. Hoxley in the Sheriff's office picking apart the gristle of pig fat from fried up bacon, she especially never found pleasant the chewy white strips and would, with small fork prongs, pull off the edges of the meat and leave them for the dogs over at Ganz's farm to crunch on during her daily walks around.
    Sheriff sipped a cup of coffee and stared deeply into his wife's eyes, he stroked her chin from across the desk and pulled her close and slipped a kiss upon her cheek and smiled. She herself giggled and grabbed her fella and kissed him on the lips, sliding her tongue around his mouth and as quickly left him amazed and got off her chair, slid it back across the office and grabbed

The Ferryman Upon The Plains

the plates, putting the gristle in her basket and covered it with a napkin and waved her husband goodbye. The Sheriff licked her taste in his mouth and thought of how much he wanted to lock the village up and take her upstairs and embrace her for the whole day, but he soon came back to Earth as his eyes were drawn to the empty office, the unused cells and the chairs waiting for deputy butts to make their presence known again, and he knew he had a bigger job to do than simply be a loving husband.

  They pulled their horses up and their loud gallops became significant trots as the four saw Cranham on their direction and walked their horses down the street, citizens took notice but tried best to carry on their days. Four more strangers looking rough and stern would not lead to anything good, and not one of the folk around wanted to ignite that tinderbox. They hitched up before the Sheriff's office and hopped off saddles, Abraham then Ezekiel then Jedediah and finally Zachariah. The four marshals had come far over the seasons, caught wind and lost track and heard steps and fell on deaf ears and just a few days prior thought they had smelt the last gasp of one of them, but the hint of mint took them off from any grasp, only a poor farmer and his dog left without. And then here they were, near another riverbank with another land dormant and uncertain about the evils that have been, that will come, that could always be. They walked up to the office and stood before Hoxley.
  Can I help you?
  The four Marshals took off their hats with respect to fellow law.

Andrew Jones

    Sheriff.
    Heard you had sum rumblin's.
    Things no soul should do.
    Unlike what has come before.
    The sheriff nodded as he picked a piece of pork from his teeth with his tongue and chewed it once again.
    Well'sir yes, it's been a rough time around, certainly. How does that involve you?
    In a flash of fabric the four men pulled jackets to the side and showed badges on their hips.
    Louisiana.
    Mississippi.
    Arkansas.
    Kentucky.
    And y'all came all this way, together? Mighty far from things.
    Hoxley stood and offered his own respect to the badgewearers. The Marshals looked at the empty office.
    Where are your men, Sheriff?
    On the trail.
    How many?
    Two.
    Poor souls.
    What?
    We've seen armies.
    Soldiers.
    Forts worth.

Face up.

Nothing left of them.

Hoxley stared at the men as his stomach quietly grumbled, the acid dissolving his breakfast was boiling over and turning within him, he wanted to release it all through his mouth, remove the taste, the weight, the memory of minutes before. He grabbed a key from a drawer and walked to a locked cabinet, entering it and turning to open, inside sat ten rifles ready for use. He took three out and boxes of ammunition sitting next to the weapons.

Well, I best get to goin'.

It's no use.

Firepower begets firepower.

Hoxley locked the cabinet up and pocketed the key and pushed past the four men, not listening as he left the office.

It's not to be stopped, Sheriff.

Hoxley turned to face them, close.

Are you aidin' them?

We're simply preparing you. For what's about to come.

Hoxley dropped the rifles onto his desk and sighed then looked at the four men.

Y'all come here lookin' dusty and dry and speakin' so empty and broken, warnin's to be heeded, what good does that do? Let it happen, let it be, cain't be stopped. Well, you go to the river now go see those who saw what I done saw, who knew the poor man taken and how he was taken, and how rotten it was to look at his father seein' whatever was left of his child, you go there and see about the mother, the wife, all they had and now lost and then you say there's no point trying, tell me there's nothin' to be done, warn of somethin' that you're not deepin'in' down on. Are you messengers for them? Bit late now, boys, my men are out there and they'll stick to it until they come home with justice, now I suggest you run yerselfs out of this place and chase those, God forgive me, bastards down and help heed the word of the law, the word of God Himself, because what nobody round here needs right this moment is word that things ain't all good and happy. We know that, too right do we know, is we aware of all that's broken some in this land. Shoo yerselfs until you make good of that metal on yer hips and catch them men what ruined e'rything and e'ryone round here with their evil.

    Hoxley clasped his coffee cup and refreshed his mouth as the four Marshals donned their hats and left the office. He followed them out and watched them unhitch and saddle and ride off out of Cranham with nary a comment or a cough or a sigh made. Hoxley saw them off but good and walked over to the Trading Post and found Kelso Harding-Grant having a little sip of water between lifting and stacking boxes of Herman's fresh crops for the next wagon.

    Grant.

    Harding-Grant, Sheriff.

    If you must. Have a particular request, can you fulfill?

Sheriff, I can move mountains, nary a thing to worry, what can I procure?

The Sheriff began to inquire about heavy duty firearms, en masse, ballistically brutal. Harding-Grant didn't bat an eye as he noted the requirements and prepared a letter to a few of the forts he often sent goods out to, a man whose fingers were found in too many pies but for once might be of use beyond the economy of the village. They shared a bottle of sarsaparilla and Kelso got one of his drivers to ride on with the letters, to gather a few folk from nearby towns to take message and response swiftly for decent coin.

Less than half of an hour after they left Cranham the four horsemen rode up to the riverside and saw the ferry port and came to examine whatever was left as Colin Maclaine sat patiently and watched and waited to be talked to like a human. He asked if they wanted passage over, just for courtesy but the lack of humor in their responses made him stand and wait to be spoken to. They wanted more information, the lack of result sitting on the ground near them stopped the marshals in their tracks, and Colin's claims that everyone wanted to bury their friend, their son, their brother, their spouse and erase the image of the end didn't mean much to the lawmen. They weren't interested in the person, they wanted only the horror, the destruction. In the brutal remnants they could understand evil, and remove the humanity from it. Here, with people caring, it only sought to distract from the destination, from the hunt. Once you care you can't see clearly. Emotion blinds the brain.

Andrew Jones

    We still kept the prints of their feet, of the man and the horse, headin' upriver like.
    Colin pointed beyond the stool and the ferry and the bush and the four men looked over and saw the prints on the ground. Abraham looked over the river, Ezekiel looked downriver. Jedediah looked back towards Cranham. Zachariah looked at the prints and followed them with his eyes to the distance.
    Many men.
    Ain't just the one.
    And his horse.
    Many men. If they're to be called men anymore.
    Come from afar.
    All over.
    North and South.
    East... and West.
    Yes'sirs, well, they's come here and did what they did, had to of been from West this one, didn't come through Cranham, wouldn'ta got close to Bartholomew North or South neither, 'less you know this area that river bends back and forth asudden and you find yerself splashin' somethin' silly and weren't no wet nearby, cept, Christ alive, blood. Came over on the ferry. Played all good and human and when Bartholomew, bless him, went and did his kindness, they done got him and took away his God given life.
    The West.
    Dangerous place.

The Ferryman Upon The Plains

Gettin' worse.

And comin' back here.

The four men nodded to Colin and hopped on horses.

You gonna catch them? Sheriff's sent his deputies already, and Bartholomew's pa and his brother, poor Noah, well, they're out there too, and good on them. If it were one of mine I'd be out there, wouldn't see me until I brought home these monsters. Best seek them out, better all together than all higgldy and piggldy and chasin' one another's trail.

The men rode off and Colin sat back on the stool. He waited. His shift ended just in time to grab a last drink at the saloon before a nice sleep at the widow Westington's and then a day of horsewrangling and training and care. He'd offer custom to five horses with eight men and two women and four children and a wagon with a family and a guide determined to see them off to somewhere far West where they say gold was spewing from the water. Lars was back on for the night shift, he was happy to man the ferry again, especially when company like Doc or Herman came by and sat for an hour and drank their fears and thoughts and memories of Bartholomew and Cranham away.

*

Jenny Wright spent the day pacing about the house, her footsteps thumping out the noise of her mother-in-law still loudly wailing across the estate. She didn't want to think about it, she couldn't bare to continue thinking on things, it wasn't about processing the information yet, it was impossible to come to terms with, and she hadn't been able to speak much since they told her, since she watched a box be placed in dirt, since she sat in the kitchen she sometimes stomped through and had a sip of deep, fruity wine. Jenny refused to let facts feel true, she wanted her body to be strong, to be good for the beautiful baby inside her, and every time her brain touched Bartholomew's possible passing the shivers that ran across her system, that spurted her armhairs upright, they turned her stomach all manner of directions not conducive to internal childrearing, so ignorance for the next months was to be the bliss of the prenatal mother.

  The stomping was so frequent and loud that it took Hazel Worthing some five minutes of rat-a-tating on the wooden front door before she just gave up all manners and opened up and popped her head in, spooking the pacing widow a minute later when Jenny had turned over the house and returned to the living quarters and mid-stomp seen the light come in and the face of her friend staring at her antics. Jenny lowered her foot delicately and beckoned Hazel in and offered some wine, she'd thought as she poured them both a splash that maybe in the coming days another trip up to Fort Oak was on the cards, a few more bottles for the house, it'd been a boon to her week thus far and perhaps wine was the way to handle the coming months.

They sat and drank and Hazel held Jenny's hand and Jenny shook her head before Hazel broached the subject hanging over everyone's heads. Hazel kissed Jenny on the cheek and nodded in understanding. She brought her bag up onto the table and opened it excited to share, with all that had been going on, since the party on Sunday she was wanting to put something together for her friend, the ride back home on Monday helped her ferment the idea.

Two little mittens came out of the bag, knitted with a pattern zig zagging across the palm and back in yellow and green wool, too tiny for either of them. Hazel held them out on her index fingers and waved to Jenny, Jenny's porcelain white face began to redden with drink and laughter and she gasped at the detail on the tiny gifts. Hazel handed them to Jenny and reached back into the bag and took out similar-patterned socks knitted for Baby Wright. Jenny hugged Hazel deeply and held onto her for dear life. She laid the gloves and the socks on the table, picturing the baby laying there ready for the winter chills. A blissful break in the brain from all the sadness, all the past, this was the future gifted in four woolen items. They drank a little more and made jokes about baby names and Hazel offered to knit an entire wardrobe for the little one before it joined the world. Their joy drowned out the intermittent wails of the mother lost of her family across the way.

*

Andrew Jones

    They had ridden all day and into the night, a crescent moon above shone slightly down and gifted the two Wrights a little help at coldest and darkest. The sound of the river fell off at moon's height but the horses seemed content carrying on forward endlessly. Nearer dawn than dusk they came across a still-smoking pile of wood and stopped up, feeling the last warmth from the small pile of sticks and dry leaves. Noah laid snake rope around them as they laid nearby, heads rested on a roll of blankets Samwell saddled up with now over a day prior and they took a small blink from the world. The sun broke open their eyes in what could only be an hour later and Samwell ached himself up to his feet, feeling like he couldn't lay down any longer on the hard surfaces of the ground. He rubbed his back and took a look around the land in the morning's clarity. Noah sat up and smelt the ashen droppings of the fire fully, such a vast difference in his nostrils from the fresh water and the mud and the desirable liquids mixed with metal and glass.
    Up ahead a little ways the land turned greener, there were tops of trees dotting the horizon, waving in a light breeze that wasn't yet reaching all the way to the dirt. Unspoken, the two men hopped on their rides and headed towards the natural life, a landscape unexplored by a Wright for many a decade.
    Entering the woodlands all sound outside seemed to fall away, blocked by wood and leaf, the

rays of golden sun shimmered the dew on the ground and basked the bark with warming love. Clover and Midnight huffed and crushed sticks under hoof as they trotted through the land, slowing down as their nostrils flared. Samwell sniffed the air and held Clover tighter on the rein to continue on. A sickening mix of metal and bile hit Samwell's senses, he looked to Noah, and followed his son's gaze off to a thick trunk with three red stripes cutting down it, and half a palmprint of crimson just above. The horses slowed, trepidatious to a halt, and the men climbed off slowly, made themselves crouch and took out revolvers. Each step careful, the crunches smothered by soft pressing to the ground, they walked the horses slowly through a leafy blanket. At the threshold of a clearing Samwell and Noah found themselves a pair of legs tied around a tree, previous owner laying a few feet away, their spine and guts open for wildlife to examine with tongue and tooth. It was not a clean break, the pelvic bone covered in muscle and tufts of flesh made a tempting treat on the leafy bottom for curious omnivores.

    They stepped further into the open woodland, letting the two horses stay back, together, and caught more red on the leaves below leading them deeper. Two small trees had arrows sticking out, through the wrist of one arm and the palm of another, the rest of the body unfound. A scalp was hanging from a tree branch next to some unripe fruits, two particular hangdowns lacked the sack they usually came in, but the flaccid addendum hung atop it keeping shape to the jewels. A pile of charred bits still smoking covered the land with grey and sickening ash, wafting clear for view Samwell caught sight of a figure on the other side of the massacre. He held his gun and yelled 'Halt' and the figure returned verbal clearly stating 'Sheriff's deputy' and Samwell and Noah holstered and walked around the grave to find Ransom and Kent examining a messy puddle of blood and digits.

    Mr. Wright? Whaddya doin' all out here?

    Noah found himself staring at the horrors around, he absorbed the evil deeper as he breathed the sickening end of so much life.

    Much in your vein, boys.

    Wellen, by the dismantled nature of these poor folks we're somethin' close to a few hours their trail.

    Danged if we shouldn'ta rested up in the end. Heard some screams like nobody'd screamed before.

    Unhearable. Unforgettable. And we were so dang close too.

    Ever seen somethin' like this Mr. Wright?

    Caint proclaim observance of horrors reachin' this level boys, no.

    Yours ok there Mr. Wright?

    The three men looked at Noah as he paled and eyes widened and jaw dropped.

    Well now, Deputy, I do not believe he is. Though given what has befallen here, could any of us ok?

    No I could not, sir.

Mr. Wright, an aside if you'd allow?

Ransom took Samwell away from the scene a little, in a wooded hiding from all noises. Kent touched Noah on the arm and brought him back to the world of the living, he handed a satchel of water to the young man and watched him drink.

Ransom spat on the ground and popped tobacco in his mouth and offered Samwell a little pile, the old man shook his head.

If I may be so forthright, you and yours is lookin' for some sort of vindication, right? Trevailin some ways off to seek out that which you feel is rightfully owed?

Is we beyond our purview to ride on t'wards them that took so much?

Mr. Wright, with all respect you best leave this case with us. We're out for justice, by the laws of the land, and were you and your boy to get in the way, or take matters into your own - we can't rightly pass a side-eye.

Ransom chewed and spat and chewed, Samwell looked at the clean woods around, and the hints of horror hidden back beyond them.

What kind of man would I be if I didn't seek retribution for somethin so heinous? We're not here for any kinda self-fulfillment, deputy. Think of us as four extra hands, extra eyes, to help apprehend.

And not dispatch?

God-willin', no.

Ransom nodded and patted Samwell on the shoulder.

We'll take the help Mr. Wright. But yer boy looks shaken somethin fierce, you certain this is the way to be?

Andrew Jones

    You saw what they did to my Bartholomew. Ain't no other way this is goin.
    Samwell walked back to the clearing, he passed the scene and found Clover and Midnight and walked them around the clearing, Kent walked with Noah away and Ransom took the deputies' horses around, they met up further in the woods and the deputies started riding slowly off. Samwell hopped atop Clover and steadied Midnight as Noah climbed up. They shared a look, the horrors too clear in their mind now.
    Son, look on. Here'll do nobody's soul good.
    The four men rode on through the woodlands, spots of red kept them hungry for the hunt long into the night.
    We could drag em to a fort, give them to the army, a firin' squad'll send them down holey for once.
    Why don't we burn them alive, let'em feel hell on this plane like they done did to all in their path?
    The deputies sounded oddly excited to deal death to people. Samwell saw them coldly and callously contemplate ending life God gave to all. Noah gritted his teeth.
    I'd like to look at the man capable of this, face to face, and watch him remorse for all the evil of the world. Take parts of him away as he apologises for the hurt. Let him know slowly the pain he's caused all this time, to all these folk. Then, once he finally knows what he's done, see

him off. Not kill him, let him go on with whatever he still has attached. If it takes half a hand for him to understand, he lives pretty easy still. If he gotta go on with a knee exposed and one eyehole open and spat in, hell, he ain't gonna be able to do this shit again ain't he.

Samwell turned away from his son as the night blackened the world.

We find this monster, these people, if they's a they not a one, and we do what's right by the land. Before the people. Justice, not vengeance, no evil, pure. Whatever's ok by the world, ok by God, nothin' else. A rope round the neck and a swift drop from up high, as in life so in death.

The men stopped talking, they stayed silent for the next day of traipsing across the land. Noah never made eye contact with his three riders after his outburst. He stayed in his own mind, Samwell worried but he had no way to reach out, to bring him back, he was slowly watching his only living son fall away.

*

It was many days of grief and impossibly gripped by the small comfort of the bed before Anna felt the strength to escape her room, her house, her estate. Boosted with the power of the Lord she made her way to church Friday evening seeking solace and contact clearer with Him above than she could find at home. She sat on a pew and clasped her hands together and closed her eyes and briefly, quietly, called out to God for assistance, she asked for strength and focus and a little light in this dark week that she could no longer see from her Earthly realm.

Andrew Jones

She hoped that Father was ok wherever he was, and that Noah was to be safe, and that Jenny whom she had yet to see since the funeral was healthy and the baby was, once again, looked after from Him please. Amen. She sat and stayed clasped and quiet and eyes closed, no senses to distract her from any potential word from Him. Father Langston sat a few pews back and watched, a rarity still outside Sunday mornings to see someone sitting and wanting more guidance and word. He tried patience as Anna waited, she didn't get a response as one would expect from humans, but hoped perhaps somehow there'd be another way He would show his love and kindness.

Father Langston stood and walked the aisle watching Anna and leaned on the front pew before her and awaited her eyes opening back to the world. She felt his breath near and opened and he smiled warmly and reached a hand to her.

Come my daughter, let us talk together to Him.

She clasped his hand and he reached his head over, resting on her forehead. They closed eyes. Father Langston believed his additional calls to God would be heard clearer, for he had spent so long in His duty, for he was in his mind purer and closer to Him, in the hierarchy of humanity he had spent so long elevating himself up towards the heavens, so he thought in this moment of need he had the opportunity to use all he had worked for to benefit the Wrights and lovely, God-fearing Anna.

The Ferryman Upon The Plains

Amens were whispered again and he caressed her hand softly before letting go and standing up. Anna felt strength ooze into her, a shiver ran down her spine and she stood up swiftly. Father Langston gave Anna a candle and walked her to the shrine. She kneeled and lit the wick and laid the candle next to several others and whispered love to Bartholomew before standing and walking out of the church, leaving Father Langston alone with His candles and His statue and his thoughts.

    Anna walked down the hill to Cranham's street as Liza-Beth Hoxley lit up a few lanterns down the way, gifting light the sun was taking from the sky at that moment. A smile began to sprout on the young woman's face but she stopped it midway, her eyes watering a little at sight of the grieving mother. They shared a half-wave of acknowledgement before Liza-Beth blew out her match and walked up to the Hoxley house. Anna walked on, the saloon nearby was loud with laughter and song. The piano fell quiet followed by yells of want from customers. Madame Westington loudly declared she simply had to get on home, stir the stew and check the meat and she'd return in no time to compliment their drinking with sound. The aged widow stumbled out of the saloon giggling at a crack from one of the patrons and saw Anna standing there, away from the fun, away from the people. Madame Westington straightened her dress and hair and walked down to Anna and held her arm out, locking Anna and began to escort her down the street.

    I sincerely hope we didn't disturb you Mrs. Wright.
    It's not a problem. I was enjoying the rambunctiousness.

Andrew Jones

    Them men can be a handful sometimes. The free drinks make up for it of course.
    Aren't you going the wrong direction? Don't you have to attend a meal?
    Hush now sweetheart, them boys won't mind a little burn or boil on their plates one night. Heck they probably'll be too tired or too deep in the bottle to even notice.
    They left the village road and walked in darkness towards the estate. Madame Westington looked at Anna and held her tight in the lock.
    Those first days, that first week, many weeks. You probably were so busy with things in your life when Mr. Westington left us all, what with the babies back then. Those months. Years. It was hard, that big house suddenly fell quiet. I was expected to exist and had no rhyme to my life no more. Them nights when the wind howled past and the moon shone like a demon, them mornings Ganz's cockerels screamed out, the strangers ridin past all hours of the day and me without any defence lest they come accostin' us. My whole life I was livin' with som'un, Pa, Mr. Westington, and suddenly I was in my adult years and all alone and had no way to know what to do and how to be and just struggled daily doin' normal things, rememberin' what to do when I wasn't doin' things for others, cookin' and cleanin' and lovin' someone else. I had no self I was meant to care for, no self to be even aware of. Folk stopped by to console and to trade and to try to care for but I wasn't there, in

The Ferryman Upon The Plains

my head I was but a shell with no life inside. And at night it was at its worst. The bed so cold, so empty. It were hard to rest up, somethin' always felt missing, which it was, but I thought on it and would be awake rememberin' it weren't missin but comin, but missin and never returnin. And then the noises started. Some night in the first season alone I started hearin shufflin on the floorboards, I heard the doors creak slowly, not from wind or nothin, but somethin where someone, or somethin, were about and creepin and lurkin. I hid, under the blanket I hid and closed my eyes and shook my head and felt the chills of the empty bed. Until the sun rose. I didn't sleep. And the next night more of the same. But it weren't somethin in the house. Every mornin when the sun gave strength to good I went room by room and saw nothin outta the ordinary. The little noises outside, the horses, the animals, the people, but nothin creepin me out. And then at nights I would lay and struggle and wish for someone to come and look and help and be there for me. But after two months without rest I had to realise I wasn' gonna do much without nobody else, and I werent to find nobody to lay with, my death til we part I firmly believe, I had to just do somethin about it. I threw my covers off me as the doors squeaked and I stood on the floor as the boards creaked and I stepped towards the door and heard shufflin and I touched the handle and pulled it open and somethin screamed at me and I fell back and the door opened in front of me and I saw in the moonlight my house, empty, and the door stopped squeaking, and I stood back up and walked on the boards but they didn't creak. I walked the house at night and found nothing and heard nothing and I went to bed and pulled the cover up

Andrew Jones

and felt a little warmer. I slept nice that night. And the next night. And the next. I aint ever heard those noises again. Then I started walkin outside again. But it took me a year. All that within, when I was entirely without. And now for the many years I've gone about like a new person, I exist on my own terms. I am and I can be and I will be. I miss and I grieve, but I live and I do. But look at yer, Anna, not a week and you're out here. I don't know where you found that strength. I wish I had that in my time. Hold on to that. Life is always struggle, it'll push us down with every opportunity. But when you're able to live on, to walk on, to be in this world with the rest of us, it can't beat you.

They stood outside the houses and Madame Westington unlocked her arm and stroked Anna's cheek softly. They looked over to Jenny's house.

Will she be ok d'ya think?

Y'all have somethin' to live for still, a few things actually. With that hope anything is possible.

Madame Westington kissed Anna on the cheek and waved off, walking back towards Cranham. Anna stood and thought about knocking on Jenny's door, but the lights in the window were blown out as she pondered. Anna walked back to her house. She would wail again, but it wouldn't last all night.

*

The Ferryman Upon The Plains

    At the ferry that Friday night Colin punted his last across the river and put the fare into a sack that once had some of Ganz's potatoes of the previous harvest. He'd been at the dayshift all week now and gotten into the same rhythms of mooring and unmooring, of punting and rowing and slowing and feeling the river, of hearing the waves lap and feeling the breeze from the flow, of listening to the birds caw and seeing the ropes that carried from here to there above it all give and fight the wind and the sun and the life around it. Colin Maclaine was as good a Wright as any had been at that post before. He sat on the stool and rested up, a week of it and his body was already asking for a little rest, that Samwell Wright was something else with decades non-stop. Finally the sounds of footsteps and laughter made it clear he was being let off for the night, and Lars Skellig and the good Doctor Augustine came about, with that old belly roaring and happy drunk farmer Herman Ganz in tow. They had enjoyed an evening at Christian Olsen's watering hole and brought enough supplies to continue their time whilst doing diligence to the good people of the land. Lars took the oar from Colin and shook hands and handed him the still-mostly-full bottle of whiskey he was sipping from, Doc laid his jacket on the ground and sat on it and insisted Colin stay a little. Ganz rolled up a little tobacco and began to smoke, he paced rather than get on the ground, like the other aging folk of the town he knew once he was down it'd be hard pressed to return to feet without making a fool of himself or his body.

    Y'know it's kind of y'all to do night watch in tandem and all, strength in numbers, but mayhap the

Andrew Jones

boozin' ain't fixin' fer smarter awareness or aimin' if things go all wonky and dangerous-like.

Back home if people come attack or act foolish I did not need many men with me, little roar, grab of shoulder and they stop and run away, no harm.

They don't have guns over up there in them cold European lands do they Lars?

Sometime they have weapon, but the man holding it not as strong, as fierce as me without any. Not the gun that matters, the man is all.

Doc raised a half-empty bottle in salute to the Scandinavian man, Ganz roared with big belly emphasis.

My good boy Ranger'd bark loud like and all them animals, don't matter pig or cow, sow or bull, they don't talk back, they march where they gotta go, they do as they must, they all know, deep within, who best not to mess with.

Y'think Noah's got that in him?

Samwell does, for definite. I've known him 'fore all you and longer, he's got that in there. Don't use it nothin', not sure sometimes if he knows he's got it in there, but I seen somethin' in his eyes from time and he don't speak on it, he don't think on it, but there's somethin' there. The kid though? I caint for the life of me imagine either boy ever capable of doin what for to make sure.

Doc rolled his own cigarette after that ponderance, the other men considered for a moment.

The Ferryman Upon The Plains

Will they return?

Poor women, not fair to them. If I had people back home, would not simply go hunt.

Even if your entire world was threatened?

This not threat. This terrible. But not threat. This about righting a wrong. Selfish.

Ganz slapped Lars and the group stayed silent in shock.

Ain't selfish boy. Don't you say that bout them men. They knows we all gots their backs, here to look out fer more than ourselves. That poor Anna and poor Jenny over yonder ain't alone. They's out there seeking justice as we all would, were it our boy, our brother, our kin. Heck, some of us would be ridin' out with them right this now if we could, if we didn't have our own purpose here. God knows I'd be side by side with Samwell if I could, seekin them fools what did this devastation and seein good them lynched up until theys blue in the gills fer what they done did and fer what theys plannin on keepin doin till someone stopped them. God help Samwell and that boy Noah, they out there doin what they should, what any of us should be doin. Aint no man worth their salt could wander round this place head held high whilst doin nothin fer what happened to em. Would be an embarrassment of masculinity. The bible always tells us an eye fer an eye, them sumbitches took more 'an that, whatever comes of em aint even close to balancin the book, but so long as Samwell sees them done for what they did thats fair as all can be in this world. Then it becomes His work for eternity, and they gonna wish they

Andrew Jones

didn't cross paths with the Wrights and this place, that's fer damn sure.

Ganz's cigarette had turned to ash in the time and fell to the ground. Lars looked at his feet, he apologized. Ganz placed his calloused sausage fingers on the younger man's shoulder and gently patted him like a calf. Colin and the Doc looked at one another then away to the world.

How long you think they'll be gone?

Gettin' tired already?

Mannin' the ferry and lookin after the horses, it's a lot of a lot.

Should probably send out for more hands, those twins ever do a shift?

Colin shook his head.

Course not, caint be separated, they'd only ferry one person at a time lest the platform sink.

Laughter permeated the night's silence.

You think Kelso might lend a hand?

I don't think he'd lend anythin' without expressly demandin' somethin in return up front and in writing. Could you imagine him rowin' folk across, all dusty and dirty and tired? He'd take one look at em and scoff and shake his head and make em bathe for an hour 'fore he considered given' them a ride.

The men laughed uproariously, the world felt warmer for a moment.

I'm riding some horses up to the fort in the morrow, will see if they can send a few spare to help out around.

Army men? That'll never do, they'd start rowing all regimented and organized and the first sign of the river flanking them they'd panic and look for their commander and then just turn tail and run off only later to claim they were outnumbered but rowed valiantly then receive a dumb piece of metal.

Mr. Ganz, I was in the army a little.

A little? So you knew it was all foolish and left?

Colin stepped to the thick farmer, a foot taller, slimmer though, not as muscular.

We some of us prefer peace and tranquillity, not built for the fight as much as for seein' to the mounts that ride in on. Weren't much fer shootin', but I could tame the wildest, found my callin and my people and my purpose in my time. Met good men in uniform, sir, a lot of brave men, some aint comin back anytime soon neither. They didn't flee when things looked rough, they stared in the face of it and gave what fer so you could farm without fear of folk.

Yeah, well, I never met no native what didn't care bout the land and animals. May not have spoken words the same, but we shared a lot of similarities.

All men can be kind and good. All men, if they try hard enough. Seems its too easy fer folk to fall into some animalistic way.

Wild animals, e'en bears, ain't as sick as what befell Bartholomew boy.

Doc finished smoking and laid down, looking to the sky, the bright moon.

God what I wouldn't do to get my hands on those bastards.

Andrew Jones

What you do, doc?

I seen so many die before I could see them healed, the light leavin eyes. I'd like to impart that fear, that realization, unto them. Grasp my hands round their neck and see them gasping and pleading and struggling and realizing and accepting. These hands, what were meant to be healin, healin the land by riddin with them, windpipe, throat, clasped, gripped, crushed, turnin red then purple then blue then pale.

No man should get to take em down hisself, Doc. This ain't revenge from one man to another, we all just take em out back and line em up and we each take a gun and aim and we let fire onto em. E'ry one in town, get a shot at takin em out. Leave nothin fer God, bullets and burn em, erase from history. Less than animals.

Tear them apart, make show of it. Drag through behind horse, let people see, then split them between horses, let them feel unGodly pain and pop, scare everyone thinking of hurting, never again. Stick heads on signpost, see off anybody, never sin again.

Colin swigged the bottle and handed it back to Lars. He wiped some whiskey from his chin and gasped.

All this, what'll it achieve? Bartholomew's gone. They've done their evil already. We do to them what they did, we're just as bad. We become the monsters like they are. We start thinkin and picturin and imaginin and considerin it, and soon

The Ferryman Upon The Plains

we desire it, we want it, we need it. Bad road to go down. And ain't no tribute to Bartholomew, a good man, a kind man, to seek his killers and make devils of ourselves doin so.

But what when more turn up? How we stop?

Y'think there's more out there like them?

History of the world, Maclaine. Folk out there willin to do things unspeakable for purposes unknown. All societies have evil inherent. Caint stop it, just gotta hope you avoid it, and when it comes acallin', be ready to send it back to hell summin' fierce. So that it don't come back round here no time soon.

The farmer sat on the jacket next to the Doc and necked from his bottle.

Maclaine, when you go in the mornin', you think you could ask nicely for a few firearms and the like? Paid, course. Might do nicely we all had little bit more than these finger holders and huntin' rifles.

What you thinkin, Herman?

I'm not sayin Cranham needs a canon or nuffin, but maybe we four out here in the edge of darkness might do well with somethin offering a couple barrels of safety.

The Doc nodded, Lars seemed in agreement as he sipped some whiskey. Colin stood above all the other men, looking down on their drunken bluster and considered the realities seeping from their liberated lips.

*

Saturday wore on and the woods fell into grassland fell into rocks and wellspring and wildlife and grazing fauna, the deputies and the Wrights rode on. The deputies never rested for fear the Wrights would consider them lazy or unconcerned with the cause. The Wrights never rested now they'd seen more damage so close, could almost taste the chance to capture their killer. They pressed on. A ripped animal carcass on the path, slashes on tree bark, bullets in rock with blood surrounded, little lumps of gore helped confirm they were always headed correctly, and in their bellies the unGodly feeling of gripping evil lured them deeper and onward. A small bloodstreak on the dirt path betwixt grassland keyed them in as the evening sang its twilight chorus and they carried on hoping at once to see the men and not see the victim soon. The line continued on at a three-point crossing, up to the right though the makings of a small town, alive and boisterous for its weekend evening festivities. The horses held up and the deputies looked at one another and the posse.

    Deputy?

    Yes deputy?

    Is a rest, and perhaps even somethin' to imbibe, outta the question?

    Kent looked to the old man tired and aching above his poor horse, his hair knotted in wind and sweat, his face craggly with wrinkle and stubble grown out over a week already. Ransom took in the younger Wright, baggy eyes of flesh sagging his face into a sour anger, a hard stare at the blood beyond, uninterested in communication, in being human, he was all focus and devastation.

I'm thinkin', Mr. Wright, the local law might at least aid us if we ask polite-like.

You can't stop now.

Noah's outburst turned all heads to him.

Son?

We gotta be close. We can't stop, they... They need to pay.

Kent took his hat off as a mark of respect, as if the hat held all authority and office, rather than his badge or gun or wage packet.

Son, we're been on this path near a week now. We go runnin' after em much more, we'll be dead 'fore we even catch sight. My partner here and I'll make haste to town and see what's to be done.

Noah clutched the revolver's pearl grip and unholstered it.

We're goin', we're gonna put these monsters down. No diversions, no distractions.

Ransom reached for his gun, Kent put his unhatted hand in the air and shook his head to his fellow deputy.

Woah, woah to the both. Hold yer pieces.

Ransom took his hand away from his weapon, Noah held his, he didn't aim at anyone, but in an instant he could if he wanted to. Samwell trotted Clover across between the deputies and Noah, a wall of human.

Noah, boy, you don't want for this now.

Andrew Jones

    Par, we gotta keep goin. They're out there right now, and we…
    And we are four very tired, weary souls unready for what's to come. The deputies, they're correct. Takin a moment, regainin ourselves, seekin aid, help, is not weakness, is not failure. In others we can find strength to continue.
    We coulda caught them before, we're so close now, y'all seen what they could do, so many out there innocent and pure and to befall their hand for no reason but the way evil is. Why are you so willin to give up.
    This ain't given up boy.
    Ransom touched Kent's shoulder and shook his head, they trot a little away, leaving Samwell and Noah to talk.
    The deputy's right, son. We're not givin up by going off. We're none of us right at this moment, no rest, no calm, we're husks. A little water, a little sleep on a bed made not of soil or saddle, mayhap some extra eyes and ears and hands and guns and a little extra law of the land to will us to the righteous way. We're huntin' monsters of men here, we don't need to become same as we give chase. We'd lose them and ourselves in the melee. You want to return back home less than human, we've witnessed unGodly things already, we can't go back from that, but we can prepare to be better, to be stronger, to retain ourselves rather than fall into their tracks.

The Ferryman Upon The Plains

Samwell turned Clover towards the path to town, Noah watched on, revolver in hand.

Onwards.

Samwell and the deputies began to set off to town. Noah sat atop Midnight, holding his gun. He looked at the trail continuing, and the men, his father of all people, leaving the hunt for a world of humans unknown to the horrors they've witnessed all this time. He holstered his gun and slowly walked towards town, in the dust of the men before him.

SIX

FORT OAK IN THE MID MORNING was ahead of the world around, activity festered since buglecall hours back and the soldiers had paraded and eaten and marched and stood watch and by the time folk were coming by to trade or talk or find their new station in the service most men were fading in the heat and hunger and waiting on that lunch to come sooner and sooner each passing minute. Colin Maclaine rode six horses into the fort, the conversation by the riverside the night before weighed on his mind and his sleep was stagnated by visions of friends and acquaintances gleefully executing people in the most grotesque of ways. His pacifism wasn't lauded in uniform but the peace he found with the animals, in a small village removed from society's growing ills, had made him complacent. The casual conversation had punched him in the stomach and his ride whilst full of scenic wonder was lost on him, his eyes glassy and his mind actively internal the entire time.

  He halted the horses in the center of the fort and grounded himself as the Major and a few soldiers came over to see to the animals. The Major stood before Colin and examined his thicker physique, the straddles of stubble on his lantern jaw, the tanlines between forearm and upper where Colin's sleeves were unbuttoned and rolled for purpose. Colin looked back at the older authority figure, he felt an instinct to salute but halted his hand and reached out to shake instead. The Major grabbed his hand and clutched it tight, shaking hard and staring into the eyes of the former enlistee.

    Fine beasts, Maclaine, they're looking right ready to see about the land.

    Thank you Major, some of my finest work keepin them alive and growin them big.

    You have a gift.

    The Major released Colin's hand and nodded to the soldiers who took five horses away and to the stables, leaving the Major alone with Colin and his own saddle.

    How's your next year's lookin?

    Bout twenty born this season, hopin fer at least seven.

    E'ryone always knows, round these parts, the horses reared from you compared, e'ryone always can tell. Y'sure we can't convince you back in blue, work exclusive-like?

    Nothin' doin Major, ain't my place to be. Can we confer a little aways from here?

    MacLaine? What're you ponderin'?

    Little o' this, little o' that. Need summin in the metallurgy fashion.

    Goin' full deep into smithin'?

    Colin stayed silent, the Major smiled with interest and walked the horseman towards his residence. Away

Andrew Jones

from the formality and structure, the Major poured out two glasses of deeply brown whiskey and handed one to Colin. They sat in his parlor, the sounds of the barracks and the trading post and the mess hall's bell ringing its first unblocked by the thin wooden walls.

    What can we do for ya?

    Man to man, as folk who've seen action at a time, I hope you'll understand.

    Maclaine, you baffle me.

    We had some nefarious deeds down our world of late, somethin' vile, truly brutal, got the whole populus afeared. I hasten to ask, down in my gut I know it's wrong sir but...

    Colin looked at the Major and asked about buying a batch of shotguns. The Major smiled and nodded and gave a price-point to Colin, called it Veteran's Discount and offered up rifles surplus to the fort that were rode in only months ago and weren't gonna see much use anytime in the future. The Major relished in bringing weaponry to Colin Maclaine, he saw the opportunity and pounced. Colin drank his whiskey and gurned at the bitter kick in his throat and down his body as he negotiated and was walked to the armory and brought a plethora of arsenal to peruse and purchase. They hid the trade with some smithing equipment, the poor horse found himself carrying a man, six shotguns, three long-range rifles, ten revolvers, two faster-loading pistols, five bars of iron, two hammers and a wagon's tether, carrying a new anvil behind. Subtlety incarnate.

Colin almost forgot as he sat atop his horse and looked towards the exit, but witnessing a collection of soldiers seemingly idle in standing post-meal he asked the Major if they could send any men over they didn't much have use for to man the ferry. The Major accepted the notion and waved Colin off from his view. He saw a man come in with livestock and leave with death.

He eyed each rider passing by, seeing if they could tell what he was carrying back, to see if they had any reaction to such danger, to see maybe if they had any questionable intent. It wasn't until her third callout when Colin realized that Hazel Worthing had ridden up to match pace with him, and poor Jenny next to her too. Hazel's stock less metallic, less potential for destruction, she had textiles of grounded and earthy colors, Jenny had a basket of grain and food for both human and horse. Colin smiled at the ladies gently, his smile weakened at Jenny with a hint of sadness and concern breaking out of his gaze, but to Hazel the smile held nothing hurting underneath. Only aching.

You fashioning some shoes for your friends today? We both found ourselves making attire lately then.

I wish I could craft a clothe as exquisite as ones you make Hazel, master smith couldn't forge a cut as pure as your seamin' skills allow.

Mayhap I should come by your stable a time and teach you the fineries as you hammer away at your molten metal.

Andrew Jones

    I'd encourage that very much but fear you'd mess up the wondrous dresses you find yourself adornin e'ry day.
    What's the use in wearin' things if you caint sometimes get it a little messy? Minute you step outside the dust and the mud and the animals come all over with their business, you'd be stuck indoors lookin all good with nowheres to go. Might as well be nekid in that case.
    Miss Worthing you hide a devil within your purty facade doncha?
    Elegance and manners are all about hidin in plain sight what you truly are, out here betwixt worlds, just us and our horses, is where we can most be us.
    Hazel winked at Colin and Colin's heartbeat almost spooked his horse with its sudden intensity. He monitored the affixed wagon and the gear covering the weapons and distracted the thoughts in his head of Hazel with paranoia of being spotted for what was being transported in the height of day under God's very nose.

*

    They weren't far off from the town as sun dwindled into fabric of purple night draped across the sky yet the noise from Saint Richard on a Saturday night was overwhelming. Laughter, yelling, a piano loudly enveloping all the discourse and hiding any ill repute from any passing the other path. Immediately at the outskirts the four men sensed a bigger town then they'd been privy to for years, at least three streets paved in cobble and lined with wooden fencing telling everyone exactly when they fall upon someone's piece of land. Strangers better keep to theyselves.

Outstanding.

Ransom gawped a singular word from his awe-struck mouth, jaw agape at the town ahead. So many buildings of wood and stone, at once built for the weather and the location and yet intended for permanence, to stand long after everyone here would perish.

Y'all ever see a place this big?

The deputies could barely take it all in, Samwell wasn't much for sightseeing and kept himself to himself, checking on Noah a little every few paces as the youngest Wright lagged behind, mute and bitter. The siren call of the playful piano led the men through the streets, passing folk finding refuge on the ground after a day of perhaps too many sips of their poison and plenty of horses roped up to buildings and posts, scattered about with no rhyme or reason, their saddlers sure to have trouble hopping on the right one after they'd reached their ground-resting limit. The saloon was surely boisterous from outside, a few folk pushing and punching with laughter but a little anger ingrained within each motion, a woman flashing her thighs to all passers by, getting glances but no offers still. The men found a safe place and hitched their rides and steeled themselves for the night ahead. All except Noah, who sat atop Midnight and stared out towards the

Andrew Jones

path through town and back to the world beyond, Samwell stood by Clover and looked up at his son.

    I'm thinkin if I just scout on ahead. Less chance of bein' spotted alone.

    Get yerself down or I'll drag you meself. Ain't no use none of us goin out tonight.

    Noah turned to the saloon as Ransom and Kent made way in, the doors swinging and loud cheers and laughter emanated out. His face screamed a pain internal, clutching at the reins of Midnight to withhold the agony and desire and fight not to just gulp down the entire stock and free himself from all thought and feeling.

    Pa.

    Son, come on.

    Father.

    Just water'll do, but better in here than out there in state you're in.

    Samwell reached his hand up to Noah and held it open, quivering with worn fatigue and ache of aging. Noah relented control of Midnight, handing the reins back to his father and hopping off, making contact with the stoned street below as Samwell moored his vessel to the fence of the saloon. The two Wright men entered the saloon together, safe alongside one another.

    The immediate blast of music and chatter and bawdy laughter hit the ears of the tired travelers and broke their exhausted trance, the pungent smells of ripe men unbathed for a week and sweaty from work and heat and whatever activities they'd been getting up to of a night punched their senses into overdrive. Ransom and Kent pushed through the crowd and found the bar, Samwell and Noah nestled in a little corner of the room where the acoustics seemed to bounce noise away and hide them thoroughly from the weekend bacchanal already in motion. Samwell clocked the deputies but when the barkeep pointed onwards and they nodded and walked in that direction he lost them in the crowd. So many burly folk, big broad shoulders, muscles and fat mixing into hefty fellas courting dames wearing few garments and huge smiles, sometimes being herded upstairs by the fair ladies of the venue for ample viewing of the land, or other sights they so wished to take in. Near to the hidden corner an old fella and two young skinny twitchy-types sat and tried to play a little cards, calling and folding with knocks and hand gestures since their words wouldn't carry beyond the brim of their hats. The stakes seemed low, the piles of coins on display real lackluster, about enough for a few drinks rather than a week's respite in coin form. The huge gorilla-shaped barkeep came to the edge of his station and poured a couple of glasses of whiskey and whistled to Samwell to come over.

    Courtesy of the sheriff.
    Samwell stared at the brown liquids, Noah looked at the glasses and shook his head. Samwell leaned in towards the big barkeep.
    Can we make for water switch?
    The barkeep chuckled, a few folk within earshot laughed at the prospect.

Andrew Jones

I can put a l'il in there if it'll make ya's less queasy an' all. You from the East or somethin'?

The men livened up their laughs of derision. Samwell looked at the mocking men and his son.

A snifter won't hurt, then.

Samwell took the glasses and handed one to Noah, he scoured the tavern for signs of the man responsible for the gift and caught Ransom and Kent beyond all men of the crowd, talking to an old man with a grand white beard and a badge on his dusty jacket lapel. He raised his glass to the town's sheriff, and received a distant nod. Noah raised his own glass and clinked it onto Samwell's.

For Bartholomew.

Never truer words, son.

They gulped down and slammed glasses onto their table, in the quiet chamber of their hide the clank of finished drinks rang louder than the piano could ever chime. They sat opposite and looked away from one another for a spell, letting the poorly aged slush this place sold as drink burn their throats, stomach and eventually their liver. Ransom and Kent and the old sheriff waded through the crowd and found the table.

This them?

Yes'um Sheriff.

Sheriff Branch grabbed a chair and sat down, back to the crowd, face to the town, between the Wright men. The deputies stood, hovering over his shoulders.

The Ferryman Upon The Plains

    My sincerest condolences on your loss. We make good with many kinds of folk up'in round here but ain't no time for those which remove goodness through evils.
    Appreciate the contemplations.
    Branch laughed at the quiet wording of the broken old man and looked over his shoulder, to the men making merry.
    We ain't much a damn sight of civility and prosperity round here, but we make our souls true and proper come Sunday be sure of that. Stick around til morn and witness.
    He turned to face Samwell, two old men seen many a day more than they have left to know.
    Sure is law round here ain't much for the chasin', we're more keepin' peace than huntin' war. I can no more hand you men than I can summon the Lord to smite your wanted, however as I was tellin' the deputies here, if you have some coin then there's a wealth of men round here happy to pick up arms real swift-like. I cain't vouch for them as shots, but if they made it this far they can't be too bad.
    Branch stood and turned to the barkeep.
    Another round for these men, they've had a long week, see they get a good night.
    He dropped a bunch of coins on the bar and walked back to the tavern's riotous land, men raising their glasses to him as he passed by. The barkeep landed a bottle of whiskey on the table and the deputies sat around and poured out into four glasses the bitter juice.
    Money ain't buyin' much of worth with people like this.

Son, we can't deny what we are offered if there ain't nothin' else in the offing. We spit on chance and get slapped by fate.

Yer pa's right, Noah, we four can't go doin' this ourselves, what we can pay for we should get and go about huntin' in the morrow.

The deputies sipped at their whiskeys and hissed from the taste and burn. Noah looked to his father, in the dark of this strange landscape, tired and aching and hiding the truth of his feelings, Noah grabbed his drink and slammed it into the back of his throat, then poured out another. Samwell witnessed his son's indulgence and let it go, he sipped slowly on his glass and found himself lost in thought, in this journey he was on, this place he was at, his wife and his daughter-in-law at home, his son six feet underground, and this husk of a figure before him adopting the shape of his other son but feeling so removed from all he trained and taught and tried to turn away from. Samwell felt more of a failure in this moment than he had ever known.

We'll see this town good at church in the mornin' and from there find folk adhering to the good word to ride with us. Mornin's a long way though, rest now. End this horrible week.

The four men drank on, the bottle would dry quickly, the barkeep made sure never to let them go too long sober. The night wore on harsh and Samwell made his way to the barkeep and enquired about rooms for the night, after an eyebrow raise at the old man the barkeep offered a roof for the night, but only the one since Saturday's his busy season, and the four ascended upstairs for rest and quiet. They were each propositioned on their way to their private chambers and whilst the deputies gave a second thought to it not a one went anywhere but the safety of their own closed door in this alehouse of a raucous evening.

    Across the land the bells rang to call parishioners to prayer on that Sunday morning that seemed to come crashing into the long Saturday evening of no consequence and loose memories. In Saint Richard Samwell shuffled off to join the dazed drunkards and the respectable sobers on the walk to the stone church sat on a hill above all the noise and passing by of everyday life, whilst Ransom, Kent and Noah were left to rest. Samwell considered bringing his boy to the church but saw his deep embrace of the hidden goddess of sleep and felt that rather than bringing him back to this world to be talked at by perhaps a droning priest or loud, pompous parish head the world of nod held more spiritual rejuvenation and hope.
    Saint Richard held a wide swath of souls who sat on pews and prayed that morning, the elders and those who operated the more industrious side of the world in town seemed to find their own corner of the church to abide with thee whilst the many drifters and day laborers kept to themselves and filled many pews without noticing or considering any other member of the flock they were inhabiting the world of, and Samwell felt cold just being a

Andrew Jones

part of this empty, transient congregation. He sat and waited for the pulpit to enrich his spirit, engage his heart, fill his mind with notions of help and love and reasons to do right and put only positivity into the world beyond, but the man who wore the cloth that day was a tall, thin fella who seemed at once glued to the bible he clutched in his spindly fingers and unable to speak a full sentence without stepping his tongue over a word or two, no line read from the book flowed naturally as if God was trying to strangle the man before he butchered more of His work, and here he was fighting the Man Himself to yell at a collection of concerned and kind-of-conscious civilians in his mitts. The sermon delivered was on caring for one's neighbor with the quotes of passage about Samaritans and singing a hymn of love that could be used for any purpose with the right preface. Samwell sat and tried to listen but found his mind wandering. He thought of the people around him, if any of these men might be taking up with his posse come nightfall, are these the flock he will be shepherding towards justice. He couldn't feel connection to the men around or the spirit in his heart. He left that morning's sermon and trudged back down to Saint Richard and found himself back in the room where his son and the Sheriff's deputies were still sound asleep. He rested as the sun woke more of the world up and closed his eyes and could hear not God or his mind a desire for helping anyone, but only his muscles and bones and body pounding an ache something fierce.

The Ferryman Upon The Plains

There was half a bottle of whiskey still left. Samwell found the holy spirit.

In Cranham the church wasn't as full as Saint Richard On The Pathway To Justice, with Samwell and Noah and Ransom and Kent on the trail, with Bartholomew permanently seated six feet under and twenty feet outside, with Colin Maclaine at the ferry, with Herman Ganz and Doc Augustine resting from another night's exuberance, with Lars Skellig nocturnal and unable to be woken by Madame Westington on her way to the church, it was a poor showing for Father Langston and he had little to offer those in attendance. The grief and the pain and the loss and the absconding of souls had been unspoken but loudly felt before he made his way across the aisle and up the pulpit to commence, but as he looked down at half a congregation, all familiar faces and none of them in a state of joy or love, he couldn't find healing words that fell on open ears. He read about the pain of loss and the trials of Jesus and ushered in acceptance to all that heaven waits at the end of their journeys, but not a soul wanted to think of an end anymore, not one that only brought them to those they missed and could no longer be with on this day. The collection plate was near-barren, only a few coins out of politeness and societal expectation and all filed out and back to their lives saying nothing to one-another, barely glancing at Father Langston at the entrance as he wished them well for the week, praise Him. Father Langston sat in a pew after the last of the congregation left and sighed and blew out a candle in anger.

Andrew Jones

*

    Samwell opened the door of their majestic suite of eight by twelve by eight onto the wooden balcony that oversaw the street below and lit up a cigarette as he took in Sunday's noontime. The stragglers coming to the tavern for a spot of liquid lunch, the elders making their way on the cobbles to dine finely with good conversation. Samwell leaned on the wooden fence and took it all in. Noah arose at the slight breeze from beyond and got to his feet and walked to the balcony to take in the image of his aging father smoking in the heavy light of noon.
    It's only Sunday, right pa? I didn't just skip over many a day?
    Tis, boy. If you wish to make peace with God best do it by yerself, service is long over.
    Damnit, why'd you let me sink into that?
    Son, last night, after a few bottles I admit, you stopped seemin' to be ill in the head with notions, weightless in anger and bile. I see my spawn enjoying themselves I cain't say no to that. I'm only human.
    I ain't good for nobody in that mind, can't shoot fer nothing, can't do much but sit and sleep and slowly let life fade.
    That's as we all. Somedays, son, we just need that away from it all. Best keep resting, we'll be on our way come nightfall.

The Ferryman Upon The Plains

Noah looked over the balcony and to the town in the daylight. He shook his head.

I'm seein' what your mind is coordinating, settle it for now.

Better we go down and raise arms with what coin we got and deal with folk what have no skin in the game short of lining their pockets?

We can over this many times talk but point stands, Noah. We're not to hunt like that, only more of the kind whence y'do. I sat with folk in church today. I felt their nature true as it was. I don't like what we gotta do neither, but I'm not partakin' in this chase with so many vulnerabilities. I'm gettin' old, I can't stand the idea of you in the firin' line, and them boys behind us ain't ever seen action, don't know how they'll be when the first gun goes off. Sure as we need their authority, rather have some bodies what know of trouble and ain't scared of facin' folk head on for good and right in time of callin'.

What will a strong hangin' really do anyways?

Samwell tossed the last of his cigarette off the balcony, it hissed on the stones below and burnt up.

Nothin' for us, if that's what yer hopin'. Sure as it's better someone else's hand gets blood on it than yours or mine though. How to live with such a sin? Unforgivable.

Noah coughed and spat over the rail, people avoided the mucus and kept going their business never looking up at the man.

You're somethin' sometimes pa. If I were in your spot, I had the chance to kill what done took my child, no hesitation. Straight shot to them.

Andrew Jones

    Samwell looked his boy up and down and shook his head.
    Well, if that's how you is, perhaps it's fittin' you never much sired another.
    Noah's face burst with anger in an instant, his hand instinctively balled into a fist and he swung at his father, stopping just before contacting the old man. Through gritted teeth and heated soul he spoke.
    We do not go down that well.
    You best drop that hand and walk.
    I'm not to drinkin', until you need me to. I'm not to huntin', cept we're on the trail. And now to even givin' someone what they deserve when they're talkin' all kinds of evil.
    Noah shook his fist away and returned the fingers out of their spherical shape, he stepped away and stood in the doorway of the room.
    Your tongue spits more venom than a snake.
    I may be blunt but I'm never untruthful, remember 'fore you do something foolish.
    You rest that mouth o' yours pa, rustle up your mob too. I'm fixin' to scout ahead, maybe for once I can be of somethin' beyond your shadow.
    Noah walked through the doors, Samwell leaned over the balcony and watched as Noah unhitched Midnight and hopped atop his stallion and rode on out of town. He wondered if this was the last he'd see of his son, he felt a pain in his stomach that he couldn't place truly, he sat on the

wooden board of the balcony and knowing he was removed from view from all but God he almost let out a tear.

His sadness and isolation loomed large and Samwell seemed within himself until a large clap of hands broke him free, finding himself standing with Ransom and Kent on the town's streets, having pushed some boxes together to form a stage of sorts, and accrued a gathering of passers by with come ones and come alls.

This will not be a lynch mob, make no mistake.

Winging is acceptable.

The deputies had festered the bloodlust in Saint Richard whilst Samwell was within himself, and the crowd they formed seemed less like Cranham's calm and collected group but many big bulky men with scratches and scars and lives lived that they'd never speak of again, some, Samwell thought, could be killers in another life.

Who is willing to ride for good and justice?

And twenty coins.

A few folk raised hands as most of the crowd waved off the men and walked back to their Sunday existence. There were eight men in all from Saint Richard who were for a low price willing to be hired to do right in a world of danger. Samwell looked them all up and down from his heightened position, not the biggest or burlliest, not the oldest and most well-fought, the smaller, younger, twitchier ones. They reminded him of the son he only an hour before watched ride away. He shook hands with the men as Ransom and Kent settled each one's verbal contract in the eyes of the law. The eleven men gathered up supplies and prepared and began riding out of Saint

Andrew Jones

Richard on the hunt for the bloody trail and perhaps Noah Wright by evening, as the tavern's piano started once again and another night of merriment commenced, all as it was when they rode in the night prior.

*

    Saint Richard was another blur on the ride for Abraham and Ezekial and Jedediah and Zachariah who passed by whilst the Wrights and the deputies were sleeping the night before, they had followed the trail through the bloody woods before that and seen terrain change around them three times over since meeting Sheriff Hoxley. The first sign to slow down was a foot lacking its body snapped within a beartrap, the leg and its subsequent torso dragged towards a cavemouth covered in moss and blood. Zachariah lit a match as Jedediah picked up a few leaves and wrapped them around a large branch, Ezekiel took out his service revolver and held it over Abraham's shoulder, as the four commenced entry into the dark, dank cave. Each footscuff on the dripping rock ground echoed back and forth in the almost-dark and the horsemen slowly descended, gripping the ground as best in the disorientating opening. They lost the entrance's light swiftly and were many feet below when the smell of char and burning meat wafted into their nostrils. The torch flickered as the four held steady against the diminished air and dank squalor and redded rocks and blanket of barbecued bodies that were forcing their every moment in the cave into a hell nobody knew could exist.

    In the bloodied walls were handprints of size from childlike to beast, the creators of the cave's current standing leaving a mark for whomever should uncover their desires, nothing more evolved than the singular palms that echoed back millennia. The horrors the horsemen were chasing seemed devilishly new and yet in their deepest core they each to a man knew everything undertaken was once and was again and will always be somewhere out there. It had just fallen onto their land. And now they stood in a land beyond, in a making of only the darkest, deeprooted, unforgivable.

    Squinting in the darkness, as the floor settled to an even keel of moss and rock and dirt, Zachariah stood back and watched the torchlight unmask a cavern that seemed to reach out many yards on. Abraham and Jedediah took out their guns, Zachariah looked back at where they had just walked and felt the air between the chambers, it was drier here and hotter, there were no crevasses for wind or water to rush through. This was a dead end underground. He slipped his gun from its holster and turned back to watch the scene from the exitway. The cavern housed the remnants of a maelstrom but picking detail was hard between the last embers of a fire that had charred and burnt through many bits of meat and the bloody wash the walls and floor had received, covering so much of the piles of viscera sitting and waiting to be found in the aftermath. The torch couldn't reveal much of anything, there were flanks of meat and bone, there were strings of organ and muscle, there were layers of skin and fur slathered over one-another like welcoming rugs in a cave home of horrors. Bear and bearcub and human and humancub alike were ripped and eaten and flayed and cooked and scraped and sent around for all to taste and spit and gorge upon, the only sign of clarity was found sitting in the back of the cave, as Jedidiah wandered closer to a twinkling reflection of his torch. Two eyes gave sirencall sitting in the head of a young boy not more than ten, his body that of a small baby brown bear, but two legs of a woman and two arms of a deer. It was not placed together well and Jedediah barely took in the Frankenstein-ed creation before his foot stepped back in disgust and kicked one leg out. The body tumbled, the arms collapsed and the head began to roll towards the fire, smiling a gurn of agony or ecstasy, it would never make sense.

    The four men stepped back and shook heads and sighed, this was becoming too normal a sight and still shocking to witness, another day they would not be able to sleep was coming from this, and they all knew it. The men began to head out again, to get some clear air, when the baby bear torso beat, the heart maybe, or was it still breathing with no head attached? The men stopped and stared, guns drawn to the big body as it moved again, and again, and suddenly a hand pushed out of the neck hole of the bear. A small, feminine hand. Abraham grabbed hold and pulled, and Ezekiel held the body down and pulled from the hand, and an arm started to protrude, and a neck, and a torso, and a head with long brown hair covered in blood and gore, and a petite body of a woman perhaps in her twenties at oldest, stripped bare, and her other arm wrestled out. And as the men cleared the body from the woman it became clear in the torchlight that there was no more of her to come. She was bleeding from the waist down, her legs torn away. She screamed and yelled and it echoed and harshed the eardrums of all in the cavern, as she looked around at the men and the scene and then saw the head of the child and screamed and cried and screamed again. Abraham tried to hold the woman but she threw her arms around in wild panic and screamed until her mouth rasped and her throat pushed all the air out and she could no longer make a sound. Zachariah and Abraham took their belts off and made tourniquets for the woman's legs and dragged her out of the cavern, Ezekiel took one last look and began his ascent to the world. Jedediah walked last up, taking the light with him, leaving the massacre in the darkness forever more.

 Outside, Jedediah and Ezekiel made quick work of burying the cave entrance in rock and tree branch as Abraham washed the woman and Zachariah wrapped his jacket around her to cover her from God. The four men waited for hours for the woman to come sane and talk to them, but she was removed so thoroughly from coherence that even when her throat allowed more air to form sound it was only babbles and screams and cries and vomiting. Night had fallen and the woman still offered no information and the four men knew each passing second they spent was losing time to catch the perpetrators, they

Andrew Jones

consulted one another away from the woman and considered the options. There was no assurances out here for any healing or help or refuge, they had no more time to offer, she was not the witness that would key them into clarity, she would never recover from all that had befallen. They nodded in agreement and walked back to the woman and prayed to God and held their badges aloft to inspect in the moonlight one last time then each took out their revolvers and pointed at the woman. They buried her shallow near the cave entrance and placed a branch atop and began riding off again, it was sense they had to track once more.

*

      Kelso Harding-Grant welcomed each guest at the porch of the nearly-finished three storey eye-sore of a statement he and his wife resided in on the outskirts of the one-road village of Cranham, he stood outside with the lanterns lit and bowed and removed his hat and shepherded each guest into the foyer and through to the living room, where seats of various cushioning and size awaited, as did a tickling fire and a glass to be filled with any of many fineries Harding-Grant bestowed upon his liquor collection through trading luxuries. Kelso was the face of the evening only to a point, as the hostess herself Lauren had the doors closed off to the kitchen until all sweating and frustration and boiling and burning had finessed into the night's presentation, and she could splash a little water on herself and retouch her visage and present only the best impression to the elite status of Cranham's collection. The skeleton staff over-managed and under-paid were near-captive in the back rooms of the building as the night took hold.

    Kelso led the guests through the foyer to the dining room opposite and there sat everyone in their chosen places. Anna Wright and Jenny Wright sat next to one-another, a seat left open should Father Langston free himself from his eternal requirements, Hazel Worthing was sat in the middle opposite Jenny, and the Mann twins sat either side of her. Kelso took one head of the table and they waited for Lauren to fill the other.

    Lauren brought in a silver bowl and laid it in the center of the table and removed the top, a steaming cloud puffed and floated across the room and out the window, to reveal a lobster surrounded by a bed of oysters, with carrots and potatoes chopped and roasted and peppered around the offering.

    We have a room here where ice never melts. It's a delight, I shall show you all after the meal.

    Kelso beamed with pride at the indulgences he and his wife had invested in, had been able to financially procure, and share among those most likely to care in this land. Thomas and Maxwell stood to spoon out meals to everybody, they started Thomas on his right to Lauren and Maxwell on his opposite with Anna, and in a mad rush to get to Hazel first found themselves fighting to scoop up shell and vegetable and meat with speed, clattering cutlery at the quiet disappointment of the table,

Andrew Jones

none of whom dare raise mention for fear of making anyone else uncomfortable. Hazel declined both men's scooping and opted to handle the ladle herself, she then asked if either Mann would like any, and the twins decided to wait for her to sit and serve themselves. Lauren and Kelso glanced at one another and felt like maybe not all this evening would go as planned.

 The conversation was intermittent but the food was absolutely delicious, flavors many of the younger side of the table had never known exploded in their mouths and washed down with a comfortable, chilled Sauvignon blanc that didn't match palette so much as battle it. When the final fork had finished and rested on its plate Kelso and Lauren stood together and thanked everyone for coming and hoped they had a lovely meal and led them back across the foyer and into the living room for another nip of drink and a game of Animal, Vegetable, Mineral. Jenny and Hazel sat together on a two-person seat, Anna was made comfortable in an armchair and the twins and Kelso leaned on parts of the furniture that could suggest dominance but looked mostly like three lost boys looking for someone to take them in. Lauren, meanwhile went between sitting on a seat and getting up and whispering asides to her husband until finally Kelso clapped his hands and drew all attention.

 It has been a wonderful night, thank you all so much for coming. My lovely betrothed and I would like to thank each and every one of you for spending this warm Sunday evening in our beautiful abode, and we wish to welcome you back every month for more meals and games and talk and time. But we didn't ask you here just for fun. My magnificent bride and I have an intention for Cranham and we'd like to make you all aware before we go ahead, out of manners and courtesy. We intend to pave the street towards the church, with stone to fight weathering, and we will pave several more roads in the village, from my trading post up towards the outskirts, and down past the Wright estate, and up to the river. And we wish to build houses and buildings and warehouses on these streets, with the roaring trade and the need for more farm workers, and now more hands at the river, it's time to start expanding this village from how it was founded into a more thriving society. We have taken losses lately and it had put into perspective for all of us how much we come to rely on one-another, and when one of us, or now many of us, aren't there it seems like the horse drags along a one-wheeled cart. We wish to make Cranham as inviting a location to live and work as any western boomtown. We might not have gold running in our veins, but perhaps our kindness and love and Godliness are valued as highly as rush locales with no law or structure.

    The twins cheered Kelso and Lauren, Hazel and Jenny held hands and didn't speak. Anna thanked the hosts upon leaving but never spoke or looked at them beyond that. She warmed up some rabbit stew when she came home and enjoyed the simple warmth and flavors of that meal, washing away the evening.

Andrew Jones

Across the village that same evening, Madame Westington finished up some lamb on the spit and carved plates up for Colin and Lars to share with her, the three sat and said grace and split a bottle of whiskey out on the porch, watching the first men sent from the Fort come wading in for work. Stragglers, weedy folk, not the cream of the crop, not army caliber, but looking for quick coin and a chance to find footing in the world, they waved as the diners ate and yelled out to them, one every twenty minutes or so for three hours, the population of the village was growing so rapidly and only one place had rooms for anyone to stay. Madame Westington laughed and ate her meal and told her two patrons they might have to share a bed, or maybe one could share with her, but she wouldn't give a discount. The men seemed to walk back as a group, finding the Doc at the ferry for the night, and all came to see Madame Westington to settle in. Colin and Lars oversaw the men and helped show them around and fed them all the rest of the lamb, and Colin and Lars decided to share one room together. Colin revealed one of the shotguns he had purchased from the Fort to Lars that night, the rest, he told Lars, were at the stable, Lars would get his tomorrow. They examined the piece and considered how to fire should any of the new men be a problem for the household. An hour went by that night when the men listened to the snoring of strangers before

The Ferryman Upon The Plains

they settled down and felt comfortable once again to sleep under the roof of Madame Westington.

*

The Monday morning wagon rattled across the dirt street of Cranham as it made its way to Kelso's supply warehouse, dodging young men walking and standing and finding their way in the new landscape of the village. The thunk of heavy items against wood and the creak of the wheels trundling on axle, surviving another journey before needing tightening, greasing, repair from various groundstuffs that the roads from the five days of riding before pulling up to Cranham had offered all left their marks on the wagon, the horses and the rider, but the good were immaculate. Kelso shook hands and handed a sarsaparilla bottle to the rider, oats and saltlick and water troughed and ready in the warehouse for the horses to enjoy and rest up with. Kelso Harding-Grant began unpacking the wagon's goods. He moved boxes of fabrics and drinks and speciality meats and laid eyes on the first large armament for Cranham. A gatling gun of iron build, ready to be applied to any vehicle strong enough to wheel it. Kelso and the driver together lifted the weapon and hid it at the back of the warehouse, along with five boxes of dynamite, which they walked and lifted very delicately across the warehouse, not a one daring to breathe until they laid each box on the ground properly.

Hoxley finished his wife's delicious breakfast and walked across the street, staring at the many new men around with curious and uncertain eye. At Kelso's

Andrew Jones

warehouse he waved off the wagon rider now carrying meats and vegetables and dresses and suits and goods from around the area and shook Kelso's hand, they closed the warehouse doors and then were alone away from all of Cranham.

    Was that some of the goods?

    Was it ever, Sheriff. Come, look.

    Kelso gleefully walked the sheriff to the hidden guns and ammo, Hoxley clasped eyes on the heavy duty equipment and his breath poured out in a gasp.

    That's a lot of power.

    Such is the times.

    We must keep this hidden from all, dead of night you and I transport these across my office.

    Perhaps things'll be safer here, for now, what with all these strange folk amassing around. I'm good at keeping my own to myself, your office, no offense, is a little more open to the general.

    Hoxley considered and nodded and looked at a box of dynamite.

    And more to come?

    Certainly.

    How much am I owin' to ya Harding?

    Kelso looked at Sheriff Hoxley and considered reminding him of his correct double-barrelled surname but thought it wasn't the time, and instead offered out a shorter consideration of his idea for the town before. He pitched to the Sheriff no costs, but instead a quid-pro-quo, overseeing the expansion of town under the eyes of the law, and ownership of many nearby strips of land as yet unfounded besides removal of any original dwellers since attacked and murdered through evil means of other men. Hoxley agreed to the terms with the understanding that his role as Sheriff was firm and fixed and he would have all the armory a man in his position could ever require.

    The two men parted ways that day both feeling stronger in their place in the world, and their intentions in their part of Cranham than ever before. Hoxley examined the strange men around the street as he walked back to his office and saw no potential in new deputies in a single one of them. He was not surprised to see them all finding root in the saloon come evening, and was grateful that he could handle any one of them who stepped out of line now he had such heavy equipment resting across the street in times of crisis.

    That evening as the new men were having drinks and becoming acquainted with the barman and a few regulars, Lars took up a shift at the ferry. He was not alone. Colin rode up with him and brought along the weapons bought at the fort, and in the cover of night he handed Lars and Doc Augustine and Herman Ganz their big barrelled beasts, and they each except Colin waved around their weapons and looked down the sights and examined them and checked the ins and the outs of their new guns. Colin gave a box of ammunition to each man and though they didn't load any in each one felt a lot more confident all of a sudden in handling the strange business of manning the ferry crossing at night and considering the

Andrew Jones

collection of folk who had in the past day come by and talked to Colin and to the Doc and to Herman about working the crossing and maybe a few extra gigs to make payment around here. Herman was worried with new faces for the first time in a year coming to see if they could help, knowing any one could be a rustler or a rotter come scrambling for quick harvests and abscond with half his crops, he'd been a good judge of character all his life but even then had seen some folk use the better part of his nature to lull him and from under his nose steal. Lars was the last in his labor pool short of the cowboys roaming north for the summer, and a good man he had been, but Lars was finding himself at the mercy of every demand in Cranham, and Ganz was feeling the aches and wear of age hard lately. This weapon might see off a good number of imminent predators, and find new workers to help the coming season, he figured. That, and it felt good in his hands. He felt like a new man.

    The Doc just enjoyed being one of the gang, with the weapon he didn't intend to use unless pushed, but he liked the company he kept, and that night he didn't much drink, imbibing the energy of the four of them hanging out by the ferry. It had been because of horrible circumstances, but they all felt closer than ever as they waved shotguns at the riverside in the nighttime.

*

The Ferryman Upon The Plains

    They had ridden a full day and a half and not seen hide not hair of Noah or the men responsible for Bartholomew's murder, but the partial patterns of blood and body had found them a shallow grave of a bloody victim, it was strange for Samwell to consider maybe one of the beasts might have felt a compassion and sadness for what they had done, and felt the need to hide their shame or in a moment of reflection ask God's forgiveness by committing half-way a Christian burial. Not a useful one, as a few animals had dug up the poor woman and it seemed like they ripped her legs off and bit through her face and festered in the wound through the back of her head. The men dug a deeper hole and prayed and sent the woman to heaven as best they could, building a big cross with tree branches, tied together with spare rope. They rode on and into Monday night, wherein the darkness lost sense of anything around them in a clear moonlit blue world and open, grassfilled lands offering breeze from three different directions somehow simultaneously, cool and hot and wet and dry and lifted the gait of the horses pushed and propelled by the winds from worlds beyond.
    Ransom and Kent insisted on settling in for the night when one of their horses began whinnying and panting, and the men laid rope and built wooden stacks and rested by a fire in the dark and the moon and the clear. Samwell sat and looked away from the bright burning light, towards the direction all winds pushed, the way the smoke trailed off covering the blue hue of the disc above. The mercenaries sang in a round and made merry their journey, even those still reeling from the

Andrew Jones

discovery of body and parts relinquished dark thoughts and feelings and felt communal in spirit. The horses rested and the deputies cared for the many men's steeds as they made chorus into the night. Samwell looked out, in the darkness he hoped he could see a figure of his son, returning to him or near enough to join him in the journey. The moon tried but illuminated only what was there, an empty land ahead, beckoning to them all to continue on, when their song had been sung and their fire had burnt out.

     Noah Wright bumped and jolted atop Midnight as they made their way down another bumpy path, a dirt and stone and weed-ridden route that he didn't contemplate existed much purpose besides getting folk from one small encampment to another over a few days of walking and resting and carrying water just to survive, before filling up again at the next stop and hitting the trail of another weed-filled road. Noah wished for cobbled stones or pathways of comfort and ease where Midnight wouldn't find his shoes scuffing clumps of dirt in every step, where Noah's butt wouldn't ache after twenty miles of bouncing on the saddle, where people might live around and offer help or guidance or put up a fight against those that might turn up just to hurt others, and see to evil with goodly violence. Better roads, he thought, might alleviate the pain of evil.

The Ferryman Upon The Plains

    Noah seemed lost in his thoughts of destroying evil through infrastructure when his nose picked a burning sensation in the atmosphere, not of fire or chili peppers, but something sweetly hot that hit the back of his throat. Mint, it was. He perked right up, that smell took him back to a week prior, and his good kindliness on the ferry that started all this off. Noah reached in his pocket and felt the two coins, he rubbed them for luck and hoped the connection between them and their owner might bring him closer than ever to fixing everything that had gone wrong in his life. He reached to his hip and felt the pearl grip of his revolver and slotted the grip in the palm of his hand and pulled the gun out, he slowed Midnight's run to a trot and squinted in the moon-blue dark to see anything on the upcoming. There was a small silhouette bouncing, wading, waggling back and forth and growing smaller as it moved. A man, of sorts, wandering, scuffing feet on the hard dirt ground, as if he had been running for miles and ran out of life. Noah rode up behind him and called out.
    Mister? Hey mister?
    The figure didn't respond, just kept on moving. Noah hopped off Midnight and followed behind, the silhouette clearer from ground level, a scrawny figure with hair growing out and clumped in mess and sweat, twitching and shaking and moving constantly, no awareness of their surrounding.
    Hey, you, you better stop or I will shoot you.
    Noah held his gun aloft and trained it towards the figure.
    You think I ain't gonna do it?

Andrew Jones

    He pulled the hammer back and looked down the sight, directly at the silhouette of a human. His hand shaking a little in nerves and saddle-ride.

    God ain't gonna forgive you what you done, and I don't need to neither. As long as you ain't around to do no more like you did my family.

    He squeezed the grip and the trigger came up to the top of its mechanism, the hammer slammed into the barrel and shot out a bullet. The silhouette disappeared in a blinding light and an ear-smashing blast. The air smelled of mint and gunpowder and metal. Noah walked over to the figure, in the dark he could only find it kicking the ground until he felt body. He lit a match and held it close to the figure, a bullet hole in the back of the person's head.

    Better'n you deserve.

    Noah grabbed the scalp and lifted the head up, to gaze into the eyes of Icriss. He squinted and wiped the face free of blood and realized in that moment this was not the man he was hunting for. He had never seen this man in his life. Noah blew out the match and quickly hopped back onto Midnight and rode on in the darkness. The stranger's body would be found in daybreak and buried by eleven men hunting evil.

SEVEN

EVEN IN THE DEAD OF NIGHT the blackness of the storm clouds could be seen against the pitch of the world. Only the intermittent flashes of full bright and forks of electric jaggering across the above and hitting out at the Earth gave any light, and the shattering crash of the thunder seconds after the fact screamed a too-late warning to any in its path. The rain fell heavy to the ground, it was out of season and came so suddenly that nobody was prepared. The single building in the area housed all those lost and seeking shelter for the time, and thank the good lord Himself of all kinds of businesses it could have been it was, of course, a tavern. Over the night men found themselves at the doorway, shaking off the rain and wiping the mud from their boots onto the wooden boards and wandering in, sitting down, putting a finger up and gulping down the desperate glass of succulent juice the barman held in plenty within his domain. All horses, poor things, had to hope a lean-to shelter on the side of the bar could house them and hold off the sky's violent cursing.

A crash rattled the boards and the windows and the bottles and the liquids and the horses whinnied together outside, cold and scared and stuck together in tight quarters, and at the flash of another great light in the sky Noah Wright appeared in the doorway to the rest spot, covered in muck and grime and damp and shaken with cold and more. He didn't slink his jacket off or wipe his boots on the wood, he traipsed his mess in with him and sat right at the bar proper and for a moment seemed silent, still, then his right hand raised, shaking, and his index finger slowly unspindled from the other digits and rose and the barman slammed a glass by him and poured out a long glass of whiskey. Noah stared at the glass and lifted it up to what little light the candles offered, he sniffed at the drink and put it back down and sat still again.

    Ain't this one fancy, what he checkin' for, any bugs is dead soon as they hit the drink, boy.

    The men laughed and drank up and watched Noah.

    I killed a man tonight.

    Noah's voice screeched out of his throat, it was a whimper struggling through the clasping of his windpipe, determined to admit his sin despite himself. He waited for reaction, he wanted so badly to receive a punishment for his awful behavior. A large bearded man with plaid jacket and never-washed jeans sat next to Noah, on the frail man's right, showing the one good eye, the one eye not patched over, and stared at Noah.

    Jes the one? Storm slow ya down?

    He raised his finger and the barman filled his glass, he kept his eye on Noah and slammed back his drink.

    I know how it is, somedays you get into a good thing, poppin' a bastard over here, two on the way to knockin' down another five and then, hey, there's a gorram wagonload ripe fer the pickin' and suddenly you find yer six shooter's out twice over and you just gotta go get a drink or a girl or if you're still in the lust of mind get yer hands close, but then somethin' like this comes over and yer horse starts wailin' and buckin' and you cain't control that and get on a good hunt and it just stops bein' fun. Myself, I ain't done much killin' lately, sadly. No call to. I envy you, boy. So many out there beggin' to be rid, they don't know it yet or nothin' but they're beggin', and I aim to please.

    Another burly man, his stomach larger than Noah's entire body, leaned on the bar on the other side, he removed a leather strap around his neck and showed a collection of ears degraded over time.

    My collection's not been amassed of late neither, but ain't stopped me just for the fun of it. Sometimes I see a young boy on the way to play by the river, or off to send news of his pa, and I'm already pouncing and letting loose. It's instinct, they're out there and what are they gonna do about it? I wish sometimes I wasn't so immediate, it's nights like these I sit around and drink and think about watching their moms and their papas when they find out, what sounds they make, what faces. I'd love to be witness to that one day. Maybe watch them discover their boy, layin' there in parts, all out of sorts, broken and broken and broken again. Lookin' into the eyes of their baby boy all ripped from life, that kinda sight is ambrosia, destruction beyond destruction. Goddamn. Curse my impatience.

Andrew Jones

    Noah turned away from the burly monster of a man, the one-eyed guy kept himself trained on Noah, he was the focal point of the stormy night. An old man laughed behind everyone, Noah sat facing the barman as everyone else looked over.
    You all are a buncha weak sorts, boys, families, ain't you ever faced off against savages? Get a bunch of men thirsty for your blood on your scent, you hide away, up a tree or dig a hole or find a rock and wait, and wait, and when you know they're near, and you know they're near cos they stink like there's no nose ever known a stink, you jam yer blade into their ankle and their hand and their mouth then they cain't walk nor talk nor getcha with their blades and bows and claws, and then they're yers fer the takin'. The look in their eyes when they know it's all over, but you ain't gonna make it quick. All their spirits and all their trainin' and all their bravado drains out and there's a fear in them that pales that dark skin of theirs, and you start up picking off bits, and keepin' them aware that you're not stoppin' for a while, and they scream but they got no voice so they breathe and they spit blood and their warpaint washes off in blood and in tears and in sweat and you start takin' off more. You go for their bits, ain't no chance of bein' no father after that. Then you go for their back, just take that skin off them, show them inside we's all the same, rub their face with their insides, then you open up them, just pull out their ropey innards and shove em in their mouth

and watch them ingest their intestines, and slowly they shake and they pale and they struggle and they stop strugglin' and they're still goin' but they cain't do no more but watch and weep. And you keep at em until ever part of themselves inside is out and outside is in, and finally when they're friends come upon you, and they see what you done did, and they see the last of their man go out of their body, they cain't even come to kill you, they're all so out of their mind in what you did, you could breathe on 'em and they'd collapse and die. None of yer babies or yer families, you bunch of boys. Whole country's gone soft on us.

    Noah sat there as the others took in the old man's horrific deeds, he raised his glass, shaking a little.

    Here's to the old ways.

    Noah started sipping his drink as the other men raised for the toast, and he slowly reached his right hand towards his pearl gripped revolver.

    He took the weapon from its holster.

    The storm raged loud and dark.

*

    Anna had been looking after the horses and feeding the wildlife and nursing the flowers and grass and vegetation on the Wright's sliver of irrigated land, tributaries from the river leading to their estate made by herself and Samwell in the years long before Cranham was a vibrant land, when it was the Ganzs and the Wrights and the Augustines, when owning land meant planting yourself on there and building fences and staring

Andrew Jones

at anyone come riding over lest they intend to make trouble or see to stealing from under you. Folk riding through were like Anna and Samwell when they came across the emptiness, intending to just ride on and find life beyond. But now, it seemed like life in the West was moving East and people living East kept wanting to move West, and Cranham was finding itself in the perfect meeting of it all.

 The evening sky painted clouds of gray and white in orange glow and light blue tinging into a darker purple across the entire world above, another dry day in the dirt and riverside, nary a hint of precipitation in the atmosphere. Anna washed herself from the sweat and dirt and animal muck with a quiet bath and dressed herself in a comfortable dress before making her way across the estate and knocking on the door to Bartholomew and Jenny's house. She waited and knocked again and waited and knocked, then opened the door and called out for Jenny. She cautiously walked in and closed the door and called out again, and popped her head in the front room and the kitchen dining area and the bedroom and realized as the sun fell behind cloud one last time that day she was truly entirely alone.

 Anna sat at the kitchen table of her eldest and recently-buried son and cried, a wail so loud in a world where not a soul could hear her.

The Ferryman Upon The Plains

Earlier that afternoon Jenny found herself drawn away to the tailors and sat with Hazel as she worked on the train of a gown that Lauren Grant had ordered the same time she invited Hazel to the past Sunday's dinner. The Mann twins found themselves staring out the windows in unanimous sedentary, no new suits to be fitting and yet so many new men making motions on the street, not a one considered looking anything other than unkempt and dirty and in everybody's way. Come four in that afternoon Hazel took Jenny over to the tavern and they sat with a couple of sarsaparillas and began playing gin in the warming sunlight by the windows, the brush of each new customer blowing cards over, but their game wasn't to be stopped just because they each knew where every card would be found, friendly is as friendly does.

It's not my place to concern, and if it's too imposing please push me back a step before I fall upon my face, but the other morning from the fort, did that Colin fella have a look in his eye for you something fierce?

Hazel giggled and turned a little red, she looked away for a moment then stared at Jenny.

I know I felt something, Jenny dear. That it was so clear isn't so surprising, he was practically looking over his shoulder lest anyone else notice. Subtle that man isn't.

You like him.

I do?

You do.

Hazel was a strawberry in full bloom, Jenny and Hazel giggled with glee.

I do. Oh, forgive me for looking but I do, don't I? Something about a man who loves animals, there's a deep

Andrew Jones

beauty to it, a true caring that breaks all bonds and beliefs. Never tell a soul, Jenny dear, but some days I've absconded my place at the store, foregone filling my stomach in the midday sun and feasted instead on the man running his stallions, riding them, watering them, holding them, reining them in. Oh gosh Jenny, with those sleeves rolled up and those forearms bulging with tan and tone, I sometimes think of him wrapping me up in them, and I perhaps play with his suspenders, or unbutton a few off his shirt, feel the fuzz by his heart and the rhythm of his beat and his hard breathing as we gaze into one-another's souls. And then I'll make my way back to the store and continue on a gown for some lucky bride or a fascinator for a wondrous event and sit indoors, never having anyone to take anywhere to share a time with.

    Jenny reached over and put her hand on Hazel's, they held one-another for a moment and smiled.

    You ever notice his form when he's riding atop his horse?

    Jenny! My gosh. Yes I have, and yes it's kept me up many nights.

    Something about a man on his beast, moving to the rhythms of another, harnessing the power of it all, flowing and thrusting. Oh, my Bartholomew would –

    Jenny stopped herself and felt the words that didn't make it out of her mouth crumble into her throat and block her thoughts. She suddenly burst water from her eyes, her face a red of raw pain. Hazel gripped Jenny's hand hard, squeezing and stroking, and offering quiet care and compassion.

I'm sorry.

It's ok, it's natural, let it out.

They sat in a stalemate of sadness and hope across the table, the cards laid out before them both.

The Mann twins gave it their longest wait but by the time the sun had glowed into its burning final hours they locked up and walked the excruciating twenty steps down the street and entered the tavern, filled more and more with strange folk than ever before. They both tipped their hats to Hazel and Jenny and made their way to Christian Olsen manning his bar before returning to sit opposite one-another on the only table with folk they knew. Jenny and Hazel left the last game of cards stay uncovered on the table before them to attend to the men who decided to occupy their space.

Tis an odd feeling today.

All this upheaval, cannot feel settled around so much strange.

Are you ladies doing alright?

Neither Hazel nor Jenny offered verbal communication, the Mann twins thus felt obligated to feel the table's silence with words.

All of this and Harding-Grant's big ideas, one wonders what Cranham will look like this time next year.

God help us, what these men'll look like lest they comprehend a little fashion and decorum upon their lives.

Andrew Jones

Has word of bathing not spread beyond our fair little settlement?

     Quite indeed Maxie, a blight upon all with sight.

     Though I do like the notion of a proper street, liken that time we visited East for the season, the racing and the suits and the hats and the food and the streets made with stone and level and welcoming to the feet.

     We could then invest in superior shoe options, cobble together a cobbler's station, a haberdashery, mayhap venture into scents and balms, a complete restorative and luxurious living location, all under one roof.

     No Tommy, multiple shops. A plethora of places for people to visit, come from afar for the finest in all this big country. A calling for the high and the mighty to abscond from their metropolises and explore the great beyond for such wonders.

     Yes Maxie, what a novel approach, build a place so majestic that simply all must come to us, a veritable wonder of the world housed in the very center of the newest and greatest country on the planet.

     The twins raised glasses to their decision and drank heartily, the women sat in silence, unable to leave because manners, unable to speak because tedium.

     I'm glad we have someone living here determined to bring this place beyond its existence, that Kelso's been a Godsend to our trade.

Well now Tommy, he's the face for sure but you mustn't think he's the brains of the whole operation now, surely? The Harding family are the real means, Kelso bless him is a lucky man married far above his trading post.

I don't think I see that there Maxie, he's always seemed on the right path and talking the good talk all our times.

Maxwell leaned towards Hazel.

He's just saying that because one time when we bought some textiles he had a spare bottle of your particular choice to imbibe tonight and he gave it to Tommy since my arms were full with fineries. Tommy here's very easy to buy.

Thomas leaned towards Hazel.

Maxie's just jealous because the richest man in town likes me more than him.

That's a falsehood.

Tis not, green gills.

The twins gave a little go around with one-another verbally then quieted down and drank. Jenny and Hazel felt the sun falling from view and took that opportunity to take leave of the location. The twins walked them out and sat back, looking over the many strangers around.

I didn't wish to say this in front of the ladies, but perhaps we should consider sending out for some denim.

Maxie, I was thinking the very same.

Andrew Jones

A few tables over, in the middle of the tavern, Avery Bedford sat and nursed an ale warmer than any he'd tasted before. His chapped lips were like all his body, dry and desperate and quivering with want. His green eyes diluted through wear and tear and many years of mounting and riding and carrying and fighting and looking for a place to rest. His blonde hair losing its yellow in the land, the sun and the passing of time, and his grand height of over six feet stood him out whenever jobs were being offered, or questions asked regarding missing objects of people. He was happy in the night to sit with others who weren't so demanding of reason or explanation, letting him sit and think and slowly lap up the amber-brown water that was better pissed than drunk.
I like it.
His voice rough and deep, it cut through silence and shook the ears and the made hairs stand on end. He needn't say much to take focus, his resonance and its staccato drawl, a not-quite-Cajun, not-really-eloquent mix gave all around moments of uncertainty, contemplating which words were meant in the homophones of language garbled in the mouth of the big man Bedford.
Last place I were at were full of loudmouths and folk always starin' and questionin' and wantin' you to 'splain yerself if you were out in the dark. Ain't nobody here yet given me a stare weren't wavin' or noddin' or smilin', maybe they don't

know better, maybe they don't know what kind of people is out there but maybe that's how it should be, sometimes, just makin' a little pocket of paradise away from all the bad shit. I'm more than happy to find a place to rest myself from the bad shit I done and don't wanna deal with no more. Just make a new life.

    A new life? Boy, you come lookin' for a new life tryin'a get into uniform and they send you to some nowhere spot to row a boat back and forth for some dead people and you wanna plant a flag and lay your hat? You're as mad as they come.

    The shrill, broken wisdom stemmed from the rotting mouth of Christopher Wolfe, he wasn't as tall as Avery but his bravado and attitude made his reach further and whilst his frame was slighter his words would pack a suckerpunch, and then his breath threw out the killing blow. He had lived out in the harshness of the fields and the farms and the endless nothing of dirt and dust and sand and grass that the world offered all across the country, his skin cracked all over and his color deepened each summer until he was a deep orange brown, his blue eyes the only thing people would use to consider him one of them and let him in establishments, that and his verbal barrage of hatred for anyone who didn't fit his pure specifications of goodly race.

    You gonna make your life sittin' on a river and just wavin' folk over followin' word of shiny gold and jewels in the ground? No way to live.

    I weren't thinkin' much about that as a long-time, just fer settlin'. Man came down to the river today, not to pass, said he was from here, sized me up nicely, he

Andrew Jones

wanted to see all us folk in our prime, in our duty, said I might have a regular guardin' his goods and stuffs.

      Guardin' from who? The rest of us? Few days here and already folk are gettin' scared. Folk never seen a stranger before, livin' in their little hideaway from the world. Ripe fer the pickin' is what these folk is, find a spot and lay yer hat if you want, all this land ain't claimed fer, go build a house and make a trail and plant some seed and rear some livestock and ain't nobody here gonna tell you to get. Fact there's animals and plants just down the way, y'seen that old guy who lays claim to all that? Might as well just go throw him down and take it all, we could do a better job than farmer death.

      Christopher hushed his voice a little as other men wandered past to refill their glasses. Avery sipped his ale and watched the bubbles in the glass rise and fall and float around. In the time away from speaking Freddie Graham finished a big glass of whiskey, got another and finished that. His eyes fell away into deep thought, into daydream, into sleep and then returned to the tavern in Cranham.

      I got my first shift later, that doc gave a bunch of us a whole talk about the way to greet folk, this crazy place and its old customs. They never heard of a bridge before?

*

The Ferryman Upon The Plains

In the light of another morning, two days removed from a torrential storm that flooded fields and left paths muddy, removing all sense of life and violence that led the posse somewhere out of the way of everything they'd chased Samwell, Ransom, Kent and the eight Saint Richard mercenaries found scattered horses saddled and dragging reins, no sign of owners whatsoever. Calling out they found no return, but the hoofprints in the gungy ground led to a wooden building bursting with chips and holes and breaks, the smell of metal and flesh and liquor gagging the nostrils as the posse came closer to investigate the out-of-the-way open house.

Samwell and Ransom were first to wipe their feet on the boards and step in, Kent and the mercenaries opted to stay outside and stand guard. The layout of bodies laying on the ground, or over tables, slumped in chairs or upon the bar, all hands holding guns, all bodies holed several times over, made it clear how things shook up. Ransom checked the bodies as Samwell stood in the center of the building, where it seemed all guns were pointed towards, where it seemed all bullets had flown through before hitting wall, wood and flesh.

They all got all their bits attached, Mr. Wright.

Just one of those things, deputy. Men done each-other in fer the sake of killin' time I guess.

Folk are gettin' more and more trigger happy these days.

Bunch a men sittin' round, drinkin' up, gettin' on one-another's last, bound to spark a fire eventually.

Andrew Jones

    Them horses all bounded from the gunfire then, Mr. Wright? Scattered at the sound of shots?
    Perhaps, deputy. Though if I were out drinkin' in some place like this I'd surely tie my Clover tight, cain't be trustin' some stranger wouldn't up and ride off with the leniency of moorin' that'd let a horse go runnin' at slightest sound.
    You is in the rope-tyin' business, Mr. Wright, though.
    Maybe so, deputy. Maybe folk these days don't much consider their saddle worth savin', or maybe they think who'd be so stupid as to steal their saddle out here, would surely be shot several times over 'fore they make it clear of aim. These folks clearly quick to firin' upon things they deem not what they want.
    But not the men we're huntin'?
    Probably not, deputy. Just another mausoleum on this accursed plain.
    A dead end.
    Samwell nodded and walked out, to the fresher air. Ransom finished examining the men and left them as they were, he walked out too and they mounted up and continued on. Their direction uncertain, they just went opposite of the way they came, that was all they had to guide them for now.

*

The Ferryman Upon The Plains

One wheel still spun on its shared axle, the connecting wood once under the wagon was there for any and all passing by to see, only the slightly spinning wheel to show what once was transport for a family across the land. Shattered wood, not lacquered and varnished, not painted and rich in love and care, red only through acts taken after disassembly unto those inside no longer finding an inside to reside. The back end of the wagon with its wheel squeaking and rotating laid on the grass and rock by the trail's dirt path, the rest scattered in splinters and boards over and beyond the pair of metal tracks leading across the land, from sun's rising to sun's fleeing. The arms and legs and heads of the family that found themselves in the collision with unstoppable force were separated from one-another, pooled in ruby red water drying in the baking sun. Entrails from each formed a string directly to a jabbering soul festering and gnawing and biting and gulping and ripping at the still-warm innards. His teeth jagged, sharp, perfectly cut for purpose. Prip's whole body was covered in the blood of his victims, his straw hair now strawberry blonde, his torn clothes making blotches of blood on his skin, his eyes cold and focussed on the gnashing of the meat and juice he was encircled with, a nirvana of his own.

Abraham and Ezekial and Jedediah and Zachariah had been riding a while since finding the cave and waiting for the woman to make sense and giving up on her and sending her off and they had ridden through a passing storm and pushed on and never once uttered a word about what they had done or what they had seen or what they were hunting for, it was no longer clear, like the world after the downpour it was a muddy trail. They saw the debris up ahead and slowed, the wheel's squeaking groan flew towards them with the wind that brushed and stopped and brushed them again, covering the horses' cantor for Prip as he mashed and fed and tore apart his prizes. The men took out their guns each in preparation and began to split up, two from the trail, one flanking the easterly and one covertly riding on and heading back down, no way away for their first catch.

    It hadn't mattered that Jedediah rode upwards and returned, or that Zachariah went east and returned following the train's tracks, Prip was lost in his massacre. Ezekial and Abraham knotted their ropes and lassoed the cannibal quite simply, only when the ropes slipped over and pulled back on his legs and body did he snap out of his singular focus, the organs half-digested fell to the bloody ground and Prip was pulled up and restrained. Zachariah wrapped another rope over Prip, bending his arms to his side as Abraham and Ezekial pulled and kept the blood-soaked bastard upright and, whilst wriggling, at bay from attack. Prip bent over and ferociously gnarled at the top of the rope restraining his arms, chewing at the material and fraying parts of it, the three rope-holding horsemen walked their steeds back a little each, Prip was lifted off the ground and felt the constriction in his body, crushing some of the capillaries in his arms and legs, were it not for the bodypaint from the wagon family the men would bare witness to a blue and purpling of Prip's skin as he was elevated and held, his gnawing and bending struggling with the entanglement of the lassos.

    Jedediah got off his horse and walked up to Prip and stared at him, the monster roared and bit towards the lawman. Jedediah turned his gun around and began smashing the butt into Prip's face, he knocked the man in the nose and the forehead then grabbed the back of his skull with his other hand and began smashing onto Prip's mouth. The butt smashed on the purposefully sharp incisors and bloodsoaked molars and forced them out of their sockets, the power shattering parts of the enamel and sending them in fragments down Prip's throat. He began choking and coughing up the teeth, down his body, onto the ground, as Jedediah finished smashing each one out of Prip's mouth.

    They dragged Prip away from the wagon and the bodies and the train tracks, the four horsemen rode a little up a hill, towards the shade of leaves green and yellow, the storm had livened up the harshness of the summer hitting the branches and vegetation for so long. The blood had mostly dried from dragging Prip, dirt and grass and grit finding purchase on the sticky coating of the shaking and angry prick attempting still to shake the bonds of the law and return to the sanctuary of the innards and goop from recent victims. Abraham and Zachariah kept their ropes tight around Prip and pulled from north and south, Prip captured in the middle of it all under the tree. Ezekial walked towards the great growth with another rope and threw half of it over some branches. Jedediah held the bloody grip of his gun and kept the barrel aimed at Prip and grabbed the thrown rope end, the two men yanked at the rope and the branches refused much give. It'd do for justice.

    Jedediah looked at Prip as he wielded his weapon towards the criminal and began to orate. Ezekial tied his end of the rope around his horse's body carefully, patting and stroking his saddle calmly as he did, and then took the rope end from Jedediah and knotted a noose.

    It is in the eyes of the law of these United States and God himself that you are sentenced to death for the murders and desecrations of many humans male, female and child across the lands we find ourselves in, you who has only sought destruction and devastation to anyone and everyone along your way. You hold no regard for human life and will be relieved of your own with the authority of the states of Mississippi, Arkansas, Louisiana and Kentucky. Your time on this Earth is at an end, for your crimes you will not be welcomed up above, the closest you'll rise is with this here rope attached. God can't help you now boy.

    Abraham and Zachariah gave a little on either side and Jedediah grabbed Prip and pulled him closer to the tree, closer to Ezekial, closer to the noose made for his neck.

    You ain't got any last words, has ya?

The Ferryman Upon The Plains

Ezekial mocked the beast, Jedediah laughed whilst holding his blood-splattered gun towards Prip. Prip spat blood at Ezekial and a slew of red fell down Prip's front, over the ropes holding him together. Ezekial reached over and put the noose around Prip's neck and tightened it a little. Prip shook and vibrated and the rope around his chest and holding his arms to his side broke with the fraying a little, the blood freshly spat and dripped helped slide the rope's knot open a little and Prip bulged his arms out a moment, the rope around his feet still tight pulled him down. His arms broke out from his side and Prip grabbed Ezekial as the lawman laughed in Prip's face, unaware of the moment now passing swiftly. Prip grabbed Ezekial's throat and clutched tight, his fingers clawing into the lawman's skin. Before Jedediah could fire off a shot, Prip crushed his hands into Ezekial's windpipe and pulled out part of his esophagus, arterial spray a fountain of warm red across the leaves and the grass and the tree bark and the ropes and the lawmen and Prip. Jedediah fired a shot into Prip, his top ribs broke with point blank impact. Abraham and Zachariah swiftly fired shots themselves, one through the spine and making Prip spew froth and saliva and blood, the other in the back of the head, his skull exploding, his face stayed staring out at his final victim. Ezekial sputtered and paled and fell to the ground without a throat. The gunshots didn't spook a single horse, it wasn't until Jedediah slapped the ass of Ezekial's saddle when Prip was formerly sent on to the law's final resting place.

  The men stared at their fallen lawman and the twirling monster rocking in the slight breeze that kept the

Andrew Jones

wagon wheel in motion long after its time had come. They untied Ezekial's horse and tethered the rope to the trunk, leaving Prip on display for any and all. Abraham and Jedediah and Zachariah stood above the body of Ezekial, they looked at the gasp-laugh final face of their trail partner and took off hats and silently said prayers to Him above and set about giving the man a decent but swift burial, no time for luxuries out here, one might be down but they to a man knew it wasn't the only monster they had to put down before their journey was over. That night four horses rode on, three men atop them more determined than ever to hunt the monsters of the plain.

*

      Another night on the riverbank had seen the Doc, Lars, Colin and Farmer Ganz drink and sit and watch as new hands tested their ferrying skills and passed the punting oar to one-another in the warm summer air, before the first hours of sunless sky ceased the heat and cooled fast everything below. The Cranham citizens eyed the new folk up for a while but felt comfortable enough to let them ferry and hold down the fort free of oversight, the four men headed off back to their homes a little sauced up and walking stiffly with shotguns hidden behind jackets and tucked into the backs of their pants, not loaded lest their butts get blown off from one drunken trip up on the unlevel dirt ground.

    Ganz had walked up Cranham's street and seen the Doc to his house, the four men looked towards the tavern and its nightly glow revealing a plethora of incoming men drinking and talking, they felt unwelcome in their own place. He walked towards the church and waved off Colin and Lars, splitting to the right towards Madame Westington's boarding house and their shared room, and he walked left, towards the acres of land beyond that made up his farm. Ganz was a little limp-legged and swayed more than walked as he made his way past the small stone wall that sealed his boundary from the rest of the world. He was feeling the top of the stones with his fingertips, letting the coarse texture ripple across his calloused skin to guide him beyond in the dark and the drunk, and as he reached the wooden gate that opened to a pathway between crops he stopped and took a deep breath. The cold air awoke his spirit and fermented his belly, the hit to his head was at once clear and euphoric, he felt free and floating but knew exactly where he was and what he had left to do. Just open the gate, walk through, close it up, walk up, walk up, walk up, door, house, bed, rest. Simple.

    The wooden latch was unlocked and Ganz swung the gate wide and walked through and turned back and locked himself off from the rest of the world, the gate only came up halfway to his person but the sense, the meaning was clear even in the dead of night. He was home. He turned and began walking up that pathway, just walk up, when he heard the first bark of one of his dogs crash through the silence of the farm. Another bark, then three more, from both his hounds, and not from the farmhouse up the path, from his left, away from Cranham, deeper through his acres. Ganz turned from the path and walked through some crops, the barking continued and increased in volume as he lost himself in the tall growth of leaf and stem and unripe crop. A gunshot shattered the ears and was followed by two more just as loud, and Ganz wondered if he lost all his senses immediately when the barking seemed to disappear all of a sudden. He made his way through his field, the leaves batting him and he could hear their attack on his person as he pushed on and knew it wasn't deafness that struck the barking. He felt around his back and began to pick his pocket the lead that he now never left his house without.

  The Wolfe on Ganz's property had leapt the stone wall and snuck through many of Herman's crops until he felt completely out of sight before he began pulling at the plants, not the leaves or the vegetables but uprooting the plant wholesale. He didn't care for the security plan Ganz had with his hounds free to roam the land at night, and he made quick work of them before they raised too much alarm, or at least before they turned their bark to worse. He was covered in dirt and speckles of blood and the night's darkness made him feel invincible, free to rid the land of ownership and animal outright. Ganz crouched as far as his aging body could take him and loaded his shotgun and peered through crops, the smell of gunpowder called him closer and the shuffling of Christopher Wolfe's hands on the plants he was pulling up keyed the old inebriate towards the right direction. Wolfe mumbled a little about the bloody dogs and felt victorious in his destruction of the animals and sly removal of Ganz's property for his own doing. Ganz pointed the shotgun at Wolfe from his righthand side.

You best stop what you're doin' sonny.

Wolfe dropped a crop and pointed a gun back towards Herman Ganz. Herman could just about see the shaking, twitching, last gasps of life in his beloved pups as he held the criminal at point.

Put that down, you thievin' bastard.

You besten' step away, old man, 'fore you end up like yer damn dawgs lyin' in their own self for the last moments.

Wolfe moved the gun a few times, near towards Ganz but not always directly at. It was clear things were too dark to see.

You can leave now yerself, boy, walk back to town with me and tell yerself to the sheriff, give you a few nights for hurtin' my dogs and diggin' up my crop. I'll accept you workin' it off too, under guidance of others, o'course.

No, I don't think I'll be doin' that.

The gun searched and searched as Herman spoke, and finally came to a stop. Christopher Wolfe pulled the hammer back on his gun. The blast of Herman Ganz's shotgun threw him back a little, his feet stepped a few but he kept upright. Which was more than Christopher Wolfe could do when both barrels exploded towards him, damn near close enough to feel the lead leaving the gun proper.

    The Hoxleys were entwined in bed, Sheriff lovingly mounted atop, his wife's body bouncing and rippling with the effects of the pounding of body on body, two loving people absolutely bathed in the glory of one-another and the power of their passion. It was a mutual completion they were coming towards when the first gunshot rang out. The Sheriff slowed his thrusting and leaned up, his full weight on his beautiful soulmate as the next shots popped off.
    Gorram.
    The Sheriff pulled out and apologized to his wife as he rolled out of her, out of bed and threw on his uniform in a flash. Mrs. Hoxley lay in bed, unsatisfied and alone as her husband darted out of their house and his bootsteps down the wooden stairs and onto the street of Cranham below left her wanting and saddened. She compelled herself to completion, waste not want not she thought as she remembered moments ago the feeling of her man kissing and holding and thrusting into her.
    On the street and from the tavern men were coming out and looking on towards the shots' direction. Sheriff could sense from them all to head on up towards the Ganz farm. He rode out fast, and saw the flash of light a moment before the crash of a big shot spooked his steed and he hopped off and

The Ferryman Upon The Plains

over the stone wall and towards the blasts. Hoxley lit a match and made his way through crops until the reflection of his flame from metal came into sight. He took out his revolver and held it out.

Drop whatever you got there.

It's Ganz, sheriff, I'm over here, I ain't droppin' nothin', this is my land, I do with it what I need.

The Sheriff holstered his gun and walked towards the old man.

What you got there in your hand Herman?

What I need to defend myself with, turns out.

You can drop it, can't ya?

I can do whatever I wish to do, none o' you can tell me otherwise.

Ganz stomped his foot on the ground.

This my land. This what I say goes territory.

That so? Who said that?

I did, what makes our country so great Sheriff, uphold your own self, fight for what you need.

Hoxley got closer and in the small flame's light could see the torn apart body of Wolfe and the dead dogs on the ground.

Gorram, Ganz, what in the hell'd he do here?

Man came to steal my stuff, he came and killed my pups. I did just what I had to do. Justice.

Folk from town started to walk over by the sheriff's horse, a few carried lanterns and led the way. They hopped the wall and followed the small match's light through crops and lit up the entire scene.

Jesus, that guy killed a man and two dogs.

Andrew Jones

Look at all the blood, goddamn.
Murmurs and gasps and shock at the ruination of life before them spread, someone noted they had just been drinking with the now-deceased Wolfe hours before, how he was a nice guy, is this how Cranham treats outsiders, newcomers? Are they next? How dare this man kill one of their own. Words become yells fast and Ganz and Hoxley found themselves circled by noise.
Sorry Mr. Ganz, gonna have to do this to ya.
Sheriff Hoxley took out some rope and tied it around Herman's right arm, pulling it back. The shotgun fell to the ground as Hoxley grabbed his left and pulled it back, tying them both together.
Goddamn you Sheriff, what gives you the right.
I'm doin' this for your own protection, Mr. Ganz, give me a little help here.
Ganz wriggled and fought against it but Hoxley was too strong and had already unhanded the man. He walked Ganz out of the farm and took him up to the office, followed by a gang of outsiders holding lanterns, watching and yelling. He walked Ganz into the pristine jail cell and untied him and closed the cell up. A few folk came to the doorway to look at Ganz in jail, Hoxley told them to go home, get out, he tried his best not to overwhelm the moment. Two bolder men stayed at the doorway and took out revolvers.

The Ferryman Upon The Plains

You get that man outta your cell, Sheriff, he ain't rottin' away in there after he killed one of us. We want retribution of our own kind.

Get yerselves away from my door, the law will do as the law will do, that's how we keep it in this land.

In this land you kill us and we have to just like it and move on?

We pass trial and judgment out of the way of emotions and bloodlust, boys.

Ain't yer boy Sheriff, ain't none of us yer boys, so you best be openin' that cell and givin' up that old man for him to be receivin' the punishment he deserves.

A few yells from outside emphasized how alone Hoxley was in this town.

Old man, you're hangin' by yer neck before dawn, best believe that.

A blast of gunshot rang out from the street, scuffles of mens boots on dirt and suddenly a silence.

Drop yer guns boys, don't play foolish round here, this is a peaceful place.

Colin Maclaine and Lars Skellig held shotguns out, pointed at the backs of the two men in the doorway. Lars' gun still smoking from the blast, he loaded it up again.

Gorram, where you all gettin' this heavy duty arsenal boys? Did y'all rob the army? Put that stuff away!

The Sheriff reached for his gun in the distraction of the standoff, as his hand was on the holster the doorwaymen put their guns away and raised hands and walked off, muttering and spitting towards Colin and Lars. The shotgunmen watched them clear sight and walked into the Sheriff's office and stood by the jail cell, Lars handed Herman his shotgun dropped from the farm through the bars and the men stood and eyed the doorway for swift retribution.

    We'll be here all night Sheriff, heat up some coffee.

    Gorram boys, what's happened to this place?

    Whatever happened, we make sure it don't come take us with it.

    From across the way, Doc Augustine had barely gotten to sleep before the shots rang off and he hopped out of his chair, wiped off the drool and grabbed his gun, watching the world ride off and come back and a standoff occur before his house and clinic. He quietly grabbed his shotgun and felt the cold of the metal heat in the palm of his hand, his whole body raging with red looking across at the uncertain scene. He gripped tight the weapon and stared through window over the dirt and wood that was Cranham in width. He heard his breath gain speed, flashes of white and red in the dark of night and in a moment let go of his gun. The clunk of metal on floorboard broke him out of the focus the Doctor had flung himself into, and he caught his lungs a kinder pace in the heavy night air of summer.

    Augustine turned from the window and overseeing it all and looked at himself in a mirror, the red of face unrested, overindulged and prone to emotional sway a beaming beacon in the blueblack of his clinic at night. A splash of water, nothing settling, he splashed a little something heavier onto his tongue and felt a little calmer, a little better about things. Augustine picked up the heavy duty double barrel from the floor and hid it upstairs, under blankets, under cloth, soft over hard, and laid back down. He closed thin curtain over the window and tried best to ignore the across-the-way, and the under-the-bed, and hoped inside he'd find a little easier, a little respite, in the darkness he created, not the one the world was pulling across the landscape whole.

*

On his back the sun was waking and reaching its warm grip across the cold land, he and Midnight had gone through heat and rain and wind and thunder and gunfire and mud and blood and raced away from every demon that came across his path and now he sat by a river's bank once again, as it always seemed to have been, a return to the flow of the water. Noah dunked his head into the cold stream and held his breath, shaking away the muck and clumps of mess that had attached itself to his and his stallion's every inch. He ran those long, slender fingers through his hair, across his face, feeling the pricks of his stubble as the dirt and evidence washed off, and then he sat back up and shook the water off of him, drips fell frequently from the overhang of his hair and onto his nose, down to his lap, and rolling back to the river to flow onwards. He cleaned off Midnight and watched as the horse played around the water, hoof in and out, head dunked and lapping the water then out and shaking the

Andrew Jones

moisture off, Noah couldn't cease the beast to clear the underside, just let him play with the water and find some rest and comfort after such a long, perilous few days.

    Quickly now the sun's heat strangled that cold night gasp and the drops evaporated and Noah was dry from his knees up, dangling his legs over the bankside and feeling the roam of the water in his feet, his boots caked still and struggling to succumb to the water's cleaning wash. With the light he could stare into the water less clear than it was moments before, yet moreso. For the first time in a week he could see a face staring back at him that he, kind of, recognized. The greying brown stubble, the messy wetted hair needing a comb or a cut, the saggy eyebags purpling and haunted, holding the sleep unoffered to the rest of the body, the cheeks gaunt and pale, Noah was not ever the person he thought he should be, when he saw others, when he saw himself, when he thought of his place, he never belonged and here in the river's reflection he struggled to see rhyme or reason for his own existence. He spat at himself, the ripples of the impact turned his face funhouse and his eyes expanded and compressed, his cheeks smiled and soured, his hair condensed and grew out, his nostrils flared and fleshed up.

    Noah looked away from himself and took in the land he found himself hiding upon, a grassy, rocky region suited more to Midnight than his kind of folk, the first flight of the day came over, the stunning wingspan of an eagle brown and white in the morning light flew fast and flapped infrequently, hovering, monitoring, observing, hunting. Noah watched the majestic bird operate the skies, scaring off any smaller animals from finding feast in the morning air, as the crack of a gunshot flew easterly and the eagle flapped a few times in surprise, turned and made haste away from the violence. A second and third shot rang out, followed by the guttural screams of bloody murder that pierced Midnight's ears and had him slamming feet into the ground and whining with shock. Noah looked west, over the river, in the direction of the violence. He felt the pearl grip of his gun in its holster and clutched the reins of his horse and stood up, reaching out to calm his stallion. In the sickening silence after the surprise, Midnight ceased and Noah sat atop his saddle, they turned to face the river and his kicked his spurs into Midnight's side a little, they began to swim the river. Midnight's underside would be clean by the time they saw shore again.

*

    The tracks led first to the small town of Rockwood, its sizeable station building from the outskirts glimmered with glass and goods sitting and waiting for the next transport. Abraham, Jedediah and Zachariah rode in as the morning commenced, the journey out taking them longer than planned, diverted off course if any course could be found anymore, and they made first to dispatch the last letter to Ezekiel's wife, and each took time to

Andrew Jones

write a little correspondence to their own betrothed in the break in civilization. The three men walked the sawdust and gravel plaza as the world woke up, the buildings of stone and wood turning out good business at great frequency, for a small locale the transport link had certainly turned things from blip to bustling and the town was yet to truly capitalize. The sheriff and a few deputies were walking the area, overseeing, scanning, checking on the locals and checking the faces of all the new folk, they made their way to the horsemen quickly, their posture upright but their presentation disheveled and long in the tooth.

    They showed badges, the town's law acknowledged and the deputies went about their duties as the sheriff was caught in conversation.

    We had another. He fell in the good fight.

    Condolences, Marshal. Marshals.

    Zachariah described the location of the hill, Jedediah the nature of the beast hanged, Abraham the placement of the body for marking.

    Gotta warn ya Sheriff, this hanged fella, he wasn't but part of a much worse cascade rollin' cross this land.

    You see or hear somethin', anythin', peculiar, start up and give chase and ride out, the moment they begin's the moment we lose.

    The sheriff laughed a hearty laugh, blasting across the plaza, men and women and children stopped to look before moving on with their morning.

The Ferryman Upon The Plains

Fellas, sure as shit ain't nobody on this here world as bad as the folk round here. Worst you can find, you betcha, we do one of two things to 'em. Some end up my deputies, put their monstrous nature to good use.

And the others?

The Sheriff pointed to the platform erected at the far side of the plaza, a wooden step-up gallows. Three nooses whispering to the slight breeze in elevated air. The lawmen took time that day to rest in town, they watched to people happy in their lives, friendly, courteous to one-another as they passed, in conversations of pleasant and sometimes deep thought, and as the sun turned to the tip of the sky and the bell rang out for noon the Sheriff ascended the steps along with a rotund old man who would introduce himself to the crowd of folk big, small, young, old, with knitting and rifles equally as the mayor and they welcomed up the deputies who dragged along three strange, twitchy men with bruises and blood and dirt and shit and feathers and grain all on their person each, and they stopped these men before the three nooses and wrapped their necks and checked the ropes around their legs and the wrists tied behind them were tight and the deputies stood on the stairway, overseeing the platform, the crowd, the horizon. The mayor called out the men for their abominable crimes, animal husbandry was the euphemism thrown out around the daytime oration, causing laughter as well as the first of many rotten crops to be thrown towards the criminals. The Sheriff pronounced they were to be hanged until death as justice in the eyes of the law and God Himself and the crowd roared with glee and excitement, there was

Andrew Jones

clapping breaking out across the way and one man threw what smelled and looked like shit up at the middle hangee, his last sense on this planet was to be of man-made manure, and then the lever was pulled and the bestiality bastards began their final dance. The horsemen watched on as the crowd erupted with joy and hollered at the dying men, their necks cracked quieter than the words thrown out among the crowd. Not a one of the three living horsemen had witnessed such excitement and enjoyment at the death of another, good or evil. They rode off before the crowd dispersed, and as ever not a one spoke of what they witnessed.

*

    The wheel still span in the wind, whenever the wind would find the wheel, but the smell of metal had been replaced with a putrid punch, the bright red had darkened crimson on the wood and the ground, the entrails had been found by many animals of size large and tiny, fly and coyote each got their taste of the family's flesh, and the shadow of the tree and the hanged man covered the world in dark as the sun was setting beyond the scene. Samwell was not first to see, nor was he tenth, Ransom and Kent each matched the quickening gait upon seeing the sights ahead, the many Saint Richard mercenaries gathered first around the wagon's scene before making their way up the hill to join the deputies and the hanged man. Samwell took his time examining the crashed, splintered wood and dried blood, and the train tracks rumbling between the mess.

On the east smoke plumed singular and large, a tower of black puffed and rose and the trundling of the oncoming was gaining volume. He rode Clover up the hill and saw the crowd gathered around Prip and he made his way off his horse and clutched at his back and tailbone and his arms and his neck in all the aching and exhaustion of the long ride and short rest he'd received. The men moved to clear space so Samwell could see the shot, smashed, bloody dead man hanging from the tree. Samwell looked at the open mouth, the smashed gums and broken teeth, the slashes of clothing and skin on his body, the fingernails clawlike and with bits of meat still in his grasp, and the milky white of the eyes. The face had bloated and paled, veins to the surface of the skin, and the eyes had lost their color and life, and in the orbs Samwell could see a small reflection of himself in white. His hair grown out where it could grow at all, wisps of grey and white had become like a horse's mane, his wrinkles saggier, his skin red and orange and brown and white in the sun and the eye, he noticed his fingernails like that of the hanged man were growing out, unchecked, unclipped, they were claws more and more. In the reflection he was in a world of white.

The train trundled louder, the black plume covered the land to the east, and the train slowed as men and their horses rode off and made their way up the hill towards the men. The train recommenced its ear-piercing screechy commotion and ran west. Rockwood's Sheriff

Andrew Jones

and some deputies saw to the crowd and the hanged man and when Ransom and Kent showed their own badges to the lawmen the Sheriff wondered how they'd got so far away from their land, and their place, and what on earth they thought they were doing up here, maybe it's time to return to where you can do something important, leave the real work to the law of this land.

 The deputies cut down Prip's body and one began to ride back eastward with it as another walked the hill and found overturned dirt and nodded to the others and they hammered in a nicely made wooden cross in the ground and closed eyes and prayed to God. In that quiet moment all men on the hill closed eyes and spoke to their Lord. The deputies and the Sheriff finished their business up the hill and rode back to the tracks and began to clean up the wagon debris, as the Cranham and Saint Richard men stood and watched, and soon the Rockwood men rode back up the tracks and they were all alone again.

 Sheriff's right, we're too far gone now, cain't do much of much up here.

 The deputies took themselves aside from the pack, a little downhill, a little downwind.

 We have a duty to uphold the law, and see to it right is done, justice delivered.

 We ain't the only ones out fer justice, some point we all get lost lookin' for it, we run into one another and lose it altogether.

The Ferryman Upon The Plains

Look here Deputy, we got Mr. Wright's whole family to think of, and Cranham as a whole, lot of good people back home we owe it to handle.

We don't owe it to anyone, Deputy, we were just meant to be trackin' and catchin', but we traced and we caught ourselves a mess and nothin' to take home for dinner. Some point you gotta think whether your job is to hunt or your job is to protect. Out here I cain't do my job.

Goin' back I cain't do mine.

Ransom took his badge and handed it to Kent, they shook hands and Kent went to Samwell and shook his hand and began riding south again.

Sorry about my partner Mr. Wright, some's made fer this, others - -

We all lost a lot on this road already, deputy - -

Just Ransom, now, Mr. Wright.

Very well, Ransom. We all lost a lot, too much for any one life, but we who keep on have our bearings and our purposes. Out there, somewhere, Ransom, our men are still taking air, taking life. Whatever we do, we best see to it they're stopped for good, otherwise all this, all we lost, been for nothing.

The men rode east, in the wake of the Sheriff and his deputies, as the sun descended behind them. They wouldn't see the town until dawn, and in that night Samwell rode through the aches and pains of his body, his heart and his soul. He thought of Deputy Kent heading home, of Noah Wright riding off, of Bartholomew Wright buried in the ground, of Anna Wright wailing in their bed, of Jenny Wright collapsed to the ground with grief. He didn't know where he was heading, he didn't know who

Andrew Jones

he would find, but he knew if he stopped, if he turned back, if he returned to the river and the ferry and the house and his wife and his daughter-in-law and the village and the people and his friends he would never be able to forgive himself, and he would never be able to see his eldest son again.

EIGHT

 THE COFFEE FOUGHT OUT the last of the whiskey in their system, Lars and Colin sat nearby Herman, separated only by iron bars, eyes firmly gripped to the doorway, shotguns on their laps, pointed at walls but ready to draw at moment's notice. Hoxley, meanwhile, between barrel's aim and the doorway sat at his desk, eyes on the farmer in the virgin cell, sipped slowly on his cup of joe and thought of his wife above him, and how she was below him only hours before, when things felt a lot better. He longed for the innocence of the marital bed and the deep love and the years of joy and comfort that in the last few weeks had slipped away from him and Cranham and left him here in the middle of the night slowly taking cooling coffee through his lips as men held heavy firepower to survive a night. Footsteps outside on the dirt scuffed and a few cries of disbelief and anger threw out from drunken throats, followed swiftly up by Christian Olsen's booming response, clear and sober, telling stragglers to find a hole to hide in 'till sunup. It wasn't long after when he gently, slowly, popped his head in to see all the hubbub and hearsay proved true, Herman Ganz was indeed in lock-up. Olsen left and came back within seconds holding a bottle of whiskey and poured a few glasses out for his fellow townsfolk, Lars and Colin greeted it kindly but partook slowly on the alcohol, trying to keep wits about them. Ganz gratefully slurped back his

Andrew Jones

share, grumbling to those within earshot of the whole predicament, whilst the Sheriff sat firmly with his coffee, a crutch he held onto as he contemplated and feared the change that lay at his feet in this small community. Olsen spent a good half hour with the men, supporting their vigilance, before he felt a yawn break out and called it a night and wandered back to his tavern.

    The sun was up shortly after and the whiskey worked to negate all the coffee, another round was warmed up by Colin as Herman rested his eyes, age wasn't good on stamina even after so many years of hard labor on his land. Hoxley fell away second, the snores of the old man guided him to his own state of unconsciousness. Lars and Colin silently caffeinated themselves and stayed prepared for any incoming threats as the world outside began lighting up from the sun behind them, through the wall. The doc's place slowly shone, the sign above it aglow in burnt orange reminding them both of the man's offerings of remedies, cure-alls and general practicionery.

    You think he slept through all this?

    Doc? He's old, he's not deaf. Maybe he just not wanting to rock boat.

    Maybe ol' Herman here's safer over there.

    You want break him out of jail, you on your own, friend.

    Colin looked over to the sleeping lawman and leaned over past Lars and gripped one of the iron bars holding Ganz, he gave it a few fair pulls and it all stayed firmly in place.

They did a fine job buildin', shame they filled it wrongly.

The first rumbles of horsehoof crashed through a half hour later, Cranham still felt the call of night despite summer's early sun insisting on being so bright and risen, and Colin and Lars gripped their guns and started sweating as the noises ran closer. Shadows danced on the walls and facade of the buildings opposite, through the window and the doorway only hints of horses and hats and human figures passing on down the still village street. The two men tensed up, brows firming and moisture ran down swiftly as steps sounded closer and closer. Slowly a single open hand appeared in the frame, and a second, the Doc made his presence known.

Lo fellas, rest ya pieces.

Augustine slowly stepped into the doorway, monitoring the aims of the guns still at opposite walls, and the four men in different stages of consciousness and he made his way fully into the building. Staring mostly at the imprisoned farmer a picture so wrong his head remained baffled and uncertain this wasn't still him in dreaming phase, he loudly kicked the desk to bring the Sheriff back to life.

There's men out here, stragglers and strangers keeping vigilance up and down the street. Saw some folk ride outward and they got themselves a staredown somethin' harsh, these guys is waitin' on to do somethin' and I'm takin' it witnesses ain't to be bared. I'm not for sayin' let's get some folk from the fort to help cos that only ever landed us in this here predicament in the first place, God help us, but maybe we deputize a few us here in the room for good measure and wire out some private folk, pool together our investments on keepin' from getting killed keeping peace in this place?

Ain't that a bit excessive, Doc?

If you left last night up to the Sheriff, Ganz'd be hanging in the middle of town right now and the lawman'd have five holes in him. Then where'd the rest of us be? Hidin' in our hobbles 'fraid to go out and live with these new folk around. We're none of us to a man capable of bringing the fear needed to these men, and they're a growin' group of sorts.

Colin shook his head and stood up, holding tightly to his weapon.

How long you thinkin' of employin' em?

Damn, Maclaine, how long's a river flow? They'll stick around until this place feels safe to live in again. Or money runs out, I guess.

A yawn burst from Colin's mouth, the Doc found it contagious. Hoxley poked his head out of the jailhouse and looked at the figures making groups of loiterers down past the tavern and up t'ward the trading post, waving off men coming back from ferry duty.

You're not bringing more men here with guns and desires and intents to disturb or uphold or mess with my town, boys. I don't care if you mean well or can't sleep from worry, this is settled between us and between just us, we don't need to buy out men or seek beyond. We can't handle somethin' like this, what gives us right to build a world entire? No more talk foolish like, and I ain't to givin' deputy badges out like dust in a storm. My deputies hop the trail of evil, they see to banish monsters, that's what makes them worthy of the badge.

What makes the badge worthy of them?

Hoxley looked at the Doc, up and down he examined the older man rested from his night in his own bed, and spat dregs of cold coffee and warm spittle on the floor.

The promise of freedom and justice. For all.

Doc sat himself down next to Herman, a non-violent vigil, as he told the ailing young men to take a little respite, their eyelids drooping heavy as dawn turned morn. They took guns with them, despite pleading the Doc to grab one for good measure, and made way past an ogling gang of folk ragged and twitchy and whispering between themselves. The men silently stumbled up to Madame Westington's, the footsteps of the last man shifted at the riverside subsided as they made their way onto the porch.

The boardinghouse was quietly rocking with snores from several different rooms when Lars and Colin quietly crept in, the screen door and the wooden one creaked and rattled despite slow and steady movements, and the floorboards echoed their hinged counterparts with every hint of weight ladled atop them, the men slowly took to the stairs and wandered down the hallway towards their shared domain, and sat on the small bed together, back to back, as the noises of the new men of the area overwhelmed them in unsynchronised symphony.

    We cannot stay here.

    We can't leave the widow alone with these folk, Lars.

    I fired this near a few of them hours ago, I cannot stay here.

    Where the hell are we gonna live, I ain't sleepin' with the horses again, buddy. Too old for that.

    A quiet moment fell upon the house, it felt like everyone awoke in unison and floorboards creaked around them. Lars gripped his gun tight.

    The farmer's house is unoccupied.

    The two men quickly gathered the few garments and mementos and coins they had and burst out of the room, down the stairs and out the front door before any of the other residents rose to begin morning ablutions. They took shifts in Ganz's bed, Lars took first watch as Colin rested, he listened for any noises outside, the silence of the world drew him into a light doze only half an hour after his resting pal. The clunk of his shotgun falling from his hands and onto the wooden boards below arose no suspicion from anyone, well out of earshot, and the two men wouldn't wake for a solid eight hours, in their trip across the unconscious realm they each felt happier than they had the past month.

*

    Jenny was feeling heavy as she rose that morning, the pull of the world as she laid her feet on the floor below her bed and pushed up, as she washed herself she grabbed and pinched at every sag and blubber and meaty chunk on her body, the days of her being skinny as a rake, tight to the bone had passed and the freckled-orange and brightly pale skin bore more weight than ever, her cheeks seemed inflamed without any sickness, and she sat and ate some oatmeal and drank a glass of water and considered her diet and her lifestyle and it distracted her for a moment from the emptiness of her house and the silence of the place she'd lived around for years now. And then, in one remembrance of Bartholomew holding her close and kissing her tiny, frail body, Jenny released tears and broke the silence with a cry pained and riddled with desperation. For a while she thought Anna would burst in to see about the commotion and comfort her, but as she looked to the door between bouts of emotion it seemed less and less likely that any soul was coming to rescue her from the despair.
    Jenny rinsed her face of her tears and applied a modest collection of make-up and clothed herself in a nice dress that allowed the heat of the summer to flow through rather than close in and made her way towards Cranham, as she got closer to the single street strange men walked past and nodded at her and watched her pass

by, and Jenny felt uncomfortable at all the attention after such a broken morning. By the time she saw Hazel's shop down the way there was a collection of strange men standing around, with scruffs of clothes and lacking any fineries leaning on buildings, looking over the jailhouse and whispering to one-another, only stopping to nod and ogle Jenny as she passed by. She took in the sight of the jailhouse and the strange men, but couldn't see much clearer as she walked on inconspicuously. The Doc left the jailhouse as Jenny passed and nodded to her, she politely smiled back and kept on, Augustine caught up with her and walked her the last steps to Hazel's shop.

    Mrs. Wright, how're you feelin' lately? Been meanin' to drop in and see to ya, any sickness in the get up? Tiredness? Sudden changes of emotion?

    Jenny stopped and turned to face Doc Augustine, his eyes baggy and his skin ashen.

    I'm doin' just fine Doc. Nothin' ever to worry about. Everything is damn perfect.

    Jenny clutched her mouth and shook her head.

    I am so sorry, that was not intended for your ears, Doc. Please, I'm sorry.

    The Doc shook his head and grabbed Jenny's shoulders and squeezed her gently.

    Mea culpa, Mrs. Wright, I meant no offense, beyond the obvious situations, it's an awful lot of weight to lay on your feet alongside all this. Come by some time, let's check you out proper. See to remedy what we can, medicinally or elsewise.

Jenny nodded and gently touched Doc's hands, removing them from herself.

What's all the business over in the Sheriff's place?

Ma'am, you've got your own things to handle, this ain't worth investin' in.

The Doc walked off towards his place, the whispering gang watched him. Jenny walked up to the tailors and entered, the ringing of the bell atop the door called Maxwell over first, then Thomas who had his neck adorned with a tape measure.

Morning Jenny, have you seen what's going on out there?

These windows were a great investment, front row seat for the theater of Cranham.

It's utter madness out there.

Farmer killed a man.

Man killed farmer's dogs.

Men wanted to kill farmer.

We've been watching it all.

Whilst working, of course.

Thomas pointed to his measuring tape as proof, Maxwell looked past Jenny and out to the street, keeping an eye on the whispering stragglers.

They wouldn't be foolish enough to make a move in daylight, would they?

Folk like that, Maxie, don't think like that, first instinct only instinct.

Fools, but it's free entertainment I guess Tommy.

Andrew Jones

That it is brother.
Jenny walked past the twins and found Hazel deep in knitting together a scarf of green and blue wool. She looked up as Jenny broke into her periphery and she beamed a smile.
Morning. I'll get some tea on once I've finished this tricky bit.
I was thinkin', actually, care to make a walk to the church?
Hazel stopped her knitting and stood to meet Jenny eye-to-eye.
Are you alright?
I don't think anything's right.
The two women left the shop and walked up the street, towards the church, as men watched them go by and nodded and stared at their passing persons. Father Langston was snoozing on a pew when the pair walked in and quietly knelt and sought prayer. He spluttered and coughed and the echo of his own noise woke him rudely to find the two young women before him in concentration with the beyond. He waited patiently then invited the women to his chambers and began pouring out a warm bottle of red wine, the incense had whetted their appetites and the three saw to indulging the deep berry with aplomb.
I pray constantly, ladies, for this place, but I see no change suiting my wants, my pleas. I watched last night as everything happened, as men conspired to steal, conspired to kill, and now there's no room for God out there between the

dangerous villainy of men. Not a one of these fellows coming by to heal the ferry's plight has come up and called out to God for guidance and aid. What am I meant to do with those that don't seek themselves? I can't reach out if there's no hand wanting to grab back. If we are to persevere as a place we need to unite and connect and be as one, as God intended, to live in peace and harmony with one-another and the world around us. All this violence and evil, it upholds the devil's wishes, to disseminate fear and uncertainty among one-another, the wolf dressed as a sheep pouncing upon the herd until not a single sheep believes any other is actually sheep, but is the danger it is most scared of. We cannot live like this, we cannot simply be broken apart and seeking to hurt and only seeing the darkness in one-another. We must find the light together, to be as one, in the name of Him, but I fear the fracture is irreparable. I, ladies, am not sure I can mend this rift, and if I cannot aid, of what use am I in this world?

    Jenny and Hazel held the Father's hands and consoled him as they silently considered their own problems, unable to put further weight on a man at the threshold of his own crisis. They consumed his wine and left him to watch from above the village all of the mess that was occurring and Hazel walked Jenny home, safely away from the mess ensuing but at a stalemate in the center of it all. Hazel cooked up a lunch of salted venison and vegetables and they heartily fed together, telling jokes and distracting one-another from everything, filling the house with light laughter and not pausing for any reality to rip apart the facade of hope and humanity.

Andrew Jones

Jenny only sometimes looked towards the door expecting Anna to come in and see about the noises. Anna who hadn't been seen for a few days now, who had been so removed from all life that not a soul even thought to reach out about the men working her family's ferry, or the new security measures in place in the middle of the village. Anna who was as forgotten already thanks to the maelstrom of events hitting the community as the cowboys who were still out herding Herman Ganz's many cattle in the plains for the summer, and who were starting to turn around and walk them back for fall, and were going to find the land they left quite different, their employer jailed, their favorite hounds deceased and the house they would celebrate holidays in being used by the stable master and a Swedish immigrant.

*

    Midnight ran across the land, the brief foray in the river had been forgotten within minutes of the two figures shooting across the west, backs to the sun, as heat and adrenaline ran the moisture dry. Several more shots rang out and then a silence deadened the world, only the stomps of Midnight's gallop on the dry grassland rang out. Noah sat atop his saddle and looked around as far as he possibly could, his awareness of the sounds lessening in the closer proximity they rode, now it was time to engage other senses, whilst his fingers twitched and clutched to the reins of his stallion and the pearl grip of his revolver. Smoke rose in sudden black plumes a little onwards and died off quickly, Noah slowed Midnight and steadied his horse and dismounted, whipping his revolver out and pulling the hammer back, and he began to tread closer to the incident.

Heavy breaths came through from the sudden quieting of Midnight's gait, and grunts, and groans. Noah crouched and took large steps, slowly placing his boots on the ground, crunching a little grass underfoot with little noise flowing out, and he moved forward upon three tented blankets, the sun still on his back, forming a shadow on the textiles bigger than his person. He covered the site in black for a moment and ducked down, scrabbling on the ground. Just a cloud passing over, nothing worth investigating. He rolled a little and caught a glimpse of gap between blanket and wood where he could peek through. Two eyes stared out at Noah, looking out with their green glow and white plumage, they didn't dilute upon his reveal or follow his movement. He beckoned himself closer and saw the mouth open, still, and the throat slashed open with blood still.

Noah closed his eyes for a second and let out a breath of remorse, and slowly made his way to his feet. He peeked over the blanket in his tall frame and could see three men gathering items and supplies from the travelers' wagon and examining them, throwing some on the ground and pocketing other items. Noah stepped slowly around the tents, gun pointed out, and peeked into another tent, two young children lay in a pool of their own blood, gunned down in their sleep. Noah looked over at the men still unconcerned with his presence when there was loot to be found. He looked at their holsters, the three men, two with guns haphazardly thrust back in unbuttoned, the man in the middle without such. A grip of a gun and a handle of a blade shoved into the back of his pants, a little red formed around his ass where he didn't quite clean it all off. Noah quietly took a few deep breaths and readied himself.

    Hey, which oneo' youse done this to kids?

    The three men turned around, guns ready. Noah shot the throat on the man on the left, ducked down and hit the man on the right in the stomach and took the ankles out on the middle man, they all fell to the ground. Noah walked over to the stomachwound and shot him between the eyes, staring out at one-another as he removed evil. The man in the middle, anklewounded, struggled to reach his gun from behind him having fallen on himself, his own blood sprayed on his pants.

    Goddamnit, stoppit, I'm sorry.

    Noah stood over the man as the throatwound gurgled, drowning in his own blood. Noah kicked the throatwound in the face, caving his nose in with a swift stomp and watched him seizure a little before life drained. He grabbed anklewound by the back of his scruffy hair and dragged him across to the woman whose throat was slit. Noah could now see she was ripped open not just in the throat but this man had made several entrypoints and, looking at how she was splayed, used them before releasing her from the horror. He threw the murderer down onto the corpse and made him face the face of his victim.

Respect her, let her go.

Wha...?

Close her eyes from this Godforsaken land.

The man shook as he reached out and closed her eyelids, he tried to reach back to his gun and his blade as he honored the poor soul. Noah got to the knife first and stabbed the man through his sneaky hand, impaling him on the ground before the dead woman. Noah grabbed the other arm and smashed it to the ground and trod on his hand a few times, fingers spread and ran in directions no bone should. The man yelped and screamed, echoing through the plain. Noah looked at his gun and the man stabbed and broken and unable to move from his position and he holstered his weapon. He went to the dampened fireplace in the middle of the camp, reached in and took out a white piece of wood, smoking still. He tossed it between hands, only able to hold it for seconds at a time before it hurt too much, and he walked to the man.

Open yer mouth again, boy. Scream out for mercy.

The man did as he was ordered, and yelled please and help and Noah grabbed the man's head and shoved the wood into his mouth and pushed it beyond his tongue. The man screamed and yelped and coughed and spluttered and blood began drooling out as his voice burnt up. He spasmed so hard the blade ripped through his hand, still in the ground, tearing three fingers off in the process. Noah stood and watched as the man pulsated

Andrew Jones

and twitched and then laid, struggling to breathe, writhing in unknowable agony. Noah pulled the knife out of the ground and waited half a minute, staring intently at the man, before he leaned over and slit the man's throat. Smoke bloomed from the wound and puffed into the sky, and slowly ceased. Noah spat at the man and dropped the blade and walked to the ashes of the fire and sat, looking over at the dead in his wake. He held his head and closed his eyes and quietly prayed.

 Footsteps shuffled and Noah opened his eyes, two young women and a boy no older than three stood nearby, their eyes glistening with water, paled out, aghast.

 Did you do this?

 Noah raised his hands.

 Ain't what yer thinkin'...

 The boy came up to him and hugged Noah. The women tried not to look at all the blood and death around.

 They came all at once, if I weren't off to relieve myself... Oh god.

 The other woman came and picked the boy off from Noah and held his hand and stood back.

 Sir, thank you.

 I didn't do anything good here.

 You did exactly what they deserved done.

 I'm a monster same as them, ladies, no good to anyone.

 If that were so we'd be like Junebug over there right now. You're not like these bastards.

The Ferryman Upon The Plains

    The woman holding the boy's hand reached out to Noah and lifted him from his sitting, he stood tall before them, bathed in the light of the dawn. Behind her, the other woman began to cry openly.

    I can't believe this, we'd barely set off and now all this. Can't go back now, can't go forward. We're done for, Sis.

    Can we step from this site, please?

    Noah led the survivors from the scene and some ways into the grasslands, where the stench of blood and gunpowder no longer ran through their nostrils. The boy stayed silent, but he clinged on to his mother deeply, dragging her back in steps as she strode fast from the horror. The other woman kept crying and wouldn't cease. Noah couldn't confide in any of the emotions and connections, he stood in the grim understanding of his monstrosity, thoughts still of dispatching the men dancing on his mind.

    Sir, what you did, you did rightly.

    Ma'am, I ain't proud of that, I ain't right in what I do, nobody should get to choose when another dies.

    They chose when our Junebug died, when her Lily and her Tommy died, thank God someone gave them taste of their own, quite frankly. Goddamn, I heard rumors of what life out here was like, but we'd barely been on the month and look where we've gotten.

    Her voice choked as she thought on her sister dead back behind them all, and the pain thrust onto the shoulders of the survivors. She held Noah's hand and caressed it gently.

    Sir…

Andrew Jones

    I ain't no sir, if yer gonna use a word, I'm Noah, that works fine.
    Mr. Noah, we're grateful, of what you did, it might not look like that...
    The woman reached out to her sister and held her close, still on Noah's hand.
    'Sides Tommy and li'l Paul here we ain't had any men on our ride, fitting given all we're getting away from, but we knew we'd be in the path of something dangerous and here, it's come.
    Yeah, out here ain't no place for anyone, man, woman, hell even a vulture makes a second thought before flyin' out, world's gone to hell already.
    Well, we can't make our way back, we got no back to make our way to, all we have is here, had I guess.
    And now? You wanna carry on?
    Sir.. Noah, we're not staying here just to bury Junebug and Tommy and Lily and live out in this patch of nowhere remembering them and living only for their tragedy. Goddamn, we can't be that, we already got from that twice over, we gotta start a real new life somewhere.
    Why not East, why not where it's safe, hop on a boat, go to Europe, people been livin' there for centuries no problem.
    We're American, we're living in America, we're gonna make our world in America, as is our God given right. We got money. We got lots of

money. How much for you to ride with us, personal protection?

Ma'am...

I ain't no Ma'am, Noah, I'm Kirsty Hollander, that there's Sissy and my little one's Paul, none of us are sirs or ma'ams neither.

Kirsty, heck, I can't protect you. I can't protect anyone.

What was back there then?

Retribution. I can kill a killer, but not 'fore they do theirs.

Shit. Well, fine, can you at least give our family a proper burial?

Noah nodded, for his young age he surely knew how to bury a loved one.

He stood by the lumps of ground recently given to the departed, four graves for six bodies, and closed his eyes as the women cried and said their goodbyes and the boy unsure of all that had befallen weeped and wailed with his mother and aunt and only stopped when Midnight whinnied and caught his attention. Noah waited with Paul enamored by his stallion as the women walked off and got their wagon, rode up with their small pony and began fitting all their belongings from the ground pile into their transport, wiping blood from each item as it passed them by. Noah lifted Paul up and sat him on Midnight, his giggles and squeals refreshed the souls hurt by the morning's unforgivable tragedy, and Noah smiled as he watched the pure joy and innocence of the child atop his horse. Kirsty came to pick her child up and watched the males all together for a moment, Sissy sat in the wagon alone.

    You got yerselves any defense?

    Got a couple rifles and a whole heap of ammo in the wagon, not much for a shot myself, but if they get close, they get blasted.

    If you're not laying down or out relievin' yerself.

    Kirsty took Paul from Midnight and placed him in the covered back of the wagon. The kid waved at Noah and his horse, Noah waved back. Kirsty looked over to Noah.

    Sure I can't convince you to come?

    Sure I can't convince you not to go?

    Kirsty shook her head.

    Children and animals, they see us clearer, purer than we ourselves. You're not a monster, Noah.

    Noah reached out and held Kirsty's hand one last moment and slowly let her out of his grip. He stood by Midnight and watched the wagon ride off, the sound of the wheels fading as the wind slowly hit the grass and swept past Noah's ears. He leaned his head on Midnight's and looked at his horse's eye and kissed the side of his face.

    Yeah. Alright.

    Noah mounted Midnight and rode out in the wagon's trail.

*

The Ferryman Upon The Plains

  The tracks led towards an impressive building, a station with plenty of space to sit and consider between times, to stand and pace, and to lump goods to and from market and farmland and the train carriages, and in the dawning light it felt like a beacon to Samwell, that their long journey had found footing somewhere civilized, where humans, not monsters, lived. Rockwood beckoned the men and they dismounted their saddles each and took steps to stretch legs, arms, backs, the night ride had worn them out somewhat. The eight Saint Richard men gathered around Samwell and asked for a small amount of coin to make rest for the day in this town, to get some rooms and heal up from the long adventure, and with Ransom's backing Samwell dipped into his satchel of money and handed slowly out a little payment to the many men, who swiftly took off to the town proper, through the quiet plaza towards the building with signage of rooms, drinks, refreshments, girls. Samwell looked to Ransom and held a few coins to the former deputy.
  Money's no good to me, Mr. Wright.
  Don't wanna go get yerself a room to rest?
  Ransom watched the men speed up and start chasing one-another towards the bordello.
  I surely want to rest, but not like those boys. Sleep, hot meal, maybe slip into a bath.
  That does sound nice.
  Samwell felt around his scruffy cheeks, his nails grown out and scratching at his stubby face hairs.
  A day's replenishment'd do us the world o' good.

Andrew Jones

    Perhaps there's more suitable accommodation a little aways from the center here, quieter, removed from the throughfares.
    Samwell nodded and the two men walked their horses away from the plaza, beyond the many signs and big buildings of stone and board that Rockwood presented to rail travelers. A bell rang from the tower of the church in the distance, the only thing risen above the many single and few double storey buildings of the town, and the light hit half the tower, keeping the town in its shadow. Samwell looked up and stopped for a second, he closed eyes and took a breath, Ransom kept on. Samwell whispered an amen and followed. They found a small house with boarding offerings signed on the yard outside and walked up, hitched their horses to the porch and headed in softly. The man who owned the place welcomed them with offerings of coffee and breakfast but they politely declined, handed some coin and went straight to bed as he ate up to start his day. There were no others in the house, its lack of excitement and activity not suited to the many visitors of this town.
    Samwell took off his boots and jeans, his shirt and holster, his satchel and bag, and laid in the bed in his longjohns and closed his eyes. His body ached, every inch flexed and dragged out desire for rest, for relaxation, for a stop to all of Samwell's infernal continuance. After ten minutes of feeling his muscles and his skin and his bones

and his nerves twitching away and fighting for attention, he slipped into darkness and dreamt of nothing but being in a bath with Anna in their home, at night, hugging and kissing and laughing and smiling and talking of their children and their children's children, and everything was as it was meant to be for a beautiful hour.

    At the bordello the sun wasn't the only thing rising, the women who had spent all night handling customers found themselves at the mercy of the job for one last ride before closing for the day. The eight men of Saint Richard divided the women up one for every two men, they didn't have any qualms about their investment within minutes of removing all their worldlies and rooting themselves in the warm embrace of professional caretakers. A few good goes around and before the sun had fully awoken the town the men were spent in coin and stamina and the women rested them and left for their own bedrooms, locked away for extra safety. The snores and coughs and groans of the men enveloped by the first horses and wagons arriving through the stone streets as life in Rockwood began for citizens.

    The snores reverberated off the wood walls, back to the men, and covered the first shots and screams outside, only when the bullets began breaking through the boards and letting holes of light in, and shattered panes of glass, did the men awaken and peek through to see the madness unfold. They were quick to grab guns and make their way down to the street, but by then most of the melee had befallen Rockwood and left. Women were screaming over the bodies of friends and lovers sliced up, shot down, bleeding and muddy, covered in sawdust and their own insides, and in the dust and trail of the horses and wagons riding out of town shooting back for protection the sights of screaming, pleading women and angry, injured men could almost be lost forever.

    The Saint Richard mercenaries shot out towards the villains but their weapons lacking in range and their recent activity exhausting their muscles, they couldn't clearly hit targets. In their altogethers, the men stood weapons in their hand and in the breeze, as a woman nearby exploded in red and collapsed suddenly without half her skull. A terrific crack rocked from beyond a second later, and a flash of light in the tower overlooking the town turned to a whizz of bullet past the men, smashing into the stone of the building behind them. They swiftly made entrance back to the bordello and rushed to gather clothes, items, gear as the screams fell quieter with each crash of rifleshot.

    Samwell's eyes burst open and the remnants of his bath dream ran down his face in the heat and tension. Ransom rushed in and jogged his body awake as another shot rang out. They got themselves together and looked out from the window of Samwell's room and saw flashes in the tower, and bodies on the ground all around town through the gaps in buildings, alleyways now full of cowering folk, and the local Sheriff and some of his deputies were covering and running between

The Ferryman Upon The Plains

gunshots, peeking through the small pathways as a tall figure atop the tower laid siege singlehandedly. Samwell and Ransom kicked off from the house and stayed low. They circled around the outskirts, hoping, praying, not to be seen from the high ground.

The mercs split up, two to a path, and ran out the back of the bordello, two ran to the station, two up towards the Sheriff's, two ran across the plaza and two offered covering fire safely behind the stone walls. Twice the bell rang out, from distance and defying gravity the men managed to almost lay decent shot on the bastard, but the rifles kept crashing bullets down upon them. The bordello men drew most fire as the station men went low, slow, hoping to avoid detection from so far, and the men making across the plaza safely found another building to hide behind. The men who made it to the Sheriff's found no badges waiting to help, and all guns taken already. The jail cells were broken open, busted, blown apart.

Samwell and Ransom kept low and stayed eyes on the tower, from their angle only the hint of rifles could be seen, flashes and sound but no body. They headed towards the church, the bell rang another time as if it were calling them to prey.

Ransom took the lead and opened the back door to the church, they held revolvers out and looked at the priest's residence, a small hobble of bed, wood heater, pot, drawer, desk and stack of books, they walked on and opened up to the chapel proper.

The man of the cloth was hanging and twitching from the rafters, gagging blood and dripping from three places at once. Samwell's eyes adjusted slowly to the darkness and from the adrenaline pumping fast, it was only as they stepped closer that he could see the rope around the man's neck was his own intestines, still inside him a little too. He couldn't speak as his last breaths were covered by echoing thunderous gunfire above, his mouth was full of bloody material, and as they walked closer it was clearer that the cloth was all the man was wearing, and he had no longer parts to hide under it all, they were as Samwell was realizing ripped, sliced, cut and stashed in him. A man with his mouth full cannot call out to his God for help. Ransom prayed swiftly and took aim at the priest, he begged forgiveness and shot him in his head, the man's skull opened up, the meat in his mouth flew out and landed on a pew nearby, and his body swung in the recoil of the impact. Samwell gagged a little but couldn't rid his body of the sin he had witnessed. A further thunderclap broke their horror and Ransom ran towards a spiralling stairwell, Samwell fell to his knees as his heart pumped so wildly and he felt the muscles in him cramping up.

Mr. Wright? You stay here, keep watch.

Ransom disappeared up the stairs, his footsteps falling quick from ear. Samwell closed his eyes and took deep breaths and smelled the burning incense and the burning flesh and the burning gunpowder.

The Ferryman Upon The Plains

The bells rang out multiple times as the covering fire from the bordello was aided by the Sheriff office duo and the two men on the other side of the plaza. Six men six-shooting covered the two on the train tracks, speeding as they passed the sight of the rifles' coverage, one man with two rifles laying fire across the whole town, the shadow of the sun provided a silhouette of the man, tall and muscular in the sky, darker than any in town, moreso out of the sun's light.

A second figure appeared behind the man, and tossed a rope around him, the rifles fell out of hand and down from the tower, onto the ground and shattered. The bell rang out as the big man pushed back on the other figure, the men stayed low as they walked nearer. The bells calling them closer and closer, the grunts of two men fighting broke out from above. The two train track mercs got closer to the churchyard and could see their man Ransom, in hat and jacket, punching the other man twice his size a few times as they pushed and jostled above, hitting the bell into noise with every movement. They looked up and for a second all went silent.

A blackness broke from the tower above and span down, the large rifleman fell towards the ground, unravelling himself from the rope he was caught in, whilst above Ransom gripped the material and yelled as it burned through his palms. The mercs opened fire on the falling man as he pushed from the rope and landed on his feet, seemingly undamaged, and pulled a revolver from his side, laying fire down on the mercs. They fell to the ground riddled with bullets and the big native rifleman stumbled on his feet, he rang a shot up to the tower,

Andrew Jones

Ransom leaned over and his hat flew off and he ducked from view. The hat slowly made its way to the ground and by the time Ransom sweaty and out of breath picked it up, the rifleman was halfway towards the train tracks, firing wildly towards the church. The Sheriff arrived and laid fire, with deputies offering riflefire themselves, but the man fell into the horizon faster and faster with every shot. The surviving mercenaries came across the scene and examined their deceased comrades and took coin from their pockets, waste not want not. The Sheriff had no time to give on to their internal mess, his whole town was riddled with evil.

      Samwell left the church the way he came in and saw the man running off, he made his way back and saddled up Clover and began chasing. The man seemed to run faster than even his own beast at full clip, he was always on the horizon and never closing in for a full hour ride until he disappeared from view entirely. Behind him, Samwell could hear horses galloping and he turned to see Ransom and several of the Saint Richard men following, and a few badges from Rockwood in tow too. He felt awful leading the pack, it was never his place to be ahead of everyone, to be the one tracking and hunting and fording, he was only ever meant to help, to aid, to give path, not to take it himself. The men rode on as the sun fell into dusk, and the train tracks nearby came to a point, switching into multiples. They stopped up and one of the deputies informed the new folk of the area that one of those tracks led off to Chicago, to the East, to the world.

The other?

There's a quarry down the way, coal minin'.

The consensus was heading to the mine, and in the dark they found a freight train overturned and derailed and burnt out and riddled with corpses and debris from wagon crashes, and in the low lanternlight of the riders several men were found nailed to wood and flayed of their skin and posed on a cross, if any were still breathing they were not making sounds as the posse passed by, evading looks with the devastation as they rode on, stomachs growing fearful and twisted by the foreboding senses tingling across the country.

The further they rode, the stronger the smell of piss and shit and burning wood and blood and gunpowder and at last coal pure from the ground, and lights across the ground below seemed to glow and rise, and the men slowed their horses and leapt off and crept close to find land's edge, and a quarry full of men laughing and flaying and eating and hurting and men and women encased in cages and mocked and beaten and slashed and fucked and crying and screaming and in their own circle of hell. The posse blew out lights on them and walked their horses away and took all the weapons they had and gathered to scout from above, gazing into the bowels of man's evil laying before them. Samwell looked at the fire below them and knew he had a duty to himself, to his family, to his son, both his sons, and to his world. He did not believe he had the strength for what was to come. Ransom reached out and put his hand on the old man's back.

    Mr. Wright?

    This cain't be what we're meant to do on this world. This ain't right.

    None of this is right, we just gotta see to doin' what we can for the sake of others.

    I shouldn't be here, I should be back home, with Mrs. Wright, with my boy.

    Life put you here, Mr. Wright. If that were wrong, God'd said so by now. We're all where we're meant to be at this moment.

    Ransom walked low and quietly away, with several deputies, as they assessed the entry points and assembled ambushes, Samwell looked at the surviving mercenaries, still around even after death, for coin at least, and closed his eyes to pray. He heard whispers from the men gearing themselves up for a good fight, for a shootout, for action, but he heard nothing from above.

*

    Avery Bedford's grand belly rumbled as he stood by the riverbank, watching his fellow straggler making his way towards, a symbolic handing over of the oar kept Bedford at the station, casting a grand shadow over the land before him. Freddie Graham took the oar from Bedford's outsized hand and patted him on the elbow to move him on, and Bedford's belly rumbled further.

Git, see to that noise of yours.

There still those men waitin' and plottin' round the streets?

Freddie nodded and Avery's face dropped.

They ain't gonna hurt you, big guy, nobody'd try and shoot you down, look at ya, bullets couldn't do shit to ya anyway.

Folk been sayin', sayin' around the rooms, men's round here aimin' to hunt us down.

That's just bullshit by idiots with mouths bigger than brains, buddy, them men ain't got you in their sights less you make them look at you, just go about your business true, that's all that we can do.

What about Wolfe?

That fool ran his tongue dumb-like and went ahead doin' things ain't no person shoulda done, as long as you don't rob a man, hurt someone, kill a goddamn dog, shit. Idiot got what he deserved, no respect for others.

Freddie patted the small of Avery's large back and moseyed him onwards, his shadow leading him towards Cranham. He walked down the street, eyes on the three boarders grouped together keeping watch, it seemed a second group of them had walked over and swapped out spots, it was quitting time all over the place. A few folk near the Doc's spot were standing and staring over the jailhouse, they beckoned Avery over but he insisted on walking on, straight down the center of the street. As he passed the trading post, Kelso Harding-Grant closed his doors and kicked up a skip towards the big guy.

Andrew Jones

Hey fella, how's the place treating you?

Avery shrugged.

You thought about our conversation yet? Room and board provided, you won't need to live with everyone else anymore.

Avery stopped and looked at the rich fella before him, looked down.

I ain't good with violence, what use would I be?

Kelso laughed and grabbed Avery's huge forearm, patting it hard.

Look at you, sir, won't be any violence whence bandits take sight of you in the dark, men'll quake in their boots just at your stature. Come, let me show you your future.

Avery's stomach growled, Kelso looked at the noise's source, nearer eye-level than the man's face.

We'll handle that while we're at it, what say you?

Avery went on, Kelso by his side, and walked towards the nearly-finished mansion down the way. Kelso stopped Avery on the porch and sat him on a bench overlooking the path into town.

Wait here big man, I'll get you a veritable feast, fit for a king. Just think, take this job and you'll have every meal made for you, right here, every day.

Kelso walked into his house and returned shortly with a plate of hot meat and cheese and a cold bottle of beer. Avery ate up heartily as Kelso watched, and once the meal was finished he showed Avery the grounds beyond, foundations dug for plenty of houses planned to be built after his own was complete. Avery was not invited into the big house at all, and would return to Madame Westington's for sleep, the snoring symphony of the many stragglers surrounded him like it did everyone new to the small settlement.

*

    Christian Olsen sipped at a small glass of whiskey as he watched another night in Cranham pass on by, his usual customers lost to time and place, and these new folk soaking up plenty of booze but offering little company and companionship. Word of extermination spread around, men drinking and complaining about the law of the land, and moaning about the aches of the job they'd been gifted in this cursed summer, he longed for the old guard and their pleasant discussions and the piano that burst to life when Madame Westington made her joy known and even the Mann twins who happily showed face between closing shop and going home for dinner didn't give Olsen a boost to his morale. Here was a man who oversaw the merriment of others, who was standing in a world of his own building, and he felt lost to the flow of time.

    His big, booming voice bellowed time on the gentlemen of the tavern and began escorting them out the doors, much to their chagrin. Protests and pleas for one more round quick fell on deaf ears and he took glasses from hands and watched as man after man made way out the doors, down the street, passing the strangers on guard and towards their temporary residences. A couple of men staggered and slipped as they met opposite the tavern with a few folk who seemed to have been standing around for days now, watching the jailhouse and waiting, coming into the tavern in shifts and returning to their corner of the street to eye the jailhouse.

    In the empty building he collected glasses and ran a wet rag through them all and put them back under the bar proper, and gathered some spare sawdust and threw it on a few piles of regurgitation from some of the imbibements. He offered a little care as he gently put chairs under tables, as if waiting patiently for their next guests, and he sipped on his glass of whiskey between each chore until it was empty, rinsed and back under the bar with all the others.

    Christian threw some dried leaves onto paper and rolled it with his stubby fingers, licking and sealing it up before chomping down on one end. He ran a match across the bar's surface and lit his cigarette with the flame before blowing it out and inhaling deeply, finding a relaxation in the infusion of tobacco, air and silence. He grabbed a half-finished bottle and a couple of recently rinsed glasses and made his way out the tavern, tossing the match on the dirt street before him, eyeing the men still standing watching the buildings who should be home, asleep, away from here by now, and he walked to the jailhouse, exhaling smoke and handing glasses to the men. He handed a glass to Sheriff Hoxley who grunted as he entered, already a new routine firmly implemented, and he handed a glass through the iron bars to Herman Ganz who had been in jail too long already and resented everything but the kindness of the barkeeper in the middle of the night. He poured out plenty of drink until the bottle was mostly done and took the rest as his own glass, swigging freely as he leaned next to the cell, by Herman's side only divided by metal and law.

    Y'all been seein' them men o'er the way still, they're looser then they've been past few days, fellas, seen to that myself, not by purpose or nothin', but whatever they's thinkin', hope you're keepin' them in check for when they do.

    Hoxley drank fast and kept his eyes more on the men in his office than them outside. Ganz reached out to Olsen, his calloused, deeply tanned hands patting the barkeep on the shoulder.

    Think them folks is gearin' up to put one over on us all? First they take the crops, then they take the people, then the land, and what becomes of this place? Men like that, movin' from place to place, ain't no idea how to survive, to live proper, take and take and take and finally move on to the next place, nothin' left to grow in their wake. We wanted army men, proper men, salt of the earth, capable, smart, followin' orders. These folks, damn them, ain't nary a one know what to be done in society, out for themselves, out for right now, not the future, not for others, just now and them.

Andrew Jones

    Ganz drank up and handed his glass back to Olsen and found himself laying on the floor, closing his eyes to it all. Olsen drank from the bottle and pocketed the dirty glasses in his pants and leaned on the wall near the Sheriff, looking through the window, the darkness of the street helping nobody.
    Your men ever botherin' to come back, Sheriff?
    Hoxley shook his head.
    I ain't got no idea about them. Want a job done right or want a job done right away?
    Their job's been done by now rightly, ain't it? They've been gone some time, everyone's been gone some time. Call me old fashioned but when a man leaves longer than a few weeks time to say they ain't but fer visitin' here anymore, no longer callin' this place home.
    Hoxley spat at Olsen's feet.
    They's good men, all of them good men, you know it well as I do, they're comin' back soon, and with righteousness and the law behind them.
    All of them? That Noah Wright ain't much for nothin' no more, none of them Wrights had much goin' fer them cept Bart and look where that got him.
    Hoxley stood up and socked Olsen in the stomach, his big figure took it without pain.
    Watch your mouth there, them Wright men is upstandin' citizens, whole reason we're all here

cos of the old man, whole reason you have a bar, have customers, have a life, don't you forget that.

Olsen grabbed Hoxley's glass and finished the drink for him, pocketed the dirty tumbler.

I could pick up and run bar any place, ain't much different to now round here, you offer alcohol any part of this country you'll be flooded with custom, the cornerstone of the world, maybe it's time I sold off and went onwards, whole place is runnin' low of reasonin' to be Sheriff, when fine men like the farmer over there are still at risk just fer bein', ain't no sense in the world.

Olsen shuffled out of the jailhouse, the Sheriff sat back at his desk and sipped at a cold cup of coffee, he didn't look to the sleeping farmer still behind bars for no good reason, he stared at the wall opposite, waiting for whatever was going to happen to finally happen, or pass by completely.

It had been a time in the jailhouse, Olsen slowly lurched back towards his tavern, the darkness of the town a shroud every direction, no clear sight beyond a lamp light at the front of his business. Olsen blew out the candle as he walked past, opened the doors and put the glasses on the bar. His feet creaked the boards below as he walked around the room, around the bar, to get the rag. He kicked his impressively sized foot on something in the darkness and stumbled, a yelp of pain from whatever it was caught Olsen's ear and in the black his eyes adjusted slightly to see the whites of a man's eyes huddled behind the bar. Olsen fell to the ground, his body slamming hard, and two other men were made out with eyes and teeth and shushing one-another.

What are you doin'?

Olsen's bassy boom shushed the men but he was flat on the ground, drunk and tired, and they quickly clattered about and grabbed a few bottles of whiskey each, one made a break for it, Olsen grabbed the other two and began yelling for help. A pain broke through Olsen's stomach, the punch took time hitting him, but it wasn't the feeling of a fist on him from earlier, it was smaller, more pointed. A few more hits and he gasped and felt the warmth of liquid rushing on his body. Suddenly he felt a whole bunch of points pressed, a piercing pain that became euphoric and empty within seconds.

The squelch of meat and liquid splashing and sloshing echoed in the empty tavern and Olsen began shaking, his grip released and the men took off clanging bottles together as they escaped the building. Olsen tried to get to his feet but he began slipping on the wetness surrounding him. He stumbled and reached out and rested hand on a wall as he pushed forward, on his knees, slowly towards the door and out to the street. The world was dark outside, blips of white broke out, spots around blinding him from the empty darkness of Cranham. He coughed and spat out, it wasn't sick, it wasn't alcohol, he tasted the warm metallic concoction and finally knew. Christian Olsen fell to the ground on the dirt of the street before his

The Ferryman Upon The Plains

tavern, nobody could see him in the darkness, not the Sheriff nearby, not the Doc opposite, not the Father in the church on high. The tavern was empty, was silent, was dirty, was closed.

NINE

DARKNESS WAS THEIR ALLY. The Rockwood sheriff's deputies traversed the bowl around the quarry in total blackness, rifles clutched to their chests making no sound as they shuffled along and took positions, using magnification lenses to best see into the mayhem below, the fires of the small pockets of activity bright in the dark coalface of the land. The screams of agony from prisoners caught, waiting or brutalized for evening's entertainment twisting the steadfast guts of the men who thought they'd come across all manner of evil on their turf. Staring down, waiting, perching. The mercenaries of Saint Richard, freed of coin only half a day before and lost of two of their compadres not long after that checked their revolvers and ropes and knives in the dimness of the lip of the quarry, hidden in bushes, their eyes adjusting to the darkness, prepared for descent into the heart of the mania. They hadn't long-range gear, those that survived, they were happy to force upon those that saw to their fellow riders close enough to see light drain from their eyes. They lived for the moments of personal destruction, the added benefit of coin from their employer served only to advance swiftly their desire to rush down and see to the monsters that were making women and men alike cry in agony.

    Samwell fell back from the men, his arms and his legs and his back tensed and pulsated and shot aches and pains and pins and needles up towards his brain. His eyesight eclipsed the world, his peripherals enveloped a deeper black than the world gave with sun's rest. He took shallow breaths in and threw them back out into the air and clutched his hurting hands to his breaking back and with a small click felt all his body move from pain to emptiness, his lungs suddenly gasped in the atmosphere and his vision expanded out, to see Ransom checking his revolver, removing each bullet from its chamber, blowing on it and putting it back and spinning the six shooter in its place and pulling the hammer back and checking the mechanisms with only a burning match for guidance. The former lawman eyed Samwell every few movements and watched the old man lose all fear and focus into something not quite human.

    Mr. Wright?

    Samwell grunted at Ransom and clutched at his pearl-gripped revolver, holstered on his hip, and walked slowly towards the edge of the land, Ransom dropped the match as it burnt out on his fingers and followed. They parted the wave of mercenaries and crouched over the edge taking in the screams and cries and laughs and the merriment made by monsters below, eyes seeing pockets of fire, of glow and glare, and silhouettes and shadows but no figures, no clarity, nothing to rush to. A closer look would be the only way to begin imparting justice on the evils living below their foothold.

Andrew Jones

    Samwell followed Ransom followed the six mercenaries seeking vengeance as they began a quiet, crouched descent slowly on the curved, slanted ground spiralling down the outskirts toward the quarry proper. The deputies and their rifles circling above were lost to height and light, faith was all the men had that their back-up was watching over them. One-by-one the men met with a track of dirt dug around the rim, flat and welcoming to see properly. They walked slowly the outskirts of the quarry and could see closer, clearer, the men that were pulling people from make-shift cages and hacking at their flesh and hammering them to wood and putting people onto fires and burning them and feasting on them and engulfing and engorging.

    Samwell could hear his breathing as it quickened, his heart beat fast and pulsated his neck, his arms, his chest, the brief window of focus evaporated as he laid eyes on a man screaming on a pyre, failing to flail from his premature cremation. It was all he could do to stand upright and not collapse and make a noise behind the Saint Richard men. Ransom turned to face Samwell, feeling the breath of the old man upon him.

    Damn, Mr. Wright, you better seat yerself, fore you exhale a lung.

    Ransom gripped Samwell's wrist and Samwell took a knee, wheezing a little. The mercenaries descended and hid in the shadows as best they could, glimmers of blades and guns flickered the eyes of Ransom and left spots for seconds after.

Be honest with you Mr. Wright, I'm gladly takin' to bein' up here by your side than down there right now. Never been much for a fight, to see to a killin' at least. None's down here seekin' justice in the way we been meanin' to make do.

The first yell of a man gutted by a mercenary changed the air. Gunshots above rained down, cracks echoed within the quarry against one-another. Metal whizzed past and from below blasts of light pocketed in the darkness shone their way to flesh canvass, painting a gory portrait on the dirt and rock. The ankle-busted rifleman yelled out an impossibly high-pitched call and began firing side-arms to the heavens, within seconds three deputies dropped down and splattered their insides around the arena, and men focused on such destruction of their prisoners turned quick to rush the darkness, blindly leaping and seeing out those assaulting them. Samwell's vision fell away, his breath struggled to hold on, thinner and faster, the embers of fire in the midst of it was all that clung, in foggy brightness of red and amber colors.

In a blast from all across the world, bullets hailed upon the land and the rifleman was torn finger by finger, flesh ripped from bone. From every direction they entered his body and from all angles exited in gooey balls of blood and meat and tangled connectors of nerve. He fired his final shots upward as he fell and turned to mush, and the bullets saw the heavens above before turning back towards the world and careening into the dirt near Samwell's struggling, aching body. The puffs of earth and

Andrew Jones

hisses of noise on Samwell's ears arose again the spirit that left him on the descent and he tapped Ransom's shoulder and whispered directly into his lobe.

    We'd be damned fools sittin' by whilst men took our weight upon their shoulders. If this is our end, we go like we lived, not hidden by the edge frozen from fear.

    Ransom nodded at the old man and gripped his gun tight, he began to lead Samwell down hidden by the sounds of the skirmish below them and the sporadic rifle thunder above. In the maelstrom two of the six mercenaries were already slashed and down from knife and barrel and claw and bite by the soulless deviants that harbored prisoners from Rockwood in the day, and were screaming as best in the agony of their wounds, drowning in the blood pouring from their gashes and holes into their lungs swiftly. The native rifleman with busted ankles lay near the burning victim, his blood flowed onto the fire under the near-burnt corpse and unleashed a smoke of stunning red-gray infesting the sky above and clouding the quarry from the deputies' vantage points.

    Hopeful shots cursed the coalground failing to hit any but air and dirt on their journeys from weapon to land. A merc with a blade used the mayhem to slice rope on a wood-built cage and freed a few weeping prisoners. Their escape was scuppered swiftly by a figure who blocked firelight from all and in his whiteless eyes and long blade reflected the carnage back upon the people.

    Samwell hobbled behind Ransom as they shuffled along the edges of the land circling it all with limited vision, forming small shadows behind them as the ground slanted less and found steady the floor of it all. Samwell moved his hand to grip his pearl holstered, his right arm flexed and pulsated the bone and muscle and nerves and his index twitched and froze half-open, unable to get his whole extremity around his weapon. The breathing heavied once more, the smoke and the fire and the singe and the scream and the blood and the metal and the viscera overwhelmed now, nothing natural survived in the onslaught of the senseless ahead.

    On me, Mr. Wright.

    Ransom ventured on, Samwell followed, the former deputy fell into the darkness and obscured in the failing vision, the fires fixated light away from them, and Samwell could barely make out fights ending and slaughters continuing in the haze of the heat and glow. Shots rang out, some clear, some muffled. Samwell knew only some bullets made their way to folk as he felt the wind of body slamming past him, down to his feet, warming his boots with crimson. He furthered, Ransom flowed in and out of his clarity, feet ahead at best before it fell off, and they rushed the darkness.

    They made it to a small cage unseen and Ransom knifed through the bind and let men and women and a crying child out. They all crouched and ran, some patting Samwell on the shoulder as they passed, the only understanding that he was even a part of the deed. A couple of men picked weapons from the dead and attempted to fling bullets back to their captors, but swift rebuttal was made and the explosions of weaponry from inside the quarry quelled. Ransom went on, Samwell tried to keep up, unable to see any further Rockwood citizens needing saving, the aching of the body and the cluster of smoke and ghoulish odor clogging his breathing. Samwell knew not to stop, only ever further onward.

    The light ceased in a single flurry of ember flying upward, and the scream of a man whose barbecuing was definitive in the nostrils of all around. The blast of his landing atop the fire scuppered the source and blew it out entirely. Samwell slowed his walk, scuffing his feet on the ground hitting bodies and treading carefully over them as his eyes attempted once more to adjust to darkness' entire encroachment. He caught Ransom crouched and holding his gun to the noises closing in.

    Mr. Wright, Christ I almost ended you.

    You'da been right to see only to yourself in this place.

    Y'think anyone's still living down here?

    If we are, same's as likely they.

    Samwell saw Ransom nod slightly in the affirmative, a little information seeping into him as he took the darkness' many depths into his eyes and could see just shades of difference. Which was the moment a blood-soaked man launched his body at Ransom, knocked him against the ground and began to choke the former deputy. His gun took off one shot, a small burst of white and an explosion limited to their pocket of the world. Samwell clutched his revolver and tried to move his arm but he was frozen. His arm, his wrist, his hand, his finger, all stuck as he saw the Cranham former deputy gasp and writhe and try to push back on the figure holding him down and taking his air. Samwell flexed his muscles but nothing moved in his arm. He took as deep a breath as his shallow passageway would allow and jumped onto the man, his weight knocked the strangler off Ransom.

Samwell laid on the ground and rolled quickly as a fist came down towards him, he kicked out and felt weight on the sole of his foot and heard a grunt. Something clasped his neck and the strands of hair on his head and pulled at them. He was briefly up in the air before the crash back. Total darkness.

*

In the darkest of night she was frozen to her bed, eyes awake, listening not to snores but the scuffs of boots on the wood outside her door. The old widow knew in her heart the many men under her roof would be active all hours of the day, she knew the ferry had to be manned somehow, but with the emptiness of her world, without faces she'd seen for years residing with her, Madame Westington kept still in her bed and stared at the door, fearing at any moment the outside might break in, for what purpose she couldn't begin to consider, or want to.

Andrew Jones

She just lay under a light blanket waiting for the light of day to clear the evils that lurk in the dark.

 Christian Olsen's body lay in the dark of the summer night just down the way from the sheriff's office for hours, unmoved, unsuspected. The Doc was first to see something, he took a walk around the street in the dawn's first, struggling to find sanctuary in the closing eye respite of sleep, he had taken to finding ways to use time and energy. He almost tripped on Olsen's hefty ankle when he was made away of the body, and he called out to Hoxley at rest in his office.
 We got ourselves a mighty problem, boys, something of a plague upon us.
 The Doc lit a lantern near and examined the stab wounds still on the street. Hoxley stepped out in the hubbub and saw to the scene, the two men dragged Olsen's hefty corpse from view. The Doc and the Sheriff and Herman incarcerated stared at Olsen's body in the jailhouse and Hoxley felt around Olsen's body as it oozed limp blood from wounds still, colder and firmer than he'd ever been.
 Goddamn them, Sheriff, you seen what they been like, from dogs to people in but days, I was right to cut one down, the rest you see to 'fore they to the rest of us.
 Mr. Ganz you cease that now, we rush to things and we only bring it all upon us.

The Ferryman Upon The Plains

Rush to things? We takin' it too slow already.

Fellas, we ain't but a small group, they's lookin' to come on and take us over and remove us from the space and become what we lay down, all our hard work they steal and use and destroy us fer.

The Sheriff walked right up to the Doc's face.

You can hush that mouth, we don't need you incitin' things round here. Look what we got. I appreciate you Doc but we can't just start up and run down folk for the feelin' they're comin' after us. We can catch criminals, but we can't imprison men for thinkin' about things.

So you're gonna wait until we all die to act? We can march up, the all of us, to the sweet widow's place right now and round us up some folk deserve to be in Ganz's place and not man nor God would call us anything but righteous.

The Sheriff stared at the corpse of Christian Olsen in the middle of his office, a man who helped make Cranham what it was, no longer a part of it. Ganz shook his bars and demanded the Sheriff let him free to hunt the men responsible. Augustine stepped towards the door, feeling the heat of day's first coming into the air outside. The Sheriff stood in his office unable to do anything.

*

The days from the camp and the burials of Lily, Tommy and Junebug Hollander ran long, the wagon pulling little Paul and weeping Sissy Hollander kept in motion by Kirsty, her stoic exterior fracturing with every cry of her little sister, sharing moments of touch and

Andrew Jones

babbled song with her son still finding his voice on the trail, as Noah rode Midnight near to them offering little words of comfort or a hint of smile to the kid bouncing around the wagon in front waving at him. The little caravan stopped at nights for rest and warmth in the cold plains and food for the animals long-ridden for the day. Sissy never much ceased her tears, the pain of leaving home sudden and finding her sister come afoul of monsters, along with her niece and nephew innocent in their start of life weighed too heavy to move from. Paul at those times resting hugged his aunty from her turmoil and held close his mother as she cooked and cared for all at campfire, and even came to Noah's side as he sat ready for anything, never getting the rest that the Hollanders were chancing at in the shadow of the moon. Noah warmed a little to the kid, playing games of guess how many fingers behind my back and imitating animal noises at one-another until they broke into giggles. Paul was always ready to laugh, Noah a little longer but when he did it warmed the camp more than the fire.

  Some nights he found Paul joined by his mother spending time, Sissy asleep and safe by the fire, the three of them played games and the adults shared looks uncertain but connected over any noise beyond, any change of wind direction, defensive instincts inbuilt in parents whether or not they were near their brood, and whilst the next day's ride would be impacted by this time together in the night, the world around flew past quickly still as if between the wagon and Midnight the riders were finding a home true on horseback.

Times I wonder, the money, it is yours?
Kirsty nodded in the light of the fire, brushing Paul's hair as he slept upon her, bubbling away with calm and comfort.
We didn't rob no bank or nothin', that where your mind mighta headed.
I wouldn't put that past ya, maybe not so much her, but this one and you got the makin's of outlaws in ya.
Mine and ours is good folk, honest, decent folk. Worked hard many generations, crossed land and sea and found ourselves somewhere as a people to call home. Then it transpired others not so like us did too, and got their hands all over our world and gripped hard until we were strangled out. My Horace and Junebug's Terrance both talked such and brought to start wonders and hope, then turned they was comin' to get what we had and take. They were not good men, they were not good husbands. Only thing good either ever did was bring us meaning and life beyond us. I sometimes see Horace in Paul's eyes and I feel a sickenin' in myself as to what he could be, but he ain't that now and sure as I can away further he ain't ever to be.
You think they'll come from away to bring you back?
Not to bring me back. Him certain, the money, which is rightfully and always has been ours, no doubt in my mind. Me? He'd as soon do to me as poor Junebug and

Andrew Jones

leave on the road a message to God. Ain't no life back there, best as can be an object owned rather a person. Least out here, I'm me true. She'll get there too. One day.

It's hard. To lose some close. Don't ever get beyond that.

You're not meant to. If you move from that pain, you lose them fully. You build upon a new self, find strength in the agony, all lost becomes found again in the dark, where nothin' can be and all same. Sure as time passes and healing brings new, Sissy'll be stronger than either us here talkin', the tears flow on as nature intends, and from drops grow trees of spirit strong.

So why don't you weep?

E'rytime I let myself feel true to inside, only things went worse. Moment I feel it rise up and come out my face heats hard, my body aches, I'm thrown back to how it was. Maybe sometime in the years if I can avoid such and live on I might cry for the kids, for my sister, for all fallen upon us these many years. For now, too painful to feel.

*

The wondrous, empty blue sky of summer escaped across the world above, still no sign of clouds or wind or hiding from the intense weight of the sun's shine and sweat, relentless as the days dragged everlong into the year's eighth month, and at the fort only an hour's ride from Cranham at a trot was booming more than ever with the first riders of the rail seeing the land from speed and height not offered by horse or wagon or coach.

    The men of the army patrolled and drilled for ordinance and presented a fine uniformity to the land, the superiors standing before their privates gleeful in showing their strength and masculinity to the travelers on the rail west to a new land. Major Richard Lambeth, Dick to any friends who'd dare call him such, before being shipped off to the dregs of the country for shitduty, stood before them all as the train chugged its way to the Fort's station and gathered goods, people, and swapped them for lost souls and items from up in Chicago and the Nor'east that sought new markets in the ever-growing civility of the country still so young in this first century of democracy. The ceremonial excitement of welcoming the transport's arrival was novel and unexpected by the passengers, who clapped politely, some men standing and saluting their soldier brethren before waiting for the damn train to move on to the next stop, others got out to see about this stop and gather items and knick knacks for the journey onwards, in this middle of the new world what an opportunity it would be to take something unique and bring it to the very end of the land, a place it never was meant to go, to place it in a landscape distant and alien to its origins. Sometimes it is the small ideas that travel the furthest.

    Hazel Worthing stood in the market with a collection of beautiful dresses and blouses, garments for the lighter days and heavier temperatures, as she continued to sew more clothes of smaller scale for her

Andrew Jones

future Godchild. She was joined by many from around the regions, with their clothes and tools and crops and meats and a chancing painter already on his third landscape of the train pulling into Fort Oak Station, adorning his stall with myriad sunsets and lakes and birds and deer the central figures of their own stories. The hour and a half that the train sat in the station saw more queues at the latrines than the market, but those with a little more money, and those that packed less and regretted it two weeks into the journey, went hogwild on the food and the clothes, something clean to wear after crusting their fabrics for days at a time sitting still as the train rocked them up, down, left, right, shaking them up as if the earth were eternally quaking beneath them. Hazel was light on dresses and only had a few underclothes and sunhats left to take back with her, those who didn't would regret soon the chance to shade themselves from the intense scope of the sun before they ever saw the coast of the west. As she packed up for the day, Hazel watched the formation of uniforms ease themselves back into natural living, the first plumes of steam covering their change from army to men, and watched the Major immediately become invaded by Kelso Harding-Grant with a big grin and a firm handshake and a grip around the shoulder to talk secrets in plain sight. She watched him hop into a coach followed by three wagons of men and women and lumber and stone as she took her remnants back to her saddle and rested it all on the back of her horse.

Miss Worthing? Ma'am?

Hazel turned to see Sergeant Carthage, a man of surprising youth perhaps enhanced by the small growth of stubble struggling to form on his chin and upper lip.

Sorry Miss Worthing to bother you, but you don't happen to have any o' them nice green-lookin' dresses do ya, with the goldprint flower you took back a few months ago? I've been thinkin' bout that since I met my Lucy, she'd look so beautiful walkin' in the sun, the light shimmerin' off her hair, the gold shining and the green, that green, her eyes would sparkle. I close my eyes sometimes and just see her and that's how I picture her, it'd be wonderful.

Sorry Sergeant, what I got ain't much for the colors, workin' with whites and lights lately. Shares the sun with the world. I can make you somethin' for next week though, if you can stand to wait a li'l.

Ma'am, I can wait to the end of the Earth for that.

Hazel smiled and held her hand out for a deal, the Sergeant looked askance before reaching out.

Ma'am, you are a unique breed.

For my sins. Be seein' you next week, if at least God allows it. Do a favor for a friend, you see any folk comin' on that behemoth what seems intent to come for Cranham, come down and tell, gettin' feelin's deeper in me each day things ain't settlin' right, folk bein' what they are, actin' strange, had a mess of it lately, gunfire and murder and I'm thinkin' plans are in motion before they been much thought about to where they're headin'. You

Andrew Jones

can have all the fabrics in the world but you don't know the shape of a human how could you ever make a dress.

Hazel hopped on her horse and rode off, the Sergeant waved and returned to life at the Fort, watching the passengers who now stood idly waiting for purpose in the netherworld between the old east and the new west.

*

The burning of the sun searing onto his ever-increasing baldpatch called Samwell to rise, the caws of three circling buzzards whose shadows seemed to dance around every inch of the world gave distraction for a moment as his eyes adjusted to such sudden light, tinged with red. He felt the back of his head, warm but dry, and moved his hand up to the top, the middle of his crown, and felt gap between flesh, his finger warming and wetting suddenly. A little venture further and his ears rang, his spine twinged, he pulled out of the entrypoint entirely having tapped the top of hard bone. The old man kicked his feet out and found life once more, slowly getting up to crouch-level and looking over what he could in the quarry. Desolate, rotten with death's cycle, he could see men laying from holes, fingers and hands and heads and tongues in a sea of red dried on the dirt ground. And some mirage in the middle of it all, a man of pure white dragging the leg of a former deputy through the melee, beaming the sun's rays out to the quarry, turning redder every second he stayed exposed to the orb's power.

The man slammed Ransom's body onto some wood and methodically grabbed a hammer and a nail and pushed nail into Ransom's palm and raised hammer. With a thud the hammer slammed the nail through and a muffled scream of agony burst from Ransom. Life, what little left, still sparked.

Samwell stumbled over bits of human as quietly as he could, speed was needed but he was at his weakest. Another thud and the nail was almost done. The screams dulled in Samwell's ears already, getting used to the sounds of pain and anguish as if they were water lapping on the shore. Samwell briefly struggled with a corpse gone stiff for ownership of a blade and snuck up behind the albino turning full red. As the being raised hammer another time Samwell closed his eyes, pulsated his muscles for most strength and opened again. The blade swiped smoothly along the albino's skin, a simple slice that cut flesh and tube and vein. Spray over Ransom's body turned him bright red and the albino gasped, he clutched his gash with his hands. Among the mayhem Samwell saw a hole in the man's thumb, and that the thumb was in fact made of wood. The hammer fell, slamming onto the albino's foot and crushing two toes like ripe strawberries on a summer's day. Samwell stabbed the albino twice in the skull for measure and the monstrous figure fell to the ground finally. Samwell gasped for breath and bent down slowly to grab the bloodsoaked hammer and walked to Ransom.

Andrew Jones

The former deputy was red and pale and dazed and bleeding from the hand and the head and the throat, his clothes were scratched and ripped and torn all over from a fight long since finished. Samwell slapped Ransom's face a few times.

Son, you gotta stay in this world a little longer, gonna fix you up but right. Ain't gonna be easy, ain't gonna be without work. This right here's about to make you scream somethin' ain't s'posed to be heard by nobody but the maker, so do what you must.

Samwell took the hammer's claw and put it round the nail and pulled, Ransom winced and yelped and held his tongue as best he could. Samwell pulled harder and harder, the buzzards above cawed and swooped and pecked upon a few bits of flesh lining the ground of the quarry. Samwell pulled and pulled and the nail came free and blood flew from the hole in Ransom's hand across the sky with the nail and splattered a buzzard as it took flight from fear. Samwell put his arm around Ransom's chest and pulled him up, the younger man scrambled to his feet and fell a little, the two a sight for nobody as they barely kept one-another upright with aches and pains and broken bodies. It took ten minutes to climb the pathway out of the quarry, to see from above the crimson devastation only suited for the animals now. The men around the rim once sheriff's deputies of Rockwood lay throats slashed and heads half off and guts ripped out and lying in their own pools above it all.

The men had no time to even consider how lucky they were to have been thought dead when whatever further occurred did so, Samwell felt Ransom beat faster and slower intermittently and gathered the younger man as best he could and whistled onward.

It took a little further stumbling and more liquid in the lips to whistle Clover over, she was spooked some even seeing her rider reappear, covered red and holding a half-alive man to his person, she clopped slowly, hesitantly, until Samwell reached out and his touch on her neck calmed her instantly. Ransom struggled to climb up even with the help of Samwell, Clover wasn't the kneeling kind, and he ended up bent over upon the horse. Samwell gripped the reins and the saddlepost and by some miracle managed to climb up, seated and saddled he was strong atop Clover. He picked out the satchel of water and splashed some on Ransom, making him drink up, then used the rest on his mouth and head, wiping the blood as best he could from him before the wound spat out a little trickle more.

They rode off from the Godforsaken land, following the tracks, passing the train once more, and at the split on the tracks turned towards Chicago and rode out. The day was long already, and it wasn't forgiving.

The dirt by the tracks turned to mud and rock and the weather crashed bouts of shower and sudden dryness and Clover's hoofs clattered on every surface fast and loud, her shoes battered and bent and breaking off, the nails falling out as they rode onwards, until the forgiving

Andrew Jones

land offered a slightly-planned dirt road to follow. Samwell gripped the reins and the saddlepost and flowed in and out of consciousness as his mare did all the legwork, Ransom moaned and coughed and spat blood creating an intermittent trail to follow if any dared, but by nightfall there finally was a signpost informing the way they went was many miles towards Rockwood and forwards was many more to Chicago, and seemingly unauthorisedly hammered to the north a settlement of Granois less than a mile. Samwell turned his horse and she slowed a little and headed towards the nearby. He brushed the back of Clover's neck and held her hair in his hand, offering kindness for the sudden shift, Clover responded with a huff and snort.

 A shack lit by two lanterns came up on them, a man on a chair older than the country nodded at the strangers riding in stuck two fingers in his mouth, his whistle reached their ears even as they sped past and more lights appeared down the road. A man ran out and waved Clover to slow, he looked at the men atop the horse and pushed his frames up to his face.

 My word fellas, you've certainly seen yourself a touch of the devil today ain'tcha. Let's get youse seen rightly, come.

 The man led Clover and the men atop towards his wooden shack, a little sign above lit barely offering the letters THECARY. Samwell took himself off the saddle and with the help of the man held Ransom up and carried him in. The man laid the ailing former deputy on a table and saw to Samwell's wound and age.

None of my work's for the faint, mind if I fix you a stay before I sort on your mate?

Samwell nodded and sat down on a chair as the man grabbed a bottle and rag and doused the textile and then placed it on Samwell's mouth.

Darkness.

*

The braying mockery of the mob seeing the final dance of the pigfuckers lingered in the air still whilst Abraham and Jedediah and Zachariah rode north from Rockwood, they wouldn't hear the whistle of the train or the bawdy men of Saint Richard or the rifleman tearing through the town, however, their path was pushing on and fast to the mountains long in the distance, peaks peeking over the horizon. They were misplaced upon the hill where Ezekiel lost his life, where the wagon was torn apart by train and man, hanged and shot and sentenced in this world and the next. The distraction to a town of ill soul and little remorse to send their homes a little connection had set them back on the hunt, to escape the sounds of the world until a river again roared would be key to keeping them close on the neck of the monsters capable of such evil. So they rode north, ever onwards.

The air was sapping and heavy, life as it was burnt up in the bright sun and the horses galloped across dry dirt kicking up dust behind them, the rocks grew around them as they went on, from pebble to stone to the ones

Andrew Jones

Abel saw before he met with God. The lawmen cared for their horses and themselves but pushed on hard during the daytime, the nighttime shorter in the summer was as much time of ease as they could justify, if they weren't so burdened by livestock and need they would spend every hour awake and not riding onwards and hunting those monsters of the land. In the curse of the nighttime they could think not upon their chase, they could think of their wives and their families and their lands long left, they could think of their fallen lawman and the way they enacted justice, and ruminate in their heart and soul as to how easy it was to remove the life, but at once nothing had really changed, nothing was ended. The nighttimes were gracefully short, and their minds could return to the ride before the weight of indifference robbed them of ability to rise from the ground's grip.

    In a woodland they found a pack of wolves dead and their carcasses the restaurant for birds and bugs and beasts alike, an entire group of predators fell from atop the chain, now nothing but a buffet for the worms. The eyes of two wolves had arrows in each orb, perfect shots or target practice, the details could not be discovered, so far gone were the bodies in ruination and so unconcerned with the lives of dogs were the marshals, they passed on by with barely a second's glance at the wildlife enjoying the gift of life in death.

The Ferryman Upon The Plains

  The heavy summer days lingered as the season seemed to progress stubbornly, the fall was still time away and yet the land wished for relief from the heat, a morsel of rain or a cloud to cover from the brutal blaze would bring the green back to the grass yellow and the trees whose leaves insisted on turning fire-colored in the overeating of the sun. The men were silent and focused until the nights, and they were silent and distracted until sunup. A cycle seemingly destined to drown their heads as the moon re-enacted the sun's shape and glow in the wee hours, and spending longer above as the time ran on. In the haze of an August morn they ran across a bloody leg and torso, torn by claw and bitten into by mouth larger than human. They soon saw a scalped head impaled on a tree trunk, mouth full of what was torn between torso and leg. This was worth slowing for, staring a second time upon. They began to approach a smokey tented fabric held down by small boulders, and were once more witness to the travesties of human devastation.

  A wagon halved by brute force, splintered, pinned down the bodies of several people whose upper torso and face were exposed to the elements, flayed, and their skins laying in a pile near collections of furs and pelts. On the last gasps of campfire the hands and tongues and eyes burnt hard. The lawmen could not close the eyes of the dead for their peaceful rest, there were no longer lids on any laying there. They stayed only long enough to take in the details and find the sickening smell of burning bodies turning their guts something awful and they saddled up and rode outward more. Silent.

Andrew Jones

  Hobbling around the pathway they came across a man bleeding from his leg and head, he had a bite out of his calf still oozing. They slowed and called the man out, he turned and they could see he had no eyes left in his skull.
  Help, please, for the love of the Lord help.
  The men stopped and hopped off horses and handed the man some water and Zachariah offered to wrap up the man's leg wound with an undershirt he carried. They sat the man down and Zachariah began tending to the bite as Abraham and Jedediah held his shoulders to inform him where they were at all times.
  What happened sir?
  Did you see anything before…
  I saw it all.
  He sipped water and let more fall around his face as he drank desperately.
  We was havin' ourselves a fine night we was, had just got ourselves some decent wolf pelt, this time o' year round here they tend to be sallow, desperate, malting and sweaty and oily, but these was fine fur, their meat decent too, like they'd eaten well and been sedate from the feast. We was dancin' and singin' and enjoyin' the gift, a rare time in any season and I been through many hard and many bitter and many angry and ain't seen such like we had, we was all happy for once. Then like thunder clappin' the fallen angels for to come to hell or worse, a big beast of a bear came crashin' through our wagon and knockin' down half of us

The Ferryman Upon The Plains

dancin' by the fire, sumbitches stabbed us with wood, with arrows, impaled to the ground. I was seein' it from by the tent fire flyin' before them, saw the bear and the manbeast same size as the furry fella and I turned and I ran and the bear done got me in the leg here and hurled me t'wards it all, and I couldn't walk much with myself all eaten, and I watched em, the big man and the little one, he did a lot of talkin', and he did a lot of horrible things to my friends. He went at em with his knives, a bunch of knives, and the big one laughed and clapped as the little one sliced and stabbed and then he turned to me and the big one sat on me, I couldn't breathe, it was a world crushing me. The little one poked my leg hole with a knife and laughed as I twitched and the big guy kept me from moving still so my face I guess got red and made faces of the pain, and he laughed, and the big guy laughed, and then he told me to look at what he done did to my people, and I saw oh God I saw, ain't none of them got anything on them no more, he skinned em the bastard. And then he grabbed my head, and he pushed his knife into my eye, and I heard it pop, I felt the tears down my face but it were warm and it were thick and then he turned to the other and I didn't see anymore. It hurts so much, it's a ringin' in my body, still, I shake and I shake but the pain is always there. I wished he just did me, but I was scared in the dark, I knew he was gonna do me like my people, I could feel the cold blade, I knew he was gonna skin me. But the bear, it roared and moaned and crashed through somethin', I heard a clutter of wood and metal and rock and the blade's cold steel fell away. And I laid there, the heat of the fire and the heat of my thick tears, and the cold

Andrew Jones

of my open leg, and I laid there and I couldn't weep again, and I waited for my end. And they never came back.

    The man laid his leg out bandaged and thanked the lawmen, and the lawmen offered him coin or assistance but he thanked them again and told them he would wait for the wolves to come back round and give himself over, better use of him. They helped him up and watched him hobble around lost and broken and they rode off less one undershirt.

*

    Maclaine never settled in the few nights he'd spent in the house that Ganz built, more than ever he felt an invader, even in friendly territory. Skellig, however, hadn't found comfort anywhere since he left Sweden and even then he wasn't much for the family and world that he was born into, this new domain was just another in a never-ending tour of walls and ceilings to hide from the devastation that threatened existence at every step. The limited room and space to breathe, bigger than the small box of a room they shared in the last days of boarding with the widow, didn't much allow themselves to release, rather it pooled their fears of the new Cranham and the uncertainty of the future in the middle of their two souls. They kept eye on the windows that overlooked the crops and the farmland and the grazing fields waiting for the cows to come home, guns at hand should anyone make a move, if anyone even knew where they had absconded to. It left them both immobilized in the middle of Ganz's property, waiting and nervous, and finding the only comfort in Herman's small supply of bourbon sitting bottled in the cupboard, barren beyond that, until the harvest would come.

They ain't comin', be smart not to, but they ain't much fer brains.

There's more each day, we stay here forever out there will be overrun.

So we ride out and hang 'em all, before they do anythin'?

Lars shook his head and drank from the bottle, passing it back to Colin.

First move we make, everyone will be watching. Can we go back to normal life? Show them we're out there, show them we know, but we're not seeking some sort of... justice, revenge.

All I want is to go back to the start of summer, things were fine all over, same as it ever was, stable and content.

You were happy with the old woman and me?

Colin nodded and passed back over the bottle, wiping drips from his stubble-forming jaw.

It was a happy home, for the time.

For the time. How long more would you even be there? You been round this place many years now, you not growing old living at someone else's land, why we're all out here, not to share, not to live among many, to find

Andrew Jones

our place in this world. I struggle maybe more but even I not think of seeing gray and wrinkles under her roof. When this all shakes up, you will find place, to call yours. And you will share that with me? No, you will find your life and your purpose with someone.

What'd you do? Ride off and find a new town, a new land to make yours?

If a place isn't worth fighting for, it is not right place. I saw my family, ancestors held their place in mountains even as world grew and tried to take them with it, they did what they had to so we could live somewhere, be free, be ourselves. That never last, no matter how strong you are, how many you are, there'll always be stronger, more. In this world nothing is ours, everything is someone else's we just do not know whose. I hoped I'd find a different land here, all new, all waiting to belong, but if it is, it is not to people like us. For a few more years we may be lucky to know peace and relief, but it will come, as it has here.

So what are we even meant to do?

Find what they cannot take from you. Land, freedom, these are not what anyone ever has.

Colin shook his head and snatched the drink to feed the sickness in his stomach.

I see how the dressmaker looks at you. I think often of her glances. One day, friend, I wish to be seen like that. I feel shiver through body when I think of that. Lay down, perhaps, the weapon you won't even fire, and aim for something good in this sad time.

They can take love away, Lars, look at how they killed Bartholomew.

He died, this is true. But love? The old man and Noah hunt for love, the old woman weeps for love, the widow carries love all over. Love never dies.

The Doc listened intently to the pulsing of Jenny's body, he examined her with some manner of respect, what privacy the clinic could offer did its best to reserve the dignity of the mother-in-waiting as Augustine gaped into every orifice of the poor woman who laid there and watched his aging hands search for problems she prayed weren't there. He gave her a tonic of vitamins and oils for the next few weeks of ingesting and looked out the window as she clothed back up, staring across the way to the Sheriff's.

All things seeming okay doc?

Can never tell these days, everything's changing.

It's harder to walk, should my feet be like this? Seems like I'm inflatin' from the ground up.

The Doc nodded and Jenny stood up, shaking a little on her expanded ankles, she walked to the window and looked out at the event alongside the Doc.

You'll start showing in the next month, if this little one's anything like his uncle, you'll go to bed as you are and wake up with a belly stretchin' up to the heavens.

I ain't lookin' forward to that, hobblin' round here with another half of myself reachin' before I get places.

Andrew Jones

Don't worry bout that, by the point he's kickin about and stretchin' out, you'll be too uncomfortable to go walkin' round places.
Wonderful. Any other comforts, Doc?

Hoxley rolled up some tobacco and lit the cigarette, he looked at Olsen's body and at Herman still waiting for any freedom.
You go get the boys and see to buildin' a box fine enough for this man to rest good in the arms of the lord, and swiftlike. Fore this place erupts somethin' into a mess.
You gonna fill my space up with folk deserve to cling to these bars?
I reckon peace needs keepin' so like, if'n that'll create peace o'course.
Hoxley sucked in half his paper, burning the grass inside in thin plumage, and unlocked the door to the jail cell, Herman got himself out of that state quick. Hoxley let out smoke from both nostrils and flung the last flicker of paper and ember at the farmer as he moseyed out of the building.
Watchin' you Herman. Careful how you go.
You as well lawman, no more drinks, no more chats, your nights are gonna be spent listenin' to some awful sorts of bitchin' and moanin'.
Hoxley listened to the old man's boots clump on the wood and the dirt as he left the street fully. He picked up his rifle and checked his bullets.

The Ferryman Upon The Plains

    Outside Madame Westington's house Sheriff Hoxley shook a little as he clutched a fist and rat-a-tat knocked upon the door. After a silent moment the door opened and Avery Bedford stood above the lawman all with his towering, imposing structure and smiley face.
    Sheriff, sir, what's the occasion?
    Where's Mrs. Westington?
    You wanna come in? Some folk in the kitchen cookin' up ham.
    Where's the landlady?
    The Sheriff clutched his rifle and made a show of having it out. Avery looked at the lawman and stepped back from the doorway.
    You should come in and see to her yerselves, not no folk under this roof much cares to cept me.
    Hoxley relented on his rifle and stepped foot first, he brushed past the big man's frame as he took in the stale air of the foyer, full of unwashed man, antique cloth and wood, and the strange peculiarities of herb and spice and pork emanating from the kitchen as the crackle of fire on sizzling fat was dowsed by creaking floorboards and laughter of men chatting casually across the way. Avery pointed up the stairway and watched the sheriff go unnoticed by residents awake.
    Sheriff, hers is on the left, at the end, the door's full closed. Mind if I come?
    You best stay down here son.
    Am I in trouble?
    Not unless you done somethin' real bad.

Andrew Jones

I wouldn't, I couldn't.
Well'n you stay around and we'll both see to her safety.
The Sheriff ascended slowly the stairs, each step a thump, he tried to keep a space between to cushion the noise. He could see in two open doors men laying in beds and on the floor, overcrowded and then some, the house was barely standing from the weight of strangers taking over. He kept watchful on them as he made it to the landing, Hoxley looked right first, up to the end of the hallway where doors were open for the small bath and mirror and washbucket, two more rooms with fewer legs laying at rest and more antiques from decades of life before. To the left was one more room wide open and full, and at the end the closed door of Madame Westington. Hoxley walked softly on the creaking boards and rat-a-tat knocked on the closed door.
Ma'am, it's the Sheriff, are you alright in there?
There was no response.
I'm comin' in, if you're indisposed or requirin' dignity, say before I accidentally expose you so.
The door opened, Madame Westington had her blanket around her shoulders and a blouse unbuttoned thrown on. She looked at the Sheriff and dragged him into her room, shutting the door behind them.

Heck Sheriff, you gotta be careful out here. Those men, I don't even know no more.

Good to see you ma'am.

The widow looked at the rifle in the Sheriff's hand as she threw the blanket onto the bed and buttoned her blouse, she pulled a skirt from a drawer and fitted herself before the lawman.

You pullin' out the big guns for li'l old me? What'd I do this time, rob a bank?

We need you outta here for a time. For your own safety.

Westington looked at the Sheriff then walked to the window and looked out at the world beyond, Colin and Lars and Herman rode up on horses holding guns, the Doc behind them baring no weapon.

Good lord, what on earth's happening?

Hoxley informed the widow of Olsen's murder. He made mention the many strange groups of new folk loitering, plotting. She stepped into her boots and brushed her hair quickly and with force threatening to pull each strand from its root and stamped her small size across the room, out into the hall and down the stairs. Hoxley followed, as she entered her parlor and pulled a real old rifle covered in dust from behind a china-plate-presenting cabinet, she blew and brushed the mites off the wood and marched into the kitchen.

Wake e'ryone up and gather outside, boys.

The men stared at the small old widow with the big weapon. No movement was made. Avery Bedford watched from the doorway and stepped out to be seen by the townsfolk saddled and holding shotguns. Madame

Andrew Jones

Westington marched out alongside the big man and aimed her gun to the heavens. She set the powder and pushed it down the barrel and loaded the lead ball and lifted the rifle up and pulled the trigger, exploding with noise and a flash into the sky, horses beyond screamed in surprise, Avery shivered and clutched his ears, the horses bucked and jutted about in the sudden sound. The widow's voice broke through in croaking anger.

    Y'all get out here right this now and see to business proper, don't make me load up another.

    Soon enough men shuffled from the kitchen, Hoxley stood on the landing, glaring a little at the back-up he never asked for and watched men coming to, brushing sleep from their eyes and releasing yawns from their mouths as they were paraded out and down into the bright summer day and before the town and the old widow and the big man with a soft demeanor.

    I asked one thing of all you who out of the kindness of my heart and the grace of God were given roof and shelter and board and food. And some of you cain't even to that stay within.

    Hoxley watched the widow talk the many men down with her hurt expression, in the light with a gun she felt control of the fears of her nightly suffering.

    The beautiful soul that run the tavern you all customed and enjoyed, and I know you all did, I heard you on return and there weren't no words coherent in any your mouths, was did wrong and unjust and the Sheriff is adamant it was one or two of you folk. I am disgusted. Ours was a nice community, a family in its own way, peaceful and kind and loving, ain't never seen such horrors as befallen since recent and the only change has been in here. What that man did to the farmer's dogs, unthinkable, and what he got, not right, not right at all, but we ain't to say he didn't put himself in the firin' line like he did. But this. For what did that man deserve his end? For giving and caring and seeing to his community? For aidin' those what looked for a little life in this world waitin' to take us all down at the first sign of hellfire? You can sort out this mess yerselves, whoever done did that to the good Christian man of the tavern, but you best all know none of you is welcome back under my roof whether you split and give the law the men responsible or all fall for the same sword. My hospitality ain't for abusin', and if y'all take to comin' back and tryin' your luck with the little old lady on her own, well.

The widow nodded to the men on horseback watching the crowd with weapons ready. A few men yelled out claims they wouldn't give anyone up so easy, Bedford watched and looked at the Sheriff and down at his feet until a few men began squaring off with verbal insults and pushing and two men were flung to the ground in rolling fight before Colin and Lars hopped off and pulled them apart.

He did it, I saw him stab the old man.
And what were you doin' when he stabbed him?
Runnin'.
From what?

The man shrugged and another man in the crowd yelled.

He took a bottle, I saw it, he came back with bottles.

A few men parted way to see the yeller now plain-faced in the light of the day. Hoxley could see the two men from the scrap and the yeller were waiting at the corner for days, staring over the street all this time. He marched up and collared the yeller, Colin and Lars dragged their catches too and left the Doc and Herman to see over Madame Westington and the exodus of the rest of the boarders.

Colin and Lars saw the men locked in the jail cell formerly Herman Ganz's residence and commenced crafting a box for Christian Olsen's final departures. Herman rested in his own bed, alone, finally back away from all folk, in his own land, in his own world.

The hole was dug in the graveyard, and Father Langston stood over the site whilst folk came swift from the land over dressed in the same honorables that they had worn a month or so before for Bartholomew, as Langston talked a respect to the man gone and the silent society swallowed the truth that so much of what they once knew was being wiped away in swift fashion. Kelso and Lauren made an appearance and whispered to the Mann twins some ideas that brought smiles to the boys' faces at this most solemn occasion. The small community watched the box be covered in soil before them, knowing the men responsible were still breathing and the fun times and loving moments and quiet confinements of the tavern in its heyday were being buried with the good landlord.

TEN

INSIDE HE WAS YOUNGER. Inside he was taller. Inside he felt no pain. He stood above Anna in their house, arms wrapped around her, as all should be. He ran his fingers through her hair, like embers flying into the air they tingled outward as he touched each strand, magical and out of all worlds. Without sound he had to read her lips speaking three words warm to his heart. The boys ran past, around their coupling, Bartholomew chasing Noah, the kid always was picked on, follies of the youngest. Mother and Father held one-another as they watched the children run and play and find joy in their own little world. Samwell reached out to Bartholomew, before he could grab the kid he had turned back to baby and Samwell found him nestled in his arms, sleeping soundly, innocent and barely alive, those first days, weeks, where they shared time in silence. The baby thinned out and began to wail, his screams silent to the internal, but his movements clear, Noah never settled, never felt comfortable in Samwell's arms, was never suited for the life he was born into. Samwell planted a gentle kiss on his babe's forehead and the baby turned into embers, floating into the sky, out of reach.

The Ferryman Upon The Plains

He awoke to the pitter patter of light raindrops on the wooden roof above, the darkness of room all encompassing. Ransom moaned and snored nearby, unseen, and Samwell felt the top of his head, bandaged up. A few footsteps and suddenly light bloomed, the doctor lit a candle and threw off a wet jacket to the ground and saw Samwell's eyes staring back.

Welcome back boss, been a little trip through all my wares to best see to your man, he's fightin' a fierce infection right now before I can even consider furthering attention. How're you holding?

Samwell moaned a slight affirmative and he took in the sight of Ransom laying on the table still, covered in a blanket of red splotches and blue wool, shivering and pale in the light.

Divine providence saw you our way, I'm sure of it, any much longer and this'n'd be off to the next world right now. Take a little drink, if you can stomach I have some meat on my person too, then the doctor demands rest.

Samwell gulped a cup of water as soon as the doctor's hand held it out and bit into some jerky handed out from the trouser pocket of the doctor and then felt the rag of ether approach his lips once more and darkness fell.

The rain pattered above, he saw himself on the river, his river, on his ferry, between the two banks of land, a place all his, forever only for him. A voice called out the word Samwell clearly above the rain, he glanced across and saw Augustine standing at the platform beckoning him over. Samwell rowed, swiftly, with no pause for pain in this land, and was face to face with his old pal soon.

    Why you out here Samwell? You should be back home. They need you. That's what you're meant to be doing. Holding the fort.

    Things gotta be done, cain't be sittin' round feelin' sorry fer myself, life carries on, folk need ferryin regardless.

    Don't be a damn fool, the whole world'll see to your station gladly, these moments shouldn't be for ignoring or grandstanding, poor Noah right now could use all the love of his pa.

    I done give him love before and he saw to turn away from me again and again. We ain't for closeness, best I can be right now is carryin' on like it ain't the end of the world. Remind him we can all continue.

    Maybe it's best to think it's the end, it's devastating. Damnit Samwell, I done carried the poor things out myself, I gotta live with sights not suited to no soul. It's not just tragic, it's darn horrendous. At least you have people to love and share the pain, the weight on each shared shoulder eases. Rest of us gotta go to the tavern for aid like that. Solace does no soul good. Come, see to yours.

    Slats of light faced Samwell as he came to again, his face full of growing stubbles itching his cheek and chin, he was laying down, the wooden boards called a roof didn't hide much from elements. The doctor was sewing on Ransom's skin opposite, twin bedridden men being seen to.

The Ferryman Upon The Plains

The doctor looked over to Samwell as he released a large sigh of pent up breath and smiled.

You've been out a while, your friend I can understand, he's been through the wars, but you still have some fight left in you somewhere.

Samwell tried to sit up, metal clanked around him, and he turned his neck to see his wrists chained to the table, his feet below too, quartered and ensnared by the metal. Samwell pulled at the restraints but beyond noise nothing gave. The doctor walked over and put his hand on Samwell's chest.

Easy there old fella, your time'll come soon enough.

Samwell looked over to Ransom, the unconscious man had three less fingers on the hand opposite and one less foot than when they had journeyed in. Samwell tried to yell but the doctor put the ether rag over his face again and as Samwell's eyes closed he could see the flicker of his friend's eyes waking, and his muffled screams took the old man back to the darkness.

The street below Samwell was wooden, boards that shifted in the heat and the sudden winter frost, and made sound when strangers came calling for trouble or worse. He stood with his friend the good Doc Augustine as Cranham moved about beyond, by the Doc's place, watching the comings and goings of many. The Sheriff's place opposite was overseeing from the other, Hoxley gave a tip of the hat to the older men, the makers of the settlement, and his deputies nodded too. Kent there with his big hat and shiny badge and clean boots, Ransom with half a hand, one foot and holes through his torso. Samwell

Andrew Jones

turned away and the Sheriff's place fell away entirely, he could instead see beyond the street, and to the houses he built by his own hand, and the loved ones looking to him between the abodes. Anna was at her most youthful and smiling, a gentle wave towards him, a thumb and a little finger were all that kept it from being a stub. Noah hobbled on one foot trying to balance as he stared angrily towards his father. Bartholomew and Jenny were ghostly pale and held one-another as they looked, protecting the other from the world in their entwining. Augustine prodded Samwell's shoulder and Samwell looked at his old friend, the Wrights disappeared.

    Your man didn't do too well, kept making noise when I was fixing his myriad problems. If you do same, I'll have to see you like him.

    Augustine revealed a red hand clasping onto bloody tissue and muscle, Samwell looked to the Sheriff's place opposite and Ransom was standing, looking out, mouth agape, tongueless. Augustine slapped Samwell a few times on the cheek and walked across the street.

    I like to do my experiments with as much focus as possible. Pain is expected, but if you could please respect my needs and hush then all will be made easier.

    Augustine took a scalpel out and sliced Ransom's shirt, his chest exposed. Samwell reached out but his hand slammed back to his side with a clank. Augustine carefully made an incision in the former lawman's gut, the man stood there bleeding onto the wooden street below, sharing no emotion, and Augustine opened a hole of skin and meat to the world. He stuck a hand in and began rummaging around.

You feel that don't you? You're still with me. Good.

Augustine pulled his hand out and held a purple-red sack, vines still attached to Ransom's body. Samwell reached out again, his hand slammed against his side with a clank. He opened his mouth to yell, but only sighs of breath made it.

Samwell turned from the horror and darkness protruded, but the groans and squelching from the surgeries continued on. He saw the wooden street disappear under his feet, a red river ran across, a torrent of mouthless pleas flowed as waves towards Samwell, drowning him in the water.

Samwell woke up and saw nothing. Darkness still. He moved his arm, a clank of chain, he was awake again, truly.

Deputy Ransom?

Samwell hushed his voice, it came out hoarse, spittle more than syllable, his face itched, he had a beard, he had growth all over, and his body was limp and twinging with the need to pump blood. He could see nothing. Samwell moved his head and then arched his back, the chains clanked slightly, he slowed each movement and silenced his restraints. He felt the warmth drain down from his chest to his crotch to his knees to his feet, and up to his arms, his hands. He called out to Ransom again quietly, nothing back. He flexed his arm muscles and pumped blood about his extremities, the chains constricted his flow, the blood trickled, dripped, slowly filling back his body with red.

    You hold on there.

    Samwell bulged his wrists and his forearms harder and harder, the feeling in his fingers returned, and he felt the chains clamping him in giving a little. He flexed more, it ached him entirely, he felt sixty years of rowing and riding and living curse his physical form. The chains clanked a little and rattled and in a flex of arm burst, clanking to the table. His hands slammed into his chest, free of restraint, and he looked at them in what little sight he had. They looked withered, wrinkled, hairy, blue, blistered, beaten, calloused, destroyed of humanity.

    He reached to his feet and felt the restraints and ripped them off, grunting hard and loud for a split second of power, and suddenly Samwell was free of it all. He reached around his pockets and found a matchbook and struck a head. Darkness was cured in a small flicker of hot, he could see his withered body, time on the table had fallen mass from his arms, from his legs, from his stomach, Samwell had shrunk. He looked to Ransom, who stared at the light. The man was bloody and poorly stitched up and lacked two hands and two feet and a tongue and clothes and many instances it seemed of his torso played with. He couldn't move, he couldn't speak, he could just stare at the light and at Samwell with his straggly white beard. Samwell slowly got off the table and stood unstable on his feet, he looked around the room for his jacket, his boots, his holster, to no avail. Samwell saw the glint of metal and reached out and grabbed hold of a bloody scalpel. He looked at Ransom, and the scalpel, and Ransom nodded and his eyes stared at the light and wept. Samwell shook his head and hushed a strained I'm Sorry and held the match to Ransom's eyes. As the light flickered its last and began to burn his tips, Samwell clung to the heat and the pain and slashed his friend's throat. A small gurgle and Ransom fell still forever, the room was once more totally dark.

    Samwell dropped the burnt match and closed Ransom's eyelids to the world and shuffled slowly around the room, he muttered a small prayer for his fallen friend as he held onto the table to stand upright. Shuffling around he felt the wood of the floor splinter his feet as he moved, but kept on through the pain, it was all pain now, life was only continual agony. Samwell lit another match and looked around the room, he found his and Ransom's clothes piled up in a corner and put his boots on, his hat, his holster and his gun, he grabbed personals from Ransom and pocketed them for anyone who might come calling, and he looked around, to the one door in the room, and slowly stomped over. His boots hard on the wooden floor.

    Samwell tried the door and it opened immediately, no force, no locks, he found himself free to leave. Samwell stepped out, into the world, onto the street of the settlement. Opposite a lantern shone on a sign reading THECARY. Samwell hopped slowly across the street, holding the grip of his pistol in one hand and the bloody

Andrew Jones

scalpel in the other. He peered into the door and saw it was empty of life, the bottles and medicines and aid settled on their shelves waiting for another victim. Samwell looked at the other shacks in the street, all dark, all lifeless. He sighed with exhaustion and dragged his feet to the nearest one. In the window he could see nothing but a dinner table laid out for a meal never to come, he continued on to another shack. Outside, he heard a snore break the silence and gripped the pearl of his gun tighter in worry and snuck towards the doorway.

    He opened the door and it creaked very slightly. Samwell took the gun out and walked into the little wooden building and steadied the scalpel in his other hand and prepared himself for what he had to do. A smaller snore broke, a higher pitch, to Samwell's right, he turned in the shack and struggled squinting in the darkness for any image. He saw Ransom's face pleading for death, he saw Noah's face steadied to ride off, he saw Anna's face crying in the night, he saw the doctor's face, asleep before him. And an arm wrapped around, a woman laying in his bed alongside, cuddling for the night. Samwell kept his scalpel up and stepped forward, a little cough stopped his track and Samwell turned around. A little boy lay on a blanket on the wooden floor. Samwell stepped back and saw the family, at peace together, in this dark and empty land. Samwell's hand shook and he dropped the scalpel, it landed in the board, blade going through wood. Samwell backed out and closed the door and shuffled off down the street.

He walked away from the horrors, away from the death, away from all that had befallen everyone on his trail, but stopped before thecary, thinking of his beloved mare. In the lanternlight he looked at the marks on the ground, the feet and mud and hoof and followed what little marks he could see, into the trees hiding the settlement from God and man alike. Samwell lit another match and walked between trunks grown large and tall, he walked for ten minutes before he saw anything but leaf and bark and dirt.

The reflection of the light and the old, wirey, hairy man shuffling closer to the eyeball reminded Samwell how alone he was in this world and the next. He looked at the lifeless body of Clover, led out to the woods and shot in the head and left for the animals. He knelt and let the match burn out on the ground and hugged the head of his beloved mare. The maggots eating her from the inside out, the hole in the head that harbored all life, the chunks of meat torn out by fox and wolf and buzzard and hawk didn't stop Samwell seeing Clover still as she was at her prime, at their best together, at her first days of walking and lapping milk and chomping grass and the years they had spent together in tandem. Samwell in the darkness, in the middle of the unknown, truly alone, wept.

*

Of an August afternoon Jenny found herself struggling in her house. Her stomach hurt, her head rang,

Andrew Jones

her arms and legs ached, it was all across and over her echoed in the walls of the empty building. She took it upon herself to ambulate whilst she still could and made her way into Cranham and saw Hazel in the window of the tailors and dressmakers and went in.

    The Mann twins were finishing up legs on jeans and placing them in the window display in the hopes of hooking folk whilst they're still outside of lockup, as Hazel worked on the green and gold dress for the Seargant at the Fort. Jenny sat uncomfortably on a chair and drank a glass of water as she sweated out the heat of the heavy late-summer's day and watched her friend thread perfect joins in beautiful fabric before her. Hazel found a perfect place to hasten for the time and the two decided on taking in the warm afternoon haze at the horse stables, spend time with animals that weren't their own. They left the Mann twins taking a three o'clock tipple later than planned with their denim escapades and staring at the disappointing foot and horse traffic that skipped right over them.

    They'd come in if we had canned goods.

    They'd come in if we sold some of this sherry.

    They'd come in if we weren't in this shop.

    The horses in Maclaine's stable were healthy and happy and plenty, bred for strong backs and long journeys, to carry people and purpose, with plenty of room to run around and live, and space to rest in the heat and the cold of the barn. Colin's gift was on full display in the happiness of every beast that resided under his wing. He was filling up haystacks and checking on the foals as the women walked in and watched, the older horses knowing their visage and scents willingly sniffing and licking hands and nuzzling the women with kindness and care. As much attention was paid to the beautiful creatures, it was hard to take eyes away from the man sweating in the heat of the day, hard at work, no longer respecting civility in his own land he had removed top layers entirely, his glistening chest and arms danced with rippled muscle and dark hair, only two suspenders offering respite from skin and keeping the latter half covered fully for God's sake as much as society's. Hazel leered, Jenny glanced and avoided as best she could, it was hard to but some days were made for a little light sinning. Jenny patted and brushed the head and mane of a horse and felt the tickle of its tongue upon her fingers before it turned away to lick salt, brushing her with its tail as a final treat. As the horse cantored off, Colin looked over and saw the two, and locked eyes with Hazel, she refrained from escaping the grip of his stare, the two saw just one-another in a moment of electricity rippling across their world. Hazel and Jenny both blushed red as Colin nodded to the ladies and patted the horse upon the salt lick before returning to a foal dancing about in the stable testing out its legs still.

 As evening encroached, Jenny sloshed her way home on her inflating body and stopped to see the family horses in their stable, all well and fine if not as loving as those at Maclaine's, if it was the smell of other horses on her person it'd be an understandable slight on their

Andrew Jones

owner. The sun set into an orange and green-blue ovation and Jenny lit lanterns for the night, at Noah's, at the stable, at her and Bartholomew's and at Samwell and Anna's. She blew her match out and stared at the house, she put her ear to the door and hoped to hear something, weeping as awful as it would be would feel like something was still alive in there. She clenched her fist to knock lightly but couldn't seem to move her body, freezing in the last heat of the evening. She slowly opened the door in place of noise and listened inside the house, the dust had gathered across the kitchen and dining table and seating space, the door to the bedroom was closed for any and all, but there was still no noise. Jenny stepped foot in and the wood buckled and creaked and felt like it was splintering under her weight, she stepped back and looked across the way as the last light fell and the house came into darkness once more. She closed the door up and walked to her own empty dark world.

    Jenny lay in bed and felt down her body, her breasts were growing and starting to feel tingly and peculiar, her stomach was getting thicker, she was finding her fingers rising across a mountain as she moved down. As she felt around her belly, like a hit from beyond her body seemed to react, a movement, a reaction, a kick. Jenny looked down and felt for a while until deep in the night when a second kick confirmed what she first felt. Her aches and agonies fell away in the understanding.

The Ferryman Upon The Plains

Hey there little one. How are ya doin' in there? We're havin' a heck of a time here, I tell ya what there's some fussin' and feudin' and frettin' goin' about and around. Not that you need to concern yourself with much of much anyhow, it'll all be handled and forgotten about by the time you're aware of where you are. Always will be, the way people are, lookin' to the things that they want now, that matter now, they ain't seein' beyond the sunset and to the next one. That won't be us though, you and me, we'll be smarter than'em all, anything we want, we look to why, we don't go for things 'less we know what fer and how to and who won't and which way we can for best make it all. World's gettin' more chokin' and isolatin but ain't no way to be isolated when there's more than one o'us, you and me and we here together. We're all here and will be and we'll be fine when we're here. Your grandma, she's in a sorry state somethin' awful, your grandpappy, he's gone off doin' nothin' good for no-one, your uncle, well, heck, I don't even know what he's up to no more. But we're here. And we'll be here. That's as all I can for certain but I can sleep with the certain, I can wake with the certain. I cain't for eatin' and walkin' and drinkin' and talkin' uncertain, life's always been in uncertain' but for all I know I know you and I are here and now, and that's fact and that's what I can sleep on. Little one, my baby, sweet baby, whatever world you're comin' into, God knows how it'll look, but know for certain I'll be there for you, and you'll be there for me.

*

Andrew Jones

    The first rains were caught on the brim of the marshals' hats and the manes of their reins, they rode up rocky hill and down grassland, the clouds dark and the sky blue, the showers short and sudden and welcome to all. The lawmen steadied their trot through the deep forest, the patter of droplets on the trees standing above them loud and echoey. They were cocooned in a balmy humid wood and water world, atop their animals they saw families of deer resting and lapping at the droplets landing on the ground in pools of rock and mud. An explosive thunderclap rang out and the deer scattered, a piece of bark flew from a trunk near Zachariah and the three marshals took revolvers and scanned the gaps between trees. A hand reached out and a man yelled an apology muffled by the echoes of gunshot and raindrop. A bulky, bearded man in bear fur and racoon hat stepped towards the men, rifle in one hand gripped and facing skyward, his other empty and stretched out.
    I missed that big one somewhat, you fellas alright? Not many come this way, you lost?
    Abraham asked if the man had seen any men and any bears and any bloody bodies, he shook his head and told them he'd been on the scent of deer for a few weeks now, but others'd found bigger. The lawmen holstered their weapons and the man offered them a little respite, a camp, a fire, a meal. The marshals walked their horses through the forest as the bearded man deftly

traversed the endless trees and rocks and found a small group of hunters resting up, feet by the fire, watching a deer cook atop the flames.

Jedediah pointed to the bear furs the hunters wore.

You seen any them round lately?

The men nodded.

Always bears up here, they mostly keep to their-own, and we us. It's the fall when we find ourselves conflictin'. Paths somewhat together, the last rush of the season before settlin' for the cold. They don't like us in their way, and we don't like bein' killed.

They ate the deer as the rain came and went and returned again, and in a pool of rock and water rippling in the drops from above the men washed and shaved and made themselves alive again before settling at the fire with their horses and the hunters. The marshals mentioned the last campsite, and the flayed hides of others, and the men shook their heads and said sorrows to fallen folk.

Hard life this, always a chance any day's the last. But to die like that, inhumane. Wouldn't put any of our catches through such, demons, devils, monsters.

The men offered the marshals their aid to rid the world of these people, but the marshals insisted on keeping to themselves. The hunters understood and soon packed up and put the fire out as the crashing rain ceased above. They felt the last hours of day were to be lucky, they had all the reason to expect good tidings from such kindness and care, a levelling of the universe. The marshals saw the hunters off and began riding again northwards, as the hunters went west.

Andrew Jones

A few days of forest riding and they found the edge of the treeline, and a trickle of a river leading up to the mountains beyond. They rode a little ways up and out of the sanctuary of the tall trees and that night laid by the river, the sound peaceful in the pitch dark of the first chill of fall. A little fidget of grass caught Abraham's ear and in the lack of sight he focused on the direction of the noise and the river's flow fell to blur as each rustle of grassblade cracked on. Abraham heard the noise get nearer and laid perfectly still, his eyes started to adjust to the night and he could see stars above, and the clouds that flew past, blanketing the dots of white and falling away again. He slowly turned to his side and saw a beast standing next to him. In the watery dark eyeball he could see himself, jittering up and down. Abraham reached out and caught the furry hopper, a little rabbit alone in the world.

Abraham sat up and held the rabbit close and stroked at its fur, he stared at the creature and gently played with its hair and rubbed its body and tried to make it feel comfortable, welcome. Jedediah and Zachariah sat up as Abraham told them he got them a little bunny and they passed around the creature and cuddled it and found some horsefood for it to eat and let it run and hop between the three men and petted it gently, laughing and smiling and having an innocent and childlike splendor in the rabbit's company. The night was longer than it had been all summer but for the first time since Abraham first came across the body in the water it was full of joy and fun. The three horsemen rode out north with the river to their side in the morning, bellies full from a breakfast of rabbit.

*

Despite the rapturous heat on the endless days of riding on the trail before them mountains came and rose on the horizon offering hallucinations of winter, peaks capped with white and gray in the blue sky and sweltering orange burn of sun. Riding up and finding themselves in the shadows of the behemoths but never removed of the summer heaviness hiding in the darkness, Midnight and Noah ran ahead of the wagon and found first a small mining town built upon the heights and steep land of the world, wood and rock both forming buildings of simple use. Men returning from an early day's labor picking and digging and finding nothing of value laid in the shade and heat and as sweat washed muck and grime from their skin their eyes glared towards the strangers rolling past, the man and his tremendous steed less attention than the woman astride the wagon, and the sound of another hidden within.

Noah sat and watched around the passers by men and women glancing over and seeing to the new arrivals with curious glance and courteous distance, and Kirsty pulled the wagon into a patch of grass and dirt trodden by many hoof and boot before, outside a building adorned with sign upon awning simply informing all this was HOTEL, the whereabouts unknown. They opted for a single room under the guise that Noah and Kirsty were partnered in the eyes of God and brought all items and coin gently in, avoiding noise and jingle of money in front of guests and residents. The women and the babe fell upon the bed swiftly, finding comfort in the four walls and the roof and the softer than dirt kindness of the hotel's simple offerings. Noah sat on a small wooden chair unencumbered with finery and cushion, spartan as the life of those seeing to the gold in the hills could need until they themselves found the shiny nuggets and absconded with hope and joy to join the elite in the American Dream.

  Despite the stagnant warmth and the time being still so early, the family fell asleep swiftly and the shade of the mountains led a strange nightly darkness sweeping over the town. Noah considered pulling the curtains over the windows but instead sat by the glass pane, careful to be facing mostly the doorway, and glanced out to the world beyond during his eternal watch, seeing the folk of the town come and go, stop in dirt streets and wooden slat walkways making conversation, showing scars and items found and sharing failures and hopes and next-time-it'll-come-trues. The women away from their loves making merry together in a world they could be themselves a little, whilst others were off in the mountains or resting up it was them that had to go about handling duties and taking longer so they could share themselves thoughts and fears and hopes and news of around. But come nightfall, as the temperature fell dramatically and the snowcaps beyond threatened to bring themselves down to the town, everyone came from dirt and rest equal to the saloon playing piano and yelling songs joyous and hopeful, scraps broke out onto the dirt and fell back in with glasses of connection poured. Noah looked over those he was caring for, and down at the rowdy activity begging for his attention, his desires.

You ever sleep?

Noah turned a third direction, Kirsty's eyes groggy and slowly acquiescing to the darkness after a long nap looked upon her guardian with inquisition.

Ain't nothin' for me there.

You're free to try at least, maybe longer spent you might fall upon what you never knew you were lookin' for out there.

Noah licked his dry and chapped lips and stared upon the woman lying next to her son and her little sister, warm and comfortable in rest. The words he considered revealing through his wettened orifice stuck in his throat and he stood instead, leaving the chair of basic use and walked to the door.

I'm takin' a time, you gonna be safe and fine without?

Kirsty nodded and showed the rifle that was held under the pillow her family slept peacefully upon, she laid still in bed readying her weapon for any use as Noah slowly and quietly opened the door and stepped out into the hotel's landing, shutting securely behind him and

Andrew Jones

heading downstairs as men and women of more washed and Godly nature nodded and smiled as they ascended.

Noah stood on the wooden planks of the street and looked up to the window, hoping to see a friendly figure in the dark looking back, waving perhaps, beckoning him return instead, but the empty frame of wood and brick and glass stared back cold and still. He wandered towards the rowdy saloon, hands shaking with fear and excitement equal.

From so long the quiet and the four of them sharing nights of fire and grief and solitary reserve the wave of boisterous amplitude in the saloon hit Noah with rapid intensity, his walk through to the bar passing tables of dancing and singing and yelling and laughing and men chasing women and women chasing men and people between them all seething into their drinks silently louder than all the haphazard fun of the evening. Shivering out the sudden change of world, Noah slammed his hand on the wood to stabilize himself in this place and feel the pain of his own intention, calling also attention of the barkeep who came over and stared at the stranger and swiftly poured a glass of bourbon brown and delicious in a glass barely rubbed from the last patron's grimy lips. Noah felt the two coins of Icriss in his pocket and the noise and heat fell away and Noah gripped and sipped and centered himself in this place. His mouth exploded with heaven, with truth, with hope, with home and safety and the warmth of what he left and what left him both. He removed his hand from the pocket of payment and found coins willing to be used at this place a stop-off on a longer journey and tossed them on the bar, got himself a second filling of drink and walked with the glass from the bar proper and found a corner darker and quieter than the rest of the building and sat there, away from it all, looking upon the tapestry of indignity as folk who believed their riches lie in the mountains, in the west, in the untamed land of America before the rest might come take it from them, now drinking at a higher altitude with less money and fewer friends to share the brief time they had on this journey with. Noah saw so many who passed over the river and the ferry these many years who didn't get much out of their believed intention. They, like he, sat here and drank and waited for the reason to befall them after all their attempts making life happen. Instead, it seemed, it was all just for nothing. Long way to find out nothing at all. Endless emptiness. Noah chuckled to himself as he enjoyed his smooth comfort.

  He woke in the uncomfortable chair at morning's first light, sticky saliva drying on the side of his cheek and down to his chin, no memory of the time between the saloon below and the hotel room above. The boots of mud gave hint how sloppy the return was. On the bed sat the rifle, but no sign of any under his wing. Noah splashed a little resting water onto his face and bits and walked his messy boots down the stairs and found the family Hollander eating at the hotel's little restaurant nook, beans and eggs and bacon and coffee all except Paul sipping on milk instead. Noah sat next to the boy and brushed his hair playfully and looked at Sissy opposite slowly chewing on her pork and staring into the nothingness beyond.

    I didn't wake y'all did I?

    Sissy said nothing, Paul didn't know words to say, Kirsty on the other side of her son smiled politely at Noah Wright and finished drinking her coffee.

    You ain't graceful on your feet, I ordered a plate comin' up soon as you stirred above. Best switch shifts and keep eye on things.

    Kirsty Hollander brushed some food from her son's chubby cheek as he chewed and crunched on the small plate of food before him and then made her way upstairs. A cook came by with a plate of hot goods for Noah to feast upon and he helped Paul with his breakfast whilst filling his own stomach up. Sissy slowly ate at the food before her, sometimes she'd turn to her nephew and break a little smile in his direction before returning to the endless stare of the living dead.

*

    The heat kept beating but the wind picked up as the noons shortened and the moisture of the river lingered in the atmosphere of the land, the eighth month fell away with the first foundations drawn up and the ground soft enough to be broken in the land behind the jailhouse for Harding-

Grant's new street. The new residents were ushered to a large camp on the mansion's grounds, the houses nearing completion for all laborers, and stone and lumber began to form shape of floor. Bit by bit the walls grew and stretched out, and two oxen pulled a machine that ripped the ground from its setting, men followed and pushed the excess dirt to the sides, and others came to level the new lower, cleaner ground. Stones were placed on the new pathway down some hundred yards, they seemed to have started by Harding-Grant's mansion path and led the way to the new build. There was no intention to carry on beyond, any traveling folk would be left to their own devices, or do better spending their time and hard-earned money in the eventual businesses the married-into-money man intended to create.

 The dust clouds from the north were not some ominous sign of things coming, but the wranglers and ranch-hands leading and corralling the cattle to the end of their annual drive north, to grass and cooler air and shade in the height of the sun. The air was cooling with water droplets and it was time for the adventures to be over. The men atop their fine, well-ridden horses kept scattered distance running the cattle over the drier land, still fertile if gasping for the atmosphere's newly moistened for quenching.

 A family in their own right, the three Peterson brothers orphaned, lost, adopted in a way by Herman took the brunt of the back run, keeping the lost and diverting bovine in check, whilst Joe Amello and Charlie Reeves led on, given point and direction proper by the man on the big gray horse, Elgar 'Eagle-Eye' Ellis. All the five that ran herd with him knew from first meeting this man was the reason to hang tight and the core to trust in riding with others. Short of the farmer himself, Ellis stood for the long-life of riding and grazing and handling and taming the land and the animals atop for all future.

    The cattle were ridden across and into the gates of Ganz's farmland, Reeves and Amello counted each cow as they passed, silently enough over the trundle of hooves on dirt, and as the Petersons ran the last of the herd in they matched numbers, two lost from accidents out of the several hundred. In Eagle-Eye's time it was one of the more successful summers, nary a rustler wrangling up and attempting own-branding on hides, no illness sweeping across the cattle, no flash floods, no middle-of-the-night bouts of in-fighting and poker gone foul between the men. The world seemed more at peace with each passing year from the wars. He hadn't known the evil had spread east this year.

    They rode the final leg back to the stable together closer than any time they'd ridden since they set off, the six without a herd, listening to the silence of the air around them, the noise in distance of hammer on wood and stone indignant and intermittent.

    Ain't Mister Ganz normal out here seein' in them what we returned?

The Ferryman Upon The Plains

Eagle-Eye nodded as he observed the world atop his horse, the potatoes and corn and beans coming true in the ground beyond, the church in the horizon alone and still, he saw no people.

Boys, I don't mean to put too fine a weight on the matter but things is too quiet all over. Don't let's think down but might as be prepared to remove yer hats in condolence.

A pall was cast as they stabled up and made way to the ranch-house for rest on actual structure, in some form of home.

They piled into the barn that was their domain, the odor of sweat and grime foul in nostrils, it stumped their stampede a beat.

Goddamn boys, someone start a fire, we gotta bathe the seasons off us fore we drown in it.

But it wasn't from them emanating, and the men who shared the year together sensed it was beyond them, a new pungency into their awareness. On one of the spare cots beyond, reserved for the one-timers, the passing-throughers, the stragglers hiding and finding they aren't cut out for the harsh and the callouses, was Lars laying, skin and clothes covered in mud and manure, fresh from a morning of seeing to the hogs in their pen, cleaning their shit and skin. Out for the noon, a siesta before a cleanse. Reeves prodded the Swede with his poking finger and Lars returned to consciousness to see three big Peterson boys, the black cowboy, the Mexican and the aging legend all looking down at him Goldilocks in their bearhouse.

Andrew Jones

This what you do when we're off out, pigfarmer? Tried all of them and found just right?

Lars found himself overwhelmed and uncertain, his mouth failed him a beat longer than his brain felt comfortable with, in the wait the six sunk certainty of the abode and the land it sat upon.

You weren't told? Ganz didn't come to count?

The men shook heads before the Swede as he stood, mess shaped in his groove on the bed below.

The farmer's age, it is becoming heavy on him and us all.

Lars walked the men to the farmhouse and knocked before opening the door, Herman was snoozing at the kitchen table, drunken stupor turned long sleep off a night's lament. They shook and nudged him awake and Herman looked at the men returned and stood to welcome, acting as best as it was all normal and healthy around him.

Howdy men, standin' fine and strong, didn't hear y'all ridin' up through the country, musta been somethin' like a sneakin', horse and cow both on tiptoe.

The old farmer took a whiff of the musk of all men as he inhaled richly and sucked the drylip of the daydrunk.

Let me go off and see to the cattle you rode in on and how bout y'all head up to the river and

The Ferryman Upon The Plains

clean off whatever in the domain of God you're all covered in.

    Ganz pushed through the cowboys with a hobble in his step, an angle on his back, shrinking and aging in the clear light of day. Eagle-Eye followed the old man as the others knew to hold back and wait together, standing outside the farmhouse, listening to the hammering, as Colin, sweaty and glistening with a smile upon his face, walked up from the settlement and waved the cowboys a hearty welcoming.

    Fellas, I was sure I heard the earth move, been waitin' on you for a good amount now.

    Colin shook hands and proceeded to tell the Petersons and Reeves and Reeves of the murder at the river and the murder at the farm and the murder at the tavern, and led them to the river to wash with himself and Lars, as Eagle-Eye walked solemn to them holding the same knowledge about to unpack upon the gang. They removed all items and cleansed in the run of the water a group, full in the knowledge of the events that unfolded in their absence, aware that their peace on the plains was replaced here instead, and only growing. The hammering kept on.

    They killed our boys. Good boys them, don't nobody put down a dog ain't rabid or rampagin', unGodly. Inhuman. Man's best friend fer a reason, they is. Which one done it?

    He's dead now. Ganz saw to deliver him to his maker.

    Man's lucky it were just him came for justice. Would go dark ages on a bastard did such to our boys, tie

Andrew Jones

him apiece to horses and pull, make him live through his death.
    What 'bout them that did the barkeep?
    Been rottin' in the jailhouse for near a month now.
    They ain't hanged?
    Things down there is messier and messier, Sheriff's alone surrounded by men carryin' blades and guns and now workin' all hours outside his buildin', allegiances all over, God knows who's there lookin' after the lawman and who's tempted to take the place over.
    We're back in frontier lands here, next thing your army pals is gonna scalp us, rape us and burn us and call it victory for America the beautiful.
    Why don't we ride on through the middle of the night and kill em all in they's sleep?
    Eyes darted to Marcus, the middle Peterson brother, and the smallest, after his violent outburst. Thoughts internal of all the men as they washed grime and sweat and mud and shit from their skin and holes. Eagle-Eye cleared his throat and eyes turned back to him.
    We wanna maintain somethin' of a civilization, much as we wanna take 'em out and tell 'em what goes round just came back, straight-up huntin' won't turn well fer none anyfolk. But ain't no good hidin' out and waitin' and fallin' from the rest of the world whilst they run rampage across our world. Gotsta put a scare on 'em, men afraid'll do things stupid, and sudden, backs

against the wall they'll act 'fore thinkin'. Murderin's easy and don't do none nothin' to solve things. And peace, shit, peace ain't a part of life that lasts any longer than man sees someone's got somethin' they ain't. If they's got men hired and men loyal and men bored that means they got eyes all set different directions, means when guns come out they ain't aimin' all the same direction. All we need to do get them towards one'nother. And not at no more of us. Whoever's even left out there to aim at. Let 'em eat each-other as we feast on the land.

 Like a war?

 Eagle-Eye nodded.

 Nobody wins a war they fight, they'll be so distracted, men like that either too much pride to stop or too cowardly to start, watch them flee for life or die for money and when the dust settles we bury them somewhere and build better above. They came to our land for no good, they'll learn em if it's their last to respect those that came before. Look at us, six men ridin' hundreds of dollars of livestock through strange land and ain't much ever got trouble found us, now find us on home land, we bring the fear of God to those lookin' for trouble.

 The men finished washing up and headed back to the ranch-house for a rest-up. Herman finished counting the cows and began cooking up a big meal of pork shoulder and potato for the men. They ate in the ranch as a nine, Lars and Colin and Herman and Eagle-Eye and Joe and Charlie and Willem and Marcus and Johnny. The comfort of the group came easy, men of the land united in feasting and resting, Ganz smiled.

Andrew Jones

    This is how it's to be, always was. Look round, ain't this right? Shame on those that try taking from, try breaking apart, this right here, this how we's always s'posed to live. They come to ours and do wrong, they bring it to us and we cain't return favor rightly?
    We can't let them win.
    It's not about that, boys, it ain't about a winner and a loser, it's about clearing the pests for the sake of the crops. You gotta find the hive, the molehill, the head of the beast. And he lives in a house grander than this land ever needed, a castle in his kingdom of dirt and blood.

    In the slight chill of the dawn in September above the jailhouse, Sheriff Hoxley was holding dearly to Mrs. Hoxley, his arms tired from carrying the weight of the world for months rested and nursed upon the plump and tender body of his beloved, she laid half-asleep still, nestled in the warmth and comfort of love beyond them both, a connection made true by the universe. She moved her hands onto his and held on, hers paltry, tiny in his grand limbs, and pushed fingers intertwining with his own as she tightened him further around her, a cuddle gripping them closer and tighter. She felt his mustache on her ear and warm breath in the chilling near-autumnal atmosphere.
    You like feelin' like this?

She nodded and bristled his facial hair against her lobe and back of her neck, tickling and warming.

Ain't nobody do ya harm in this hold. Ain't nobody but us knows what goes on up here. A world of our own we got.

Mrs. Hoxley leaned into her husband and turned her neck and head to look in her periphery at her cuddling husband, just about able to kiss his cheek as she whispered return.

To have and to hold. We don't ask for much in this life. Sometimes all we need is this.

If I asked you summin', would you keep it to yours alone?

She nodded and tickled her neck again.

Hold me how I do to you.

Mrs. Hoxley turned full body, breaking a little of the tight clutch, and stared into her husband's eyes, before kissing his lips softly and longingly and letting grip loose of her in their embrace.

Turn around.

The Sheriff rolled on the bed and Mrs. Hoxley scooched to his new position, taking her form around his back and legs and pushed her lips onto the neck of her husband as she slipped one arm under his body, wrapping the other over his side and meeting around his chest, pulling him closer to her and holding him in vice-like cuddle. She nuzzled and kissed the back of his neck and his ear as Sheriff Hoxley closed his eyes and felt their united beats and her lips and breath and arms and legs and fingers and chest against him, embracing him, warming him, holding him from the abyss of the endless world beyond. The men down below locked in the jail for a month now, pissing and moaning and yelling and pleading and angry and sad and disgusted, and the Doc rotating in to help with it all and pressuring the Sheriff to handle the law he was appointed to do were distant memories. This, the cuddle, the couple, the togetherness of two souls found somehow in the expanse of the world in this moment, in this land, in this time, was all the Hoxleys needed to carry on another day. For they would return once again to this room, this bed, this hold, till death do they part.

  The sun was coming up and the first signs of chill in the light of the star bristled on the shrinking cock of Freddie Graham as he released his liquid upon the river's flow before him, another night of pittance for paddles closing out. He buttoned up and spat on his hands and the dirt below as he collected the change left hidden like all before had decided best to handle on the job, pocketing the hard work's payment and listening to it clink and move in his trousers as he wandered and wondered on the way back to Cranham's little street sitting still, the hammers over the way clinking ever always, the path up to the camp by the Harding-Grant land still best the old road than the newly stoned and cobbled and graveled and ploughed, until buildings finished and it would gain purpose for perhaps a breakfast in the hotel restaurant they'd touted for a spell that was still a few weeks of lumber away. Then, and then maybe if still, Freddie might change paths and stop thinking in his head as much as he did on this muscle memory of tedium and survival. He, as he had for a month now, stopped outside the tavern dry and dark and thought of that first month, the comfort of a place to be, a community as limited as it was, the conversations and quiet drunks made under a roof in a room built to hide from the world the darkest and most introvert moments of humanity. Settling on a bottle in a tent had less an impact, sharing was miserable when someone invaded your fabric rather than a pal popping on a chair on the table to see about, chat about, play about and drink about town. The good Avery Bedford had sometime in the nights it seemed opened the trading post for a few folk to drink and chat and play some poker surrounded by fabrics and drinks and food and that damn sasaparilla Harding-Grant insisted on gifting folk like it wasn't him throwing shit stock out with a smile, but Graham was always at the river punting folk off to seek gold and riches and lives as others turned a settlement in stasis into a confluence of confidantes drinking and slamming cards and forming bonds beyond where they slept and worked.

    He made his way to the camp of men as they woke in the sun's first bright shimmers, the fire began and coffee en masse began brewing. He laid in his tent listening to the shuffling and grunting and farting and pissing of men ready to do another day building the town they intended to inhabit for a good long time as a voice broke through with surprising clarity and authority. A call from the voice announcing that come the end of the

Andrew Jones

current week the small shacks will be ready for them, reasonable rates for all who put in such hard labor, Harding-Grant and wife welcome you and wish to share successes of the work and building with all, contracts passed around in the coming days to all who seek shelter. Freddie listened to the excitement and gruff thanks and some under-breath 'about damn time's from men who had spent damn near a month on hard ground and another few months huddled together in squalor, space, a place to exist, somewhere to call their own, even on another's land, was always to be welcomed, if not with the open arms and excitement. He thought of a place of his own. Not to sleep, but to be.

  Rumbling rocked the land as a mini-battalion rode on in colors and uniform and relented their push at the jailhouse. Twelve privates and sergeants led by First Lieutenant Anson Mills stationed themselves before the lawman's office and waited for Hoxley's welcome into town, the spurs and boots of the Sheriff echoing and scraping inside through the small doorway, bursting into the world beyond, as the hammers of construction beyond enveloped them all. Hoxley stood at the top of the steps down to the dirt street and touched his hat's brim to the army men.
  Lieutenant, Sergeants, Privates, what's the ruckus over?

Mills took a step up and another until he was matching eye-level with the lawman and peered into the dark shelter of the jailhouse, the men behind bars in a moment of silence of sleep or drained of yelling for a time. The Doc stepped out behind the Sheriff, half-in-darkness.

Word keeps spreadin' of capture and murder round here, from folk comin' to buy, to trade, to come back and forth from station, and yet we ain't seen you or any of your men come by to talk law true. Murder comes with a cost, you ain't hangin' men out here on your own is ya?

Come inside and see 'em, they're still alive as much as they can be, much as we wish they weren't some times in their misery and noise and obscenities. It's just me here to see though, can't be riding the hour up and lettin' this place without a badge.

Mills stared at the Doc hanging around behind the law.

You gettin' older deputies these days? Cain't fer no good measure do much more, so sit with a badge and get paid to be watchdogs?

Good citizens pickin' the slack of the world overburdened, my men went huntin' murderers and ain't been back for the season. Just me and my badge and my gun.

You folk need a wire and fast.

Yeah, well, I get the feelin' we're getting one whether we like it or not.

The Sheriff let the noise of construction yonder put punctuation on his point.

Andrew Jones

    Mills looked at his men and nodded, they split into three groups and walked their horses in different directions, one up to the top of the street, one to the bottom, and one went beyond the jailhouse and to the source of the noise.
    You got proof on those men done the killin'?
    Suspicious activity in the days before, they eyewitnessed each-other, maybe to save themselves but it only circled back to 'em anyways.
    And the victim?
    Buried under the Lord in the churchyard beyond.
    Mighty influx of men around here, what's happenin' over yonder?
    Man's building half the town himself.
    Man?
    Name's Harding-Grant, owns the supply and trading post here, married into money, intent on building a bank and a hotel and God knows what over there, been at it few months now, says he's bringing the future here. Ain't seen much good in the future, always brings more of the past around again.
    He's a good man, might ruffle feathers of some but he talks good and his handshake's somethin' stronger than iron.
    Can't help but be glancin' aside at any who want to grow so much so fast. Time's as good for a tree's as good a land. They've been making noise somethin' wild for so long I cain't remember the sound of my own thoughts in the nighttime.

The Doc stepped forward and shook Mills' hand.

Lieutenant, if it do you fine we're all good and doin' dandy round here without need for you and yours comin' round and staring over our shoulders, or worse, taking arms. We're not a many sure, and we're not trained to kill like you folk, but we don't need ourselves more with intent on death round here. We're tryin'ta keep this town alive.

Mills sneered at the Doc and left the two men and walked his horse down the street, the four uniforms at the end of the path saluted as he walked past and stood still a long time. Augustine and Hoxley looked at one-another as the men behind bars returned to calling the Sheriff a 'loose-headed bastard of the lowest order'.

I best get some rest myself, night's been longer and louder and I'm sure to soon be dealin' with God knows what'll go wrong round here.

Hoxley stepped back into the world of abuse and darkness, thinking of sweet Liza-Beth above as she enjoyed a little rest alone in their bed. Augustine laid on his bed, the feeling of the shotgun under blankets came through harsher than ever before. He sipped a little sweetness to cut nerves from his brain for the time. Mills and his men stationed themselves up in the tavern laid empty and kept eyes on matters from their new spot. The hammering kept on nearby.

ELEVEN

AVERY BEDFORD, THE GENTLE GIANT, made his way through the patrolling army and the swapping shifts of ferry folk and waved a wagon coming from the trading post just off the Doc's clinic and shook hands with Kelso Harding-Grant as he finished up the post's work for the day. The businessman patted Bedford on the arm and smiled.

End of the week, big man, you'll have a place to call your own. You all will. Been down Harding Street yet? Bank'll be wired and safe and full of money in no time, it's all coming together faster. Tomorrow another train, the lady's new maids, books, papers, food, drink, from Chicago, from the real world, where it all counts and matters. And then we'll show them, we can make a city as good ourselves, good men working together, that's all it ever took in ancient times, a bit of land, a bit of help, together to a goal, Rome, Athens, Babylon, London, New York, Chicago, Cranham.

Kelso hopped back home with joy and hope, Avery closed the doors and sat in the post near a solitary lantern for a while, listening to horses and men walk past and mumble conversations that didn't make it through the wooden walls. He took a walk around and opened a bottle of sarsaparilla, gulping it down, enjoying it unlike all his campmates, anything's a treat after nothing. He'd spent every night here for a while and felt he knew all the corners, he could see the difference in piles of stock after a wagon's visit, what came and what left, but he always saw in the corner two crates of fabrics above boxes carefully stacked that had no markings on them, boxes rather than crates, containers that had lids, that held secrets. He carefully took the first crate of materials off and placed it to a side and then the other and lifted a box, as he did he saw under it a crate covered in sawdust and hay with little fuses and packed powder poking out. Anyone their worth out on the land had seen one before, but not so many, from mining and excavating. He knew an explosive when he saw it, and Avery looked over to the flame making sure it stayed as far away from the dynamite sticks at all times. He put the box down atop the dynamite crate and struggled to remove the lid with his bare hands, gripping the edges and pulling it towards him until it started to slide off. He knew the weight of the box wasn't fabric, or food, it didn't clink like bottles of drink, and now with the booming sticks it hid his mind went a mile a minute. Seeing the first glint of metal inside he felt his stomach crush and he paled. He pulled the lid further off and in the dim light he saw a many-chambered rotating mega-gun, a weapon designed for the mass. The kind not for glory or justice, but eradication. He wasn't one to weep but at the sight of annihilation he let a couple of drops fall as he pushed the lid back and hid the monster from the world and covered it all back up. The first knocks of friends at the door told him it was darker now outside and, as he had done often before, it was time to turn solitary work into social gatherings.

Avery opened up for the men and they came in and grabbed a couple of bottles of bourbon and slammed cards down on the barrel holding the light, it danced in response and they began dealing and telling dirty jokes and discussing the houses they'd soon find themselves in. All this time together, working to a goal, as they sat there thinking of the future, Avery saw the gun turning fast and ripping through their dreams.

Kelso and his team now forming men of size and constantly-angry glares stepped into the nearly-complete bank in the middle of his new street and stood in the structure shaped with bars in windows and doors secure for threat of any fool in this well-armed road to fail at robbing. He stepped into the safe room in the middle of it all, he didn't want anyone bursting down a wall and ripping off the goods, he'd read the same dime novels as every chancer. He stood in the mecca of money he dreamt of, and he saw to every angle of employee, their blindsides, their full view, he watched his men stand and witnessed them in all locations, if he saw them not smiling he called out, this was to be eternal joy and endlessly profitable if ran as he dreamt. The only problems were the furnishings yet to come and the noise outside of the hotel and the restaurant and the other builds coming along, and that he knew was only here for a few more weeks at the most. It was all coming together so fast, this world of his own doing.

At the fort another train from out east brought the bank's desks and lanterns and the safe itself along with the first influx of bills and coins to be held. Men came and began immediately to set communications to the fort and the wire leading out across the country, within the day it made its way to both the bank and Harding-Grant's mansion. Kelso himself came to observe the arrival of the items and the money and the new workers, bank manager and clerks and hotel manager and women dolled up in make-up ready to keep that hotel full of frequent users. Three men of muscle kept the women in line as they met Kelso with charm and excitement and within their luggage the men brought enough goods to establish a little pokerhouse under the roof too. It was all coming together, the people back east would know Kelso Harding-Grant wasn't the fool that absconded west and spent his wife's family's fortune, he was the man that tamed the land and taught it to be everything the dime novel kids dreamt of and the elite society demanded all at once. A perfect unification.

Maxwell and Thomas sat and drank tea and watched the army patrol every fifteen minutes, and the men walking to the ferry and back, and Doc heading to church, and Father Langston heading to the Doc's, and Jenny struggling much more to walk looking in the window and walking to the Doc's before heading home alone, and Lars and Herman and them cowboys that loudly returned walking about, talking to the Sheriff and army folk and making honest smiles and laughs and knee-slapping from folksy men-of-the-land comments and jokes too rude for business hours, and they sipped and sat waiting for their jeans and their suits to do more than feed moths.

    Hazel Worthing wasn't at home and she wasn't in the shop. She stood in the Maclaine stable, smiling and waiting as Colin finished feeding the horses and letting them run free in the field a little. He came back in, topless, sweating, smiling.
    Well then, that's all my jobs done.
    He walked until he could smell the sweet scents of Hazel's light perfume, a brushing of lavender and jasmine, and kissed her neck to get closer to that wondrous aroma. She clutched his wet and hot back and held him close, slipping his suspenders off his shoulders and letting his pants fall a little as she climbed onto a haystack using Colin for balance.
    They locked lips and their tongues fought a battle everyone involved won as their hands felt around one-another's arms and hands and chests and backs, he felt his pants fall and he was left in long undergarments and boots. Hazel giggled and held his clothed package in her hands, playing and stroking gently as Colin exclaimed and let breath fly her hair about with glee. Colin pulled down his garments and Hazel spread herself before him, hoisting off her own underwear and clutching his

hips in her legs, bringing him to her and waking his cock hard.

Miss Worthing, I am shocked and appalled at this behavior.

Stableboy, anyone works with horses worth a damn knows how to ride good.

They kissed deep as she played more with his penis and pushed her hips on his, the warmth made things happen easier, she felt it all in the pit of her stomach and the beats of her heart, she was ready. Colin stopped kissing and pulled his head back.

What's wrong?

I just love looking at you. The world has so much beauty in it, none moreso than this moment, this image, and I'm the only one that bares witness.

You're a fool in love.

I am. I am, madly.

Stableboy wouldn't say that.

Stableboy is deeper than you might think at first glance.

How much deeper?

They both giggled with naughty glee as Colin pushed himself forward and they became one in beautiful rapture. They made love for a few minutes quiet and rambunctious, fulfilling one-another's pleasures until sweat was joined by other liquids, and they held one-another and kissed softly and felt in the middle of the stable, in the crest of war, love and togetherness and pure humanity in the arms of one-another.

Andrew Jones

*

  The ride home was long and he avoided sights still festering in his soul as he rode on, speed wasn't in his design as the land took his imagination away from the world he knew. By the time he stopped back at Saint Richard he took a few days around others, people, noise, civility, and sat in church long after the bells ceased and the priest sat on the pew next to him and just felt his presence. The Cranham deputy had a week's ride or so still on his way and the heft of his partner and their trail and the men they took north and the murderers they failed to capture and see justice carried upon strangled his every waking moment. Kent saddled up and rode out, the time he saw the Cranham church on the hill beyond was when he felt the drops of river in the air nearby, and it all flooded back, the way things were before, when it was just the three lawmen sitting in the jailhouse waiting to settle up for the night and drink, and relax, and know the world was stable and static and ever-the-same. He now knew that was a memory stuck in the back of his head, a dream to be unfulfilled the longer time wears on.
  A band struck up horns and drums and flutes and fiddles as Kent rode closer to the Cranham he knew, shadowed by buildings taller and wider beyond the jailhouse and tavern and tailors, he watched army men by the four walk down the street, and strange men walking with

purpose and muttering to themselves back and forth from beyond carrying full and empty satchels of clanging metal. He hitched his horse and walked into the jailhouse and saw Hoxley tapping away to the beat of the music, three tired, unshaved men spitting and rattling the bars they were behind against the rhythm of the music taking over the air.

Well golly Sheriff, didn't think I did much round here, weren't figurin' my absence required half an army to pick up my slack.

Hoxley looked up and saw Kent and his eyes widened, he rose and smiled and reached out to shake his deputy's hand.

Deputy, you are a sight for the sorest eyes in the land. Where's Deputy Ransom?

Kent picked his pocket and handed the former deputy's badge to the Sheriff.

He went on out of justice and honor, him and Mr. Wright and a fair few folk from north of here. Last I saw they were headed with some lawmen to a town on the trail. Was a man hanged and shot before one of many unGodly massacres we fell upon. World out there, Sheriff, it's worse than before, it's lost humanity, morality, it's animal, it's vile.

Hoxley patted the deputy on the shoulder and pocketed the badge for himself.

Well, deputy, ain't just out there. We lost the landlord to these swine now under lock and key, Farmer's dogs were put down by a fella too, and now God knows what's all the mayhem over there'n playing the music with it. At least I have one of mine back with me, these

Andrew Jones

army fellas from the fort been walkin' round for a while now putin' the fear in me things are ready to go off.

    What's all goin' on over there?

    The Hardings, in their wisdom and greed. We should show face like we still run this place.

    Hoxley turned to the men prisoners in their cells.

    Don't you be goin' nowhere.

    They walked down the road as Kent began to unfold the horrors of the trail, Hoxley didn't much take in the nature of desecration the deputy bore witness to, the music and the buzz and the sense of uncertainty beyond overwhelmed the senses.

    The band played in the middle of the stone road, a gathering of men, women and children in their finest from all round the region stood and watched and danced and smiled. Lauren Harding stood on a stage before a banner welcoming friends to Harding Street, her flowery summer dress and pale skin blinding in the sun's glow. Three young women stood near her to tend to her every need as she watched the band and the populace come and celebrate the start of their new world. Kelso left the bank in a white suit and brim hat and walked up the stage, he held his wife's hand and they watched together, before the town they were happy and together, a partnership to dream of.

The Ferryman Upon The Plains

Kelso held his free hand high and the two walked to the edge of the stage, the band stopped playing and he smiled and loudly proclaimed welcome to all. The street around them, the buildings, whilst not all finished and ready yet looked full, looked realized, the facades up, walls, roofs, floors, doors. The bank, the hotel, the supplies, the restaurant, there were twice as many buildings than the other road in town, and all fresh and new and unweathered. It was a welcome, exciting new experience awaiting all in the dust and heat and desolate plains. Kelso beckoned the men to come follow to the bank and explore the fully-finished building as Lauren stood before the women and children and excited them with new fashions coming in from across the country, from across the sea, European style dresses and hats and coats, and jewels to be sold shortly soon, a place to be seen and discover what to be seen in the next time they come shopping.

Inside the bank Kelso welcomed the men to the manager, Mr. Oliver Tuskar, who proceeded to show the system of banking, of taking coins and opening accounts to those who may never have heard of the concept, the men were excited about simplifying and securing their years of hard effort in an authoritative building with security as strong and clear as Tuskar and Harding-Grant presented. And then the communication wire began tapping away. The crowd gathered around as the manager wrote down the message being sent over, he held it up and the men struggled to admit their limited education in language. In his clearest tone he read aloud 'Hello Cranham From Fort Oak', the applause and gasps of the men boosted the band to restart their music outside, the world had come to Cranham and the town was rich with possibility.

Tables of fresh food and cold drinks were freely offered around, the oysters and lobster-tail and rib-eye and beans and yams and shallots and mushrooms and truffles met with glasses of champagne and ale and gin and sarsaparilla. A hit for every sense, the delight on the faces of strangers discovering this new opportunity brought Lauren Harding out in her happiest, she was afloat above the masses showering them with gifts and ideas and the riches she'd known all her life.

Kelso let the men feast and then in the distraction led several to the hotel and presented the madam of the bordello operating within, and her wards. A few took advantage of the first go round as he led others to the back, where the heaviest towering men the town had never known offered security for a small poker house. First round free and sarsaparilla on the house. Thomas and Maxwell Mann despite themselves followed the men into the den of inequity and sat at a table drinking free root drink and put money on the table to play with the men dressed in their Sunday best and found themselves unable to keep up with the insults and goading of holding a mid-level hand on a table of debauchers and gamblers. Discussions of fine wine and the oyster buffet were met with gruff show-em or shut-ups and asking if the twins could go fuck themselves or is that jest playin' with yerselves? They folded fast and stepped away to spend time in the decorum of women, children and uniforms on patrol.

Hazel Worthing walked behind the crowds being shepherded and stared at the grandeur of the occasion and the revelation of what was realized by Harding-Grant's ambitions, in the window of the shop rich in new fabrics and designs she saw her self-made dress elegant and practical, she fit into a world but not the window selling promise. A couple of soldiers passed by out of patrol, looking around the new locale as well and Sergeant Carthage stood next to the reflection of the dressmaker and nodded with a smile.

Not a one here as fine as you could do on a day of sickness.

Hazel smiled kindly at the man and his compliment.

You all been roped into all this nonsense?

Orders is orders, though I sometimes wonder who's the one commandin' them. Not as much the bloodshed as they proclaimed round here, not that I'm wishin' fer violence to find us.

Time'll come on all, any situation where men got their hands around guns'll see 'em fired somewhere.

Just hope it's at the right target.

Who's that then?

Not a who, if we can help it. Fear of God can do wonders, shot across the sky hittin' nothing and solving anything.

Andrew Jones

    Sorry state to see even the need to let one pop off. Sure as an echo returns.
    Well best'en keep you out of all that trouble and strife then, don't wanna see the world rid of fine artistry. Stay safe out there ma'am.
    The Sergeant left off and headed towards the hotel and made himself comfortable amongst the poker tables and the crude conversation, Hazel stepped back down the stone street and found herself at home on her own, listening not to hammering at least, just the sounds of strangers passing and loudly making merry beyond.
    Kent and Hoxley met up with the Sheriff's missus and hugged and ate and felt comfort together in the new street, the new land founded from others, and listened to the music overwhelming the world before Kent could tell more of his horrors to the innocents of Cranham who would hopefully never know such disgusting sights before they found their way to Saint Peter true. For all the prestige, the lack of founders was loud, the Wrights, the Doc, the Father, the Farmer and his many men, this was not for old Cranham, this was a new chapter happening before them all.
    The men of the ferry and the laborers and shift workers at the trading post all were absent as well, some asleep in their new builds, others keeping the world afloat with their hard work, they would see about the hotel and its exotic opportunities when the families and travelers had fell away, losing hard-earned wages at the poker

table and before starting a fight finding men casting shadow before them and choosing to concede over confrontation.

    The Sunday that came fast after brought a packed crowd to the church as Father Langston commenced a sermon slurred and red-faced with fear and anger at the death and destruction, the paranoia and uncertainty, the change and loss of focus on God and his teachings and Jesus and his life lost for their sins, he reminded in the echoing acoustics of the hill-high chamber how Job was challenged to the point of testing his faith, how all the horrors in his life, how everything perfect was taken away and he still knew that at the core of it all his love for his maker was all he needed to carry on. He pivoted looking at the faces of the many not wanting to think there was a point to the estrangement and devastation and unsettling of the land they'd known or come to around them. Father Langston let slide the quiet thoughts he'd offered Jenny and Hazel in confidence and wine in the hobble he slept in at church's back and fell old testament eye for an eye and fear of others, how important it was to love, but push that love too far and you can't turn the other cheek when there weren't any left unslapped.

    On the front row Madame Westington put her first show in a long time public, she sat silent and not feeling the spirit of the Lord, she had shrunken a little, aged a little, an old lady without the energy of her wild widow period anymore. Hazel Worthing and Jenny Wright sat next to her, looking up to the Father, seeing their private discussions coming to light in front of the whole town,

Andrew Jones

they held hands, Hazel feeling Jenny's expanding fat and skin as the baby grew clearer for all to see. Lars and Colin and Herman sat nearby, Hazel and Colin made sure not to make contact before or during the sermon, they were keeping everything as best away from others, though the energy Jenny felt in the middle of the two secret lovers was undeniable. The cowboys took the second row of pews and were glad to be back in Cranham and seeing their Father preach, but the tone was starting to sicken them too. Sheriff and Mrs. Hoxley held hands and Mrs. Hoxley put her arm around the Sheriff, holding him in public, keeping him safe. Kelso and Lauren were sitting on the far edge of the second pew, pushed out by the real locals for their late arrival. Kent sat and stared at the back of Charlie Reeves' head, he saw the forest and the clearing and the dismembered bodies brutal and ruined in the eyes of the Lord in the mess of the man's overgrown black hair. A collection of army folk stood still the entire sermon watching, searching the church for spirit. There was little room for Avery, looking over to Madame Westington and feeling guilty and scared and like he didn't belong under the roof of God. For all those that left or passed on it was astonishing how overstuffed the house of God was that Sunday, and how the Father's anger and bile at the invading and destruction and change ripped into the hearts and minds of men all across the building.

The Ferryman Upon The Plains

    The collection plate was loud with coin and heavier with each pew it passed by.
    The congregation passed Langston as he shook and hugged and saw them off for another week, he welcomed Kent back and asked him to come by to talk more sometime, he listened as Avery discussed helping out with the church anytime, with finding a space to build the community better, and let Madame Westington's silence speak louder than he had the entire hour indoors. Kelso and Lauren waited for all to leave and encircled the Father. Kelso offered to invest in the church to let more parishioners in, expand the building, more pews, more space, to bring the church into the needs of the many. Langston thanked them for the offer but insisted God would provide what the community needed, he wanted to see the back of the two as swiftly as possible, the wine was open and growing old the entire sermon and the longer he stood there listening to the devil tempt him the wine was only vinegaring more.

*

    The world around was blind to Samwell's trudging, he ambulated slow as muck through the woods and the dirt path and found once more the signpost that led to hell and lent on the wooden standing for help as he drew breaths in the dawn sun. He looked back up to Granois, the illegitimate signpost point and the illegitimate settlement. He looked west to Rockwood, and the massacre and ruination of an entire people save for himself. Onwards east, it seemed inevitable, towards

Andrew Jones

Chicago, a place he'd heard of from folk making their journeys, a place of people making lives, creating civilization in this country still so young, still so riddled with evil. He began on foot east, the many many miles on to go would wear him thinner, weaker, but was there any option else short of laying down now and waiting for life's end to catch up with him.

      The day was harsh and brutal, the clouds on the horizon refused to block the heat of the sun and the mugginess sweated on his brow, his neck, his arms, his knees. He could smell everything he'd been through on his clothes and his body, and he never walked fast enough to escape the stench. Trickles of water started to fall before him, the heavens made rain for Samwell to drink and refresh and he held his palms before him as he walked and splashed pools on his face and on his beard and his sweaty back was washed clean of the salty brine. Samwell took his hat off as the rain heavied and pooled more water in it, slurping down the moisture and refilling and slurping more. Samwell put the hat on the side of the path and looked around to see no signs of life and began to undress. He laid entirely removed of clothes and poured water on his body, on his legs, on his crotch, and rubbed in the moisture. He looked at the skin hanging off his bones once rich with fat and muscle, thinned and wrinkled and aged and damaged from the journey. Samwell reached to his head, he felt where the crack was on his scalp and it was a harder skin than the rest of his head, it felt rougher, coarser, but his fingers showed no blood from there. He sighed a little relief and reposed in the dirt with the wash from the world.

Out of nowhere a trundle rocked through the world, Samwell grabbed hold of his nethers and hid them from sight as best he could as a stagecoach rolled up and a rider looked down at the old naked man.

Howdy fella, making the most of the weather I see.

Heck, didn't see a soul all day and the moment I come undone here y'are.

Hell of a place to get caught unawares. You been walking all the day out here? Must be mighty tired sir.

I been tired years now, good man, cain't remember much from before I felt so exhausted.

Well'n you sure shouldn't be up out here all alone like this.

Got no choice, things gotta be seen to that gotta be seen to right.

Well I can't in my good conscience let an estranged fellow go alone out here like this, come up and let's get you where we can.

I have coin, enough I reckon to see me to Chicago at least.

Never you mind payment, money don't mean much over deed, get you up here next to me, I'm taking my duties to the city anyhows, fate, luck, the goodness of God, whatever put our paths together, we'll see it right onwards. Come.

Bless you sir.

Andrew Jones

 Samwell began to put his clothes back on and made his way up the stagecoach front, sitting next to the driver. He could see the man clearly from the side, a man of age but not senior to Samwell, face harsh with scars and sun damage, muscles lasting on his body filling with fat in the change of lifestyle, covered in wide brim hat and coat stopping the wetness seep into him. The driver smiled and held his hand to Samwell, keeping reins to both horses in his less dominant.
 Howdy there, names Dickie, hope you don't mind sittin' atop the coach, think a starving old man wading into the wagon proper would put the fear of everything on them rich folk. Not seen the likes of dusty, ridden men of the Earth for a dog's age and then some.
 No bother to me, I ain't fussy or proud, glad for the aid.
 Samwell shook Dickie's hand and told the man his name and the coach began its journey eastward.
 Dickie offered up some water and some jerky and some dry biscuits to Samwell who fed well as the coach roared up the road and rallied against the heavens' weeps, and Samwell was offered time to sleep for his troubles but he declined the comfort, he had slept too much too long, he wanted to be awake.
 You mind conversation whilst you drive?
 I'd welcome it, lonely up top. It's a long way to go in silence, or without others, can turn a

person to madness you know. Seen plenty lost to the travel in my time, folk unable to tell the real from what's in their heads no more, terrible situation, like they see ghosts that only haunt up in their brains, they speak to them like they're there, shoot at 'em sometimes too. That's when it's real bad and you gotta handle them something fierce something fast, a man lost to mania like that's a danger to everyone.

There's times what's up in here is better than what's waitin' out before ya.

Maybe so sir, but hell if anyone should be out here livin' up there. If you're in a place you better be a part of a place, don't be makin' your own worlds out onto others' land, didn't work out well for no-one in the whole history of man, such mania.

And it's to you the hammer falls, the man ridin' on past?

If I don't do something, who else will? If we pass the duty onto another each time, nothing ever gets done. Best to put an end swiftlike and move onwards.

I ain't ever been much for getting involved in folks' lives, keep to oneself, live in the good graces of the Lord and love who you can as much as you can, nothin' more, nothin' less.

Well, when you find yourself passing by strangers all dangerous and ready to cause chaos at the sound of your wagon, to shoot and to harass and to throw themselves under the horses just to live their life in place of yours, you start to consider taking steps first, handling business before business handles you. Ever seen a stagecoach get pulled over and robbed?

Andrew Jones

> Seen plenty in my life ain't good for the soul.
> But you didn't step in and make good to the Lord against those that trespass?
> Make it no business of my own what happens, live and let live, it's others to pass judgment so aggressively. That's the lawmen, that's the folk being robbed, that's what they all gotta handle when it happens, man passin' by is just passin' by to live his life. We all stop and put our noses into other people's, we lookin' to destroy all we built before by way of uprootin' ourselves into another's pathway.
> That's a mighty selfish way of looking at things mister. If someone came and held you up you sure you wouldn't look out to passers by pleading for help?
> I handle my own, I know what I'm gettin' into, and I see it out proper. I don't go pleading, I don't go cryin', I don't go thinkin' why in God's name ain't nobody helpin' me. Shoot me if I ever do, I built myself a damned life and I wouldn't have nobody take it from me, and I wouldn't have nobody come see to it for me. That's my life and mine alone.
> Sounds lonely, buddy. Worse in your life than up here for five weeks with just these horses for talking. Let someone in, at least, life's a shared experience, ain't none of us here for ourselves and ourselves alone, that way lies madness.

The Ferryman Upon The Plains

I shepherded folk across a river some thirty years now gladly, not a one thought of me the moment they rode off the ferry and onto their new lives. To them I was ten minutes on a three month journey that saw everything change. I don't matter to nobody, and that's alright, I never intended to be important or change the world. I just wanted to do what's right.

All on your own out there? No wife, no children?

Of course I got them.

So you ain't alone pal.

I am now.

By your own doing it seems. What in the hell made you leave all that you had?

Samwell began detailing the terrible situation of his loss and his second loss and his continual losses and how he had got from Cranham to a dirt road in the middle of nowhere entirely naked and the man rode on fast and hard as he listened over the screams of the coach and the horses and the wind and rain against them.

Permit me a curse atop my coach? Shit sir, that's something nobody should come up against in their life, you sure are hellbent on hunting those bastards, christ alive. You think they're out Chicago way now?

Mister, I don't got no clue where in the heck any one of them got to. We followed a trail of blood to its bitter end a few times over and now I don't even know if I'm chasin' monsters, demons or ghosts. Maybe nobody's up in the big city, I don't have a clue. I just cain't be goin' back home emptyhanded after all this time can I? What's that say about me as a protector?

Andrew Jones

If you need a weapon to handle what you gotta get done, I have a rifle under my seat. You're welcome to it, I can always go buy another no problem.

Samwell showed Dickie his pearl-gripped revolver.

That's kind and all, but I got all I need. Never had requirement to use proper though, thank the Lord.

Count your lucky stars, I've gone and been the last moments of many lives and it holds onto your soul when you look for peace. The first especially lives forever. The worst part is how easy it becomes in the moment once you deal your first death. Pulling the trigger is easy, the meal afterwards though.

I've killed people, God I pray forgiveness every second, I done 'em in, just ain't squeezed a trigger to do it. A man went on beatin' my friend and hurtin' him and turnin' him into an effigy of the Lord and I saw to his blasphemin' swift, felt his warmth trickle out his throat onto my hands. All those men in that mine did horrible to so many and all I did was cut one throat to save another. And not fer long neither. Poor man Ransom, good man, strong man, lawman. He had no need to go out onward with me, went huntin' these monsters like the law ought to do I guess and continued on way beyond his job, for what, humanity? For what's right? He held by my side, fought by me, for me, and got himself hurt so bad, so hard. And what'd I do? I killed for him then took him to a man what meant to heal him up decided to experiment on him like a corpse freshly dug, whilst I lay there in my own world. He plead and he bled and I was asleep next to him at peace. And when I awoke and broke free all I could do was relieve him from the journey I led him into. Then I went to seek retribution and I couldn't even satisfy that. I stood before the monster depraved enough to mutilate a patient and saw the love he had in his life, the people that cared for him, that he cared for, that he created, and who was I to walk in and remove that from this world? I'm not God. I ain't got no say in that space. That's only for Him to decide.

    Lord might just work through you sometimes.

    If the good Lord decided to use me as his vessel I pray He uses me for kindness and love, not for some abhorrent abuse unto others.

    Love and death sometimes balance the world all at once.

    Samwell felt his eyelids sag and he closed them and the trundle of the coach and the roar of the wheels sent him into a sleep more comfortable than the ethers ever offered.

*

    The whistle blew first and Samwell felt the rumbles of the metal beast rolling closer as he opened his eyes. The middle of the night, in darkness once again, the furnace of the steam engine glowed in the distance, coming closer, louder, heavier. Samwell and Dickie

Andrew Jones

watched the train coming closer, bound for the west, with carriages of candlelight and folk together in compartments bracing for the adventure yonder distant from the stagecoach, a blur out the window of these people on their way out.

    Ever been on one of those?

    Samwell shook his head.

    Mighty things, pull at a hell of a clip, nary a horse I know can match it at its best. Course the trouble is it's stuck to its rails, you only go where people wanna send you, no way to go out on your own, to find your place besides the rest. Those folk in there paying a hefty coin to travel out, probably hearing the stories of gold and land and tales from the fights and conquers and the open plains free to roam and exist and explore. Ever come across a gunslinger, a bandit or a hero?

    Ain't nobody only ever one thing, even in the briefest time spent with others, all contain multitudes, shades of many.

    Damn right. But try telling it to folk only lived out there in the city longing for the dream of America the beautiful. They want the stories, the excitement, the romance, the money. Most on that train won't see the west before setting back to Chicago, the others, God be with them.

    Samwell watched the lights fall away into the distance behind them and closed his eyes in the darkness once again.

The Ferryman Upon The Plains

*

A week passed, they stopped for food and relievement sometimes, the weather abated and returned and nights grew longer, chillier. Dickie kept to himself, Samwell watched the world pass by high above in his perch, the grass longer and the trees orange and the land turning hilly as he grew his cocoon of thoughts.

Y'know who we got back there?

Dickie broke his silence another week onward, the night darker than ever before, the breath falling out of his mouth in cloud as he spoke. Samwell shook his head, he didn't get much a view of the companions in the coach any time they stopped, he did best to remain silent and still and hidden from them, save Dickie a problem explaining.

Man's name of Hatcher, with wife and two children well behaved to the point of no sense of fun or play, bred I guess to be heirs rather than people. They got themselves half of Montana for pennies on the dollar and went off to see about their landgrab and the men they got handling the men who see about the men who force the men to build them the rails and the houses and the world they're creating for their future. Now they're off back home to tell others what it's like out there in the big country, and rest up with people they can talk to, who drink fine and eat well and hold their noses up at folk like us who do the hard sweat to make their lives important.

You don't like 'em much?

Used to be I'd take folk like them for a ride and teach them the reality of the world with a little holding up

Andrew Jones

and bartering for freedom. I have my sins, gotta live with that. Now, though, hell, can't fight it anymore, it overwhelms us, might as well make what you can from it and carry on carrying on, keep the mouth quiet and say the things up here, ya know, the opposite of folk on the road.

  I was in the war, not for nothing but I can't from your voice reckon if you were too and for which side if you did fight with. Not for long, though, felt right in the moment to use our power to free the world, big ideas in the head and the heart but as we all see didn't much amount, folk aren't free even if pieces of paper say so, we're all chained to something, all we were doing was putting the hurt on folk too loud and too violent to handle things with words, when talk fails and fighting starts we've all lost. That's how animals do their business. Two bucks locking horns, so they can mate with a doe and create another generation of bucks locking horns. Inelegant solutions to never ending situations.

  I was riding up for years cleansing the land for all these folk, never found a bother in my head to scare or chase or kill an injun, but soon as it came to one of us it felt all sorts of useless, like looking in the reflection on the lake, same as me back again ready to blast barrel through my skull. When we kill our own for any reason at official level, as ordered by men sitting in rooms eating good food and drinking fine like, it all becomes a failure in our existence. We playing cards in a deck dealt out for the masters to play or fold without care. I did all I could to make the lands safe for folk like the Hatchers to grow and build their fortunes, and here I sit atop their world taking them back from there to their happy lives hidden amid the masses of masters that chose to make everything hold value only to their interests, to their wants and needs. I'd surely kill folk again if I found them doing things directly at me, against me, but I wouldn't ride out with colors anymore and see to things that don't directly face me. Crazy folk out on the road, nothing but trouble. Entire civilization spent centuries on their land, they should keep it, we don't need more, we got all the good Lord provided and we always call out for more still, Greed, or maybe Envy, blinded by Pride. A deadly cocktail.

    I've been in service to someone or someones all my life, I did what was asked and I didn't question why, the good soldier always. If you can find a place to live beyond their domain, their power, to be free as all men were meant to be, to find happiness even if it is fleeting, that's more than any I know ever get. Very few can right the wrongs of the world and live, most get lost on the path and drown in the mud.

    And the rest?

    I get to them before the rain.

    Chicago came slowly on the horizon, buildings of grand size blocked the sun and in the daytime the men rode in black land, Samwell couldn't quite take in the sky disappearing before brick and glass towers stretching many humans high, he felt his neck ache as he gazed upwards evermore trying to see the epic grandeur of this human society built up beyond all needs. The stagecoach

Andrew Jones

pulled up at a row of houses taller than a mountain and the Hatchers stepped out and their manservants came to collect all belongings for them, never lifting a finger themselves. Samwell was transfixed at the way these folk treated other humans, disgusted at the sheer indifference they seemed to have to everyone that offered help.

    Ain't they even gonna pay you?

    Men like that, they don't pay directly to you. One of their servants'll take a bunch of coin down to the bank sometime, if not already done.

    You trust a bank to hold your money?

    Anyone foolhardy enough to mishandle money around here will find retribution very swift from a lot of folk who serve a lot of folk.

    They themselves won't lift a finger though?

    Dickie shook his head.

    If you could pay someone else to do all your work for you, would you bother?

    I like what I do.

    Well then, my friend, you are the richest man in the city.

    They shook hands and Dickie helped Samwell off the coach and rode off down the avenue, Samwell in his dusty, dirty clothes and mangy hair and beard and skinny frame and aged and damaged body stood as people passed by wearing furs and coats and stared and made snickering as they whispered walked past and continued their lives unabated.

The Ferryman Upon The Plains

*

    The sun was hidden once more by the mountains beyond as the warmth protruded and the family filled the wagon with their goods and walked to the shops of the town. Noah sat on Midnight next to the transport, staring down folk passing by with pickaxe and pail and grit and determination who flickered a look to him before returning to their endless emptiness.
    Let's see the goods.
    A clatter of metal on wood attracted Noah's attention to the shops and in the distance beyond a crowd of men coming and going he could see three men holding knives surrounding the Hollanders, the shopping falling aclatter to the ground. Sissy burst into tears and pulled Paul behind her as Kirsty glanced to Noah and stared at the men whilst clutching the remaining items juggling between hands before they too fell. Noah clicked his tongue and Midnight walked fast towards the shop, the horse and wagon in tow behind, and he gripped his pearled holstered revolver and yelled out a Hey calling attention to himself. The men looked over and up at the horseman astride his steed, one turned to face him holding his blade aloft.
    This don't concern you, scram or you'll be sorry.
    Clear outta here and leave them be or you'll be what these folk'll be finding in the mines.
    Kirsty glanced at Noah's hand ready to release death and looked at their guardian worried. The man facing him swung his blade, Midnight stayed still at the danger and Noah swiftly smashed the man's hand with

Andrew Jones

mud-covered boot and knocked the blade to the ground. The other two grabbed for Kirsty and Noah raised his hands from presenting more danger.

 Let us be on with them, ain't no part you need to be with, shitkicker.

 You all is lucky they don't much wanna cause a ruckus, and nobody here'd wanna have to handle the aftermath else you'd not be speakin' now already. Free the women and that poor kid and be on without further mess.

 The man facing him reached for the blade, Noah jumped from his saddle and stood on the knife and stared at him, the other men watched whilst gripping on Kirsty.

 Even without a weapon we got the upper hand.

 How'd you see that?

 Three of us, one of you.

 Noah beckoned the man without a blade close to whisper and as the man leaned in he uttered Two of us and punched the man in the gut, he coughed hard and spat up breakfast on the dirt. The men gripping Kirsty released her and walked towards Noah holding their knives ready. Kirsty Hollander saw opportunity and kicked one of the men in the back of the knee, collapsing him. The other turned in shock and swung his blade. Kirsty dodged the attack, her shirt losing a little fabric in payment for safety, and sternly kicked her foot up between his legs and landing in the soft path made for pain. He too fell onto the ground and coughed and sputtered. Noah ripped the knives out of their weakened grips and collected the three weapons and stood before them, Kirsty took Paul and Sissy onto their wagon and gathered the fallen cans. Noah looked to Kirsty.

You want, I can see to this and meet you on the way.

We already saw to it. Ain't more needin' to be done.

You sure you don't wanna see to the end?

The end is they learned their lesson somethin' hard in front of them who live here. What else occurs later don't need to be in our grasp. They didn't do nothin' deservin' more. This time, at least.

And you don't wanna make sure they never do?

That's not our place to decide. Judgment falls not to us. Not here, not now. We got places to go to, reason to move on. Don't need to fall off our plans to waste away ill men wrong in the head and the heart cos life didn't work out for them. Otherwise we'd never get anywhere.

They rode out, wagon first and Noah on Midnight trailing, keeping hold of the men's blades until long after the shadows of the snow-capped peaks fell away and daylight once more gripped the caravan.

*

The Hoxleys took the Sunday together as Kent sat in the jailhouse and watched over the three convicts. Kent lit up and stared at the jailed three.

Andrew Jones

    They're gonna hang you eventually, you know that don'tya? All the awful things men done in this world and you're in here rottin' for doin' foolish and those that did so much worse get to go on and carry their evils beyond. You was all thinkin' too small, too little. You decided to wipe all this place out you'd be ridin' out and about nobody the wiser, but you in a town of folk took out the one person that kept e'ryone happy. What fool kills a barkeep or a doctor or a priest? Those are folk you don't play with, those are folk weave the tapestry of society. Women, children, lawmen, all can be rid and nobody much cares, that's how life is, tragedy and evil come hand in hand, but the one that feeds the soul, drowns the brain, heals the heart, you don't come for, even if you wanna grab a free drink after hours. Hell, that's the worst to be done, impatience, misunderstanding how each day ever passed and will pass again. You settle down and sleep off and drink more the next, you don't kill for that. You kill cos your bored, cos in your heart you want to cause pain and ache in victims and their loved ones. You want to see what happens when you deliver a knife to skin, the eyes explode in the man you stab, you wanna witness a bullet ripping through a throat. I seen folk splayed out all over a mess, piled up, undone, not human no more, whatever they were was taken as their life was, and the men done did it still out there doin' devil's business. And instead you'll be sent up to the fort sometime soon and sentenced for good.

The Ferryman Upon The Plains

Was it worth it boys? Your last free act in this world?

Kent blew smoke into the air and looked at the men awaiting justice for the acts they wrought upon the land and put coffee on the burner.

The longer nights let Hazel and Colin sneak under cover freer, he left the ranch-house and the noise of the cowboys tired and angry and talking nothing about the crazy changes and the violence of the land, leaving Lars to listen and relay to him anything missed. Hazel lived alone and had no need to play coy, but the excitement of the ruse made her heart skip a beat, the sight of Colin lit by lantern, exposing himself and placing his lips all over her body as the horses found rest for the night, the humans falling prey to animal instincts in the house of beasts made her orgasms come harder and faster than she'd ever known. Maclaine was passionate and intense, but he could create poetry in her ear and within her loins at the same time. It was perfect, a time together nobody but Lars and Jenny really even knew was occurring. They made love several times and Colin walked her home before dawn came, standing before her pathway he snuck a kiss on her lips and held her hand, if sight struggled in the darkness then taste and touch and smell were heightened.

At breakfast, Colin sat satisfied as Lars filled in the ramblings of cowboys pent up in their cages. He couldn't take in their anger and hatred in his worldview, there was too much euphoria flowing through Maclaine's veins and soul shielding him from the destruction of others.

Andrew Jones

    Major Richard Lambeth rode up with a few uniforms, met with Deputy Kent and saw the criminals in their cell.

    You fellas been in there a while, you all admitted to doing your part in conspiracy to rob and murder a man, my men heard it, most in this town's heard it time and again, along with what I'm informed is shocking amounts of cursing. If you were under my command I'd give you something see you never say such again even as your feet burn under you. But instead, you're coming up with us, boys. Take your last around here, the platform's ready and the crowd'll be the ones making noise when you stand and hear sentence and say your last.

    Kent went and saw to the Sheriff and told him it was time to deliver justice, Hoxley said he wished to stay here, he hadn't the stomach to watch death. Kent requested he represent Cranham and Olsen at the Fort. Hoxley gave him the go-ahead and he and the Major and his men and the criminals set about riding on horses and in iron-caged wagon up to Fort Oak.

    The clouds began to cover the sky, a white and grey in the blue and orange, the heavens were growing above as they rode into the Fort, the train long-gone and Harding-Grant's latest collection of employees and supplies already on their way back to Cranham. Kent watched the criminals be dragged out of their mobile prison and tied wrists before them and tied legs, hopping around as they were marched up a platform in the middle of the fort, surrounded by onlookers, traders taking a break for the event and uniforms standing on to watch justice in America served proper.

Kent stood in the crowd and heard the Major read out the crimes of the men as the gallows below were reset from the previous sentencing, bodies wheeled off to a hole dug for a large amount of senseless fools. He could make out several of Ganz's men taking a little time off to come see this to its bitter end, those that like he weren't even around at time of incident and rued how they couldn't protect and keep safe the land.

People around Kent booed and yelled and shouted against the evils of murder and theft and ruination of society as the criminals looked down and out to a swath of humans all hating their existence for one small moment one night, not knowing how as boys they ran around and played with animals and other kids and made their mothers laugh and their fathers would get drunk and beat them senseless and they still found ways to fight through and make their way in life, across the unforgivable plains of America, through gangs and mobs and tribes and communities and found themselves lost and nowhere and looking for purpose or a reason to make the next day not their last. Then they were offered last words, but the braying mob were too loud to hear them apologize and lament and wish to have been born in better worlds and times and in money. They were hooded blind and the floor disappeared under them and their final dance snapped silence in the crowd for a brief time. And then

Andrew Jones

they yelled and cheered at the destruction of three more humans lost to God and America's dream.
    Kent tried to keep himself stoic but his heart sank and his stomach twisted and the heavens opened up to cover the tears that snuck out and down his cheek as he felt unwelcome in the middle of a crowd wanting easy and fast destruction of people who made single mistakes in a world of monsters.

TWELVE

  THE RIVER RAN WILD OVER ROCKS, the foam on the surface hiding the pure clarity of the water under, seeing all the way to the bottom in calmer times. The three lawmen sat atop their horses one chilly dawn as salmon leapt up out of the river, over rocks, fighting the tide. Their splashing turning the air wet and colder still. The men kept their distance up a hill as a bear stood on the bank, pawing and slashing at the fish in the air, mouth opening and biting at the food willingly jumping into its snout. As dangerous as the animal was to the fish heading into the unknown of the air above, the lawmen didn't find concern with it onto them, nor after pausing a little did they see signs of traveling partners on the prelude to hibernation. They carried onwards, upwards, the crashing water always with them.

  The water's cascading down rocks hid the first shot, Jedediah's horse bolted and he settled it down with a kick as Abraham and Zachariah took out revolvers and scouted the hills above. Behind some boulders a large man peeked out and fired, the smoke rose slowly whilst the bullet pinged past the lawmen and hit dirt. The three aimed and fired at the big rock, hitting shards off with their bullets and keeping the big guy at bay.

  They cain't getcha, don't let'um spook, fire damnit.

Andrew Jones

A voice harsh on the ear, pitched high for a beast in the woods, rang out. Jedediah scoured the landscape for the sound's source, but the river obscured all noise.

Give yerselves up, easy now, no point keeping this goin' too long.

Jedediah looked to the east of the boulder as Abraham's voice echoed back to them.

Goddamnit man, shoot.

Zachariah looked westward, sure the voice originated beyond the river. He could only see spray and salmon. Jedediah saw the bearman behind the boulder shake and dart off upwards, he couldn't get a clear shot on the man.

Coward!

The shrill voice screeched out into the air and silenced fast. An arrow flung out through the spray above, dripping, and landed in Abraham's hat, missing his skull by inches. The three men laid fire at the top of the river's rocky fall, splashes flew out over them and a trickle of blood fell into the flow. A second arrow flew out and grazed Abraham's neck, landing at the hoof of Jedediah's horse. Abraham clutched his skin and felt the little stream of blood drop, nothing a problem.

What was all that target practice fer if you cain't land a hit on a man right next to ya?

Zachariah silently dismounted and began climbing the rocks across the river as Jedediah and Abraham kept guns trained on the source of the blood.

If you was to stay still you would see to how good my aim is.

Abraham scoffed at the high-pitched man, Jedediah stayed somber. Zachariah darted up the rocks and gripped his revolver in one hand still. He caught glimpse of a small man huddled behind some rocks in the light flow of the stream, his lenses shattered on his face, his head bleeding. His bow empty. Zachariah found steady grip with his boots and took out some rope, he made a lasso swiftly and quietly walked behind the rock, hiding in the blue of the man's broken vision, and roped him up.

Goddamnit, getoff me. You stupid lunk, help me.

The call fell down the river as Abraham and Jedediah rushed upwards, still checking every rock and tree and hill for figure of the big bearman. They gathered around the small guy, lost of all weapons and sight and freedoms, and carried him away from the river. They found a tree raising high above the world, there way before any of them and theirs landed on the continent, and began roping up the small guy. He yelled out and shouted obscenities to the lawmen and they quietly began to pull the rope over a branch and hang the man. His calls kept on through croaking throat and breaking neck.

The tree shook as the small man danced a few inches above the ground. Abraham held his wound as Zachariah and Jedediah pulled the man up slowly, all watching him suffer. The branch began to splinter and break and the rope cascaded down between the small man and the lawmen. They gripped on tight and the small man ran off, their grips on the rope pulling him back as best they could. A boulder rolled through the rope and smashed into the trunk, the tree began to uproot and collapse behind the lawmen as the rope broke and the small man ran off. Abraham fired a few rounds off at the man but he was too small a target and Abraham a little rough from the wound. The bearman rushed and knocked Abraham to the ground, his hulking figure bruising the body of the lawman. The other two reached for their guns and fired as the bearman turned to them and darted over. Splotches of red flew and the big fella winced as he ran faster, grew larger in the eyes of the law, never ceased pace. He picked up Jedediah in one hand and Zachariah in the other and ran them to the falling tree and smashed them against the wood. They heard cracking inside and the impact knocked the trunk down faster, the tree landed on the ground and sent the earth shaking beneath them all. Abraham fired a shot from the ground at the bearman and hit the back of his neck. The bearman roared and ran off, haphazard in escape, bleeding out as he went. The lawmen lay on the ground crushed and broken. They spent hours before they could even sit up again, as the trail of blood damped in the wet and chilling air.

     They managed to get up on their horses and ride for a while in the direction of the blood, days and nights nonstop, the pain above the saddle better than getting off and resting. The horses took time to drink and eat but they were finding themselves struggling with the weight of the broken lawmen and the air getting thinner and the lack of rest.

*

They never stayed at settlements they passed by on the path winding and heading towards the sunsets every day, the safety of the four by a fire and the wagon and tent canvass was all keeping them from the fate of their kith and kin. Sissy sparked up tears and weeps from time to time but began more and more focusing on Paul's care, helping him with feeding, opening cans of food, starting fires. Behind the red eyes and pain she, like her sister, harbored skills suited to life outside of civilization. She wasn't much at maintaining and holding onto the rifle, that was Kirsty's load to bear it seemed and she had no intent to pass that to her sister or son yet. Surviving was one thing, defense and the hunt would come later.

Noah thought of his pa and holding the revolver always at his hip when he was Paul's size, how he never made much a success of a smaller weapon than the rifle that could see threat from afar and hold it back. How he felt removed and mocked from his own for not being able, more because physical growth than soul, to handle the weapon, he wouldn't wish that upon the child, or any. Paul was a baby in the hands of women capable and caring, gone through horrible traumas and still fighting on for their own and their blood, because they knew within them was reason enough to live and live well. Noah sat another night by the fire watching the family alive and fighting on, wishing he too had such power in him to live well. If he could at least help others carry on, maybe was reason enough. Maybe. He rested easier in that thought, without dabbing tongue on lip and desiring other methods to cope.

      Their ride ran through months, the sun at their backs arose later and ahead of them fell earlier, the air cooled and as the land lost green and found sandy eternal the threat of cloud in the sky dried up until blue was almost like summer despite surely now being closer to the harvest time. During days Paul had begun calling Noah *Noey* and Noah decided Paul was thus *Pawey*, the sweating of the travelers curtailed by squeals of laughter from the little one that made all the ardor resplendent for the experience of hearing each and every time. The sand fell away and somehow it seemed mountains returned with snow and rain, it wasn't known despite following the path and the posts on their way from previous journeying souls whether they somehow turned around and were back heading east, even if the sun above sat in the usual places at dawn and dusk, the bizarre nature of the land held secrets coming forth only to the caravan on their way west. They maintained the sunset ahead still, and embraced the cooler world through large woodlands and warmer embraces of lake and desert further still until the cold almost entirely ceased. Noah brushed sand from Midnight's flowing mane as they rode into the blue-orange wonder of the early evening sky somehow flowering still in the mid-winter times, and looked upon the beach they were riding near. The wagon stopped and Midnight settled a little into the water, braying and moving hooves in the sudden cold of the body of water that lay out. Noah found himself hypnotized by the water reflecting the sun's wondrous dance of color and power with ripples and splashes its own, unique a moment all to be witnessed by the few in this one time. Noah could see far with his seat astride his steed and his jaw dropped adjusting his eyes to the distance, it never ended, the water flowing inward, crashing onto the land rather than passing by, it was the very end of the world, and the light was falling below it all.

  For days more Noah and Midnight rode with the Hollander wagon along the coast, mesmerized by the sunsets and the strange changing landscape this place held, the nights Paul and Sissy nestled together and Kirsty sat with Noah each waking the other when they intended to rest for a time, after all these months they almost felt the gentle touch before it landed and were ready to be on guard.

*

  Lost and waiting for any more opportunities from Harding-Grant, sitting in shacks that were costing more the longer they sat around listening to the percussive rooftop dance of precipitation, a few of the men semi-permanently settling in Cranham gathered away from the high-cost Harding Street where dollars were handed out at the bank and given away at the hotel swifter than a

Andrew Jones

snake leaping for a fieldmouse. They huddled in the gaps of dirt and outside wall between the army barracks tavern and jailhouse and the shops of Harding Street and found small pockets blind from everyone else to tent up with excess wood a few stalls of suspiciously gathered goods and evocative mixings of powder and leaf and liquid from the clinic and apothecary that made folk feel briefly good and permanently in need to attend that higher plane ever always with lessening results.

  Passing by folk wouldn't much notice the comings and goings of red-eyed, mouth-frothing, stumbling men scratching at their arms and necks and rubbing their noses and mouths as they scuffed back and forth from alleyway to street to shop and browsing and looking around and walking with padded jacket back to the alleyway. In plain sight the back alleys thrived, legitimate business found itself there quickly with Choi Lo taking thrown out cut-offs from the hotel restaurant and boiling and cooking with flavors that scented the air. Shoppers, users and the curious all welcomed giving only a few coins to taste chewy fat and muscle on bone peppered and herbed and spiced unlike anything they'd laid bite upon.

  The days wore on, the rain came and went and the land dried fast still under the sun's lessening gaze. At the bankside the ground was penetrated with wooden poles and the first stages of bridge construction took shape. The tide rose and fell, haphazard more than the summer season with the weather adding and evaporating across each day, the men checked notes and scuffs of their boots on the dirt to prepare height for the structure, they'd settle for a few feet above land, and then the river would subside and it seemed like a little lower could save time and material, and as they made their minds the water would splash back at them and cause another consideration. All while the ferry platform stayed as it always was, no matter the river's height, above enough to float on and work.

    The ropes were secured on either side and lumber was laid opposite, at night a man would be stationed for watch, the river was overpopulating, and the construction began with several of the shack-subsisting laborers lost in the back alleys finding time to return to opportunities disorienting and a little unwelcome. Paler, wan, itchy, sickly, the muscles lost from weeks of reliance on methods to pass time outside society's acceptability. The hammering and building of supports and boards was fine enough on the land, but once the flowing water came to play the men struggled functioning, waves crashing on them slipping wood from hand and hand from rope and bodies fell in the water, the ferrymen on shift becoming lifeguards for no extra compensation. These same men turned dry dirt into the hustle and bustle of Harding Street in a matter of weeks, here they were dripping wet and bruising hands and splintered skin and jonesing for their time off to hit up the tents betwixt worlds.

Andrew Jones

    Colin and Hazel headed out and turned right at the top of the street. Their secrecy was short lived, their passion demanded more time together than ever before, and Maclaine took what he needed from the ranch-house and leaving Lars in the hands of the cowboys. All the bluster and vitriol shook Colin, he struggled to sleep some nights under the noise of men wanting to settle the land any way needed. Colin brought the gun surplus he had in the stables hidden as balance for stepping away, Eagle-Eye declared it an upgrade if anything, and out of earshot of the others wished the man well on his adventure. Love, he said, had always seemed impossible, something made for others, but he wished no ill will to any that found it, sought it and nurtured it.

    Worthing and Maclaine may no longer have required a ruse that failed to fool the any suspecting eyes examining, but it didn't mean they relented in desire when dropping secrecy for open adoration, their lovemaking rivalled the entirety of the rooms of the bordello nearby, and with greater vivaciousness. Hard working daytimes built up their wants, their needs, Hazel at home turning fabrics to fashion to sell at the fort, she declined opportunities to open shop in Harding Street and was completely removed from the space at Mann's Tailors, whilst Colin sweated and caressed and looked after his livestock, smithing for the army garrison and the cowboys and the local laborers, he was offered to help build the bridge from Kelso

Harding-Grant, but Maclaine upped his costs to make the devil's bargain something worth selling his soul and Kelso decided that perhaps cheap labor slogging for weeks or months was worth not dealing with someone who resented him. Harding-Grant wouldn't notice, it seemed, that not a single soul in town didn't resent him. Including his wife.

*

    The denim hung unworn in the window displays and the coats for rougher work and temperature were moved to be shown to passers by over the fine and elegant suits and dresses and hats and lightwear that adorned in the high sun days and the times when three of them operated business in the shop, but Thomas and Maxwell Mann still found themselves lacking in foot traffic, the outside patrols never breaking glance ahead to peer even with the set-ups changing before their very strides.
    In a dawn they ventured to the trading post opposite as Kelso took reins from his night watchman big and tall and procured small firearm for their own sake and in their quiet shop began turning leather to holster that matched best their dapper attire of any event. The holsters and belts that attached it seemed always intent to pull down a little pant, a little hip, the weight of the change in their standing a constant reminder that they as well measured as they were did not fit here anymore.
    Harding Street was a sore spot, the haberdashery brought in the clientele more likely for the Manns to

connect with, but housed all the basics required and at such convenience from the hotel and the restaurant and to get a spot of shiny gem to boot, not ever needing to step foot off stone and onto dirt to go see about fine stitching. The sound of the men's leather shoes on the hard rock floor filled them both with unease and doom, and standing around in the bank waiting in a line of men shuffling and scratching and coughing and dirty and stinky and swaying brought thoughts of superiority and disgust into both men. They were surrounded and drowning and had only one-another left to cling on to.

      They did try a few more times to ingratiate themselves with the men in their best, in the poker house, where a coat was mandatory, but a fraying vest that did its job meant no man needed think to the tailors' for a chance at the table. They sat in the low light amid red and green curtains and towering men with jackets and vests and bowties and smiles turning sneer at the first sign of cheat calls. They tried to split tables and court custom individually but talk around them was all of who to screw after and what's best to score down the alley for longest high and actually the fancy foods taste worse than something Choi Lo could cook up when paired with a few fingers of bourbon and in the end what's the point of eating anything if you could spend that money on an extra finger or a snifter or a little more to toke. The elegance and high class that Harding-Grant envisioned his little casino hub harboring faltered by presence of the wrong type of customer, but money talked and these men squandered their coin on the tables so the tables welcomed them. The Manns ended up sitting together to try and at least balance conversation to fit the world they understood, a little chat about local life between the harrowing adventures of fallen men desperate who had known raw meat rotting on the dry heat of a long summer for survival.

 I recall having to close my eyes and chew hard upon terse meat, t'was when mother-dear was upset with the sicknesses and the moods, father told us to handle our own, recall that?

 Rabbit, skinning was awful, we tried to avoid the blood by burning it off, had to scrape along the flesh as it melted and set aflame and took with it heaps of good food.

 Lots of salt to cover the taste. Wouldn't wish that dish on the worst of the world.

 Nobody much noticed their trivials, the Manns found themselves losing attention and seven dollars at the table raising on one-another only to find someone with three of a kind besting their jack-high and pair of sixes. They left the pokerhouse and were swiftly replaced by Reeves and Amello and Eagle-Eye and Skellig and the Petersons, cleaned up and wearing their Sunday best and splitting themselves over tables handing down coin anteing their pot and staring at the men of hard labor and ill posture who may or may not be partially responsible for all the woes befalling Cranham.

Andrew Jones

    The cowboys took spots across the room, the Petersons inseparable sitting in order of height over age keeping Willem closest to the middle of the action in case things started up. Eagle-Eye perched in a corner, near shade in the lowlight of the den, smoke shrouded from any staring around good cover, his sight still strong and his presence evoking tension from those aware of the man's long history, ignorance in a room like this was welcome until arms are picked up. Skellig found himself a crap hand of odds and pictures amounting to no pattern or doubling, he played quiet and folded early and watched the men around scrabbling for the next big win to score all they needed from others in the same situation, suddenly the chance of pot increased and without smiling or throwing much sweetness at all they appreciated the Swede being on their table to throw out money.
    Reeves and Amello sat opposite ends of a table of men some stringing out and some wired from work fancying their evening with respectable entertainment, six in a circle with the dealer-cum-security shuffling and watching the pot fill with blinds.
    We don't see you boys by the whorehouse, you find good together on the farm doya? Happy together? Or is it you take your herd across the land and elope e'ry summer? Pump for you then a little squeeze, udder delight?

The Ferryman Upon The Plains

The rotting teeth and scratched up face of Freddie Graham bared down on the cowboys with his crude conversation, the flicker of light yellowing the brown of the exposed enamels worn down in his months stuck in this world.

Why buy the cow when you can get the milk for free, I 'spose.

The men around the table cackled and slapped knees and wood, Amello and Reeves let them have their fun, they offered kind grins and scoffed out the disgust within them and checked their hands now dealt before them all. Amello threw in a coin, Reeves called, the others around finished the go with equal pay still laughing and cards were started to be thrown out.

I ain't hearin' no no's from youse boys. Maybe next time you all smarten up and go see yer God up in thar hill there I'll see what the fuss is about. Any tips for 'em? You tie em to the fence fore you mount or chase em down and ride em sweaty? Hell, we're all friends here, ain't no shame, finish up and let's go you put on a show fer us, lemme see which one's your favorite. I wanna know the sweetest meat you got.

Another pass and light raising to turn eighty three cents in the pot and two men folding and Amello swapping out a single card whilst Reeves stayed exactly where he was. Graham tapped his hand on the table and looked at the black cowboy who hadn't risen to his instigation and threw two cards out, the dealer swiftly dealt him his last change and the loudmouth looked at his final collection of cards.

Andrew Jones

Hell, I'll fold this now if it'll speed things, take the pot as payment and lemme get a handle on those horns. I'll brand it somethin' fierce. Succulent sirloin.
Amello laid his two sevens and ace nine four down, facing a pair of fives in an otherwise unspectacular hand of one who didn't fold when he had the chance and Reeves began to place down his cards.
You got a lot of mouth boy, none of it well looked after. Not even a dollar ain't gonna get you the runt of the herd, and even then you wouldn't know what to do with your limp prick.
He placed two eights and three tens down before Freddie, the man's smile sneered in grit and grime and his eyebrows furrowed.
Goddamn you, comin' down here and actin' like you some sort of king among men, you sorry, jumped-up...
The word fell out of his mouth full of disgust and insidiousness, the cards in his hand came to the table presenting pittance in two, three, five, six and jack high of all suits, all the bluster and nothing to show. Reeves swallowed the epithet tossed directly at him and reached for the money well won, Eagle-Eye across the way with smokey haze watched Freddie and bowed out of his game quietly, the Petersons slowly turned heads to the table next to them, Willem's fist clenching.
Maybe that I am to you but I'm at least a dollar up tonight too, you can call me that again if

you got the coin, hell let's go to the bank and make a weekly stipend then you can go about all manner of day and night callin' me one.

Oh you funny now is you? Time was I could pull my piece out and do you away and they'd not care, not no-one, you was just another animal to be farmed. Animals cain't own money.

Charlie Reeves flipped a won coin in the air and snatched it, winking at Freddie. Graham spat on the table and pulled his gun from his holster. A smash around his cheek took out two teeth and flew the bastard out of his chair and onto the ground. Willem stood over the little man, it took all five employees to hold him back. By the time they'd surrounded the biggest Peterson two tables were turned over by Graham's neighbors and they reached out and smashed and grabbed at Reeves, Amello caught in the crossfire found himself a blow or two landing on him too. Eagle-Eye stood up and picked up his chair and smashed a man in the back, breaking the wood into splinters, and took two rods that once formed the backrest and whacked away a few of the foul players. The Peterson brothers Johnny and Marcus decked out their fists and punched and slammed a few men into the tables, a snap of bone on the overturned side of one rim on arm or wrist, in the melee it was hard to be clear and in the smoke it became a cloud of splinter, dust and blood.

Get out of here, all of you.

The voice of authority from a man in vest and bowtie struggling with his peers to hold back a single cowboy didn't persuade the bloody battle raging across the den, men pushing and smashing items onto skin and clothes and kicking when appropriate men landing on ground. Freddie attempted to reach for his gun again, Eagle-Eye pushed another man into him and the two of them distracted one-another with flying fists. Willem pushed away the dealers and threw a fist out to one of the junkies clawing at Charlie and hit him in the skull, the man's eyeball bulged in the socket and rattled before he collapsed to the ground and struggled to breathe. He pushed the ball back in with a yelp but the cloudy vision and impaired atmosphere kept him swinging at two people and missing both.

  The Peterson brothers pushed on the men, Charlie and Joe dodged the last hits and wiped blood and spit from them as their foes were smashed through the door into the hotel foyer, the shrieks of delight from patrons above undercut the anger and yelling of the bloody brawl. Eagle-Eye cooly waded behind the battle and patted Reeves and Amello seeing them ok for the moment. The dust-up went fast through the dwelling and found its way to the harsh stone street soon enough, the Peterson's overpowering trifecta met the harsh constant of the ground and erupted bloody noses all round. Freddie in the mix of seven men finding new footing before the next round finally gripped his handle and pulled out and fired a shot in the air, the light of the bang lessened by the lanterns all over the street but the crash of thunder echoed in the night air for long after, and all movement ceased between every participant.

The Ferryman Upon The Plains

Y'all can love all the cows you want and you can go about yer business up in that farm together but you come down to our town and make yourselves like us real men and you can go spit, we built this place, this is our town, and you ain't welcome.

Charlie and Joe held their hands close enough to grab firearm if called on, Eagle-Eye shook his head and stared at the broken loser in the middle of the street. Behind him, coming running unheard by the perforated eardrum of those near the smoking gun were the Sheriff and his deputy and the First Lieutenant and his privates. Eagle-Eye raised his hands open and above his head no intent of violence in his hands, his cowboys followed suit and stepped back from the gathered mass of angry, bloody poker failures.

Drop your guns boys, fast.

Hoxley's command failed to resonate, Freddie held his gun aloft still, he felt the rumbles of men behind him and turned and saw the swirl of law invading.

Get it down boy, on the ground.

Graham let the gun slip out of his grip and swivel on his finger, aiming at nobody or anywhere, and two uniforms gripped him and dragged the man away. The other men raised hands and showed no weapons and the law pushed them one-by-one out down the street away from the commotion. Eagle-Eye nodded and the Petersons and Reeves and Amello followed through the parade hands held still. The old cowboy wiped the small splotch of blood he found coming out of his forehead as he stared at the Sheriff, Hoxley waited for the men and officers to leave the scene and walked right up to the legend.

Andrew Jones

    You tellin' me you didn' have nothin' to do with this?
    I'm not sayin' I didn't have nothin' to do with this. I just don't have my gun smokin'.
    If he aimed it at one of you?
    He'd be layin' still on the stone, prob'ly long with the rest of 'em.
    I got a whole lot of trouble brewin' round here, do I need to handle you all too?
    Sheriff, you mightn't see it from your place but we're on the same side.
    Side nothin', you cause chaos in my town you're my problem, not solution.
    You want a solution, you get rid of the pest.
    That what you intend to do? Kill every ant in the hill?
    Ants don't kill folk for fun.
    So you're wantin' revenge on Olsen? Well, his killers got theirs last month in the law of the land.
    Those that held the blade gone, sure, what about the man killed our dogs?
    Your boss done him to the Lord swift.
    You're lookin' at things after they happened, lookin' at the gun that smokes, not the hand that makes it in the first place. Maybe you'll pick up arms after they take your wife, but what good'll that serve her, or you, or any us? Sheriff, all your military and all you're gonna do is make e'ryone hide round and brush shoulders 'till they

start a fire that ain't gonna be put out before it burns us all.

You men got important times ahead, whole county relyin' on a good harvest, keep us all alive, don't let anger blind you from what matters most.

Sheriff, when time comes, you gonna let the uniforms take our town from us?

If time comes, and God help us all if it does, I'll see true justice found. I ain't stupid and I ain't a push over, but the more mess you cause out here, the more gonna come all over to take away what we spent our lives makin'. See your boys good and right, they'll follow you anywhere, that kind of respect you can't buy.

Hoxley walked the old cowboy down Harding Street and past the old street and saw him to the farm's gates and watched him set up to the ranch house. Lars Skellig dusted himself off and left the hotel absent from all other souls, he looked around and the blood and teeth on the stone street and dragged himself back to the farm alone. His winnings jangled in his pockets.

*

The route down and round from the outskirts towards the streets bustled with wagon and coach and horse and foot, but the noises were broken by symphony reaching through the walls of the widow's house, the gentle fingering becoming chord and melody and branching from hymnal familiars to compositions written for the kings and queens. People passing took moments out of their journey to stop and cease all around them and take in the heavens on Earth that pleasured their ears and tingled their brains. It was easy to invoke smiles in passers finding beauty and magic in the empty expanse of the country, and Madame Westington's wondrous hidden talents brought forth waves of joy and heartbreak with caressing of key and dextrous reach. She played piano all the day and into the night, and the next and the after, each and every with people taking time in their day, amassing small crowds staring to the still building beyond and thinking of the old woman bringing forth such wonder into the world, and they each were connected in that moment with one-another and her and the entire universe from creation to completion in the vibrating strings of the wooden ivory instrument.

     Sheriff's Deputy Hartwell Kent came to stop outside and listen everyday at sun's highest, the chill and the rain and the crisp and the unseasonably warm all he came and stood and listened. In the music he lost the sights of bloody bodies in trees and hanging monsters and braying mobs seeking violence, he found the sky clear in the grayest days and the air warm on the coldest breezes. He in the moments with strangers and locals all felt alone but not lonely, within a world of pure and hope and light and beauty. It was not coincidence that his eyes would fall often too upon Marie Delphine who also took brief respite between errands working hard to satisfy Lauren Harding's every want and whim, the most personal of her staffing, as close a confidante as the help would ever be deemed under the over-built roof, a young, quiet girl squirreling away funds to send off to her large family back east for another winter's survival. Eyes down, chin up, ears open, mouth shut, she was perfectly suited to care for someone who had no ability to live without five extra pairs of hands at every step, but Marie could for small moments passing the widow's abode live free for herself, to think and feel and exist away from family and service and expectancy. And she too found herself looking across the crowds to the ever-present figure of the deputy. They each smiled back.

The church was still outside Sunday service, Hazel and Jenny's frequent advances uphill to see the Father slowed when Jenny's body took her to bedrest and brief waddles around the grounds, and Hazel's time was better focused on the sewing and knitting and drinking and lovemaking. The aging leader of the spirit was a relic in his stone temple alone with drink and candle and books of suffering and tests of faith. His footsteps around the chapel echoed into one-another, he became legion alone waiting for purpose or sense to return to the land. He walked the grounds at times, looking down at the busy streets below lost to their own selfish desires, he stared at the marks embedded in ground reminding all of those who once were and now laid at rest below. He looked to the heavens when it rained and to God when it shone, he cricked his neck upright and locked eyes with the universe and waited for guidance, for something to point him purpose or reason or a way to carry on, and he drunk

Andrew Jones

himself into many a stupor as not a sign nor a hint came forth. Come Sundays they'd pack his house and listen to him irate and hurt and lost and unfathomable at humanity, detached, removed, broken, and they'd feel fear and uncertainty and leave for the week to rebuild purpose and reason below, in their worlds, whilst he walked above between the human and the spiritual, among the dead.

Sweetest Mother Wright, it has been long now and I sit and I lay and I in my best days stand and walk and feel the child moving with me and I wish most of all to share these moments with thee. I once and sometimes heard but now even sound has fallen and I have on occasion found myself in yours and listening to the silence hoping for more, for sign, and I am scared. I am scared of losing all now. What without you is there here, the horses perhaps but they as lovely as they are are not for talking or holding hand or remembering the gone and capable of embracing the hope of return. Father and Noah will make their way hence and with great reason to celebrate, ridding with might the evil vanquished upon the world, a sickness not unlike what took so much before, and will be welcomed too a prize of grandchild, of being uncle. It is hard though alone, we both are, yet so close alone. I am scared to tarry further in and find mayhap there is only one of us here now, I cannot for now impose thought of fear or definite end upon myself and baby, for without I would bring into the world only heartbreak and destruction. We a family should together stay and hold and keep firm for the world, for the men, for the future of us, and for if so selfish ourselves in this fast approaching winter. Please Mother Wright come to the world again, to me, to the Father who misses you on the service, to the Doctor who comes by to see me and talks softly of the days before, the years before, and wishes to see you as you ever were. I will be here in the house beautifully built beside yours with the grandchild coming sometime, and we three for the now as we wait on Father and Noah's return can forge the darkest season united and stronger for it.

    Jenny waited for the ink to dry and folded the papers up and walked next door and knocked, she waited and entered as she had done many times before to the darkness of the empty house, and stared at the closed bedroom door and creaked the boards below her swollen ankles, each step she felt the swishing of stomach and child inside. She reached out for beam and table and stability within the house and came to the closed door. She placed her hand on the wood and tried to rat-a-tat but stroked instead, the harshness of even soft finger on the surface seemed loud in the silence. Jenny dropped the pages to the floor and with her heavy foot stood on it and slid it under the barrier between worlds, until she could no longer see the white of the paper, even if seeing anything in the dimming light was near impossible anyway, a feeling of it fully crossing the boundaries flowed through. She waited by the door for a moment, listened for any movement, reaction, anything, then turned and began her arduous journey back across the houses.

  Hazel came by and sat with Jenny on the bed as Jenny's weight crushed her another day, the infectious aura of joy and love emanating from Hazel kept spirits up in the hardest of days and Jenny was delighted to hear of the adventures with Colin Maclaine like bedtime stories for hormonally overwhelmed adults. They managed to get Jenny back on her feet for a little air and stretching and went to see the horses in the Wright stable, Hazel with more knowledge than ever before about caring for the animals and seeing them bred well, she picked up a lot in her brief time close to the horseman and Jenny watched her friend take the reins of the animal care with wonder and goodness.

  He'll have you partnering in his work before long, the two of you breeding horses across the land, for men of all sorts, perhaps one day for the president.

  I hasten to imagine spending more time in barns than I do already, wouldn't get anything done but one another elsewise. Amongst them we certainly become animal.

  Ah, and civility and Godliness is what you both under the same roof get up to? Even with the family so close, when Bartholomew and I were ever in ours alone we weren't but two entwined and deeply forever. You two ain't more than animals rutting for the good of the feeling.

Oh, heck, is it so wrong?

In no way. It is as natural as the dawn comes.

And far more frequent.

The women giggled and blushed but within their outgoing the warmth of the connection and their honest adultness strengthened their connection. They talked with the privacy of the land of the good sex and the better love, being held and being wanted and feeling and wanting and how good it was to for such time feel stable, feel connected, tethered, to another human. Pockets of silence crept in as Hazel tiptoed around glorifying her moments as Bartholomew's ghost haunted their thoughts, but Jenny's child kicked and they felt together the offspring getting impatient to enter the world, not all gone, the father there in some way still, nobody was truly alone.

In the window of the Wright matriarch as they wandered the mud and watched the horses run for the time the women glimpsed a face briefly. Anna stood looking out, still, frozen, her eyes red and raw, her skin paling and ashen, she stared in a single spot beyond the women and beyond the horses, the sun breaking through cloud shimmering among shadows on the ground light that came and went, ebbing and flowing darkness and orange glow on the wet mucky soil and the horses as they danced and ran and the women who talked and glowed with love and onto the window pane that held beyond the widow, the woman lost of child and husband and all the world she once was with. Jenny and Hazel waved and smiled with soft kindness but it changed nothing on Anna's stare, their faces dropped and they took the horses

Andrew Jones

back before cold swept over the land and headed back to Jenny's for a warming drink and a rest. There the two considered names for the growing baby, Samwell and Bartholomew and Anna and Jenny were first up and all thrown away, levelling a child with the weight of things past was only inciting cycles that shouldn't be repeated.

    You could go presidential, inspire the child to beyond this, Abraham, Millard, Franklin.

    Hannibal Wright, he could ride elephants across the country, from the coast to the Potomac. What of the Bible? Lot's Wife Wright, she's a salty lass.

    Looking for girls in the good book is one step towards mania, they aren't much for the taking.

    Rachel Wright, Eve Wright, it just doesn't settle me.

    When you gaze into the eyes of him, your babe, you will utter purest the name right for him.

    Right Wright?

    The ladies giggled and held close and spent the evening further contemplating before Hazel made her way to meet her lover at the tavern for another wonderful night of connection through conversation and intimacy. Jenny laid in her bed alone, in the dark she saw the face of Anna Wright staring out, staring beyond her and the room and the world she lived in.

*

The Ferryman Upon The Plains

Avery Bedford listened to the piano of Madame Westington alongside the crowd as it played on, the mass of folk disappating at the early signs of evening this mid-afternoon, and smiled at the knowledge of safety and the power of the widow's skill and soul rising beyond the wood walls she encased herself in. He walked on before his shift began and came to the jailhouse and sat with the deputy on watch and looked at his old friend Freddie now prisoner of the town's making.

How on earth'd ya let this happen?

Them boys up there on the farm, I just wanna make enough to get mine damnit, they come by with their smug faces and their good lives and their togetherness and all we got is ourselves and a debt to the man Kelso what seems intent to go about buildin' an empire on the backs of slaves like it's the old times.

I can put good word get him to come and sort things out, might as free ya if the Sheriff and the Deputy here see kindness and you agree not to cause no more trouble. Come spend your eves over the way with the bunch of us, cards and drinks and no fightin'.

I gots to run ferry and stop fools fallin' in the river in the nights, ain't no-one take the dark shifts round here, all lay on me and my foolish head keepin' myself important enough to carry on until finally they put rest the need for the entire ferry.

Well'n you think about it, clean yourself up a little and make good with Him and with him and maybe things'll fix up to score a life true to bein' worthy outside of these bars and those'uns.

Andrew Jones

Avery nodded at his old friend through the cell and shook hands with Kent and went on to take on duties at the trading post, he pointed to Kelso the situation and the rich man said he'd handle swiftly and by evening proper he brought sarsaparilla and steaks fresh from the hotel to the jailhouse and sat with the Sheriff and the Deputy and the prisoner and reminded the lawman in charge what he held within his walls and organized and saw to when he was at his lowest and most desperate. Kent didn't much know the euphamisms explored by the wealthy Kelso but he was enjoying the food and the drink and thinking more on what Marie would be up to in the moment to much care about the machinations of his boss and the fella across the office. Freddie reluctantly stepped free and shook off Kelso's handshake kind and devilish simultaneous and wandered to the ferry for a shift tired and miserable.

    The rains returned and Harding Street was dampened with footsplash and horses making speed to get through as fast as possible, those determined to shop and gamble and settle still made use of awnings for cover, or had their service staff hold aloft parasols drumming droplets above them as they leapt across the stones below. From the back alley three men came jawing at their latest hit and pounded their feet hard purposefully pushing past the elite and their special shops of frilly fashion and beguiling jewels and headed right for the bank. They each wrapped cloth around their mouths and noses as their senses and adrenaline rose from kick of cocaine and pulled out guns from their holsters and walked right in the door. Blue Cloth Mask kept on to the barred window as men and women waiting in line watched their place taken by mania, Yellow Cloth went right and into the corner and looked over the whole room as Red Cloth stepped next to the guard on duty and pushed barrel into the man's back, he took out a blade with his free hand and stuck it into the guard's belly and dragged it along, spilling red and pink onto the wooden boards. Shrieks and gasps were raised from the customers and Blue Cloth Mask stared at the teller, waved his gun and with eye and brow pointed to the safe held firmly in the middle of the building, behind the bank clerk.

 This won't end well for you.

 Blue Cloth pointed his gun at the teller.

 It'll end sooner fer ya you don't get goin' now.

 The guard gurgled and spat blood and fell to his knees as he tried best to keep guts from falling still. Yellow Cloth waved his gun at the queueing customers and pointed at them all one-by-one, then at the ground. They fell to their knees and faced the ground. The clerk stared at the gutted guard and moved his hands slowly up to show empty to Blue Cloth.

 Ok, ok, get that man a doctor.

 Open that up first, maybe we'll all come out good.

 The clerk backed away, staring at Blue Cloth and Red Cloth and the guard and turned as he got to the small safe, twisting at the knob until it opened.

 How much?

Andrew Jones

    Are you a fool? All of it.
    The clerk began taking out papers and coins and bars of gold, all he could carry, and walked it back to the window, passing it under for Blue Cloth to grab. The robber held his gun at the clerk's head and shook his own.
    A bag, a sack, somethin', you idiot.
    The clerk nervously nodded and scurried around under the window, rustling of fabric and wood and boot came out as Blue Cloth bobbed on his feet, the drugs distracting his system.
    Y'know you won't much get away with this, bank notes is for the banks.
    Don't matter none, put it all in and see to shuttin' yer yap.
    Red Cloth looked to Yellow and chuckled at the gold sitting before them, Yellow Cloth nodded to Red at the guard's near-death pose, hunched over a stomach that was already escaping. The wood blew apart and Blue Cloth's knees ripped open in a mighty roar of buckshot, through the gap made the clerk loaded again and aimed his shotgun at Yellow Cloth. Red jumped at the noise and squeezed his trigger in the shock, the guard's brains met his guts on the board. Yellow Cloth shot at the window before seeing the man hiding under the wood, firing a second shot at Blue Cloth. The vocal robber's knees and legs fell off his body and the second blast took a hole in the middle of his torso, his red splattered all around the floor and to the door behind. Red and Yellow turned to aim

down in the hole and fired many fast. The shotgun impacted with the floor and blood ran out from beyond the window's floor. The two approached carefully from both sides, the customers screamed and stayed still to avoid worse as Yellow and Red peered over the window through bars and saw the lifeless body of the clerk riddled with red holes. The two men grabbed as much paper and gold that was sitting on the counter and looked at the scared folk, Yellow aimed his gun but Red tapped him and shook head, pointing at Blue Cloth's body. They started running out of the bank through the door made red by Blue.

Red slipped on the stones on his escape, Yellow left him as the army came fast through the back alleys, pushing through the men drugged and queues of folk wanting food for the day. Yellow ran into the empty world beyond, his figure in the distance growing smaller. Guns were raised at the Red Mask picking himself and some gold off the ground. He aimed his gun at the uniforms and began firing at them, they ducked and dipped and fired back. Red was winged and hobbled onwards as blood joined rain on the stones. Shoppers gasped and ran into buildings, finding sanctuary in commerce. Red became holey fast and dropped gold and paper as he lurched towards the hotel and poker house he frequented most of all. Yellow had taken his mask off and took in the wet and cold air of the empty land stretching eternal, no space to hide, he had to carry on forever. Within minutes the sound of rain crashing on the ground before him was overtaken by noise of horse hooves giving chase behind. Sergeant Carthage on horseback throw rope around the man and dragged him to the ground, tying him and dragging him back towards the town.

    Carthage dragged him out to Harding Street as Kelso and his men walked up to see the mess laying out before them. The businessman stepped right up to Yellow Mask and locked eyes with the robber.

    I know you. You work for me. You owe me money.

    Kelso looked at the bank riddled with hurt.

    How will you pay for this?

    Yellow spat at Kelso and looked away. Kelso looked at the army surrounding and nodded, Mills ordered his men to step down and move away, many did. Carthage atop his horse stayed.

    Step away, Sergeant.

    Carthage kicked heel to his horse and pulled reins, the steed stepped back a few, clopping shoe on stone in the wet. A moment of rain splashed all and rinsed the blood from stone. Kelso leaned down and picked Yellow Mask's chin up, they locked eyes as one of Kelso's men took out a knife and gutted the robber. Hoxley and Kent rushed to the scene and from a distance saw groups of men surround the criminal, they found no purchase on the street. The criminal suffered and gasped and groaned and yelled in agony as he bled out slowly, the stones covered in red and diluted swiftly. It took a long, painful time. Hoxley and Kent walked up to Kelso as the customers of shops fled and bank's survivors absconded in fear.

What d'ya think yer doin' Grant?

Sheriff, this doesn't concern you. They took from me.

Law don't come and go because it's direct to you.

Farmer shot a guy and he's free, we all get to dictate our justice.

I uphold justice, Grant, round here.

Don't put on a big show in front of the town, in front of all these fine people. You aren't fooling anyone but yourself. And maybe that boy by your side with his daydreams and distractions.

You're gonna get us all killed.

Only if you're in my way, Sheriff. Stay on your street, stay home, better use of your time anyhow.

Kelso walked away, his men followed. The army walked them up the street, Sergeant Carthage hopped off his horse and walked up to the Sheriff.

The whole fort loves him, he has the ear of the Major.

Christ, we ain't got much hope to hold onto round here.

There's still something of a community hidden between it all here. Harvest's comin' for us all.

*

He walked the avenues, the trees bare but branches stretched out across the sky, the houses huddled up shoulder to shoulder reaching up high, the noise of the horses cantering upon the road three, four

Andrew Jones

passing at a time, a constant activity to watch as the sun began to hide behind the buildings and cover the world entirely in darkness. Samwell wandered down, feeling his holster, his satchel, the noise of his spurs and his coins and his bullets rattling as if to warn others of his existence, that he isn't of the ilk around. Folk passing kept a wide berth perhaps from the state of his clothes or the state of his body or the smell pungent and ripening the air before and long after his appearance on any given avenue. The darkness of the sky above was only witnessed briefly before the many illuminations of the city fought to drown out the very brightness of the stars that screamed from the heavens beyond, stretching to the seeming infinite of every street and pathway and up every building a lantern for every life in this burdensome inhabitance, rich with humans and empty with purpose.

  Samwell found the sound of flowing water and walked onto a bridge and peered down at the river flowing under, through the built up land of humans, the water continued onwards, unstoppable even in this world. He closed his eyes and the lids couldn't remove the fullness of the lamps around, the sound of the water lapping at the banks and waves continuing their journey harkened him back to the safety of the world he lived in, but the redness of the skin over his eyes lit up still by the flames all around him restrained the old man in this metropolis, this strangling settlement as he longed to just be back where it all had worth and meaning for a person. He walked the streets, passing men of similar age and build and gruff unkempt hair asking passers by for a little handout and huddling together by flames for another night of life against the harshness of the frost ensnaring all. Samwell kept on, head down, eyes avoiding everything, sickened to his stomach, and found himself upriver so far that light finally fell away. Behind him the city, the world, was alive and alight, but here before the great lake there was a darkness across sky and sea, a blackness inky and easy to fall into. He stood before the emptiness and listened to the lapping, the simplicity of nature's cold listlessness beyond the hubbub and endless activity. A serenity called him, the air cold, the water steady, the stars beyond glowing softly, afar from the world he was anchored upon. Samwell put a boot into the lake, he felt the cold rush through the leather and he kicked away and returned himself fully to dry land, his heel sending shivers upward, he let out a gasp, powder of air relenting from his mouth and nose into the sky beyond. Samwell lit a match and took out a cigarette and stood before the infinite smoking in, steaming out.

THIRTEEN

THE FIRST BUMPS ON HIS WALL broke illusion of darkness and dream but Augustine lay still on his bed comfy despite the gun both-barrelled below blanket. It was the smash of glass that sat him upright and made him reach and pull on the fabrics to see glinted back shine of the weapon for protection. He clutched hold and loaded up the weapon quietly as several stomps the floor below moused across the world. Stepping, sneaking as best on wood, downstairs and crouched he looked in the darkness at silhouettes made from army barracks lantern light across the way and the jailhouse's lamps too three men thin and all about his clinic grabbing at items and tools.

Scram, fast, or worse!

The men turned tail and dropped items and scurried off past the light and into the dark of the back alleys leaving the Doc to parse the dark house and business of his self rummaged and rampaged and ripped apart. He put match to candle and saw to the items dropped righting them on the shelves and looking at cabinet doors snapped open on hinges, and the glass of his window now adorning the wood of his floorboard and sat up until light with gun in hand keeping vigil. In the dawn he

The Ferryman Upon The Plains

walked to the jailhouse, clutching shotgun without much thought, and stepped in to see Kent half asleep and bubbling from mouth murmurs of dreams and nightmares both. A knock and the deputy came to and saw the sawbones with death in hand.

Doc, what offers thee in the way?

I'ma to lookin' fer somethin' along the line of needin' watchdog or guardman on mine now it seems, behind you in the nethers of the town them men gettin' more and more bold with the night drawin' long and needin' themselves heavier fix. I'da welcomed them some ether into their end if it meant cease of situation but I'm not interested much in the destruction of any, even with this affixed my station. If you cain't to the situation make headway I swear I'll out of pocket myself and call in men what will at least balance scales of justice to my side.

Last thing we need here Doc is more folk with intent only to self and damning others when they come by. Might as well all head up to Ganz's farm and find ourselves lined up for slaughter the good it'll do.

That as may be but I'm down a window, a lock, good ether and a decent night's rest and sure now they've exposed the opportunity they'll see to many chances further to test the odds. If there's a pile of men thin and broken up and ripped through with this gun here come morrow, it's on all you here and next to us not doin' the right and seein' this town for good, lettin' whatever they're playin' with take over our everythin'.

Well we're spread thin here Doc. Maybe call up some yourself, everyone on guard round here anyway sure they'd welcome a little coin to do what they'd always.

Andrew Jones

And I to trust any else?
If you cain't come trustin' nobody round here then I guess what are you even doin' livin' about? Time's as come to close up all and head to the next.
Augustine spat onto the floor by the doorway and stepped out into the cold blue light of dawn.
Some good you all is to us down here in the real world. Who even does that badge protect?

*

He felt the coin in his satchel, it weighed heavy on his person, more the longer he stayed in the city. Samwell walked the river path back to the men reaching out for help and asked them to join him for dinner. The several vagrants wandered around, each doorway filled by men shaking heads and staring intently at the horde of humans as they silently received answers to unspoken enquiries. Blocks and blocks, wards and wards, until a small place with limited menu, splinter-rich seating and a cook-cum-owner who held no snobbish injustices upon his fellow man, coin being coin, life being life, the food being at a stretch categorized as food. Hot plates of corned beef hash salted to heaven and tastings of bratwurst to side with the beers the men indulged upon, a cold treat from Europe having made its way across the ocean, the land, to end in the stomachs of men thirsty and bypassing tastebuds for the burps and gas it inflicted upon the atmosphere within seconds of its final destination. Samwell sat with the men, eating up meat and potato and welcoming every little morsel as his lost souls sopped up their beers with the offerings and told half-cut tales of life in the times before they were stuck in the center of a land unforgiving, where they too once were kings of their existence, they rode and they hunted and they explored and they made the country what it was, only to be thrown away when use of their bodies was over and their minds had been riddled with horrors and broken by regiment. Useless to all and unable to make the leap from then to now the longer the then falls away and the faster the now catches up to itself. There were no folk dressed up and whispering and staring and guffawing at the table, this was the one haven in a city unforgiving that Samwell saw the humanity he knew still beating, begging for warmth.

    He paid up and still felt a weight on him, the meal was rich but cheap, his years of toiling could never be spent up so swiftly. He considered finding a place to rest, but the men so revelrous from the drink and the community gave him lift of spirit and offered fine free holding for the night, nothing fancy but a warm fire, friendly folk aplenty, the mercy of man. They walked their way back through the city, towards the parkland and a large fire, seen from all parts of the world here it seemed, a towering flame that punched the cold of the air with heat wrapping all men in sweat and ash. They showed Samwell third base in a playing diamond used during warmer seasons and rested coats on the ground, a nun

Andrew Jones

did the rounds with blankets of sheepswool, itchy but thick, and they lay on the wet and cold near the blaze and had their heads on the plate. Samwell kept one hand on his satchel and another on his holster, a guilt within to even consider, but the world suckerpunches enough and your defences never drop. The lids returned over his eyes and the darkness danced red and orange through the skin, he saw the sun in the sky of a late summer upon the river, the shuffling of feet and brushing of blanket became waves, constant and arhythmic, he was home and stayed there a healthy night next to humanity.

    The cold snapped him awake, the fire was gone, the sun dim in the winter sky of gray and white, a threat he heard of snow swiftly, nobody wanted to hear that prognosis. His satchel was still on him, it pulled the same weight. His hand moved from his holster. As he stood and flapped his jacket out the wet and the chill, beholden to the blanket for coverage and towel, he watched a strange figure in a top hat and cane and long jacket with forked back tail make his way to the collection of men and shake hands, reach out, showing coins and beckoning them to follow him. Samwell stood by some of his new friends and watched the man speak his piece.
    Morning fine fellows, hoping this brisk day sees you true. I'm the Great Hiram, you may have passed by my theater, I present many fine acts to

the distinguished citizens of our fine city. I'd like to offer you stage time this night, do you possess strange and fanciful talents to show the city? Can you recite a sonnet, can you dance the Waltz, can perhaps you lasso a horned beast from miles away?

    A few folk mumbled yes and presented, staggered and aged, renditions of tying rope with a short cut the man brought with him. The Great Hiram held his hand out and they each managed to snag him from inches away, he handed them each a coin and sent them towards a wagon where many already sat. The theaterman stared at Samwell, his blue eyes chilling in the morning frost.

    Here sir, snag yourself a showman.

    Samwell shook his head.

    I ain't ever been no cowpoke, you keep your rope and all it does to folk.

    The Great Hiram's face broke with huge teethy smile hearing the ferryman's voice.

    Well, howdy there sir, you're not from this fair state are you? Not from this half of the war neither, I take it? Mayhap you have stories to delight my audiences? From a world long lost? What say you come upon my many and find yourself lit up and the center of attention? A star recognizable to all who walk the streets?

    I get plenty o' attention already, lookin' to make myself less so and get outta this godforsaken land. You see to those men right, they're good folk, salt of the Earth, true folk tryin'a get on by round here.

    The Great Hiram patted Samwell on the arm and walked away, handing rope to others and getting snagged fast, leading them to his wagon.

Andrew Jones

*

Ganz and the ranch-hands and Colin and Hazel and Mrs. Hoxley and Avery Bedford came to the fields to help over the week harvesting the potatoes and carrots and the ears of corn before the frost came, the chill of the air coming in each sunset but still a little away before the dawn healed all. There the community as it were worked together to gather vegetables for the winter, rows and rows cared for across the seasons coming to fruition. Herman couldn't keep pace of the younger men, his movements stilted and his aches pronounced at each reach and bend. He took to rest earlier than the others, laid out on his bed, Maclaine came by to see the man he hadn't much spent time with since making moves in life and saw in bed not the strong, capable man who had all his time in Cranham made his way and seen right on land, but a husk withering under blanket and losing mass on body and muscle both.

It's gettin' on, Maclaine. I'm not much more, only so many crops a plant gives before you gotta dig it up and plant anew.

You're still here, in all this you're still here.

Winter comes and frost kills, could might be my last, son.

Don't think like that.

It's hittin' fast-like. I maybe should see to Doc but I don't wanna know what's comin'. If it does, rather look to my farm when it gets me, not stare it down until it takes my everything.

You'll be here on your land a long time, might forever be yours.

We all pass on through, get to mine and you seen it so many, stops even bein' sad, the heart scabs over. Just becomes rote. Impatient for the inevitable.

Don't rush things, we all ain't wantin' to see ya not here no more.

Herman smiled at the man before him, standing above, a man with hope and love and clear purpose.

When time comes, and say otherwise it will still, y'think you and yours might want to, since I never'n kept my tree goin', take upon ye this whole?

Colin Maclaine sat in thought at the proposal and looked around the little farmhouse and the man drifting slowly in the bed.

I am grateful, of that make no thought else, the notion kind, warming of heart and soul. However I am not the man who can, I am not even who should rightly be first called upon to hear the opportunity.

What of Skellig? He have it in him to make this his home true?

He's a good man, an honest man, a hard worker, but he is still young, ropes need learning, loyalty needs to be earned yet. Mr. Ganz, if you are determined so to move land on already, you know the man to hand over.

You think he'd take it all on? I trust him to the next world and more, always been right and good and true but you think he'd even consider the whole? His place always fit right atop a horse, headin' into the wilds.

Andrew Jones

    I think even a cowboy gets old, wishes for a place firmly lay his hat. The boys in the ranch house'll take charge of the drive no problem, they are a family unto themselves and if you ain't there to be papa no more then Ellis will sit atop and command the respect due.
    Turns my stomach, asking a man home on the trail to pull saddle and find settlement.
    You'll gift him purpose beyond himself, a new life, for all. Kindest thing anyone can do, shine hope in the dark.

    The Sunday service was overstuffed with people, clamoring for the good word and the smell of the slow boil of beef and potato and carrot and cornbread Mrs. Hoxley had left Choi Lo in charge of as she listened to Father Langston mumble and break into yells and circle around anger and fear and with the wafts of scent from the food remind himself and the congregation of the good of God that the gifts of the land offered. Emotions raised and sank and stomachs twisted and turned, and the collection plate was lacking as the escape to the lunch offered became mad dash for hard workers and old souls the same.
    The Sheriff's wife joined the Chinese cook and finished up the meat and the sound of metal plates scraped by knife and fork amassed through a crowd gurgling with hunger pangs. The meals were dished out to churchgoers and locals and folk passing by seeing a mob and joining in, Harding

Street was silent, the place to be that day was the churchyard. Most grabbed a plate and walked back to their shacks and hangouts and ate alone in silence, but a few tried to make community still in the strange times. Jenny had come out, twice the size anyone had seen her before, and she and Hazel stood alongside the Sheriff's wife and made quiet conversation, temptation to lean into risque or suggestive was put on hold when they remembered just before tongue formed certain syllable that Jesus' spirit was but three steps and one block of brick beyond them.

    Avery Bedford found favor with Madame Westington, complimenting her piano and asking forgiveness for all involved with the mess at the boardinghouse. The widow saw good in the big fella who came asking atonement and ate with him, Colin and Lars joined and the four made kind connection with their similar love and respect of the widow and her talents. Deputy Kent and Marie Delphine shared a little cornbread together before she had to return to her lodgings to make lunch for the Lady of the manor. Herman took Eagle-Eye Ellis aside and over the hot food made suggestion, Eagle-Eye didn't see it coming, he took time to swallow his potato and asked for a stay of execution. The Doc and Father Langston split a flask in plain sight as they watched the town before them, Doc told the Father of his recent break-in, the good Father Langston shook his head and lamented, them men won't barely come up here for food but make haste to the opportunity for a quick high. Both set their sights on the Farmer with concern but neither could make the step forward, instead vigilant and

Andrew Jones

sipping in the alcohol to placate their fears. Bedford took a chance to break from the pack and see to the Sheriff.

I work at the trading post, sir. Guard it in case. I've had time and I haven't come to you and I am sorry, sir, for my failings. I came across one night in the building some worrying sights. I understand the import of trading and keeping safe certain items, but in our small town it came across a bit more suspect than if we was in a mining town or a battlefield. Sir, the man Kelso has in his possession quite a several sticks of dynamite, which maybe he's prospecting, the man's got fingers in many pockets, but there's some kind of large many-barrelled gun that I came across and hid again and keep finding myself coming back to and staring at and being very worried for whatever the means of its existence and to whom the barrels is intended to be aimed at.

Hoxley patted the gentle giant's arm and walked him away from the gathering.

He still got them hidden? I know about that, damn man got me over a barrel on that charge. That's technically the ownership of the Sheriff's department, not that we have facility to hold onto it, certainly cain't hide it in the jailhouse, no room to scratch an itch there. He's keepin' in safe, is he still keepin' it? Is it, with him, safe? Best'n actually that man shouldn't have his hands anywhere near somethin' like that. Can you, if you don't mind and thank you for comin' to me rather than your boss, cain you open up tonight and let us take our items off him?

Avery nodded.

If they's yours, they's yours, and in all honesty Sheriff I'd much rather see these weapons under the badge than that man.

Hoxley smiled at Avery and told him to wait a moment. He went and took Colin from conversation and brought him into the fold.

Maclaine, it's been a spell, I apologize for how things fell apart with Ganz, and with the weapons. I understand harborin' such heavy around here, I wish to God ain't nobody needed to ever use it, but God ain't hearin' us over the blasts goin' on frequenter and frequenter.

Sheriff, whatever's been goin' on round here, it ain't good and it ain't what this place was founded upon.

It ain't, I know it, we all do. Problem is what we know and what they want is two opposin' forces and they keep comin' a-conflictin'. I got a request to make, two mayhap, actual, if you be so kind.

Why we all hush about this? We're in the eyes of the Lord, is this against him?

He already knows it all, He's watching it play out, the rest of them round here, though. We don't wanna cause more problems. Your stable, you got space we could use for holdin' items?

Items?

Guns.

Guns?

A big gun.

Andrew Jones

    Now you're uppin' firearms?
    Now I'm havin' to bring bigger guns to handle bigger problems.
    And what happens when they fire back harder?
    We all know where this ends.
    Then we stop it now.
    Maclaine, you know well as all us we ain't gonna stop things, not like that. Already happened, shots fired before we pulled trigger, this is just how it carries on.
    I don't like this one bit.
    Ain't none of us happy. I'm just tryin' to see my land safe.
    And now I'm roped in?
    For the good of the all, yes.
    Goddamnit Sheriff, and now look at me spittin' vulgar, what kind of big gun?
    A gattlin'.
    Silence fell on the conversation, Colin thought on his time in the army and the scenes eradicated by bullet before him.
    Nobody should have that.
    It's with Harding-Grant right now. He's got it under his roof. Keep it safe, from him at least, from the world if you insist.
    Colin let out a sigh, a bubble of sick in his stomach escaped as gas.
    I'll take it and bury it would do us better, one grave over twenty.

The man's got the army in his pocket, got the ear of the Major they say. You think he can't get another one if he wants?

Colin slowly nodded his head and accepted the inevitable and they agreed that night to carry the gun from the trading post to Colin's stable, to balance the odds, Colin ended up accepting, if and when. They left the sticks of dynamite, the Sheriff had no want to destroy, just maintain peace however necessary, and the three took the gun over in darkness, leaving the warehouse unattended. In the stable, Hoxley asked another favor, he asked the undertaker-builder-blacksmith-horseman-veteran-farmer-lover to build a wagon for the weapon. Colin was on for the ride as much as he wished he wasn't, but he told the Sheriff it would be lowest priority if ever. Bedford offered his help but Maclaine wished if there was any blame to fall upon whatever happened, it'd not be shared, he'd meet St. Peter alone for this.

*

The breeze picked up but the rain held off for the evening, a blue black spread across the mud and stone and wood and brick of Harding Street and customers of distant worlds set back off with wares varying in cost and quality, the denizens of the alleys and the shacks took to the street in place and watched the patrols of uniform, no talking, slow movements, the tension nearing breaking point. Kelso Harding-Grant wore tuxedo well and in arm with his wife who slipped into a gown of light color and detailed pattern fashioned from the east, all the way from

Andrew Jones

New York by way of the continent. They passed the hotel cleaning up still the remnants of the fight the week before and the bank patching holes and came to a building on the corner with swinging doors and men welcoming entrants, as long as they could find coin to cover walking into the space. In the melee of the streets, the building slowly rising was overlooked by all until its grand opening this night, a societal landmark for the town, a bar serving drinks beyond the basic brown liquid in grubby glass, the town now thanks to its dominant landowners had a cocktail lounge.

     They sat on grand chairs as a band gently played for them, a mint julep for him, an old fashioned for her, they sat and sipped and listened and looked away from one-another and said not a word all night. There were no other customers the entire evening.

     Hartwell Kent and Marie Delphine met in the cover of the night as the widow's piano hushed for rest and snuck through the estate of Harding-Grant, Marie had found several shacks laying in wait for residents of late and as long as they were quiet and they were hidden from the light going in and out, the two could for her rare times free of the lady share something deeper.

     All she's talked of these past days has been her club, her parlor. Must be some fine drinks make you obsess over for long rather than just make yourself.

Kent picked the little lady up and laid her on the brutally harsh bedding.

There's a time when the waitin's so much more part of things than the partakin'.

Marie moved her hands down Hartwell's body and into his pants.

Well guess tonight all of us are finally at the partaking step.

They embraced passionately, his rough and lived-in hands on her soft and hidden-away skin, for all the time in ladies' chambers she erupted with pleasure in a man's hands, their night everything the Harding-Grants would never experience, but just as hushed as they fought against the bedding and thin walls to make a world of pure animal lust their own.

*

Samwell's coat was dry but it wasn't warm. He made way through the city to a tailors and made enquiry, they sized him then measured him. In the wait for the bulky coat to be finessed he found a barbers and got himself cut to size, the man threw in a few scents to mask him too and he left the establishment almost presentable, the stubble gone, the wisps of hair short and thin on the back of his head. The weight still heavy, Samwell walked into the first bank of Chicago and waited patiently to be seen by someone, he sat with a young man lanky and with brown hair, a slight nervousness to his every move like he was expecting to be shot for doing anything that might incur wrath such as asking how much money the old man

Andrew Jones

had or if the old man found the seat comfortable. Samwell put his coins on the table and the young man counted up and wrote a number and told him he could wire the money direct to the bank of Cranham if he'd like that. Samwell sat in a state of shock that so much time had gone by and his settlement had a wire, had a bank, had some of this new civility rising up. Samwell took a few coins from the table and shook the man's hand, the young man flinched a little as he felt the calloused fingertips and overgrown nails grip and claw around his unlabored extension. On the leaving of the building, Dickie called out to Samwell and casually showed the older man what the cost of their ride had afforded him, he handed Samwell a fair few coins to thank him for the conversation and humanity that spared his sanity another journey, and just like that Samwell was unable to remove the weight around him. He returned to the tailors and saw his big coat ready for the season, he handed the men some money and they handed back more coin, the tip too friendly, looking at the old man's being, he should save some for himself. A man couldn't remove the weight in this world, it only grew whilst many others wished to feel a little in the emptiness of their existence.

    In new coat, new smells, new self, Samwell passed by the theater of The Great Hiram And His Lowmen - Amazing Acts From The Wild Days Of The West, and God help him the man's curiosity proved too much to deny, he paid a few coin to the clerk and walked into the theater.

    The screeching in his ears was a pain unknown on the worlds he traversed, the moment he entered the auditorium and heard the acoustically perfect caterwauling from the stage it was obscene. He accustomed himself as best to the frequency of the noise as he looked to the illuminated stage and saw a man standing in the middle of the raised platform undulating his throat with syllables of vowel as some elder outside of the light played splendid guitar the likes of which no man on the plains'd ever be seen plucking in good company. The yodeller ceased as Samwell found a seat free several spots before the front and hid his disdain through staring at the floor and settling into his chair. The claps around were hardly thunderous. The Great Hiram stepped onto the stage and ushered the performer off with a smile and announced a tale of the ravenous, bloodthirsty land west from a true gunslinger, at which one of Samwell's dining vagrant friends stepped up, swaying in a drunken haze and slurred an accent one might kindly call authentic if their ears were still recovering from the previous act. The bullshit spouted was a mix of dime print child story and disgust of the other attacking the notion of the native and their own land, Samwell shook his head and stared at the man, he had no hatred for the performer, it wasn't his doing to be there, puppets can no more stand trial lest their strings are tightened.

    The man was listened to by most and whispered over by some bored of the solitary figure stationary, with

Andrew Jones

a little swaying, detailing nothing for a long time. The claps when he left were more thankful than congratulatory, and The Great Hiram presented his star act, the Lowman to end all lowmen, a genuine native to rally them all with ire and shock, a man presenting his skills worth fighting up against. If we, he decreed, could best him and his kind, what couldn't the white man do to America. Already the crowd were cheering and ready to enjoy some for-real action upon the stage, as the native man wearing half-cut pants and no shirt stepped out holding a tomahawk, hair tangled up, face painted with shadow and blood. Samwell squinted, his eyesight dim and in the smoky, flickering room struggling to see clear, the figure from afar felt familiar, he had seen this man in the distance run, in the distance shoot, in the distance kill. The rifleman of Rockwood.

    The rifleman began by waving around his hatchet, faster and faster as a steady beat of a drum increased tempo, he rolled and leaped and almost came towards the audience, with gasps and jeers and claps aplenty encouraging the performance, and then span around and threw the weapon towards a piece of wood upstage. It lodged perfectly in the thin beam, the crack of metal on wood exploded more applause and a man stepped out with three knives and gave them to the rifleman, before dragging out a painted board, giving the impression of a street in daytime out on the frontier. The rifleman juggled the blades to more drumbeat as one of the vagrants was walked onto the stage, and stood by the wood. The rifleman suddenly threw a knife. It lodged into the wood by the man's hand. The audience gasped. The drum continued on. Samwell gripped his armrest. Another knife flew in the air. It landed between the man's legs. Excitement turned to tension. The drum stopped. The rifleman turned his back to the wood and the man. He tossed the knife behind his back. With a slice, the blade landed in the wood by the man's ear, he let out a little yell and red came from his skin, a slight nick. The rifleman took a bow and the vagrant and the wooden board were dragged off stage. A man handed the rifleman a bow and some arrows. The drums rolled off more excitement.

 Three homeless men of Chicago were stepped onto the stage holding a pumpkin, a melon and an apple, all starting to show signs of rot, the people and the vegetation. The men held their food aloft, on their heads with hands maintaining balance and weight. The rifleman took a ribbon from his pocket and placed it over his head, covering one eye, and took his first arrow. He pulled the bow back and the flight touched upon his cheek as he aimed. The snap of the string returning from stretch was quickly eclipsed by the smash of the arrowhead flying into the pumpkin, the homeless man holding the squash shook but held tight to the orange lump, presenting to the crowd the front with arrow end sticking out, and turned to show the rocky head pierced through the other side. The applause was solid if not electric. The rifleman removed his ribbon and wrapped it around the head of

Andrew Jones

his next arrow, and dipped the fabric in one of the lanterns on the stage floor, setting ablaze the arrow itself. He pulled back as folk around Samwell gasped, the ferryman's teeth gritted and he tried to look away but felt compulsion to witness what he paid for. A twang of string, a drumroll ceasing, an inhale of the entire audience. The melon exploded into gooey red and yellow across the stage, the homeless man once holding it had his hands free with splits of rind left on his tips, now covered in mess. The arrow fell to the stage floor and a man tipped a bucket of water on it and then splashed the homeless man clean. The applause and the hollering invaded Samwell's ears with agony and fury. The apple was still standing.

  The rifleman aimed his arrow as the drumroll recommenced, then shook his head and let the arrow fall to the ground. He put his bow down and took a revolver out from his pants, and aimed it across the stage. Samwell felt his forearms tense, felt the armrests shaking, starting to splinter. The rifleman looked to the audience and with a ferocity leapt over the lanterns, out to the crowd and dashed up to the back of the theatre, roaring at members of the crowd as he went by. People around Samwell turned their necks, stood a little to see the rifleman. Samwell watched the homeless man he slept next to last night alone on stage, haunted by the endless procession of drumbeat, holding a small fruit above his old head, shaking as he stood above the crowd, for

The Ferryman Upon The Plains

everyone's enjoyment whatever was to happen. Samwell watched as the crowd yelled and clapped and whooped with excitement, yelling slurs to the rifleman, goading him on and baying for blood. A crash of thunder from behind overwhelmed the drum noise, and in a flash the apple disappeared above the homeless man. He stood there shivering, his hands on his head as if prisoner of the show, as the crowd roared and applauded and stomped feet at the rifleman's perfect aim. He hopped back on the stage, passing Samwell and roaring at him. Samwell could see marks on the man's skin where holes had healed, his ankles bulbous and deformed. The rifleman took a bow and picked up his weapons and walked off stage to the standing ovation of the audience. A stagehand dragged the homeless man from his position and The Great Hiram stepped out to eat up all the undue accolades as he closed the night's performance with a little magic and a recitation of the Lord's Prayer before curtains closed.

    Samwell got to his feet and filed out of the auditorium with the rest, as everyone else made it to the brisk Chicago air, he turned and burst into the backstage, unstopped by the tired staff of the theater focussing on a little drink and food and sleep to come. He walked through the darkness and saw the homeless men handed a little potato and bean meal and a mug of ale as they sat together on the ground, he passed the yodeller and his guitarman packing up for the night and picking a few coat pockets for good measure, he passed a young woman not maybe of age removing black paint from her face and hands, and found The Great Hiram smoking a cigar and

Andrew Jones

leaning on a wall, counting coins and tossing them into his tophat with glee.

Some show ya got here.

Hiram turned to see Samwell and burst with delight.

Oh, a fan, good day.

Lot of hot air and nonsense, but you got somethin' you don't shouldn't have here on stage.

What's it to you, sir?

Your injun, that man a monster, I seen him do awful to many fine folk. I saw him fall and fall and fall and he ain't possible to return, yet I seen him like you did stand and dance and shoot still. He ain't to be put up before folk, lest it fer the noose.

Everyone's a critic, my Lowman's a fine man, sir, he's a good man, in actual fact, to break the facade of the performance he's a wonderfully sweet fellow, best kind of guy. Your disparagement isn't welcome here.

He's not a man, he's a monster, you should set him to the sheriff, or I will.

Sheriff? Where do you think we are old timer? This is the city, not some Godless land of fools with more guns than brains. Why don't you go have yourself a nice drink and forget about what you saw.

Hiram held out his tophat of coins and shook the change at Samwell.

On me.

Samwell shook his head.

Very well.

Hiram nodded his head. Samwell turned to look behind, the rifleman in his imposing glory stood high above the old man, he grabbed Samwell by the neck and began to throttle him in plain sight of any who cared to look.

Darkness fell and the curtains closed.

*

Night came faster than ever and the lawmen had to let their horses rest. They hobbled and hopped and put together a small fire and sat around it and watched their horses sleep and looked at their bruises and bones still broken and looked at one-another's faces through the fire, the determination, the unstoppable demand of themselves, and all they had done, and here in the fall of the year atop a hill, a mountain still in the distance, failing at their single task.

Never seen a fall like this'un, y'all ever witnessed such cold, such wet? Down'n the Mississip cold as it gets ain't feelin' like this, e'en at night's longest, always a li'l heat up high give to the land and the folk, enough to fight on till dawn. They's snow up in them hills yonder already, might as always be white up there, when we're sweatin' and watchin' the fireflies dance it's frozen. When we been cursin' the night's strangle on our air, hotter than some days, it's frozen. I member back some a night so bakin' we, and I was young then, we lay mostly naked on the roof of our shack, my brothers, the three of us, sweatin and cursin and gaspin for a li'l breath in the heavy. We us

Andrew Jones

weren't even tryin'a be secret about bein' up at that hour and on the top of the place, we all knew ma and pa weren't asleepin' under neither, nobody round was, nobody but could curse and lay in the sufferin' and sweat out as much as possible, beggin' the sky to send some rain or some breeze or somethin' to distract from the heat. Then there were a scream. That did the job, that scream. Us three we got up on the roof and looked around and heard nothin' more but that scream I still hear in here e'ry day. Few folk burst from their places and looked round, saw us and I guess figured we was bein' loud and naughty and young, but some others certainly didn't see it that way. A few folk came on runnin' past, all red and puffed out, fast as their feet could in this heat, they tried, but weren't right for em, and they was felled past our place by a man in a hat, lassoed one and tackled the other he did, in one move he took two down. Maybe it wasn't like that, but in the heat and the dark and the lack of sleep and the tales we us brothers continued for years that's how I member. Man took two down and tied one up and knocked one out and demanded us nearby to come see folk who red-handed were caught from slicin' a girl somethin' awful. He hanged them both on the same rope before us all, and we all walked, half-naked and sweatin' and cursin' the sky, with the man to the sight of the woman, she weren't much older than my biggest brother, fifteen maybe, her throat open and her eyes pleading for help. Ain't nobody could sort her out, too far from a doc, too hurt for life, we

The Ferryman Upon The Plains

crowded her and the man held her hand as she died and we all just watched and wept and I looked back at the hanging men and the man who did all for the right.

    My papa's brother walked our town a sheriff, or what was the sheriff back then, a man I guess decided to determine right and wrong, folk around came to him for advice and help and he saw to hearing and seeing and talking through things, at home, on farmland, whatever needed sorting he'd see to. My papa talked little of him but I'd run off anytime I could and watch him help, sometimes people yelled and sometimes people took up arms but he never raised his voice or his gun back. I saw power in him, not control of others, but respect, acceptance, understanding at least that the man before them had foreseen the every option and handed them the best for all involved. Papa was callous, he'd hit us all any time something annoyed him, the door squeaked, the dog barked, we'd all lose out. I didn't wanna be that man, I wanted to not have any of him a part of me. When I was old enough I spent my days with my uncle proper, a disrespect my papa held against me even when I was as big as him, as tall as him, maybe bigger, but I loved being a part of that, being there to see to the world as it was meant to be. Then my papa came to see my uncle and shot him there in the head in front of the whole world and turned the gun to me and told me to decide, who do I follow. Fool of a father, let his anger hold him from sense, he stared at me with his gun and he couldn't see I'd already handled my blade and stabbed him in the heart the second he turned his violence in my direction. It wasn't revenge, it was justice, for my uncle, for my mama,

Andrew Jones

for myself. Nobody else would suffer his foolish fire. I took up to the army for a spell after that, made good on the land proving I wasn't some inbred hick trying to kill my way around, and found my way to law proper when the opportunity came. My mama didn't much live to see me come good like that, she never got to see me be the father my papa couldn't be, the kind of father my uncle was for the world.

    We didnt fight in our family, too much outside all times, we kept together besten we could we was stronger a group than alone and e'ryone b'yond our place was always feudin over this or that or any moment to take up to the others and fire off a few. I watched all my child years not runnin off from ma or pa or my sistah, we was as close as can get and always together, when one gone we all afeared and looked together, and when pa went to get supplies we three sat with a rifle at the door in case and prayed hard he'd come back again, never didn't but we couldn't stop prayin just in case that one time he did and we'd take that foul-up to the grave. Time came my sistah went and found herself a husband, how she escaped us anyhow I'll never know, secrets in a family can bring it down, but she hooked herself some man wantin' to take her with him out of the hollars and away from the feuds and we three, ma pa and I, we couldn't much to stay away from her, so we all had to take up from our place and not barely we left our house and walked away the fightin' loudly exploded, guns afire all over. Read in a paper some thirty men, women and chil'un shot before the families ceased to be and the land lay lonely, they wiped themselves out and I don't know what for. I asked my pa and he shook his head and sighed. I asked my ma and she cackled and spat at the paper. I asked my sistah and she never understood neither. I even asked her husband, I guess my brother for best term, he told me he knew one of them men when they was both kids and that kid was rushin' to fight anything, you look at him off, you say somethin' as he passes, he'd try and gut ya. Whole mess of folk exist to do harm and when it comes to it they achieve their goal and leave nothin' for the understandin'. Some people just is, some people will always be and no amount of talk or threat or jail'll see them a new perspective. The fear I felt all my life because some men need to be put down like dogs, well I never wanted nobody to go through that if I could.

  The men silenced up again and looked into the fire and felt their pains return in their bodies, and in their souls. The first snowfall flurried as they slept that night.

*

  Kelso Harding-Grant was well rested when he rode over in the morning and saw the finishing boards laid on the bridge. He thanked the men and let the ferryman on duty know his time was up. The man had little reaction to the news, he and his others had watched the building for a while and were happy enough surviving the last days of

Andrew Jones

their time before setting off to the next land and the next opportunity. The ferry sat unoccupied.

 Hazel waited in the clinic a while as Augustine remained comatose, all his worldlies surrounding him in his bed and vicinity above the shop. He woke to hear visitor below and clasped his gun, brandishing it as he descended, seeing the dressmaker in her morning glory bathed in low sun of dawn and offering not but kindness and community. They sat in his room above and he slowly returned to the clear and conscious world over coffee and beans and potato, Hazel ate a little but let the Doc devour, she complained of aches and a light sickness.
 We all got that these days, round here.
 The attempt at joking wasn't welcome in the moment, and the truth within seemed bitter to all ears. Doc took her down to the clinic and examined her properly, his breath of beans and coffee and whiskey and sick and rot made her gag, her condition worsening in the time in the clinic. After ten minutes of questions personal and feeling and looking around Augustine stood back and congratulated Hazel Worthing on being pregnant.
 I'll keep it to mine but you might want to inform Maclaine, if he don't outright drop and make an honest woman of ya there'll be souls uncleansed all over this land.
 Hazel sat gobsmacked, she slowly picked herself up and walked off, she went straight to the

stable and as Colin sanded off a wheel axle for a wagon she held him close and whispered in his ear. He took all of Hazel Worthing in and smiled and asked her to become his wife. They there surrounded by the horses entered a partnership built on love.

FOURTEEN

 THEIR BODIES FOUGHT THROUGH the first weeks of cold and they found the mountain beyond coming ever nearer when the clouds parted long enough to see, but their horses struggled more up the rocks and steep hills with barely muscle left on them to walk, let alone ride. The three lawmen took a morning of bitter frost to decide before they began upon their beasts and kept their meat for the weeks ahead, and wrapped themselves in the bloody skin of their saddles. The men stumped with broken bones and aching every step carried the weight higher and higher up the mountain until they reached a frozen lake stretching flat across the land. The ice stained red both dark and fresh as they slowly balanced and slid across, the peak of the mountain further onward. A small family of bears lay carved out and partially skinned in the middle of the ice, the lawmen kept on without looking too much, nothing left to investigate or decide, up there was all there was now. Abraham looked down as he slid a little, through the ice he could see a salmon stuck, eyes wide open, mouth half ajar, about to have jumped out, now forever between swimming and flying.

 The ice was stable but the longer they stood upon it the deeper the rumbles beneath them seemed to yell. There was a stillness to the pool, the water and the dead bears and the snowdrift on the trees and rocks and ground surrounding, nothing was alive in the sky or on the branches or around the mud and earth, except the three men in horseskin coats. It took a day just to scale the steep side of the mountain, its little traversals and passageways around the hills and falls, narrow and slippery. The three men took each step carefully, single file, and they worked their way up towards the mountain's top, still obscured often by clouds, at this height seemingly always in flurry. The air was bitter and cold in their lungs, each thin gasp hurt, they slowed breathing to once every ten seconds, as long as they could between every inhale this high.

    A small near-horizontal perch gave the three men a space to stand together without fear of falling, mist cleared for them to see down at the lake below and the bloody mess visible up high, and the flow of the frozen river carrying on down the land beyond all sight, and around the horizon of white and blurred gray from snowfall. They seemed mostly lost in their own world of emptiness. Zachariah considered starting a fire here and resting for a while, he offered some bullets for their gunpowder. Jedediah looked around their point, and the side of the mountain still ongoing, and behind some logs he saw darkness, a mouth to enter. The three took out revolvers and circled the hole. Abraham called out first, the echo of his voice inside was the only response. Jedediah offered a second yell, only to himself. Zachariah threatened just for good measure, and was warned by his own voice to come out with their hands up. They went in,

Andrew Jones

single file, and in the darkness their eyes could once more see nothing.

    Jedediah lit a match and in the burst of light a bear's snout jumped out, dead on the wall, a hide covering the big bearman. He didn't react to the light, he stared into the white outside unmoving. He was pale and his face had frozen tears turned icicles, glistening in the flame. Below the man's beard, the small man with broken lenses sat, inside the belly of the bearman, bloody and pale and blue, frozen inside the man inside the bear inside the cave. They all stared towards the white outside.

    The three men looked at the end of their hunt for a while as the flame flickered down the match. Abraham stared at the beasts and thought of all the time he could have spent at home, the meals he and his wife could have shared, the seasons gone for this escapade. Jedediah thought of his kids, the world they'd grow up in without these people, he wondered if more were coming or if this was thankfully the last of their kind. Zachariah wished no more death and no more fire and no more fear, he would come back to Kentucky and find a peaceful life, maybe even hang up the hat and settle on a land to raise family and crops. The match burnt and Jedediah dropped it from his fingers as it hurt his tip. The flame landed on the ground and hissed, and popped, and sparked. Beneath the men in the center of the cave a spiral of powder began to sputter in the fire. Within seconds the light was blinding white and the noise ear-shattering.

The mountain's peak exploded with flame for a brief moment and the clouds burnt up into smoke. From above snow rolled down the side and fell with rock towards the ground. A line of fire ran around the passageways and thin cliffs of the mountain and met the frozen lake, and the bodies of the bears. One final boom. The avalanche and the explosion turned the lake liquid in unseasonable times and the world around it melted, flowing loud, fast and too much down through the river, through the ground, across the trees, drowning all around it as the water rushed on, unstoppable.

*

The wagon passed through strange collections of folk situating themselves near water and trying to hunt and gather, grow and harvest, run to the rivers and pan for shiny hope, with men mostly gaunt and weary and determined for all the miles they pushed through to prove themselves despite the reality of their situations, the few families that were around comprised mostly of women and their kids shaken and silent from all they had to pass through to get across the country and find only this, all the talk and letters of excitement and folk in taverns passing on what they heard down the trail led to these pockets of dirt and heat and sand and redwood and no chance to ever see their parents and sisters and aunts and friends and home again. Nowhere outside the caravan felt right to settle with the women and the kid and the money they held and hid, Noah felt apprehensive passing past each group looking down at them in their blind faith and broken promises, nowhere firm to build a home upon.

    Further down the land, where days were hotter still if not longer, church bells rang and a small town made their way to their dutiful respect of their deity, young and old, speaking English and Spanish together, women dressed fine in gowns suited to their outing and the heat both, and men cleaned up and looking healthy. The wagon was waved at by settlers and founders both and kids came running up beside to see to the newcomers. They were welcomed from the frightful journey across the country warmly, Noah remained with the wagon as the women and toddler were walked to church, and he sat above watching those who denied the call to prayer. Stragglers and sots acknowledged him and smiled at least, he didn't feel his hand moving to his pearl grip in any moment the town's majority sat and listened to the good word. Within the day the Hollanders were embraced and offered sanctuary by the community, two different women almost fought to house them in their own place until they could get their own residence built, the one who worked as schoolmarm for the town won out and Noah was aided by several older men carrying the wagon's goods into the stonehouse, the box of coins jingling never raised eyebrows to any and they left the family alone true enough to acquaint themselves with their new habitat.

    Noah rested outside the schoolmarm's place that night, Midnight was fed and washed and watered and slept near enough he could hear his horse snoring in the calm and serene air. Kirsty exited the house and saw Noah sitting on the ground before, lit by evening's final glow and the swaying lanterns on the porch, and sat next to her guardian.

    I brought you a few things, thank you for all.

    No bother. Good deed's its own reward.

    A better reward is to be had.

    Kirsty held out a satchel heavy in coins. Noah picked it up and looked in, then handed it back to her.

    I don't need it.

    You did something special, most folk'd take twice as much for half the work.

    I ain't most people, I ain't any kinda person.

    If you don't take it all at least a couple just so I ain't offended, a kindness for all.

    Noah relented and put his hand in the satchel and took three coins, holding them out to show Kirsty.

    If you're worried about us, we don't need much to get by, Sissy and I can make do on nothin', little Paul, he'll make use of this when he gets there and I hope well, but otherwise holdin' on does nothin' good to nobody. It's all temporary anyhow.

    Noah stayed silent, looking at the woman of unbelievable strength and goodness in the last light. She stood up and held her hand to Noah.

Andrew Jones

    Up off yer haunches, you won't permit me to pay for services, at least share in a little tranquillity.
    Kirsty winked and revealed in her other hand a bottle of mezcal, the scent filling the air suddenly, a punch burning through the nose and throat of Noah as he stepped up and followed his travel companion into the house. They snuck quietly up the stairs and into a room cool and empty from furniture, a bed all that made it different from storage. Kirsty sipped and spluttered and passed the bottle to Noah, he kicked up a cough before Kirsty shushed him and closed the door, and the two sat on the bed together giving themselves hell in a bottle.
    Pawey's fine with Sissy, sleepin' away safe and warm.
    Kirsty, that's awful kind, but I…
    It don't always gotta mean more than the moment, if that's your thought. Sometime we all us get animal in our veins.
    I cain't let myself go animal again. I cain't trust mahself to return. Don't know it's worth returnin'.
    We can make it worth it.
    Noah rested his head on Kirsty's and closed his eyes. He listened to her breathing and her heart beat, the flow of her life through her.
    You're goin' soon, ain'tya?

Noah nodded against her skin. She placed a hand on the back of his head and stroked his messy hair and sipped courage.

I ain't suited to stationary. To smiles and talk and bein' round folk happy to just be, to have purpose in their togetherness. My togetherness ripped out from me long ago.

I don't much think Paul gonna see me like a mother, a protector and carer. I see his pa in his eyes, I know he saw all what his pa did, the weakness, the breakin', the bleedin' and weepin' and nights when he couldn't hug his mama tight cos touchin' me made me wince and shriek. And when I see Horace there I shudder sometimes, at my own flesh and blood I fall pale and scared internal. I cease to be and become victim, failure, instead. He don't have that with Sissy, they share bein' all on the outside enough, witness not participant, and hopefully he'll not remember it all when he gets older, do right instead of haunt himself from his father's evils, but I don't know if I'm the one to help him get there. Sissy, she's natural and attentive, she don't lead him one way or push him off, they together make sense. I'm not sure I'm meant to be in one place and sittin' round makin' good. My feet get antsy the moment I think about putting them firmly down here. I feel like I need to be back in the wagon, even without nobody to carry on with, the ride, the journey, that's where I make sense, not the place at the end of it all.

She sipped more mezcal and winced only slightly at the searing alcohol.

Andrew Jones

    Alone is hard for all, nobody's meant to live like that.

    Noah looked upon the woman laying her weight on him, he smelt the journey still upon her body, felt her body pulsating with excitement and fear. He turned to stare at the empty room's darkness.

    You have love and meaning and reason and strength, in you and around you. You can't leave that for the unknowable, the possibility of what else ain't worth losing the security of truth and connection. All we are in this world is our connections, severing them purposeful-like is a fool's errand. I can't be a connection out there for you, or nobody else, mine were ripped. I cain't let any come back if it means doin' same to any else. No-one should live like this, especially if they never need to. Stay a little longer, see to Pawey and Sissy and make them anchored and secure at least, do right by those you love.

    They're not the only ones I love.

    Kirsty gently placed her lips on Noah's cheek and tried to move them to his lips, Noah held her head softly and kept her from committing deeper connection, he brought himself and her down onto the bed to rest and held her into sleep comfortable and with no need to wake and stay guarded. In the night he slipped himself away from Kirsty and took his boots off, tiptoeing out of the room. He looked into Sissy and Paul's and saw them asleep one last time and walked downstairs.

The Ferryman Upon The Plains

He kicked his boots on in the lamplight and woke Midnight up, they were long gone before dawn cracked over the winter blue sky.

*

    Samwell came to and felt the restrictions on his neck and wrists, bound by chain and leather that rattled softly as he wriggled, the feeling of bumps shaking under him. In the coach he sat opposite the rifleman and Hiram, Chicago's cold night alight once more with lantern flicker blurring past.
    Where ya takin' me ya Godless heathens?
    The rifleman placed his finger to lip and shushed the ferryman.
    You have denied me twice there Peter, I'm not in the risk business, showmanship requires careful planning, big ideas and a little restraint. You could have been something special, alas old fella you are simply tonight's main attraction.
    The coach pulled up to a grand mansion rising up into the heavens. The doors were opened by impeccably dressed men of silence and refinery, Hiram stepped out first, then the rifleman gripped Samwell's arm and dragged him out, and walked him into the doorway of a house bursting with light, with gilded artifacts and folk of all ages dressed beyond the means of any Samwell had ever found the fortune to meet. They who passed by on the streets now stared gleefully at the stranger chained up and paraded before them. He was walked up three large stairways until the men were found in an ocean of

Andrew Jones

cigar smoke and brandy sniffing adorned with statues nude and proud. Hiram stood before his attractions and tipped his hat to folk, whispering to them, and in time the room parted to allow the three center stage.

    Fair evening ladies and gentlemen.

    Hiram's spiel rolled out easily from his throat, the opulence of the crowd may have changed but his clinical targeting of humanity's deepest intrigues was ever-present, the eyes of the party turned to the showman.

    Many a night I have presented to the great people of our city the wonderment of the bloody and fantastic reining upon our dear country through music and story and action, and whilst it enthrals upwards of three hundred folk daily, all who leave with smiles upon their faces I might add, for this illustrious crowd of Chicago and indeed Illinois itself's finest I present to you a man of genuine continuance of the likes the land beyond the sunset offers. A man who no doubt was responsible in part to the many achievements of our great success across the country in ridding the vast problems of pest and petulance. Come see a real cowboy standing before you at this party, come ask about all the stories you have only read about before, have your visage photographed with him, gratis of course to you wondrous folk of this magnificent land.

    The rifleman pushed Samwell out to stand next to Hiram, the showman flashed his hands

The Ferryman Upon The Plains

around the old soul as if to prove no strings held him aloft, though the chains rattled and made guests a little uncomfortable. Jutting from the crowd a man of grand stature seemed to block all light as he stepped to Samwell, his head large with long chin and grand feathered brown hair, and eyes that danced with the flames reflected in them. He looked Samwell up and down and put his hand out to Hiram, the showman grabbed and shook the big man's wrist.

Hiram good sir, perhaps you're unaware but we won the war, no man should be shackled around these parts, especially not one of this fine fellow's complexion.

A sneer of a smile came from Hiram and he nodded to the rifleman. Samwell's shackles were removed from his arms, his legs were still cuffed. The big man put his hand out to Samwell.

How'd ya do there fella, hope you don't think all us Northerners are looking to chain you up just for being, I assure that's not the values we intend to proclaim.

Hiram leaned into Samwell's ear and hushed a whisper.

Man's the governor of the state, shake his hand why don't you.

Samwell stood still, the Governor chuckled in the silence and patted Samwell's arm.

Alright there fella, a little frozen in all our wonder perhaps, or maybe The Great Hiram threw you into the wolves unprepared. What say we play a game of sorts, I have maps of much of our country, perhaps you tell us where you hail from and we can seek out on the papers your land?

Andrew Jones

A sense of excitement rippled through the crowd, a palatable parlor game before the strange figures of the showman, the rifleman and the ferryman that interrupted their standing and smoking and sipping.

Through gritted teeth Samwell uttered the single word Cranham. The Governor stood before him and looked the old man up and down and leaned down to be eye-level.

You got a state there?

Angry.

Some crowd chuckled, some gasped, the monosyllabic guest proved resistant to the charms it seemed, and Samwell didn't care to be considerate to those surrounding him.

Let's be amenable, how about we loosen the man's chains all, and get him a drink, and some food. What's your name, mine's Theodore.

Hiram nodded to the rifleman and Samwell's chains were removed entirely, a glass of brandy made its way to him swiftly. Samwell stared at the Governor, he saw his cleaned up, wrinkled, aged, thinned, sundamaged self in the man's eye looking back at himself. A hit of brandy and a gasp of the burn in his throat and Samwell gave them a state. The attention went to a man across the room scrambling through papers to find maps of the area and ran them over to the Governor. He was an old fella for a scrambler, he could have been an old man when Samwell was young and yet he stood here still alive, dressed fancy but he had scars and wounds from harsher times. The old fella and the Governor ran through some papers and shook their heads, passing maps to nearby folk engaged in the event.

No Cranhams on the map, you sure you come from a real place?

I know where I came from. I know everything about it. There's the river run up and down, there's the church on the hill seein' to God all we can, there's the good people who live their lives honestly and compassionately, there's the road across leadin' folk yonder and back, if they's so needin' to turn tail like.

A one road town? No wonder it's not here, but a blip in our land, we might as well add it with pencil, it'll wash off soon enough.

Chortles as men chomped cigars and women derisively giggled at this strange old man from another world.

There's a fort nearby, full of good men who serve this country proper, they give their heart and soul to the land, to the people, to the way of life.

A fort? Maybe that's somewhere here.

Fort Oak was on a map, as was the river, flowing far north across the country and down to an end before the land ran back to the ocean. There was a track drawn on the map from the Fort up towards Chicago, and continued on west towards California, it seemed to run right on through where Samwell knew his world sat. The Governor clicked his fingers and the old fella who it turned out was acting currently as both assistant and Mayor of the city handed the Governor a pen and inkwell

Andrew Jones

and the Governor dropped a dot on the map for Cranham as act of charity for their guest. He held the map aloft and folk clapped the contrition of their elected representative.

An elder couple grabbed at the map and guffawed in the midst of the crowd, the husband remarked that their absent daughter had squandered many of her not inconsequential funds in that vicinity with a relative rube of a husband, to the mockery and delight of those within earshot, they laughed at the plight of those not attending for many reasons that night. The couple stood up to Samwell and locked eyes with him.

You I assume are aware of the buffoon Kelso Grant? So daft a man devoid of purpose he clung to the name we bore and carefully weaved meaning into this as if it were his own, taking our daughter to discover something like importance and power in the world out there. If you can't buy your value in a city, go out to the wilderness and call yourself king of nothing I suppose.

The man's delight in berating his son-in-law brought an agony to Samwell for the trading post landlord he never knew he felt, he thought of poor Jenny, welcomed into the Wright family in name and in love, they would never a one of them in public or alone think such sick and cruel upon her existence. He wished to be back at the estate, to reach out to Jenny and hold her crying widow with comfort and warmth. The evening continued with Samwell examined by a doctor for seeming

The Ferryman Upon The Plains

authenticity, bankers and lawyers and traders and people who held no role in labor relished the time stood before the ferryman and taking in a sense of the world they'd never lift a finger to explore or exist upon, and then returned to their drinks and conversation of empty purpose and he was a blip on their night such as Cranham was on the maps they passed around. A bishop stood before Samwell, black robes highlighting the pasty whiteness of his skin, a scarf around his neck and a hat not too tall for formal events covering scalp rather than a sense of hair on the man, he held out a hand before Samwell and reciting Latin words waved about. There was a hole in the man's thumb, and it shined in the light, a lacquer upon it, a false digit.

Do you believe in the Lord?

Samwell nodded.

Very good, He believes in you.

The Governor handed coins to Hiram and he doffed his hat and stepped out of the room, Samwell and the rifleman and the bishop and the mayor and the Governor stood together in the middle of the party. The Governor leaned towards Samwell.

I remember Cranham now. Come, let's make away from prying eyes and open ears.

*

A knock on the door of the clinic continued for minutes pounding the wood before Doc Augustine shuffled out of his stupor and in the dark and biting chill of the night looked upon Marie Delphine wrapped in layers and covered in sweat and blushed nose. He pointed his held weapon at the ground and wiped spittle from his mouth, the Doc staring into the night's shroud and feeling the chill bear down on them all. Her lady, she gasped into the icy air, ailed hot and shivered the same time. He grabbed items and threw them in a satchel and stepped out alongside the maid.

 Augustine sternly made his way to the jailhouse and Marie followed, Kent was on night watch and stood up on the Doc's appearance, somehow made himself taller when the fair maiden came into view as well.

 Deputy, if you could just for the time make darn sure no folk foolish enough do more damage to my place whilst I see to whatever in the hell's goin' on across the way?

 It'd be my pleasure.

 Kent didn't take his eyes away from his lover at any point whilst addressing the doctor, and wrapped a coat over himself and made station in the middle of the road, lantern in one hand and metal cup of coffee freezing fast in the other. The Doc and the maid made pace upwards and towards the monstrous expansion beyond.

 The lights around and inside the monumental residence struck out the blackness of night and suggested life continual that as Doc stormed into the foyer broke into hurried fret, he was led by Marie and met by several men and women opening doors and taking coat and seeing to every part of Doc's being as his job lay before him. Ascending two staircases and through long corridors that opened up to entire wings waiting for people to breathe into their stasis, just making it to the suffering lady of the manor was a ludicrous maze built for madness and oppressive imperialism. He was the first resident of the town to step foot in these parts, the interior gilded and beautifully designed that were he awake and in any way prone to distraction the doctor might find himself stunned every step at the artwork adorning the beatific walls, the lush rugs on sturdy wooden board, the fine design on the ceiling a pattern detailed and flowing throughout the house. He didn't miss a step in his march to the chambers of Lauren Harding, finding a young woman pressing warm sponge to her forehead as she shivered and chattered her teeth under three thick blankets on a bed large enough for three or four, dead center of the room, drapes closed around most of it to keep the chill at bay.

 A fire crackled in one side and large windows looked out the other onto the sea of shacks and the land beyond, the faint light of small fires and the dawn's rise glimpsed in the blackness of the vista captured by the panes of glass. Augustine and Delphine stepped to the sick woman's bedside and he rested the back of his hand on Lauren's forehead. She mumbled and gasped and he felt the intense temperature through his extremities, he switched hands and confirmed same. He laid his hand on her chest and looked at his timepiece for a moment and then finally looked into the woman's eyes and asked how she was feeling.

Andrew Jones

    Lauren murmured and rasped a hacking cough from her throat, the Doc gently rubbed her neck and told her to breathe easy and slow as he opened a few bottles and mixed them into a glass, stirring away. He handed the concoction to Marie and laid the bottles out on the table by the porcelain waterbowl and showed the maid specifically how to mix them up every six hours, before taking the glass back and getting Lauren, laying down, to swallow the strange clear-browning medicine. She coughed and spat and choked and finally let the last drops down her throat before closing her eyes, Augustine and Marie and the other two handmaidens around placed palms on the woman and felt her heat with patience and love as they waited for further reactions. The lady fell into a sleep and Doc took out syringes, he told the help to use only if things grow worse, and laid the needles near the bottles.

    Worst thing you can do is let it fester, this infection shouldn't be, she's spent enough time out here to know to wrap up in the nights, to rest up by the fire. I don't know what y'all been up to, what she's been up to out there on her fancy new land, but you gotta keep eyes on this before it grows and cain't be rid of. Any change, you come, good or bad, don't wait, God help us all if she turns for the worst. God help everyone in this town.

    The Doc stood and slowly made exit, into the grand hallways.

He was nearing the final staircase by the door when a big man stepped out and ceased the Doc's gait. He handed over coins and asked for confidence and informed the Doc of ails beyond the house, in the shacks the men were suffering, were sick and shivering and hurting and falling into disarray. He opened the door and walked before the Doc, it wasn't threatening but the old man didn't much see to absconding, straying from the path. The shacks once low and far from the window of the lady now stood before him in firelight and early dawn, the blue-green glow of freezing sky and distant sun.

Men warming by the fires pointed towards shacks with doors closed and groans and hacking coughs and sneezes nearby as the Doc walked past and nodded to the folk immune for now from disease. He saw men in anguish from frost and shivers in the drafty shelters rushed for profit, giving what little supplies he still had in his carry, and men blackening in the extremities after fighting the chilly river for building the bridge, he made note to return to them with ash spread on their doorways whilst he saw to folk too whose insides carried knives as they relieved themselves, whose short stub between their legs were growing wart and reddening over the days. As sun basked in the sky fully Augustine had made appearance at every ailing citizen of the estate and took a moment in the brisk air to rest by a fire and breathe in the smoke and ice.

He returned to his clinic and found implements and sensory dulling supplements and passed by Kent making a show of how still he stood in the middle of the street giving view. Doc patted the lawman on the back and walked him away from the center of the road as privates on patrol passed and went into their tavern barracks for the morning.

    Do no good you get trampled by tired soldiers.

    Augustine left once more and Kent sat on the steps of the jailhouse looking across, and over to the barracks. He peered down the alley between buildings and saw the first smoke of day, the smells of meat over flame, the sound of the fat sizzling as it burned off. Kent's lips were lapped and his stomach made a growl of desire.

    Augustine lit a match and held his blade over it outside a shack marked with ash and asked a few men for assistance, they held the patient down on his bed as Augustine brought in his lightly glowing metal and fed into the man a little dose of pain relief, counting numbers down and looking into the eyes of Freddie Graham as anguish subsided and a glazed cloud fell.

    If you all need to turn fer this, I wouldn't but understand.

    They did not, the men held Freddie and like summer's churn the glowing knife slipped through the blackened flesh of the man, he yelped and twinged but it could have been much worse, they there all knew this wasn't such as times prior. The stench as the ruined extremities were removed and the smoke of flesh singed and cauterized turned the stomachs of the men more than the sight of fingers and a toe lost from their place on Graham's body did.

Well done, all you.

Doc gently wiped sweat from the boiling patient riddled with fever and wrapped the wounded regions tight, he patted the men and asked to join as he continued on, seeing to the others suffering from bite and rot. Sun was setting and men coming back from the river this day were showing signs of ill as well. A few intent to head out to the hotel and see about a fuck, despite the engorged grotesqueries of neighbors. Augustine wondered if removing a bitten penis might dispel their desires, but he took what little coin he could get from the men around and headed back to his clinic for rest and drink and a nice dose of ether to clear this day from his unsettled, overworked mind. This place, this place was not healthy.

Kent watched the Doc return and settled off to Lo Choi's for a bite to eat and as he tore through gristle and grease and found the chunks of actual food he felt mana flow through his buds. The deputy leaned on the barracks' wall and smiled at the cook as the line of folk seeking cheap and fast food grew, as men from the chilly tent offering freedom through substance scratched and slumbered their way out and into the day's bright frost, and as a couple of men in uniform left their own troop to seek individual pleasure beyond, their steps splashing on mud becoming hard on stone before falling away entirely. Kent finished his food and threw the remnants and the last of his cold coffee onto the ground and headed off to

Andrew Jones

his little place removed from the world, stopping only to listen to the first notes of Madame Westington's piano.

    The cowboys short of Ganz and Skellig came down for another evening, not at the pokerhouse but stood outside the cocktail lounge as they were denied entry by a big man giving stare to any passing by. Inside the sounds of the band played out but it wasn't much noise of dancing or shuffling or conversating, the world inside empty beyond those employed. Eagle-Eye and Reeves stayed standing before the building as the Peterson triplets walked to the alleyway and bought up food for the group. Amello and Skellig gave up waiting in the cold and headed down their old street, passing the trading post as Avery Bedford welcomed in a few stragglers, less and less in each passing night, and sat with Ganz in his house for a few hours of kinship.
    The cowboys remaining began singing to beat the band, home on the range and she'll be comin' round the mountain and ain't that cow that fine horned beast, and the big man told them to cease, told them time and again, came down to give them a towering command as they kept on, it's a street, it's for the public, they as good as any could stand and be and sing and exist.
    Cept it's not. It's Harding Street, boys.
    Kelso appeared behind the cowboys, dressed and ready for a night's drinks, his and his

men's boots on stone silenced by the singing and the music internal.

Now clear away and back to yours, no place here for your kind.

Eagle-Eye stood before his men and stepped to the richman.

We could make as much noise up there and you'd hear it wherever you find yerself, and I surely pray that place is many miles away and out of all our sights.

Harding-Grant couldn't help but chuckle.

I'd very much appreciate you giving that a try.

How you intend to remove us from this very land we helped make?

By now folk from around, from the pokerhouse and the alleyway, had come to listen to music and see to the potential fun of a little blood on the streets.

I think you know how much sway I hold here, boys.

So ain't none of us have any rights except you? All us and our hardworkin' and our long livin' and our intent to exist, don't matter to you?

Kelso stepped back from the cowboy and let his big muscle from side and from the lounge handle height and put pressure.

I intend to enjoy my night as I rightfully should, if you interfere, if anyone comes in to shatter my peace, they will pay the price.

Eagle-Eye looked beyond the big men and to the crowd of new residents.

Andrew Jones

Take a look what you done built, boys. Not so much a place to live as a man's empire what we don't get to live within. You enslaved us all.
Eagle-Eye stepped back, his own men forming a crowd as the men of the street stared at the big fellas of Harding-Grant's employ and shuffled forward with anger. A whistle from the bouncer and within seconds several men in uniform filed through the alleyway and, rifles in hand, stood before the crowd and began breaking them up. The cowboys stepped back from stone to dirt and away from the lanternlight as the men angrily yelled between pushes and stepped further down the street from the lounge. The band played on.

The whistle blew and a few stragglers long of beard and hair stepped off the train, finding favor in the fort's offerings of food, drink, water and humanity, the engine itself preparing for the journey east and north to the colder climes. Maxwell and Thomas had with them three cases each carrying everything they owned and sewed and held dear to their hearts the decades living in the wilderness and finally raising hand and heading towards the world they'd dreamed of being a part of. The shop windows still held the fine denim attire that sat unsold and unloved, somebody might one day smash and grab and make use the finely stitched hard fabric whilst working good honest to make up the thievery. The twins didn't take a second glance back that morning, they finished itemizing their homestead and checking for any memories and heirlooms that might have found their way through the boards or behind cabinets that were too heavy to make the move with them, threw their cargo on the wagon and rode on, breath visual before their redding noses in the icy air. They passed by Hazel's place, the only house they much fancied giving one last knock and hold to, but kept on. The journey up to Chicago would be a long one, likely to spend Thanksgiving and the run up to Christmas in the presence of strangers angry and bitter and tired and wasted west finding no sign of glitter and hope in the gilded lands prophesied and oversold. There were no folk looking half as dapper and outfitted as the twins, the smiles on their faces and elation in their spirits as they knew they were saying goodbye to all they had unfortunately found themselves in, making the trek to their rightful place in this planet, was not the same experience as any on board.

    These fine beasts you got here Maclaine, damn fine. Folk don't treat 'em well, get what's comin' to them down the way some, see to it they do, these creatures. Respect and love pay out in kind. How's the wagon a'comin'?

    Maclaine finished pouring oats out into feedbags and wheeled out the wagon, four wheels strong holding up the gun on a triangular three-directional stand able to pivot and reload with ease, enough space all sides to hold men and ammunition and with a little more wood provide cover from fire.

Andrew Jones

    Finishing touches left, been findin' time not lettin' the horses run out in the chill and roundin' up again, and now Miss Worthing and I ain't much to head out and spend evenings drinkin', or at home even conspirin' to imbibe, fixing this up into something stable for you was most of my times.

    Congratulations on the by and by regardin' you and Miss Worthing's impending, mighty appreciate her offering place in the party for my Liza-Beth, poor woman not seen much a connection round these parts anytime, always the wife o' the Sheriff, ain't much more than that to her to most folks.

    Kent stared at the wagon and the gun built for absolute desecration of humanity before him as the other men indulged in pleasant chit chat about life and love and hope for the future. Their voices dulled in his brain as he witnessed every inch of the weapon before him being built in secret, even to himself until now. He touched and felt the wagon and the gun and examined it closely as the other men continued inane conversating until he finally broke a voice from within.

    Ya cain't be bringin' this stuff out round here. This ain't fer people, not fer the likes of homesteaders and families, this is fer yer redskins and blackhearts, this is fer them that need to be moved on and them that refuse to ingratiate themselves prompt-like with civility and humanity like'nin we be bringin and buildin and creatin out here. This is a beast fer putin' down, not for lovin'.

The Ferryman Upon The Plains

You wheel this out and aim it, ain't no goin' back, this here's a declaration of war unto itself. We need peace, soon, to cease the men out there incitin' one-another and ourselves somethin' fierce, we need to reach out handshakes and good nature, none of the evils, none of the monster and animal in us. We're better than that, we need to be better than that.

    Colin nodded with admission of guilt, Hoxley left the stableman to see to his deputy.

    When y'all were away and fine job it was to go huntin' evil out there, they came here and saw to the chance to infect our little spot, our land beatific turned sour and rotten. Them out there, them that were here already, they all heard somethin' of a call of the wild and came a'rushin', took with them weapons and intent to destroy, and they did. They did destroy, each person they ripped from us a little more of ourselves lost too. Now look out there, look at that Harding-Grant in his castle of his own design, with his knights of the round come from all over and festerin' wounds and desired for retribution and seekin' return to their violent ways in this place, a chance for easy huntin'. The time to seek for peace was before they all came, they had no designs on togetherness and community and comin' here to work with us. They see us as bugs to crush under their feet, we ants built together a world and they want to get what they can from it and move to the next. We ain't here gonna survive this winter cold and frost and sickness and them, we have to push back, remind them they ain't the only folk out there can do what it takes to survive in this world. I hate this, Lord knows I hate this, ain't right in the eyes of Him or any of us, but there's times you fall to the goodness and graciousness of the heart and the head, and there's times you have to just let your gut and your spine take the lead. Better to have something to hold onto when the flood comes than to be washed away in the hail of bullets from folk no intent to seek peace anyhow.

    Kent paled as the Sheriff outlined his deepest motivations and thoughts of the world, he let the words hover and thought of them, Colin stood looking at the transportation of death he had worked upon, sickened but understanding the alternatives himself, accepting evil bitesize over bouldered. The three accepted the monstrosity in the heart of the stable.

    Sergeant Carthage absconded from his barracks and passed by the empty tailors shop and made his way to the door of Worthing and Maclaine and knocked. Hazel opened and smiled at the uniformed man away from his troop.

    Miss Worthing, ma'am, hope I'm not disturbing. Would like to make enquiry upon your business.

    Hazel welcomed the man in and they sat before some fabrics ready for selling as clothes and Carthage asked about some fashions for his love, for when he next gets longer time away than an hour or two, for the holidays upcoming. Hazel showed some heavier material for the temperature and they agreed on simple and easy, Carthage whilst intent on gifting his girl didn't much know beyond pretty and colorful what garments mattered and how to a lady.

 I find myself, ma'am, sometimes in the times laying on bedroll on the wood of that old building listening to the snores of the men around and the shuffles of sneaks headed to meet ladies for a brief and professional purpose and think on them as men who share air and walk same path as me, and we down here far from view of any short of the Lieutenant, and then that man Grant with the name like a leader and thinks himself one without the papers and without the time spent and without the men saved to his doing to make him such. I lay there and wonder why are we here, for the good of who? Do you as resident feel safer now, feel like you're living as free as you're right to do in this land? I feel more used than those the men go visit in the hours dark and long and cold. This feels like a place not for safe-keepin' but more for keepin' together until tinder burns out, and what's left in the ashes I do not know and am finding myself further and further without rest pondering. Them fellas up in the ways, also together a bunch like us, got it more right. Seein' to theyselves and comin' down here sometimes to cause a little ripple in the stream, blow out the flames with something akin to a ruckus. A little bloodletting stops the poison setting in.

*

 The many Chicago men led Samwell out of the room, onto a further staircase leading to a small parlor

Andrew Jones

overlooking the lake beyond, a darkness outside threatening to break into the small tower the five men inhabited.

The rifleman and the mayor sat Samwell down at a table and imposed themselves in his presence, the bishop stood in a corner and removed his scarf, a red scar across his snow white skin, he took his hat off where further scars sat atop his scalp. The bishop stared at Samwell and smiled. The Governor poured drinks for all and placed a deck of cards on the table.

We did very little in your small world, if I recall my friends here may have handled one piece of business, nothing much at all.

My son.

The Governor nodded and simply uttered an Ah. He flicked through the deck, shuffling as a distraction for his body.

Astounding how something insignificant to the many can be so potent to others.

The Governor picked out the jokers and threw them onto the table before them all.

You've come a long way, that's impressive old bones, it'd be a shame to return home empty handed I suspect.

I don't care no more, I done lost e'rythin' already, kill me like you did my Bartholomew and have done with it, don't be playin' with your hunt.

The old fella by Samwell's side took a decaying skull top rotting with use and damage and poured his glass of drink into the bone, supping at it.

I'm not interested in seeing you dead stranger, the Great Hiram's a fool like all others out there, but he finds us a decent sort every so often, and you are a specimen. I put you an offer, one of my men for you, how's that for fair?

I ain't workin' fer ya.

No, of course not, you're not the sort able to do the work we require, getting hands dirty. But my men, they've seen you in action, pushed you'll fight, in darkness you bring light. Patching up our man of God there was a hell of a job, you sliced him but good, in the parlance of your ilk. You led many a man to see to our man of the land, twenty shots ripped through his skin, his bone, his muscle, and he's still standing by some miracle, or perhaps...

The Governor put the cards back on the table.

Divine intervention.

The Governor smiled, Samwell saw himself in the bright teeth and thin squinting eyes of the big man opposite.

You want to finish a job, you can't use the tools of the layperson, you can't expect someone else to do it. You hold all you need to bring them down, you just refuse to do it.

The rifleman ripped the pearl-gripped revolver from Samwell's holster and held it aloft.

Go ahead, shoot me for all it matters.

The rifleman span the revolver in his hand and aimed it at Samwell's head, he pulled the hammer back. The Governor held his hand up and the rifleman looked over. The Governor shook his head slowly and the

Andrew Jones

rifleman slowly placed the gun on the table, putting the hammer forward gently.

One hand, you win, you go home, you lose and you see your son.

I don't play games.

Call it business, a deal. A trade, the gun for your life, if you win that is.

Take the gun, I cain't use it on no-one no-how.

The mayor supped on the skull, the bishop drank slowly from his glass, lost in the darkness of the window. The Governor stood up and pointed to his seat, the rifleman switched and sat opposite Samwell. The Governor picked up the gun and opened the barrel, he dropped the bullets onto the table, and put one back in the chamber and span it.

One hand, and this gun will go off. You don't even need to get your hands dirty unless you win. Then we'll get you on the first train out of here and back to your world. Play.

Samwell looked around the room, he wasn't shackled, but he felt the restraints closing in around him. He nodded and the Governor began dealing cards to the ferryman and the rifleman.

The pattern on the back of the first card before Samwell popped red from white card, broken up between the plain with color and shape, diamond and spade and heart and club from close up became a hypnotic spiral the harder the eyes absorbed it. The second card flew onto the first

The Ferryman Upon The Plains

and Samwell was returned from the daze, he looked at his first two dealt as the Governor continued handing back and forth the cards. A two of clubs and a seven of spades. Samwell watched the Governor as another card came over, the man wasn't looking at him or the cards or the rifleman opposite, he seemed locked on the wall to Samwell's right. He glanced over with his eyes, maintaining stillness in body. The old fella Mayor blocked a lot of view, a portrait of the Governor in white suit looked back at both Samwell and the Governor, and yet looked beyond them all. The last cards were dealt and Samwell picked them to his deck, a four of clubs, a nine of diamonds and a queen of spades. He peeked over his cards and to the rifleman opposite. The man's face still painted for performance couldn't hide a smile. The rifleman looked back over to Samwell, the ferryman averted eyes back to his shit hand and placed the two and four down, calling for two more.

    A three of hearts and a five of diamonds, Samwell looked at the Governor and the rifleman and the bishop and the mayor and put his cards down on the table, they all turned to the rifleman. He placed three cards down and pushed them to the side. The Governor slowly placed one card before him, then the next and the final. The rifleman picked them up and looked at them and placed them in his hand, and he stared towards Samwell and he stared towards the Governor, and he nodded. Samwell stared at the pearl-gripped revolver in the center of the table as he picked out cards, putting them back in his deck, and felt the bumps of the pattern on the back of the cards, he stared towards the rifleman and from afar found

Andrew Jones

a little dizzy the hypnotic spirals of the pattern, and he closed his eyes and pulled out a single card and lay it flat, face down, on the table. He picked up a new card, he removed his queen and in place got a jack of clubs.

    The Governor looked to the rifleman who shook his head and passed on, the attention came to Samwell once more. He looked at his deck, his three of hearts and seven of spades and five and nine of diamonds and jack of clubs, a whole heap of nothing transformed twice to find less than he had before. He discarded the three and the jack and received his final two cards as the rifleman passed his last go round. Samwell slowly placed them into his collection. A four of spades and a two of hearts. Samwell put the hand face-down on the table and stared at the gun and the rifleman beyond.

    Alright, men, let's see.
    Samwell turned his useless hand over.
    Nine high.
    The rifleman smiled and brushed his cards with his hands, he laid his cards down on the table before the men.
    Well, how about that.
    Samwell didn't look to the cards, only the glint in the rifleman's eye and the lack of reflection of the world back at him.
    Five jokers.
    Samwell glanced down at the announcement, the inexplicable, impossible, utterly incomprehensible announcement. Sure as

it was, the rifleman had all jokers, and had stuck with that.

The old man wins, take your prize, take your shot there.

Samwell glanced at the Governor, deck of cards still in his hands, and the Governor looked to Samwell, then the revolver.

Ain't no fair game, no way to win.

But you beat the man, do what you must.

If I win fair I'd do what I could, this ain't the way to go for nobody.

If you had to play fair all your life you'd never win old boy, some get a duff hand by default, teach them what that ends them with.

Samwell shook his head, the bishop turned to face the blackness out the window, the Governor sighed and stared at the portrait of himself, the old fella Mayor drank from his skull and sat still. The rifleman reached across the table and grabbed the revolver and looked at the single bullet in its chamber and placed it next in line and looked at Samwell and pointed the gun directly at the old man and pulled the hammer back.

Samwell stared down the blackness of the barrel, he could see himself and Anna in their kitchen holding one another and dancing gently all those months ago, the beauty and wonder of their happiness eternal rushing back to him. In a blast of light and an explosion to split the ears he felt the warmth of the gunpowder let loose.

The bishop turned back around, the Governor ceased looking at himself, the old fella Mayor still sipped on the skull. The rifleman's head was a cave of bone and blood with no face to protect the elements. The revolver's

Andrew Jones

pearl grip was all that was left in the rifleman's hand, the metal exploded in the table and the ceiling and the portrait and the glasses of drink and in the cards. The Governor looked over to Samwell.

    Man can hold his head up high if he still got it then. Get him out of my state gentlemen.

    The Mayor stood up and pulled Samwell out of his chair, the bishop waved his hands over the dead body as the Mayor and the Governor walked the ferryman out of the parlor, out of the party, out of the city.

    The train station was grandiose, built to present itself as an icon of human achievement, columns and arches and designs not for purpose but for portents, the cargo passing through was not that of others Samwell had seen, the many making their way towards the trains waiting to set off in the coming hours, to make their journeys west to riches and freedoms and the new, the world they'd heard and read and dreamt of manufactured by men in theaters and publishing houses for dimes on the dollar. The Mayor and the Governor seemed to sneak through the station with Samwell, their seats in power came with discretion amid a crowd concerned with their own imaginations than the reality around them. The men walked Samwell to a train heading to California after a long time across the land, they walked him on and sat him down in a seat reserved just for him, made for an old man to rest and eat and drink and stare at the world passing by the many days, weeks, he'd be there. The Mayor left and stood outside, looking through the window to make sure Samwell stayed until the train left. The Governor sat next to Samwell.

    Be glad you're getting out of here old boy, a place like this is a tinder box, it is powder keg and the people themselves the spark, can either go like our man tonight or like those wondrous fireworks that illuminate in summer. If you know the course of the river, you can sense the falls and the bends, but most them out there don't look too far upstream. I've seen men like you time and again, you intrigue me, enthral me. Unknowable. Unwinnable. Incorruptible. I like a challenge, but I also like to succeed. A mutual stalemate perhaps. Enjoy what you've got as long as you have it, this ride doesn't last as long as it seems. Be seein' ya, Mr. Wright.

    The Governor patted Samwell's leg and left the train as the whistle blew and a conductor ordered all aboard. The train departed and the lights and men and life fell away at the window to a darkness of night haunted by the start of the winter's sunrise orange across the land of blue. Samwell sat silent staring out the window the entire journey, as the snow and rain dried out, as the mud and tree became dust and dirt, as the elk and hawk became coyote and vulture. He looked at the road running next to the train, he saw a man atop a stagecoach riding hard, he watched an old man talking to himself, he watched a family in a wagon encircled by bandits, he saw a child alone crying for help, he saw a

Andrew Jones

horse laying and twitching as a man held a rifle to its head, and the blurs of life passing by between it all.

*

Jenny Wright screamed into the world for hours, alone. It was an abstract agony, one she was well aware the reason for and was waiting many months to suffer, but here it was and she was in bed alone when the wetness sprang between her and the mattress soiled. At dawn, Hazel rode over to check and heard the guttural violation of noise in the night, she went and awoke Doc Augustine and alerted Sheriff Hoxley for the sake of safety before heading to her friend's side and held her hand through the pains and pushes. Doc took time returning to the land of the living and gathering his effects, he watched Deputy Kent leave the jailhouse still chatting casually to the Sheriff behind him and stand in the middle of the street before he began his journey to the estate. By the time the Doc came to Jenny's room and started helping the proceedings it had been five hours of pain and the head of the future baby Wright was starting to peer through the dilation below her hips.

The sun began to shine stark and cold on the world, no rain or sleet or fog for the land today, it was a direct connection between the dirt and the sky beyond, the universe threaded perfectly to witness the birth of the next generation of Wright. Colin Maclaine came by and offered love and positivity to his lover and her best friend in the time of great stress, he saw too much the process of childbirth in his brief time in the bedroom and staggered himself to the kitchen speechless and confused. For all the horses he'd reared and brought about, the distance of nature and biology compared to humans, compared to the womenfolk he'd loved and been intimate with, witnessing the natural cycle befall one broke a little of his brain in that moment. He found the wine and took a little cup for himself.

Doc and Hazel proved partners in aiding Jenny's frustrations and pains through the crowning and the long struggles pushing the baby through and into the world, the bloody mess the mattress was in became a warm and comfortable welcome to the world for the baby covered in red and blue blobs gooey and wet. Doc wrapped the cord around his finger and held the baby aloft as the placenta made its exit and he slit the connection, the child's first gurgles and cries were set in motion and Hazel wiped forehead of mother and child before helping the baby into Jenny's tired arms, cuddling for the first time external. Jenny had a look and discovered what child she had brought into the world, she smiled.

That's his name. Willie Wright.

Jenny and Willie rested, Doc oversaw them, sitting in the chair opposite and resting. Hazel came to see Colin and held him tight, he was gathering himself still and split the wine with his beloved. Lars Skellig walked Herman Ganz into the house, the old farmer gaunt and pale compared to his summer glow, but he insisted on coming

Andrew Jones

to see and share the good times. Colin and Hazel tried best to hide their sadness at the withered state of Mr. Ganz as they helped Lars walk him to see the baby, and the sleeping mother in her wondrous glow. Doc took a look at the old man and asked if he could give him a once over. Ganz stubbornly insisted he was fine, he was more than fine, now there was something worth fighting for. He kissed the babe and mother gently on the forehead and walked out, sitting at the dining table haphazardly, the folk caring for him struggling to keep the old man's pace as he escaped the clutches of the Doc's gaze.

    I still remember when the others came. Bartholomew and Noah, and Noah's li'l babe too. What magic a baby brings, from two can come one so pure, it focuses the world, colliding creating something unique and special, and all turn their heads to see to the baby, make the world right for the baby, so he can grow good and make a world for his own, who can bring better for his own. We each our little step make better the next. Clear the path and ease the pain. We go through so much and learn from it, just want the mistakes to be known without lived the next time. The more they learn early, the more they discover later. The magic a baby brings.

    Hazel and Colin held hands tight, they remained silent on their bigger news, they to everyone were just whirlwind in love and needed to bring the year to a close with their declarations.

The Ferryman Upon The Plains

Not even Lars was aware of the little thing in Hazel Worthing made of the love of these two souls. Willie Wright would have his day in the sun before anyone needed know of the Maclaine-Worthing kiddo. Lars helped Herman up as the old man insisted on going to see Anna and get her over. They left the house and in the chill knocked and slowly entered the house, hearing no weeping, seeing no light, feeling no warmth. Herman pushed Lars away and slowly walked through the house and to the bedroom door on his own, the Swede watched from the front doorway, he could not hear the old man as he hushed direct to the figure beyond he envisioned was still there, was still a part of the world.

    It's a boy, Anna, lovely. You're once again a grandmother good and true. A beautiful boy, he is. Eyes of his pa, eyes of his grandpa, those sparks that glint and shine and see beyond the here and the now, see into the heart and soul of a man. Little Willie Wright, he lies there in bed with his mama now, warm and cosy and healthy and ready to live. Just open this door and come and see the world before us to make his beautiful and the last of ours with purpose once again. All ya gotta do is rip this wood off its block and expose the air to your warmth and glow and the world will be at peace around you. One little pull and everything can change. Join us, we're all here wantin' to welcome you back. Come see your li'l Willie. Come Spring and the flowers'll rise taller than him and you'll show him how this world works, and how he can work with it. He'll hold dear until his last the time spent with you, what it means. The moments, the little moments shared, the looks and smiles, the laughs and tears, holding

Andrew Jones

hands and hugging close, or even the wave across the street, it all adds up. I might not see much comin' but I surely hope he sees you some before life seeks its end among our generation true. Lead him into the next years as you did your own, hold him close and watch him learn, see him become his own, echoes of you and yours loud and anew in him, the eyes of Samwell and the heart of Anna and the smile of Bartholomew and the freckles of Jenny, they lay right there next door in bed right now waiting to start their journey. Lead him until he's ready, and watch over him even after, forever. It's your duty as matriarch, and your luxury as family.

  Herman waited a few minutes and shuffled back to Lars and left the estate to return to the farm, his bed, and rested up. He wouldn't find the energy to leave the bed ever again.

*

  The stableman and the Swede met in the frosty evening haze, the pig farmer fresh from washing his muck of a day off, the horse breeder bathed in the house he shared with his nearly wife, wearing semi-respectable attire for an evening beyond animal husbandry, nothing like a suit or Sunday best, but they had intention to respect the old widow and offer their best selves somewhat when they walked up her little pathway and knocked on the door and waited for her to open.

Madam Westington wasn't much for effort, she wore a nice enough dress to walk around the house and maybe step outside for a brief chat, but it wasn't the formality of the men, not that any cared, they could have all arrived and worn longjohns and nightgowns and had be it some slumbering party like children now grown.

    Two bottles of bourbon were waiting to share, she had dusted off the glasses sitting prone for months since she last had visitors.

    We hear you playin' out there sometime, folk stop all what they's doin' come to listen and together stand watchin' the house I don't know hopin' to see ya or maybe they just wish to face the music.

    Heck, I don't play for nobody but my own.

    That's what they love, it's a gift for all, comin' from place of purpose, of singular desire. Ain't about makin' folk happy, just happenstance your joy infectious.

    Ain't it always. Someone makes beautiful music and it inspires, someone makes beautiful love and it inspires. And sometimes ain't about what you make, it's just bein' there and bein' the best kind of person is all that ever need be.

    The old widow held hands with Colin and Lars and smiled richly. She poured out drinks and began playing for them. The two men found voice in the drawing room of their good old friend and together the three spent the night drinking and singing and dancing and laughing, the hangover would have to fight lost voice and exhaustion for pride of place come the sun's return.

Andrew Jones

    Hazel had left Colin to bathe and set off to see her best friend rested with child, poor Jenny had been dealing with crying and shitting and vomiting and tough time taking the tit, but Willie had settled into a nice nap by the time Hazel had come to the door. She did spend a few minutes listening to the screams quiet outside before daring to gently tap and open the front door, she was gonna deal with this stuff herself soon, to have to handle another's child right now seemed too much to cope with. Sometimes it's nice to find peace and quiet. Something Jenny Wright had just found when her best friend came in, smiling and warm for a big hug and a watch over the peaceful angel asleep, not the demanding devil when awake.

    The women held hands and sat at the dining table, overlooking the bedroom but far enough away to be present with one-another as adults.

    He is cute.

    I know. For all the mess and the stress, he's my beautiful boy.

    How much do you resent the waking and the screaming?

    In all honesty, in this space right now, havin' someone else with me is all I could ever dream of. Ain't nothin' that kid could do make me feel any less. The moments of tiredness and I just get to a wantin' to give up and I look at him and I see Bartholomew lookin' back and I see that smile,

The Ferryman Upon The Plains

I don't know if the kid's smilin' cos he knows he's loved or because his face ain't learned no control, but heck Hazel, I melt. In the coldest night I melt.

I hope I feel like that when it comes.

Just human nature, that. We all meant to feel right to them, love them forever and no matter what. Everyone deserves love from the get go. You as well as I seen the life removed of it, ain't gonna let that be the case for them.

Undo the mess that came before.

As much as we can, hold back the mess fore it comes crashin' through. We keep the mess at bay and let them carry on cleaner.

They laid with the child and rested, Hazel and her baby barely growing, Willie Wright asleep after another day on this planet and lovely Jenny mother of all, caring for them all, being held by love and hope.

FIFTEEN

IT WAS NIGHT WHEN the train came into Fort Oak and he joined a small group leaving the carriage and stood in the center of the military base's station, the warmth of the world wrapping up compared to the brutality of Chicago. People exiting the train basked in the brisk but comfortably autumnal-feeling air from their experiences, to Samwell and his withered frame this was the cold he knew to be at its lowest around these parts. He watched his huffs exit into the air beyond and embraced his coat for shelter as others passed by seeking food and trinkets and souvenirs and conversations with locals, others hopped onto coaches and wagons and horses with family or friends or staff waiting for their arrival. Nobody knew Samwell Wright was coming back, was ever coming back, and not now. He stood in his coat covering his lost mass, his hair thinned and less than ever before, his cheeks lost to a gaunt jawline wishing for sustenance, a feast beyond simple survival. He stepped away from the train, his journey nearly complete, he would have to take the last of it on his boots once more. There was no horse to ride, no wagon to sit upon, no person to welcome him.

The Ferryman Upon The Plains

The hour on horse was nearer three on foot, for Samwell against the wind shuffling his long-aching body desperate for warmth and comfort and home it seemed an age in the dark, but he was never lost from his direction, something innate in his gut, his heart, drawing him towards Cranham until the lights of the Harding-Grant estate appeared on the horizon. The garish, grand mansion blocking the world with its impossible existence drew him closer, the old man wincing at the vision of destructive change in the world he knew, and he began taking shape the shacks on the land reaching out towards him, Cranham's expansion lit by campfires and orchestrated in groans and coughs and suffering of strangers in a land lost to all.

He passed on by the mass of strangers struggling in their ramshackle shelters and the agonizing building for the elite that befitted the city he escaped from not the land he founded decades ago. In the quiet he was sought by the siren of piano playing in the distance, up at the old widow's place a joyful tune complete with three-part harmony made of drunk self-confidence that stopped him to stare and listen and appreciate, there was still something unchanged in the place he once lived. Bawdy songs of vulgar intent and gleeful humor, more suited to the tavern than the church, but in the privacy of the widow's boardinghouse a little inspiring hope that in the darkest and coldest there was warmth still. He stood among several stragglers, strangers drawn to the music who turned to see the ferryman and if they ever knew him didn't see the figure before as one and the same.

Andrew Jones

    Samwell wandered off as the crowd dispersed for sleep and shelter from the cold, he looked at the glow of Harding Street, the stone road from dirt he had well worn for years, the oddity of such sudden shift before him, the illuminated gargantuan difference from all Cranham was, yet its silence and stillness kept the old man from inspecting what occurred, he shunned the abnormality and headed towards his home true. On top the hill by the church Father Langston walked the grounds with a lantern, he nodded to the man of the cloth and saw no reaction, in the darkness below he was shrouded and removed from all he ever was and knew. Samwell a ghost wandering the plains. He turned to the old road and saw mostly what he always knew. The trading post closed, the tailors with clothes in the window, Doc's place up ahead, the jailhouse and tavern, all the buildings still stood, even if things felt strange, an energy unlike it had been. He made his first steps on the place he felt he knew as home still.

    The thunk of his boots well worn on the dirt was muffled by the shuffling soon after of the scrape back, his feet one after the other hitting the ground hard but struggling to make the launch up for the next step, he was a mess, a husk, an old soul pulled deeper towards the Earth, gravity and weight bringing him by force down. He peered in to see Sheriff Hoxley at his desk gnawing on some food the remnants of a late dinner or an early breakfast. Men from the fort passed by and looked at the man and went on their way, into the tavern some and round down the alleys others. Hoxley caught a glimpse of the passing action and saw Samwell, not as he was but saw a stranger of no ill will passing, and he stepped up swallowing and came out to see as Samwell wandered to the tavern's barracks and walked to the entrance to see in this night the complete transformation of the building he had spent many merry nights in since his children could offer shifting duty. Another piece of the soul of the settlement ceased.

 Hoxley shuffled up behind the old man and lit his wrinkled, thinned-out face with a match as he lit two cigarettes and handed the man one.

 Good God, Mister Wright?

 Samwell looked to the Sheriff and graciously accepted the smoke.

 Sheriff. Thanking ye.

 Damn shame, this. We lost ourselves a man serving the town, then the place to commune itself.

 Olsen?

 He's up there buried on the hill.

 Place has changed these months.

 As have we all, Mister Wright. Let's get you warm and indoors, away from this.

 Hoxley led the ferryman to his office and sat him down with a nice cup of whiskey for his fortune and they smoked and warmed by the fire and the drink.

 My deputy returned, he told me some what he witnessed, what y'all been through.

Your men were honorable, they were as good companions as could ask fer. Stayed with me long as they could. More than my boy, broken somethin' in there long ago, I don't know where he came to and left fer. Ain't returned here has he?

Hoxley shook his head slowly and solemnly.

I wish I could tell you Deputy Ransom was on his path back too. Thick and thin he were there, through so much.

I see.

He did you proud, even if he weren't behind the badge at the end.

The badge, Mister Wright, is a symbol, folk like us did what we had to without one for a long time, just our nature. Was it an honorable death?

Samwell looked at the Sheriff and in the silence from those words recalled the quarry and the albino and the crucifix and the false doctor and the yelps of agonizing pain and the deconstruction and desecration of the deputy by his side.

He did his duty to the end.

Samwell gulped down the warm alcohol and finished his cigarette in one long breath and kindly stood and took his leave. Hoxley implored the man to stay but he shuffled onward into the dark of the night, leaving Hoxley to his own self. He looked upon Doc Augustine's place and considered a brief look-see if his old friend were indeed in residence this night, but the liquor and the cold and the journey and the strange new world hit hard and he turned and walked towards his home, the darkness enveloped once more, the old man of thinning frame and thick coat waded through the world and returned to the nethers of the land beyond light.

    Bedford sat on guard in the trading post, waiting for someone to come and share the night, a drink and a game and a conversation, something. Fewer and fewer and somenights never now the world outside came to find respite and community in the hallowed halls of Harding-Grant's warehouse and Avery Bedford did his duty best he could, just existing was all he needed to do, somenights though even that felt exhausting. A couple of taps on the wood led Avery to open the door and look out at several men neighbors of his shack seeking something, he welcomed them in and more followed swiftly, keeping the door open long in the cold and letting the heat escape. The men came many and grabbed up bottles and bottles of drink and Avery clutched at the swag as they attempted to steal more than the allotment and as he reached for bottles men began pulling back, fighting off the big man in bulk. Bedford though big was soft, the many shards of glass and sharpened rocks that made their way into his gut penetrated with ease, he was a human pin cushion within seconds and the residents of Cranham tore the big man to pieces as they imbibed and tore apart crates, boxes, stealing items they could find, and in the last light of night Bedford saw the men find the crate in the recesses of the trading post, covered by shadow, and began taking sticks of dynamite for themselves. Avery Bedford bled out and drowned in his own guts on the cold

Andrew Jones

dirt floor as the men his neighbors absconded and left him alone in silence and emptiness.

    The small patrol lightly clattering boots upon stone of Harding Street's cold, lit, empty night atmosphere gave oversight to the nothing passing by and the limited life hidden within the hotel and the bank guard duty and the cocktail lounge unused, and with it the thoughts of Sergeant Carthage surrounded by three men of lower rank took flight. They had walked this and the dirt road parallel many times in the months since stationing post in the disused tavern building and with it had seen temperature drop and tension rise and the threat of men once working for and now deeply in debt to the man responsible for all surrounding them, for getting uniforms like themselves here full time. The bonds of servitude of all at different pressures. Carthage's fellow patrolmen gripped their rifles in the cold grasp of night and winter and walked on.
    A shatter, a break in the nightdreams of the men and their job, and several smaller crashes as glass fell and broke more on impact with the ground, and turning to face the noise's direction Carthage saw men kicking and bending down and gripping the ground, the road, and picking out stones of the floor and throwing them towards the barely-restored bank, and the supplies and the haberdashery, and the hotel, and the cocktail lounge and the doorman big. Pelted with rock and

stone the buildings stood but their facades found holes as the crowd rallied and ripped apart the street. Carthage watched taking no matter in his own hands, the privates around pointed rifles and yelled out to the gathered masses showing force and demanded ceasing, moving on, peace or else. A stone came towards the mouthiest private and the shot of rifle blasted on impact.

    Ringing of the gunfire heated the world and many men dispersed instantaneously, others threw more rocks at the patrol before scattering from aim and into the darkness beyond. The privates gave chase to the unarmed citizens of the town. Carthage stood in the torn-up street between battered buildings alone, holding his gun loosely and chilly in the breeze of the winter night. More shots rang out and yelling of pain and vulgarities aimed at those holding weapons upon them, sight unseen. Uniforms burst from the alleyway, pelted with rocks as they passed and confused in the mayhem, looking to the Sergeant staying stationary and headed out to the direction of noise beyond the blackness. Carthage laid down his rifle and walked up the street and listened to the piano of the Westington boardinghouse for a brief respite before walking slowly into the country, to his Lucy and ride away from the mess, from authority, from orders, from the stranglehold of those seeking absolute domination.

    Samwell slowly saw his houses come in through the darkness, the briefest flickering of lamps keeping life in the expanse of the plains as the sounds of the roaring river erupted around, an ovation upon his homecoming. The house of his eldest son stood with light inside, the

Andrew Jones

house of his youngest and the house he shared with his soulmate dark beyond the external luminance. He stood between the homes he had once worked to erect and craft life in a world unfounded and listened to the silence of family there and gone, the river near enough to carry over in the atmosphere moisture and sound, the wind helping it reach the ferryman it hadn't seen in months. Trembling, Samwell Wright opened the door to his house and made first steps on the familiar boards as they creaked and clattered under his heel. He called for his beloved Anna to no answer and stepped deeper in, he walked to the closed door of their bedroom and slowly opened up more dark beyond and saw in shadow and silhouette against the endless night what amounted now to Anna Wright in isolation of grief and lost to the world moved on beyond her.

  Anna. My love.

  The figure turned from the window where she had stood seemingly forever looking for the return of meaning and Samwell struck a match and lit a candle, he could then bare witness the lost, sagging, wrinkled love of his life who had spent so long unable to weep anymore, unable to sleep anymore, staring. She looked upon the wrinkled husk of muscle-less, fat-less old skin and bones and wispy thinned hair that was once the one she before God agreed to love till death do they part. Samwell offered a smile in the agony, his lips barely lifted upward from the weight of all carried, and stepped towards her. Anna was still as he wrapped his arms around her tiny frame and kissed gently on her cheek his dry lips and jowls of wasting. Anna Wright said nothing and her eyes did not focus on the man before her, she instead stepped forward, the grip of Samwell falling away in her movement, and left the bedroom for the first time in many seasons. Samwell turned and watched his wife leave the glow of flame, into the darkness of the room beyond, hearing tiny feet tapping on the wood below, furthering in distance until the river's scream overtook the pitter-patter. Samwell took the candle and followed.

Mother, what are we doing? You'll catch yer death a cold.

Anna walked on and Samwell followed, trying to bring the daze to an end, his beloved in light nightwear caught in the frosty wind-grip and flapping as she walked against the elements, towards the call of the river. Samwell followed on and the candle blew out as he scuffed his boots and struggled to match pace in wind and old age. He could barely make out his wife in the darkness of the land beyond as the river's screams increased to fever pitch.

The empty land once grazing for horse and many wildlife lay barely before the ferryman as he tried best to follow his beloved beyond him. The sound of animals racing past and the wind of sudden riders flew Samwell's hair up and shook his soul, he could not see what was moving but clear enough were his other senses to recognize outwardly more than he and his own out there

Andrew Jones

on the land. Laughs mocking and nefarious came and went and soon enough the rush gave way to silence and stillness and only the water beyond to call him over.

In the distance, in the inky blackness, amid the roar of rushing water, a man appeared atop a horse large in the world, floating, moving across the water with a lantern lit just enough to show his forward path and body of man and steed both. Red he was, dripping at least, hurt and wounded or worse with machinations of further. Planks of wood below blinked in and out of existence in the swaying light. Samwell couldn't make much of the rider somehow fording the river above the surface. He could, though, witness his beloved as she in her light cloth cover walk towards the figure, slowly drawn as he towards her, raising up above the land onto the crossing magiced before them, over the river Samwell knew better than any alive. He tried to call out to Anna Wright in her dazed state but his voice hushed from exhaustion and suffering and low under the noise of the water crashing fast downstream and passing all swiftly. He could do little more than stand and witness as the horse moved slowly and the man stared down as Anna Wright headed towards the man and the animal and the light, slipping on the wet wood below but never breaking stride, always forward, always closer.

The Ferryman Upon The Plains

    She stood in front of the man and his grand horse and he leaned in to her and whispered in her ear and in the light he was seen clearer by the old man's struggling eyes than ever before. Scarred and wrinkled and dirty and bearded, but behind all those he shared the face of the man Governor of Chicago, sure. Twins, long lost. The man finished his brief secret intercourse and kissed Anna Wright's cheek with red lips before he leaned out of the light. He looked directly to Samwell in the dark by the banks of the river and smiled a shine that sickened the stomach of Samwell Wright. He sat on his saddle and the two stayed in place watching Anna Wright in her nightgown blowing in the breeze and awash by river foam splashing on the bridge boards. She took one look to the darkness of Samwell's space in the universe and seemed to see beyond him, before she closed her eyes fully to the world and stepped towards the edge of the bridge.

    Her splash through the surface of the freezing water running rapid was lost quickly from the screams of the tide flowing onwards and forever. Samwell moved his hand instinctively to his hip and his holster and gripped the air where once his pearl revolver sat waiting. He stood empty staring at the man on the horse and the space his soulmate last stood, now swiftly occupied by water and freezing air without remorse or condolence. The man on the horse continued slowly on the bridge, the horse careful on every tread as the boards proved slippery. The light flickered as the wind caught it, the shadows falling all upon the land.

    Samwell stepped onto the first board of the bridge and found his scuffed boot slip off, he caught himself in

Andrew Jones

balance on the bankside and tried again. His boot couldn't find purchase upon the wood wet by the river and busted by sudden heavy use and slipped again, he watched the flickering shadow of man and beast in the middle of the river many feet away still slowly encroaching and looked upriver and down. Samwell shuffled himself downriver on the bank and in darkness found the poles he once planted, and the stool still sat waiting and beyond it knew the ferry lapping at the rapid flow of the river still above the surface. He could see the man and horse floating above it all beyond, close enough to make detail but far enough away still, coming ever closer and over.

    Samwell struck a match and lit the lantern on the post, the light closed from the elements behind glass, swaying in the breeze as a whole, shadows of Samwell and the post falling onto the waves as they passed by so suddenly below. He picked up his stool and flexed the limits of his husked and withered muscles and the pristine seat that stayed the same for decades, immaculately crafted by the ferryman, broke apart with seeming ease, exhaustion from Samwell unseen in the dim flowing light of the lantern. He dipped a leg onto the firelight and watched it blaze, grabbing the other parts now deconstructed and lit them from the first leg's burn and rushed to the bridge, rolling the wood onto the bridge's boards and despite the cold and wet they sat glowing and began eating into the wooden slats above the river, a

The Ferryman Upon The Plains

consumption across the water's surface eating away from bankside.

    The fire grew and made its way to the man and the horse, faster than they to the bankside. The glare and the heat and the thunderous roar against the river and the chill of the night began to spook the horse, neighing and slipping hoof on the wood below as it grew hotter and remained slippery. A few flames blew large before and began to circle the animal and its rider and in the heat the horse whinnied and bucked up and shook around. The man not governor but of kin tried to settle his beast with hand on its head and back and as the horse continued to spook he stepped off the horse and broke its neck with his large hands, tossing the beast upon the flames as it withered and gurgled and struggled to breathe. Agonizing in its final moments. The man continued on by foot, his steps clattering onto the boards burning and splintering under him.

    Samwell backed away and returned to his post, seeing the mess in the distance, and gripped the pole whose rope kept tethering the ferry to the guide across the river, he took the last strength he knew he had and pulled the rope out of the ground and out of the wooden pole's hold. Samwell picked his punting oar up from the ground where it lay dormant a while now and stepped onto his ferry platform, unmooring with haste he began pushing his platform untethered to all against the tide of the fast-flowing river.

    The water careening against him, splashing him with horrendous chill, he pushed and rowed further out and upriver holding the rope, with one arm rowing the

Andrew Jones

other began tying a knot ready to throw. The man waded through flame and Samwell pushed hard as he could against the rapid tide and neared enough the bridge to see it melt and burn under the steps of the unstoppable soul. Samwell began in his right arm a motion circling in the air the rope, the whoosh of air as it passed pushing away sound of river roar and scream of flame. He let go of the lasso and it flew into the darkness of the cold air.

    The rope came down by the man's shoe and fell into the river. Samwell's ferry fell onto the river tide and he pulled the rope back as he struggled to keep platform upriver and close to the man he wished to grab. He drew the rope close again, wet and cold now, and began another throw. He pushed a little harder on his oar and it began to snap in the force of man and water, the splinters splashing into the waves as they smashed on the wood platform. Samwell began to slow his push, the oar splitting, his ferry falling away from the bridge as the man continued on, closer and closer to riverbank. Samwell whooshed and circled and moved his arm and rope with it as the sound passed his ear every second swift. He let go and the drops of water fell upon his balding head, freezing into his scalp.

    The rope fell upon the man's head and Samwell pulled tight, gripping the neck of the man in the flames in the distance as the ferry fell further downriver. The wetness a coating against the fire, Samwell pulled the rope and the man

The Ferryman Upon The Plains

gripped back, his composure suddenly ripped from him, he gasped and coughed in reaction to his neck's pressure. Samwell saw the light of the lantern on the bank closing in and threw the rope he held upward, catching it as the ferry flowed on, the untethered rope that ran low on the river towards the other side now tied over the wire rope guiding beyond and above where bird often made sitting in the warm summer days of yore.

Samwell pulled the rope tight and watched the man on the bridge lift of his feet as gripped hard and forced downward on the platform. He saw the lantern pass by and felt the pull of the rope against him. Samwell looked back and saw the man standing again, pulling his end of the rope gripped around his neck, fraying the end.

Samwell found the tug of the man strong and with his emaciated self struggling to find the last strength in his core, he pulled with all and fell back to the wood below as it fell further from river's edge. Samwell felt hands burning against the rope as he pulled hard and the grip ripped through his palms. He yelped but the pain was covered by the river's screams.

The rope pulled Samwell up and off the ferry, he looked back as he flew into the cold air and saw the man in the flaming bridge pulling all his might onto the burning wood, watching the rope come closer to him.

Samwell was hanging by his bleeding palms above the freezing water. He pulled himself up on the rope and began to spin the tether around his small frame and tied around his stomach and chest and reached to the guidewire above and with final pressure pulled the rope out of the ground beyond.

Andrew Jones

The splash of Samwell Wright into the river was masked like his betrothed, his red hands washed into the frost and chill of the flowing water. Under surface he could faintly see the orange glow and silhouette of the man amid the flames in the distance. Samwell let out a gasp silent in shock of the icy water and looked at the light before, bending to the whim of the water, and felt another pull of rope.

He looked down to the darkness beyond and kicked his legs with the tide of the river. The rope came with him, the man above surface fell onto the fire. Samwell kicked again and the light of flame began to fall away, the rope eased its tension and Samwell kicked further to the blackness beyond. He shook and shuddered and kicked once more, flowing into the frosty emptiness.

A splash above.

Samwell turned to look to the brief light and saw the man's feet dancing through the surface of the water.

Samwell felt a little limp pull once more and instinctively kicked down until darkness enveloped. In the icy domain of the river he was blueing in his thick layers unable to sustain the landscape under.

Samwell suddenly felt in the complete darkness dirt, rock, stone, mud. He reached out and gripped the wet ground and dug into the bedrock, kicking against rope pull and tide, and dug deeper. As Samwell coughed red into the blueblack water and convulsed the last gasps of heat out of his hurting body he pulled mud above him, encasing himself below his river.

    Samwell in darkness and water and the land he knew so well and loved like his own. The body of the man hanged on the ropes guiding the burnt bridge from bank to bank, frozen and burnt and rotting and soggy and in the last glow of the fire destroying the connection his smile drooped and his body blue and red and finally forever dead.

*

    The low winter sun shone bright warming the bitter air with brisk glow, Cranham and its land beyond awoke to light and hope as the wedding of Colin MacLaine and Hazel Worthing began. Hazel adorned her self-made dress in the home of Jenny and Willie Wright and rode on over with mother and son on Sally and her close companion of the stable, stopping at the jailhouse to Liza-Beth Hoxley joining the bridal party on the final feet up to the church. Colin MacLaine arose groggy alongside Lars Skellig in the parlor of Madam Westington, the old widow had found herself rest in her bed but the men lightweights that they were collapsed with one-another overnight, and now in the bright morning clarity lamented such jubilation weighing heavy upon them. Colin helped his Swedish pal to consciousness and sent him upwards to the ranch for preparations, snuck back to the house he shared with his soon-to-be bride and checked not to catch sight of her before the ceremony, rushed a wash and a

Andrew Jones

shave and threw on the smartest wear he had and made up to the church before the party started. Father Langston was shaking from a cold night's wandering and deep bottle drowning and saw the stableman dressed up and waiting and found the potency of the winter's air in his lungs to kick him out of daze. Within the hour the widow had made out for the church looking resplendent and respectful, the cowboys led by Eagle-Eye Ellis found their Sunday best for their compatriot, eyeing as they arrived the unrest of the town beyond from noises the night prior, praying it at least wouldn't rise up to the church this day. Doc Augustine took his time to make it up the hill, another early morning seeing to sick folk rich and poor alike before coming to share, he waved to the Sheriff as he passed by and Hoxley double-stepped to walk with him upwards, leaving the town for the army and the deputy.

    Did he come by yours in the night?
    Who?
    Mr. Wright.
    He returned?
    Y'day, in the dark, thin as his oar poor thing, on foot, no sign of his younger. Lost so many out there.
    But he's returned? Did he succeed?
    He's alive, home now, resting. That's maybe all any could want anymore round here.
    I shall to see him after this, we may once more be glorious.

The Ferryman Upon The Plains

    Lars Skellig looking snappy and lanky with his blonde hair shining in the light of the sun coming in through the doorway overshadowed his muscular groom friend as they stood waiting, outside Willie Wright wailed and was bounced and coddled and fed before he and Jenny and Liza-Beth Hoxley followed Hazel Worthing in her astonishing beauty and sparkling with excitement walking in and stepping up to greet and look into the eyes of the love of her life in this land special to them all. Hazel in Colin's eyes saw herself and her friends near family as she'd known, and a warming glimmer of love and desire on the cold winter day. Colin in Hazel's eyes saw himself smiling and his friend the Swede standing by his side always, and the Father starting to welcome them all in celebration and honor of love and humanity before God. The church was full of life and cherished joy inside each soul sat and stood celebrating and partaking in the ceremony. In a blur the priest said his words and led the couple in their vows and formally announced their union and in front of the world and God and their friends as close as family Hazel and Colin MacLaine kissed gently as husband and wife for the first time, and the bastard in her belly secret now could be as welcome and pure as Willie Wright who rested in his mother's arms whilst she wept for all that had gone and now all that could come.

    The couple were led out by the cowboys and Lars and Liza-Beth Hoxley and Jenny and Willie Wright with applause and all singing We Come To Thee To Welcome God, We Come To Thee And See Your Love, A Love To Last For All Of Time, In Eyes Of God And Hearts Of Thine, some tuneless and some beautiful, all together harmonious.

Andrew Jones

External of the church the party felt the warmth of love in the cold air of day and clasped hands and held one-another and all came to see the couple in passionate but honorable connection and offer personal congratulations. Amid the rejoicing and singing and laughter and love a thunderclap of explosion rang out. On the edge of the churchgrounds below the hill a fire smoky and full of embers rose in the distance. A second and third quickly followed, Harding Street was being torn asunder. Hoxley looked across, turned to his wife and kissed her and ran down the hill as more explosions came and swiftly riflefire crashed through the world.

  The cowboys stood around the wedding party and before the town, covering the innocent and the deeply in love and Eagle-Eye looked to the women and the groomsman and the baby and the older folks and told them to make haste sanctuary of the building near. The party returned to the church and the men of the farm stood outside by the door and took arms hidden for the ceremony, Lars watched his best friend join his own family now and stood instead with the men of the land. The cowboys held firm the ground of God listening to judgment beyond and baring witness destruction abstract from the town they ever knew.

  Hoxley raced to the end of the dirt road, his deputy ran up from his own place and met looking at the stone street decimated as uniforms fired at

The Ferryman Upon The Plains

men throwing sticks of dynamite at buildings already decimated. Blood and bodies and bits of bone adorned the remaining cobbles of ground. The sheriff looked at his deputy and beckoned him off to the stable near.

In the stable of MacLaine Sheriff Hoxley took one side of the wagon and looked at his Deputy, shaken and uncertain.

Time's all we got left to do this, ain't fer us to decide good or evil, it's just the doin', the bullets'll sort out who's fer Him and who's not.

Sheriff, this ain't Godly, this ain't human, this is monstrous.

It is. And so's out there, and right now the war they wanted's here to rip through us if we let it. We have one thing to strike back and maybe stop this before it does us all in.

I cain't be a part of this no more.

Kent ripped his badge from his jacket and shoved it into Hoxley's hand and turned away, he left the door open as the bullets ripped through the air, he went to find his love in the house of the ailing woman and the man responsible for tearing the world in twain. Hoxley pushed hard and wheeled the heavy machinery out of the stable before the wagon hit a muddy dip in the road and broke.

The gun pointed diagonal towards the church hill beyond and the men firing on the busted street. Hoxley looked down the sight, at once all and nothing, and sighed. He clasped his hands and looked to the heavens and prayed forgiveness for what was about to happen and began to turn the gattling gun, the heat took summer into the cold winter of Cranham and the noise firing up roared

Andrew Jones

like a river of death spreading through. Within a minute flashing metal hot shot through the holes and towards men of the farm, the west, the fort and the town equal, they all in time looked to the Sheriff and fired at him as much as one-another.

 Inside the church the bullets pinged the walls and echoes of thunder rung through. The women huddled around the baby and Doc Augustine and Father Langston and Colin MacLaine stood before them offering protection, they closed the door to the world and heard bullets hit away at the walls, unable to make it through to God's building for the time.

 Colin came to the doorway of the church as the strange noise commenced and witnessed the slaying of many by the Sheriff and his brutal machine made solely for death. A spray flew past and the men of the farm ducked and Lars fell to the ground, reddening the dirt below, before finding himself moaning and yelling in high Swedish accent. He rolled over and the front of his face bleeding revealed more hole towards his brain, half his skull apart but connected still, barely. Reeves and Amello grabbed the man and dragged him out of harm's way, laying him on a pew as the Doc tried to bandage the wound with his own coat. Hazel tore some of her own dress off to affix the best man's head together.

 Behind the Sheriff below, silenced by the noise, men came and stabbed the lawman many times as the gun continued to stir and whir for a while, they themselves began to lift the wagon and aim with their strength, finding the heat of the metal sparking up fire on the wood surrounding it. They fired off a few rounds before the wagon burnt and began popping powder in the bullets before they could release. A crater of explosion, a bomb again in the heart of the town. Where silence should have sat after the destruction a rumble grew louder, Colin looked and closed the door fast, holding it tight.

    River's flooding.

    Thuds on the church door as uniform and man of the shack alike rushed up the hill putting anger aside for fear of life, the cowboys held the doors closed as best they could. The knocking became pushing and ramming and the doors threatened to buckle but the men held firm, outside yelling and obscenities flew and broke through the holes made from man's violence. Water trickled in.

    Outside the church stone was solid on the wave of tide crashing and flooding so high above the world, the men locked out hit by water found the frost sudden and heft of the hit pulled them from ground fast. They could survive seconds of swimming before falling prey to the frost internal. Men ran as fast down the dirt roads and clamored at the door of Harding-Grant's mansion to no help, they kicked at the door and punched and pushed, from stories high at a window a man began firing shots at invaders, their bodies stopping others getting past.

    Kelso Harding-Grant lay in bed listening to the screams and the gunfire and the rumbles of water rushing and relaxed. His wife shivered in cold, calling out for help

Andrew Jones

and coughing as her maid held the former deputy of Cranham in a quiet room unused by anybody, whispering sweet nothings amid the mayhem of the world.

    The shacks were wiped out immediately, the men inside dead within seconds. The streets of Cranham already blown up and burnt down found themselves awash and debris spread across the land, the blood wiped entirely along with the lives barely holding on before the disaster.

    In the church those that survived, the town of Cranham last, sat and stood and wept and cried, and Father Langston ushered prayer, Madam Westington held his hand and echoed his words, others joined on until the town as it was left all spoke out loud and constant a plea to God for survival, for life, for existence. The sound of water outside overwhelming the church, creaking at the sides, the baby cried out, Doc Augustine closed his eyes and saw the Cranham of older times, of Samwell and Anna Wright and their two boys lovely and sweet, of Herman Ganz and his belly laugh, of Christian Olsen quiet but kind, of Sheriff Hoxley and his deputies smiling and thanking all for peace and tolerance, of his wife holding him and warming his heart. He opened his eyes to see the last of them, beautiful in their own right, telling their own life stories, fighting the fear that could drown them at any second.

    The cold of the water trickling from the holes shook the town, they stood and stayed on pews and patched up as swiftly as they could the gaps. Lars lay covered in blood and bandage and his moaning echoed and slowed and he stopped after a while yelling and calling out in languages unknown. Colin and Hazel and Madame Westington and Doc Augustine and Father Langston and Joe Amello each took turns holding him and keeping him from falling asleep. On the second night he stared into the last burning of a candle before Jesus and blew his last breath, the darkness enveloped the world internal.

    The town such that was left stayed in the church for three days as the water stayed high on the land. On the third day they dared to open the doors and looked out at the wreckage of their land, and together knew they would have to start anew.

EPILOGUE
THE PRODIGAL SON

GERROUTTAHERE!
The yell was muffled by the ensuing blast from the farmer's rifle, it spooked the bison as much as the kids with their ropes and mischievous grins, hopping fence quickly and running out across the dusty plains as the animals kicked up dirt in clouds around their grazing land. This weren't the first and he knew too damn well it weren't to be the last, and holding his gun toward the heavens he felt it was time to do something more about things. The next morning after seeing to his herd the farmer rode out to the supply store down the way some hour and a half and told the owner as he himself dealt with customers en masse that he'd pay decent for a couple hearty and foolhard hands to take a little step towards balancing justice, any who pass through with that look in their eyes and weight in their boots were preferred. The farmer hit the local drinking hole and gave the barkeep the same wants, swapped need for need through a tipple on the house. He took to a few lean-to rest stops on the way back just for good mind and returned home to another night's vigilance.

The Ferryman Upon The Plains

Some days of waiting passed and the farmer listened to hoof and foot scuff the dirt hoping for one or two to be coming to aid, but no luck and as he sat and watched his sole existence graze and run before him in the spring warmth he felt useless, broken, as all his purpose was a joke. In the darkest, he tried to keep his eyes open and ears alert sitting in his hut but found the weight of his lids slipping them closed until a burst of groan and stomp and slamming onto the ground ripped him to waking life. He ran out with his gun and in the dark fired out a warning, and aimed then ahead. Footsteps scattered and the weak call of *wait, wait* came underfoot. The farmer glimpsed one of his beloved herd down on the ground, warming underbelly on the dirt with red and wet, and beneath it a young man flailing arms and screaming in agony of his crushed legs. The farmer aimed his gun at the kid as he begged for his life. In a moment he saw the rustler as a lost boy in peril and felt his guts twist at holding weapon to him.

Gorram you.

The farmer tied the boy's arms up and to the nearby fence and pushed the bison up enough for the kid to wriggle free and see his bloody limbs flattened. The farmer picked the broken boy up and unshackled him from the wooden fence, he walked the kid into his little shelter and tied him up proper behind doors, looking in the lamplight at the injuries.

Boy, I sure hope you got what you wanted outta them things cos you ain't steppin' foot in this world ever again.

Andrew Jones

He did what he could and made tight tourniquet for the both crushed limbs and drowned the boy with liquor until he blubbered and fell to sleep. The farmer went and got one of the cutters for slaughter and began releasing the boy's useless extremities, burning the ends as he went, filling his hut with disgusting stench of charred flesh and metal-tasting liquid. He propped the kid up on a chair and tied him secure for his own sake as well as the kid's safety and took the busted body bits out into the night, throwing them over the fence towards those that ran off. He looked at the dead animal he'd cared for so many years, gutted and wasted by rustlers unprepared to fight for their own misdeeds. It was then that the man with the pearl-grip gun astride his grand black stallion rode up and looked with his own lantern on the scene.

You the farmer that wanted hands not so clean?

The farmer nodded as he tried to push the body of his bison away from the herd. The man stepped off his horse and lent a hand, shifting the dead being from its familiars.

How's that for dirty? What got you in this mess?

Boy in there and his pals, keep runnin' up me and tryina nab my beasts from my land. This one got that kid good in his final moments, done turned the boy into a halfman with heft. He's sleepin now, when he wakes he'll see the damage he wrought and maybe he'll talk the where'bouts his gang. I hoped to see to them an end 'fore they come here and start doin' things untoward, but it's already gotten so darn far.

Y'know these animals ain't meant to be locked up and farmed like this? Meant to run free and live true on the land.

All animals can be farmed, all can be turned to food and money, if you're lookin' at somethin' free out there it's only cos nobody ain't got to it yet. How's a drop of drink do ya while we wait the kid out tell us somethin' might serve well our endeavor?

You're speakin' the kinda words I love the most.

You got any issues killin' folk?

The farmer poured a cup out and passed to the man, they drunk up.

Depends on who. I look at someone holdin' a weapon and intendin' summin, I don't blink. Sometimes though, gotta sit here in the moments fore and think on the times after, whether it's worth the cost, on my self, on the world.

Well'n, you seen what these is capable of, you think you'd be alright doin' some retributionin'?

Sir, I came from across this land and heeded yer call. When you're the kinda soul in need that the man what hands fruit by the can to folk passin' through's putting their time out seekin' to source men of action, it ain't some passin' desire or domestic dispute rollin' out into the land. I'm here to see about settlin' scores that others cain't.

Andrew Jones

    Settle away.
    They drank themselves into the sleep the kid fell upon already, and woke to the screams of the boy realizing all below his crotch was lost to foolishness. He went on for a while as the men watched and let the noise permeate the atmosphere. The kid's eyes wept with shock and horror and realization and ultimately his voice raspt and throat tore itself to hoarse gasps until he was gifted a little drink of smooth alcohol salving his internal rips and tears.
    Whatcha done ta me?
    The farmer moved his hand back to slap sense into the kid, the man with the pearl-grip gun calmly reached his hand to hold the offending back from attacking and looked at the kid in his eyes.
    You can look around the room to blame your sudden limp on but ain't nobody more at fault than thee, the farmer here's well within his right to do more and with less relief for your ills. Be thankful I'm here to keep somethin' of the peace betwixt y'all.
    You killed me, look at me, I'm a halfman, a gorram monster. Dead man walking.
    The farmer retracted his hand as he casually mocked the lack of walking of the dead man, the kid locked eyes in fury and reached across to grab the farmer but the man with the pearl-grip gun broke them apart and pushed the kid back on the chair and stood imposingly over him, staring down upon the broken boy.

The Ferryman Upon The Plains

That ain't to say I'm seekin' peaceful conclusion here by any means, I got plenty blood on my hands and what's a little drop more in the ocean? That you're alive is two-fold kid, you're lucky you got your youth still, folk my age, farmer's age, we're set in our ways, you can turn your life around and do better, make amends. You also, of course, might like to live well if you ain't hounded by the boys you done pulled the stupid with last night, and them nights many over.

I ain't tellin you bout them.

Well, here's the thing kid.

The man with the pearl-grip gun pushed the chair over a little, the kid gripped the sides hard to stop from falling.

I'm here to see to clean out the mess for the farmer here's safety and well-bein'. I'm effective and I'm ruthless and I don't stop until I've done exactly as folk want done. So if I go on out there and round up a group of kids lookin' like they've been rustlin' bison and killin' and slaughterin' and abscondin' with 'em and bring em to their retribution, and maybe a few hear me and hide and come find the farmer, and they see you and he together here, before I come to bring my final judgement they see the two o' you best of friends sharin' the house together, they lookin' to their old friend they left for dead and thinkin' they'll free you and take you to their next adventure? What they'd do to this man here ain't half what they'll do to the kid squealed. So you're already dead in myriad ways. We're just offerin' you the path without pain.

The kid relented and pointed in the direction the kids ran from the farm the many nights before, a start if

Andrew Jones

not much detail. The man with the pearl-grip gun picked the kid up from the chair and carried him out to the field, the kid pointed always to the same direction.

    You best know how to navigate then, boy, silent-like, or that pain is about to come from every angle.

    The man with the pearl-grip gun propped the kid on his magnificent stallion and tied him securely to the saddle, he hopped behind and sat uncomfortably close to the boy and looked at the farmer.

    If we don't return, get yer gun ready for what's comin'.

    I should really be ridin' up with you both after what they did.

    That's what you hired me for.

    The man with the pearl-grip gun kicked his heels and the stallion rode off from the farm, the kid held tight pointing the way. They headed into the horizon and kept on going for a while, the two atop the horse being led by a finger. It slowly turned west to south, to west, to south as the world passed by and came across a small forest breaking out of the dirt and dry, and the finger pointed towards it. The man ceased his horse's ride close by and listened to the noises of young men talking and scuttling about in the crowded woodlands. He patted the horse and the kid and tied them both to a tree trunk and headed into the woods, pearl-grip in his hand.

    He snuck through the growth, his boots finding solace in the soft grounds shaded from the sun by tall greens, and he trod slowly to listen to the increasing voices of boys scoffing at food and laughing away at memories of the fool they left the night before, got himself into this mess didn't he? The man peered from a trunk primed to hide his form as he approached and could see six boys not yet twenty around a small fire ripping apart meat still bloody. They were thin, desperate for any food, twitchy and beaten broken to uncertainty and eternal fear. The man prepared to leap out, he pulled the hammer back slowly on his gun, he could do all boys in one chamber no problem, they were close together. He stepped out and as soon as he became visual to them all, the kid on the horse started yelling in the distance *HERE HERE SOMEONE COMIN'*, they looked over and the man fired his pearl-grip hitting three swiftly before the others fled and lost themselves in the woods and trees. The man put three new bullets in his chamber and followed the first runner deeper into the shade, listening for footsteps soggy through the growth, sloshing. He dipped and ducked past every trunk, looking all angles around and carried on, dipping and ducking and following the slosh until he turned and dipped and a bullet flew into the trunk near his head and the man looked directly at the boy who was on the ground holding a revolver and shaking. The man looked at the hole meant for him and the boy holding the gun and brought his weapon up to aim.

Andrew Jones

How loyal you think your friends might be?
The man shot the kid's gun hand, it exploded in red and the gun fell to the ground, the kid screamed in pain and the man waited near his bullethole trunk, watching.

It'd be easier if they cared for you like real folk do in this land. But then you might not be the type to go stealin' from men who put in all the hard work. I seen your type before, talk all big game and act like you're nice and polite and good and when it comes to things you just band together with monsters and hide behind them, lickin' up their remains so you don't have to do nothin' and survive. But you are doin' somethin', you're helpin' destroy lives, every action has a response.

The kid never stopped screaming in pain as the man spoke his piece and when nobody else came to see, the man spat on the ground and looked at the wounded kid, shaking his head.

Sorry boy, nobody came to save ya. Greet them in the next as they deserve.

The man fired two between the boy's eyes and silenced him forever before walking through more forest, listening out for any sign of movement. It was a futile hour of hunting until he returned to the campsite and sat with the dead and their poorly cooked meal.

You still with us boy? You happy what you did? I got most of em anyway.

The Ferryman Upon The Plains

The man left the forest and looked at the kid on his horse, laughing atop the black stallion in the sun.

You think it's funny boy? I offered you kindness and you spat back at me. That offer ain't here no more.

The boy kept laughing as he shrugged and showed his arms covered in blood, dripping, sliced. He paled and shuddered as the man grabbed him and slapped to keep his consciousness.

What happened? Who did this?

I don't feel no pain now. They weren't as mean as you said they'd be. They ain't like you. My friends like me. They don't like your master though.

The kid laughed and convulsed and laughed and spat blood and laughed until he died in the man's arms. He put the kid gently on the ground and began riding his horse back across the land to the farmer, gun in blood-covered hand as he gripped the reins and kicked his heels hard. He ran across the land fast, the man covered in liquid saw red in the sun's basking glow of afternoon heat. As he approached the field and listened to the herd of bison moaning low he heard the single shot of a gun rip through the land and rode faster, leaping from his horse and heading to the farmer's hut. Smoke fogged the building and the heat of the weapon's discharge sweated every pore, the man looked as best he could through the mess and saw a boy splattered onto the wall dripping in red, his stomach lining the ground now, opposite he could make out the farmer with a knife on his neck and a boy peering back at him, locking eyes.

Drop yer gun old man or the farmer's history.

Andrew Jones

The farmer's gun was lying on the ground still smoking, the knife pressed into his neck made him flinch through his wrinkles and blood dripped from the light wound.

Shoot the kid, don't give a second thought to me.

You ain't even gonna let the fella free. If you did, I 'd just shoot you then, how you gonna get out of this?

I don't need to get outta this. You shouldn't have messed yerself with all us.

The man let the pearl-grip fall from his hand, hanging the trigger guard on his finger, loose.

I tend to do that, works out well for me, clearly.

He killed my friends, he took all from me, this is only fair.

The man shook his head and backed to the door of the hut.

Ain't no thing as fair in this life kid, just what we do and what happens afterwards. Think about the next moment and how you'd like to get there.

Through you both if I have to.

The man stepped out, illuminated by the sunlight, the gun loose still in his hand.

That's a shame, I saw a different ending for all us. So be it.

The man swung the gun around and it began flickering light into the eyes of the kid,

The Ferryman Upon The Plains

direct bright white into his squint in the dark, the kid yelped in pain and winced as he closed his eyes. The farmer felt release of pressure on his neck and pulled away from the kid. The man gripped the pearl of his gun and fired a bullet, it went right into the kid's eye, exploding the house with more red. The kid dropped to the ground gripping his knife, by the shotgun that stopped smoking. The farmer stepped out and looked at the day with the bison around on his farm still.

    That them all?

    That's them all.

    Boys, just boys.

    Boys are men waitin' to grow up, they can still do damage, it ain't playtime, they knew the rules and broke them and got what they got.

    What now?

    Don't see anyone else comin' by to mess with you after this, sends a message long and far. Maybe think about freein' those that shouldn't be kept like this. We all deserve a chance to roam free.

    Thank you.

    The farmer tried to hand the man money but he shook his head and shook the man's hand and hopped atop his horse and rode into the setting sun, for whoever might need help next as the farmer looked after his herd and cleaned up the mess left by the rustlers.

*

Andrew Jones

He leaned on the bar and watched the barman pour brown liquid into his glass, taking his coin placed by the drink and leaving him in peace. The leaning man clutching his hat brim and the bar's wood to keep the world together. He supped at the cup of warm whiskey and gasped at its comfort and joy, and dropped another coin for his next fix. He'd been there for hours just plying his throat with juice, as people came and went, talked kindly to the barkeep or sometimes angry, demanding speedy service with a smile. Folk who came in groups mostly took to the acting like they deserve such service whereas the loners were casual and weren't about to get caught short in a bar in the middle of nowhere away from the world's eyes. This was a place to go missing in, nobody would find you, nobody'd know where to look. He leaned on the bar not looking.

"Here for a good time?"

The man looked over his shoulder, a weedy figure of nervy energy wiped his sweaty brow and breathed his disgustingly minty breath.

"Just here for the drink."

"Place ain't known for its whiskey."

"Place ain't known, that's for good reason, right?"

The thin man smiled and gasped a little chuckle.

"You're more than welcome to keep us in business a couple coins at a time, but maybe you fancy samplin' some of the delights not on most menus."

The man turned for the first time in hours and looked at the nervy fella, he raised an eyebrow to the offer. The awkward propositionist waved a hand and two large men came over.

"You'll have to forfeit your weapons, of course. Cain't be havin' nothin' go untoward in our house of luxuries."

"There's a house full of 'em?"

The man took hands to the man and felt his ankles for hidden guns, and his pockets. The man took his pearl grip gun from its holster and handed it.

"Only got the one on me, never much needed more to do its job. I best see it back in as good condition though."

The nervy man grabbed the customer and walked him from the bar, the heavy fellas followed, pocketing his gun. They left the back entrance and found themselves in the nighttime in a courtyard dark and dank, he led the man up stairs as the two heavies sat in the middle of the yard and stayed watch.

"Don't you worry about nothin', we'll have you and your gun out of here better than ever, you'll both shoot straighter than y'all ever done. Tell me sir, what's your pleasure?"

"I like em young."

"So do I."

"Untouched."

"As God made 'em."

"I got a desire for a native, this land is fertile, I bet they is too."

Andrew Jones

The nervy man laughed, the mint of his breath somehow sickening more than any stench. He patted the man on the back and stopped a few floors above the world, before a door.

"Well, I think I can do somethin' like that. I appreciate someone who knows what they want. Follow me."

The nervy man opened a door and beckoned the man to follow. The man took a moment to breathe before heading into the dark beyond. The door closed behind him and a candle was lit. The nervy man blew out a match and stood by a bed where a girl barely pushing her teenage years was laying, tied by rope from all limbs. The nervy man ran his thin, prickly finger on the girl's dark skin and licked his tip.

"Homegrown, pure. Ain't ever been used. Like she was waitin' for Mister Right to sidle up to the bar tonight. You are one lucky man. How about it?"

"She'll do."

The man stuck his hands in his pockets and jangled some coins. The nervy man clutched his hand on the man's arms.

"Don't you worry yet about that. Have yourself a run, we can handle business once the fun's over."

He patted the man's back and pushed him to the bed, opened the door and waved goodbye, smiling into the dark beyond. The door closed slowly and the man waited a few seconds before covering the girl up and looking at her in her near-comatose eyes.

"Wake up sweetheart, we gotta get you free. Your ma's been all over ain't had no success gettin' folk to find you, free you. What they done to you, hell, it'll unfold upon them ten times over, once we get you back to your family. These men think they can exploit y'all, get up now, we'll show them together what happens."

The girl murmured and smiled at the man as he grabbed the candle and began to burn away at the ropes, freeing her wrists and ankles and wrapped her up in the blanket, carrying her to the doorway.

He slowly opened the door and peered out, the nervy man, if he was there, hid in complete darkness. He could hear the men below talking to one-another. He pushed the door open and carried the girl out to the landing. He felt the cold metal of his own gun on his forehead and he saw the sickly smiling nervy man holding his pearl-grip and whistling. Heavy steps raced towards them.

"Man, I hoped this wasn't the case. I thought you was a good kinda weird."

The nervy man smashed the hero on the head and his men grabbed the girl before he fell to the floor, dragging her back into the room, her screams numbed from whatever she was still coasting on. The nervy man looked at the unconscious hero and spun his gun in his thin, long fingers poorly.

Andrew Jones

He was splashed with liquid warm and stinking, on the wet dirt floor of a dark room. The nervy man smiled at the bleeding fella who used to have the pearl-gripped gun and took his own member out to add to the waste cocktail thrown at the man.

"What a relief. Listen sir, thank you for your custom. We'll take good care of the gun, the money and the girl. Enjoy your stay, not like you've got anyplace else to go."

The nearby man finished himself off and walked out of the room, closing the door and locking it. Footsteps rose up and in the darkness the man covered in piss started sinking. He grabbed at the wet ground below and felt it break easy underhand, he dug a little as the blood on his head returned, blinding him. He yelped and gagged on the wet still around his mouth and sunk into the ground. He pushed out of the mess and with it he took chunks of dirt flying, kicking and scratching up the ground before it could take him.

He swam across the room in the wet mud and urine, kicking up clumps and rocks and heavier things that he didn't want to look upon, the darkness a gift in hiding what and who he knew would be there. He reached the entranceway and what steady footing there was. Climbing up and coughing up his strain and the mess he swallowed, he thought on the knowledge that he was definitely not the first to be locked down here, but he would thus be the first to break free. He stood on the small wood walkway and put his back to the door itself. He breathed in a little before the fumes of human disgrace knocked him out and pushed hard on the door, it budged enough to compel the man to try again, and again, and after five hits he burst the door off its frame and he began treading his piss and shit covered clothes up the stairs, squelching quietly each step stinking higher and higher to the heavens.

    He peeked out at the top of the stairs and saw the courtyard beyond, the man and his heavies laughed in the middle of things waiting for another customer. The nervy man span the pearl grip revolver around playfully as the two heavies counted coins from the man's pockets, in stealing his goods they took away his jingle jangle, no weapon but no noise now. The man looked around nearby for something to use, then felt his pockets empty, but full of muck. He gripped the mess and turned it into a ball and threw it across the yard. The men all turned to the noise and the nervy man nodded to the men.

    "Go, go see."

    The others went off to have a look as the nervy man played with the gun still. The man darted up and covered in mess was shrouded in darkness, he stood behind the nervy man and clutched him by the mouth, his shit fingers smearing on the man's nose, sickening him. He let the gun loose and the man got his weapon back.

    "If I make a noise, how many of you is there to handle?"

    Through gagging the nervy man laughed.

    "Take one out, five come to replace, this business don't end with you and me here tonight buddy."

Andrew Jones

"I know where this ends, don't you worry."

He smacked the nervy man in the head with his gun and patted around the fella, sure enough there was a blade in his ankle and the man took it out, hiding back in the shadows as the men came to find their boss knocked up and covered in shit.

"Gorram!"

One of them ran down to check the room of mess, the other looked around and as he scoured the darkness the man covered in mess slashed the heavy man's throat and let him gurgle his last to the night sky. The man wiped the blade on his coat of shit and stood at the top of the stairway, the man went to look at the mess saw him casting shadow over him and ran upstairs shoulder-first. The man planted his knife in the shoulder but was knocked down hard. The heavy fella ripped the knife from his shoulder and branded it to the shit-covered hero.

"You had an easy way out and now you're in for a horrible one."

The hero got to his knees and felt the rush of the blade by his face, slicing hair and skin, he fell to his back and kicked out, hitting the knee of the big man. He tumbled and the man rolled over, gripping the knife in his hand, wrestling it out as they rolled in blood and the smell of shit overpowered them both.

They rolled down the stairs, hitting each step and smashing their hands failing to get grip of the blade. The heavy man landed on the shit-covered fella on the final step and smashed him down. He held the knife up and prepared for a good final blow, the man looked up at the man covering the light with his heft, and reached back, into the messy room, and grabbed shit. He splattered the man with waste and he coughed, spat, swore and dropped the knife in the mess. The man grabbed the blade and stabbed the heavy man several times in the side, releasing blood into the world, and freeing him from the pressure of the heavy man's weight. He rolled the gagging, suffocating man off him and picked himself up, looking down at the struggling beast. He dragged the man into the room and pushed his head into the mess, holding him there by his boot underground. He watched as the man struggled and waved his hands and spluttered and stopped moving.

    The man returned up the stairs and picked up the nervy man's unconscious body, light as the girl, and walked upstairs to the room she was found in. They had retied her, but with the man's bloody and shit-covered blade he swiftly freed her properly. The nervy man came to at the smell of shit and the scream of the girl shocked at all coming for her.

    "You ain't gettin' outta here alive, either o'you."

    "We're all gettin' out, she with her dignity, more than either us can have. Where's her clothes?"

    The nervy man spat and the hero put his shit fingers under the man's nose and made him gag until he told her. The three walked a floor further into the sky to the top room of the court, there from the stairs could be seen the whole town, asleep at night, unaware of any gone on. Sure enough in the room there was a dress for the girl, and rope, and money and goods and letters and items from past victims. The girl put the dress on and the man roped up the bastard and they walked down a few flights, looking over the town asleep. The shit-covered hero stopped the girl running too far off.

"I gotta look somewhat respectable, people will talk about the fella covered in mess."

The man and the girl looked around and found nothing for water, the girl found a few bottles of whiskey sat around the courtyard and in her innocence assumed the liquid was water. The man poured sweet bourbon over him and washed off the mess wasting his favorite liquid as he went.

"Damn shame."

He cleaned up fast and grabbed his coins, his jingle jangled once more as he and the girl dragged the unconscious bastard of a nervy man through the bar, the stench of alcohol wafting past, an aroma helping to camouflage them in the place, and he sat himself and the girl on his beautiful horse, the tied up man behind him trapped for the journey. They rode out before anyone knew, before dawn came. The man and the girl rode up to the reservation and she screamed out to her family, they came from all tents with excitement and delight at the reunion, they cried and hugged and were happy she was alive, she was safe, she was protected. The man brought out the bastard and he and the girl explained who he was and what happened, and some of the men dragged the man still tied off, to judge on their own land. The mother hugged her daughter and the hero profusely and she offered thanks every second, asking the man to rest the day and feast with them, a celebration before a judgment. He thanked them and held the girl's hand gently.

"The world takes and takes, they don't see you as someone, they see you as something. Show them you're more than that, never let them forget it for a second."

He smiled and let the girl go to her family and hopped on his horse and rode off into the sunrise.

*

The kids of the town more than any recognized Midnight's grand visage on the horizon. The jingle-jangle of coins in Noah Wright's pocket was symphony on the plain. He was the man who rode in around these places, sometimes for a day, sometimes for a week, but more than any around it was the kids who knew every story he starred in and kept them alive, passing them back and forth, adding to them each time. Noah himself listened to their effusive recreations and smiled, relishing the love and fantasies of the youth.

As he rode in he waved at the kids and hitched Midnight near the Sheriff's office and knelt in his dust-weathered outfit to see eye-to-eye with his fans and rub their hair and pat their shoulders. Eventually he sent them back to their homes and headed to attend business in the moment.

"Howdy sheriff, how's things fare ya?" Asked Noah.

Andrew Jones

"Not good Mr. Wright, thank goodness you showed up." The sheriff spoke with worry in his throat.

"I always come about where I'm most needed." Noah's confidence cooled the air.

"Ain't that the truth. We got ourselves a mess of a gang come around here, courting chaos and messing with our people. Leader's a real buggy boy name of Death-hand Driscol, thinks himself The Devil himself, running through our streets and chasing out folk, we just don't have the manpower to handle him and his. Can you help Mr. Wright?"

Noah smiled and nodded at the worried lawman.

"I surely can, don't you worry yourself Sheriff, foolish boys playing in the fire find themselves burned."

Noah walked out of the office and walked Midnight down the street, everyone he passed smiled and felt safer in an instant. They rested outside the saloon and Midnight drank up on water as Noah washed his face from the dry land and welcomed the children excited once more to spend time with their favorite cowboy.

"Is it true you took down three bank robbers with one bullet?"

Noah nodded and laughed.

"Didn't need to shoot anyone, neither. Fired up into the roof, hit the chain on the light and it crashed on all three o'them fools and sorted them out but quick. Crime don't pay, kids."

"Did you and Midnight really stop a runaway train?"

"Midnight here don't need my help stopping a train, he might as coulda roped up the back on his own and ran reverse until the train settled, I just put out the engine fire and freed the carriages to save the passengers. We make a good team."

A shadow loomed over the group and boots hit the ground with quaking amplification.

"Is it true you came to town to get yerself killed?" The voice low and growly, grizzled from years untamed on the country.

Noah looked up and saw Death-hand Driscol, oily and angry with a weak mustache and sweat all on his person, surrounded by some fifty fellas all kids barely grown and lost on the range, just boys playing gang before a legend of the west.

"Driscol, I presume." Noah glared and offered, knowing exactly who the figure thinking himself outlaw was.

"Death-hand, cos this hand here, it delivers only but one thing, and it looks like you've come seekin' that."

Noah stood to match the presence of the many, the kids around sidled away, watching from a distance as the gang enveloped their hero.

"Don't go mistaken' me for some fool who just fell out of the stagecoach, you come square with me and it ain't gonna end well for any y'all."

"This is our town, Wright, even the Sheriff knows that."

Andrew Jones

"Might be you walk in with your many men and yell and shoot at folk to scare 'em into letting you do what you do, but that ends now. Cain't be spookin' me noway, I seen and done things'd make you go home to mommy and weep fer the rest of yer lives."

"Maybe your missin' somethin' here Wright, take a look at my gang, we got some fifty men here."

Noah smiled and nodded.

"Yeah, you're right, it ain't a fair fight. I could give you a few days if you wanna round up more folk."

Driscol grabbed Noah's jacket and pulled him close, the hero of the west could smell the rotten stink of the man's ugly breath.

"You wanna do this, Wright? You and me, at sundown, right here." The proposition echoed through the town, everyone heard the challenge.

"Alright Driscol, we'll handle it then, see your men oblige fair, don't wanna lose a fight to a broken cowboy do ya?"

Driscol pushed Noah away and walked away, the gang followed and the kids came back to cheer their hero and here more stories as Noah Wright watched the men grow smaller in the distance. The sun still shone for a few more hours or peace and tranquillity in the town. Noah took to the saloon proper and raised glass immediately with the crowd, men and women alike came and patted his back and celebrated the heralded return of their hero, come to put good the bad in the world and clear shadows from their life. The doors burst behind all in the saloon and a rotund man with white suit, white beard, white hat and white boots walked in and right up to Noah Wright.

"What you doin' makin' mayhem in my town? As soon as Driscol takes you down he's back on my doorstep and I have less chance makin' amends and seein' to a peaceful negotiation Wright." The Mayor's voice cracked under pressure and his presence a mere fly in Noah's ointment.

The town stepped to the Mayor and backed up Noah.

"He's doin' what you cain't. Finally someone found a spine out here in this land." Called one person wanting to see right done for once.

"Easy folk, the mayor's fair to be riled up, it's tough enough handlin' a town without folk comin' in and out actin' like they own the place, ain't no one man own any place, we all is a part of this together, and should act accordin'." Noah said, making diplomacy in an untamed world.

"Wise words Mr. Wright but you ain't got no stake in our quiet little place, come round here and bring folk need to be jailed, you ain't no hero, just a bounty hunter with a conscience."

Noah stood up, taller than the Mayor could reach, and looked down upon the elected official.

"And that's what separates folk like me from folk like Driscol. I might bring bloodshed, but I don't intend to cause no more than to those that lay the same on others.

Andrew Jones

Your fella and his gang will get what they put out and then some, after that this town is in your hands mayor, and you won't have nobody but yerself to put the blame on when it all goes foul."

    Noah tossed a coin on the bar and told the barkeep to pour one for the mayor, he had to go prepare for the duel. The mayor sank his free drink surrounded by townsfolk angry at him for putting weight on their hero and not supporting him in the fight, and walked out as quick as he could.

    Noah brushed Midnight's fine mane and looked his horse in the eye, the orange embers of eveninglight tapered the sky with magic and warmth, a day so hot starting its nightly chill with a last hug of sun and land. Noah kissed his steed and let the animal lick on his face and hands, two old friends long on the journey together sharing a moment's peace before the world would once more change.

    Noah took his pearl-gripped revolver from its holster by his side and opened to look at the chambers, checking each bullet before putting them back. He popped his hand in his jacket and took out two coins separate from the ones in his pants and rolled them in his hands and held them against the dying light. The reflection of the sun's glow hit the ground and flickered onto the walls, flying into the sky before he pocketed them once more and jingle-jangled his walk from his horse to the street main, where all had evacuated in prep.

The bell of the church began to ring out in the distance and the air of the world seemed to have been sucked out from fear and anticipation of the many. Dead-hand Driscol's shadow reached long as the sun set behind him, the tall, thick man leading the many weedy, nervy lost boys walked slowly up the street, glaring at Noah Wright who squinted into the sun to see.

"Alright Wright, the bell's chimin' fer ya, holster yer gun and prepare yerself for facin' yer maker, in the next few minutes you'll be nothin' more than whispers on the wind not good fer any kid to recite tales of. Just another old fella turned to dust out on the plains." Driscol yelled.

"I gotta hand it to you Driscol, thought you'd fer sure bring your posse to foul up the experience, you're more courageous than you look, and a whole heap dumber." Noah responded.

Driscol grinned a maniacal smile and stood before Noah Wright in the middle of the town.

"Ten paces?"

Noah nodded, they turned and walked a step apiece, looking over their shoulders to make sure each were keeping right and true. Ten steps away, Noah stopped and turned, he could barely see Dead-hand Driscol for the bright kiss of sun and horizon by him, a man lost to light.

"Alright Wright, say yer prayers."

Noah stood, hand hovering over holster, watching the shadow in the sun. In the pause, a light wind blew dust and debris and weed of the desert across, obscuring Noah's sight of his enemy. He squinted harder and saw a glint of light bouncing from metal moving to the right of his aim, and to the left, slightly higher.

    Noah gripped the pearl and fired three shots, smoke rose from his gun and he looked hard in the distance. A figure fell from behind a barrel, another rolled off from a roof, and in the center the man standing dropped to the ground. Noah put three more rounds in his chamber as he walked slowly to the men and listened to the silence of the streets. He came to the men as the sun left only darkness and blue in its wake and saw three young men from the Driscol gang guns gripped to their last breath, but no Dead-hand.

    "Where's yer spine then Driscol? Sendin' boys to fall to my gun instead of facin' me like a real man." Noah Wright imparted as he looked, searched, for his duelling partner.

    Noah stopped and took a breath and heard a hammer click back. He fell to his knee and turned, firing two shots out behind him. Two more young men fell, one screamed in pain, the other already dead.

    "You really wanna do this all night Driscol? Go down the last of your men or come out like a real leader."

    Noah was on the ground, looking back to the darkness of town and all the alleys and roofs men could be hiding. He put fingers to his mouth and whistled. Midnight let out a whinny and ran through, guns blazed as he ran past each alley and from roofs. Noah shot and reloaded and shot at each blast of smoke and bullet and men came falling, in pain and dead from their positions hidden, and Noah jumped onto Midnight's saddle. He patted his horse and looked at the roofs from his heightened position.

"How many ya got Driscol? How many you willin' to let go? I'm still here, I'm still standin'."

Noah walked Midnight slowly down the street, looking into the alleys and hidey-holes. No more popped out as he passed the fallen and looked at them, all young men thin and lost to the world. They reminded him of something, someone, somewhere.

Noah Wright rode Midnight through town. He saw in the windows of buildings townsfolk peering out with trepidation, hoping the man with the pearl-grip gun would rinse their town of this infestation this night. He nodded with a touch to the brim of his hat as he passed, keeping eyes open in the blue haze of twilight, listening beyond the crunches of Midnight's hooves on the dirt street seeking Driscol's men and an end to all disaster on civility in the west.

He passed a window and saw movement reflected, Noah turned to see the action when a shot rung out. He felt warm pain hit his side and fired, Midnight picked up speed and ran off as Noah shot and shot and shot until the revolver clicked. The dust kicked up and the smoke of the guns gave cover for an escape as Noah sat properly on his steed and touched his new wound.

"Gorram." He muttered, wheezed a little.

Noah squeezed the bullet from his side and clutched his shirt to the wound as it bled lightly, dropping onto the ground below, and let his fabric mop up the

Andrew Jones

mess. Noah padded his pockets for bullets and found two more, loading them up and spinning the chamber. He patted Midnight to slow and behind the buildings he leapt off his horse and rolled into a crouch walk, listening to the footsteps of the gang.

"The horse went that'a'way." One of Driscol's men called out.

Men ran past and chased Midnight, he poked his head out to see them go and looked from whence they came, seeing Dead-hand Driscol standing above his dead gang members, firing into the air and laughing manically.

"So long Noah Wright, your story ends with a whimper. Look upon me, townsfolk, I have defeated your intrepid hero. Ain't nothin' to stop me now."

"Oh really?"

Noah fired into the dark and Driscol yelped in pain as his right hand exploded from bullet hit, his gun dropped to the ground and on impact fired another into the air. Driscol grabbed his bad hand and looked to Noah Wright coming from the back of the buildings, as the town watched the wounded hero come up on their malicious monster.

"You think you'll kill me and that'll be the end? All my men will tear you asunder, you shoot me now, they'll come runnin' back and won't leave you alive to see mornin' light."

Noah put his gun to Driscol's head and heard the rumbling of footsteps coming closer.

"There's been many like you round these parts, Driscol, and many fallen before. You may not be the last, but your time always comes round, more than those who fight for what's right, you selfish beasts swallow each-other up until there ain't no more left to eat."

Driscol sneered one last smile into the night as he looked at Noah Wright, the gang came around and held guns to the hero.

"Let him go. Or we'll kill ya."

"What now hero?" Driscol sneered with his breath stinking of rot and pain and blood and evil.

Noah closed his eyes and heard in the air the sound of rain hailing fast. He looked up and saw glimmers in the dark. Bullets rained down on the gang, from up on high the bullets of Dead-hand Driscol crashed back to Earth ripping through every boy saddled with their leader. Driscol's grin turned.

"Move you fools, run." Driscol yelled.

But it was too late, all had fallen to his Dead-hand, and Driscol was on his knees looking upon his entire gang wiped out. He looked at the pearl-grip in Noah's hand.

"Do it, then, kill me, wipe me out, let everyone see how much of a monster you are."

Noah shook his head and lifted his gun to the sky. He fired the last bullet into the air.

"I suggest you run. Give you two minutes."

Dead-hand Driscol looked up into the sky and got to his feet, he was sweating and yelped and ran away fast. Townsfolk came out and cheered, Noah whistled for his horse and Midnight came. He looked to the mayor and the Sheriff.

Andrew Jones

"Come on folk, let's go round up the Driscol gang." The Sheriff called out.

Men cheered and saddled up and together the town went and grabbed Dead-hand Driscol and brought him to jail. The man would rot until the governor came to personally execute the vermin of the county, but Noah Wright and Midnight would not wait to witness. The next morning, after being seen to by the doctor, celebrated by the town. And regaled once more by the children, Noah Wright and Midnight rode off into the land, and were never seen again.

*

The land closed in around, the sound of water ceased and any lakes dried in the heat and merciless strangulation of roads and rail and buildings and townships and civilization as it was called by settlers firming their foundation on places now inhabited more and more by those not from near. The uncertainty was cleared and in its place a certainty of ownership and expansion, those that had accrued further and those without continued to be hitched to the wagon of subjugation, the freedom and possibility lost once more to the inevitable structures and hierarchy of power that borne time and time again in known sentient civilizations. It was as it was and always ended up being. The opportunity for change gone completely for the sanctity of the known.

The Ferryman Upon The Plains

  The man was a misnomer in the horizon always, riding on his struggling horse as the years wore on, never settling, never speaking, always onto the next place but never the final place. The noises from his ride were jingling of metal, coughing of lung and gasp of horse in its last years of strength. Folk paid no mind to him or his never-ending journey, a fly on the carcass beaten by sun and rotting slowly in the endless land.
  It was a night cold in the eternal plain, a fire barely burning against the battering of the desert breeze, frost in the air and the man rested himself with a rock for a pillow. He had let his face lose to the hairs breaking from inside, keeping cover in the harshest of seasons, and warmed his insides with deep breaths of leaf crushed and rolled and burnt and inhaled, he hadn't much more time for liquid insulation but in lighter form it still served purpose, even as he coughed each exhale out into the cold air above. He listened to the whistle of the wind and the crackle of the fire consuming its wood, a clarity fell upon him and in the dark he saw beyond the world as it was, in the firelight and inky black of starless night he felt shivers not from chill flow through, eyes descended upon him from elsewhere, familiar gaze each, from blood and from the heart all. He was certain this was a welcome return with open arms after all had been and all was said, he laid down and looked up and listened to the crackle and the whistle and waited for his soul to fly beyond and join those looking down. Instead, loudly collapsing by his side went the horse, a slight gasp and a gust of wind against the breeze that flickered the fire into darkness for a moment. He looked to his side at his companion all these

Andrew Jones

years and put his arm on the gasping creature, breathing hard and heavy, and massaged its face and brushed its mane with softness and love. They looked into one-another's eyes as the creature slowed its panic and relaxed into the final breaths, and the man held his beloved close and breathed slow with the horse, turning desert wet with his eyes until both he and the horse closed and held close and he kept breathing slow and the horse stopped for its last. He lay cuddling his companion into the sunrise and the burning embers floated skyward and the fire was just white and ash, and he knew he had to continue on with those looking down now grown in number once again. He knew not where he was to ramble, his speed reduced and his destination foggy, but in his heart he had a sense to return somewhat to the place he always knew he was meant to be. He tried for a day to break the cold hard ground and commit his companion to the rites of his family and all before, but alas it wasn't to be, the world refused to give. He kissed his passed goodbye and shuffled his wounded knee and broken body onward, the animal would give itself to the land and keep it alive a little longer.

*

    Noah Wright walked slowly through the world, the years grew long as his beard, he watched in reflections of water and glass his face

The Ferryman Upon The Plains

wrinkle and his hair thin, though taller than his father he couldn't help but see more and more of Samwell Wright in his eyes and his stubborn insistence to continue onward, he became older in this lost land than his father was when they last crossed paths. He collapsed with his tricky knee in one town and the doctor saw to him swiftly, checking the wounds all across his failing body, wounds accumulated and unchecked too long blackening the skin and internals, his cough a worry too. He insisted on continuing on when the doc begged his rest, and despite all hope the doc gave Noah Wright a stick to keep balance on the path further and waved him off as was hit eternal wont. Coaches and horses and trains and grand buildings tall and wires strong against the elements became daily and trapped the beauty and wonder of the world in cages around their encroachment, where Noah Wright was comfortably situated as he let his boots break away from further wear and tear, he couldn't find reason to rest in the towns and meet the people, he was just another old stranger with no place to settle and nobody wanting to talk to him. Stories and tales fell away into myth and legend and instead talk was turned to magic and fantasy and possibility of the world built up, science and human invention took over from fighting the old and making safe land untamable. It was tame, it was fought, all was safe except the new, and that was exciting, not terrifying, and was embraced even beyond the reaches of the rails. Noah Wright was a relic walking.

He shuffled through a dry land sweating from the beating sun, wiping his brow and matting down the wispy

Andrew Jones

hair on his head that seemed thinner each and every day. Noah stepped to the edge and looked down a deep slope to a dry expanse, he looked up and down and saw shade south, a tree grown grand in the deep emptiness and a wooden bridge above and covering the width of the land's groove to the beyond. Noah carefully made his way down and leaned on the trunk of the tree, breathing in the hidden cool from the sun's beat, the leaves plentiful and green and offering apples bigger than the old man's fist, he plucked one from its branch and bit in. The spittle of tooth and flesh cooled the air and he chomped calmly into the sweet gift of the tree as he sat under its protection, looking out to the dirt rising on either side, back and beyond. He groaned as he got back up and prepared for another long walk, but first gently patted the bark and thanked the tree for all its kindness and aid, taking sticks for kindling and pocketing them. Noah Wright walked with the sun on his back and climbed up the dirt to a silent world of dry grass and dirt paths unused for years, and looked at the other side of the bridge strong and stable. He looked back over the gap from this side and felt something strangely familiar in his stomach. He stood for a moment and closed his eyes and listened to the wind lapping up at the ground and the gap beyond, with no calls of bird or deer or rabbit or snake, just the breeze flowing and leaving swiftly. The weight in his coat pulled him a little and he gripped his cane to balance and slipped hand into his pocket, feeling the two coins separate from all others and they almost burned in the heat. Noah turned and continued onward.

    The evening fell on the land and he continued, almost instinctively he walked east and north, putting the sun to his back and his side, he'd felt that angle many a time but not much for a while, it was familiar in warmth and bright, but he couldn't place it. Noah felt his knee tricky each step, a wobble on his foot and he clutched hard the stick as he put weight upon it and swung further onward, and in the distance he looked up and saw in the encroaching darkness of summer's night a cross in the sky and a building of stone silent below, atop a hill that he felt he must climb. He pushed up the way, following a path long since used frequently and rested at the door of the chapel. He knocked a few at the wood and heard echo from inside, but nothing came. He wandered around and sat before stones sticking from the ground but in the lightless world could make nothing of the etchings upon them. He closed his eyes with the understanding inside his lids was as clear and bright as outside and grabbed the sticks in his pocket and pulled them out, rubbing fast and hard until through his skin he could see red and orange and felt heat burn as if the sun's setting state was permanent.

    Noah looked upon the grave markings with his light and saw names from long before. Before him was planted Paul and Mary Westington, one lived into their sixties and the other saw her nineties well kept and loved before finding the ground her forever home. He touched the stone and gently caressed the ground and moved to the next, Lucy, Christopher and Jacob Augustine, the

Andrew Jones

husband and father outlived all, kept the world alive when it was dying many a time. Noah pressed his head to the stone and whispered love and kindness down and to the heavens and continued, his stomach sinking as he stood above familiar ground. He waved the light over the stone and caught glimpse of the word Wright and closed his eyes, he blew at the flame and began to weep onto the dry ground as the darkness ate the last flickers of fire and laid atop the ground his family rested below. He took his jacket off and made a pillow from it and rested above, crying and coughing, once more with his family. The night enveloped and he slept released from pain.

    Sir, you got some place to be?
    Noah opened his eyes and the sun beamed in the new day's sky, silhouetting the lawman standing before him, looking down.
    Sir?
    Noah squinted and coughed and in the light's glimmer could see in the man's holster a grip of pearl like the one he carried, he looked to the face and couldn't much make clarity. He slowly rose and on his aged body found himself just a little shorter than the lawman before him.
    Can we take ya somewhere?
    Noah raised one hand empty and open and slowly showed his gun's grip to the lawman.
    Where'd you get yerself that?
    My pa.

The Ferryman Upon The Plains

The lawman put his gun's grip next to Noah's and saw they matched.

Goddamn, you'se one of us.

Noah nodded, still finding nothing of the man's face in the bright glare of sun.

Is you Jenny and Bartholomew's boy?

The lawman nodded and brought Noah close and held him.

Shit, takes forty years but I finally got me an uncle. Guess I cain't lock you up for disturbin' the peace or doin' voodoo shit on these-here graves then.

Noah smiled and put his gun back.

I know this land well, but heck if I couldn't make hind nor hair of these here new stones.

New stones? Hell, they been around almost as long as me, since the flood wiped all out had to make markers stronger, some ended up for many to fill in the spots of families and the like.

The lawman walked past Noah and stood before another stone, he touched it sweetly and closed his eyes, Noah could see the man rough-skinned and tan from life out in the sun, not like Jenny's complexion, but hair burnt brown and red. Noah stared at the lawman as he turned to look at his uncle once more.

You paid yer respects too?

Noah nodded and squinted, he couldn't see his brother in the boy who was already a man older than his own father ever made it, and he couldn't see sweet Jenny there neither, the man with a badge and a pearl-gripped gun was a mystery before him.

Andrew Jones

Come ride with me, let's get you some food and a nice place to rest, on me.

Noah nodded slowly, taking in the visage of the future he never knew he'd see.

Where's my manners, uncle, you don't never know me didya? I'm Bill.

Bill Wright held his hand for his uncle to shake, Noah placed his long, thin fingers into the grasp of the man and was brought close for a long undue hug. He breathed in the smell of his nephew, it didn't smell familiar either, a distinct mix of tobacco and mint on the man's breath. He freed himself from the connection and followed his nephew to his horse and sat behind, they rode away from the church and down the hill and through the empty lands where once Cranham existed, now long desolate.

Where'd it all go?

All what?

This town?

Ain't been no place here for many years, flood came and wiped out half the state what I was told, settled further from the water, before the river ran itself dry, nearer to the railway, easier to keep life lived with the comin's and goin's of the trains.

They rode on, Noah looked at the land eerie and alien from all he grew up and all he fondly recalled, as he looked at his nephew a full grown man before him handling business as natural as anything.

The Ferryman Upon The Plains

They rode into the town after some fifty minutes and the sound of the train whistle gave welcome to their arrival, and many others from the carriages. Bill settled the horse outside the Sheriff's office and helped the older Mr. Wright off and walked him in, sat him down and poured a couple of cups of coffee for the two.

You the Sheriff round these parts then?

Hell no, still a deputy twenty years goin' now, Sheriff Bell's been law since always, he's got the ear of the mayor and a seat on the governor's shoulder and that's thus how it'll be until someone younger and just as comfy heedin' their calls comes by. I'm not for politicking, happy to make the days safer and see to them what live in this place. That, alas, don't make for good leadership in their eyes. Bell wins the election and I just take my pay and keep the balance best possible for all those wanna live round here.

Your pa and I, we often talked bout seein' the world, getting out of around here, not that we could with the river and the ferry to be kept and manned all hours, he'd have wanted you to explore, to discover.

I didn't know him, cain't say to have disappointed him by stickin' by ma's side all these years until her last. Someone had to, she deserved as much, hell she deserved more. You saw the world though, I guess, was it worth it? Find anything out there?

Noah shook his head and sipped the warm drink.

Everytime you think you escape the shackles, you discover another chain wrapped around. All is illusory,

Andrew Jones

the dream is only ever meant to be, cain't live like we're meant to, none of us. Not forever.

    Well if you wanna stay for a while we'd welcome ya, got no space at mine of course but since Jessie left to Chicago and Hannah crossed our threshold Mr. and Mrs. Maclaine have had spare to board, I'm sure they'd welcome an old friend for a few.

    I ain't stickin' round, not much left on the clock, so much more to see to, best be makin' tracks and swift.

    They finished drinks and Bill helped Noah stand and walked him out into the bustling town, nodding and smiling to folk as they passed by. He offered his uncle some money for the journey but Noah rejected the charity and shook his hand and shuffled off away from the last of the blood he knew of.

    Noah sat patiently on a hard wood chair looking backwards out the window as the train began to chug and jump and move on from Fort Oak station, unrecognizable to the old man who had come in his youth to collect supplies with his mom and see the men in formation and uniform prove rigid structure in a world of formless desire. It flitted away in a blur as the train picked up speed and soon the land became desert and the sun moved west and on his back as he watched the shadows grow and the night chased his view.

The Ferryman Upon The Plains

California called and the train pulled in to the final station, the lapping sounds of distant ocean and the golden hue of the sun blazed the sky in yellow and blue magic, many came from the carriages and breathed in the wondrous air clear and pristine and listened to the seabirds cawing and the bells of the church rang to celebrate new life. Noah left his hard seat and took time moving his joints, his aching body, from the vehicle, coughing with each step. He held out and watched many find transport for their own destinations and stood in the sound of the eternal water beyond until a wagon came to offer ride north. He sat in the back, with a few others on their way up, and listened to the rickety wheels trundle at speed as the hooves of the horse kicked up dirt on its sprint. He coughed some more and let his hurt leg sprawl out in the back, rubbing it to soothe the aches and pains. For a day he sat and watched folk hop off and on and heard bells chime for all manner of towns and settlements, but it wasn't quite the tone he felt in his heart. He closed his eyes as the sun beat on the cover and danced on his lids with red and orange in the darkness of his skin. He drifted away for a while in the hypnotizing magic of light and shadow and awoke to the toll of a bell familiar to his deepest dreams, he peered out and saw beautiful buildings of white stone majestic in their simple form, and he was drawn back to many years hence and that one chance he let go. Noah left the wagon and handed a few coins, he was nearly depleted of change, he felt the two coins still in his jacket weighing him down, the last of his worldlies.

Andrew Jones

    Noah walked to church and saw the town together and sat at the back to listen to the man preach in two languages, floating through them with ease and the many not lost at any step, if not understanding language then meaning and emotion was clear enough. The plate was passed around, Noah took out his pearl-grip and placed it heavy atop the plate and passed it away beyond. He watched as folk walked out and greeted their spiritual leader and he followed a small group to a house near the coast and knocked on the door nearly as soon as they closed it to the world. A man in his middle age opened and stared at the old man and asked what he wanted.
    Paul Hollander?
    Who's asking?
    You may not remember me, I took you and your ma and your aunt across the land when you was tiny, kept y'all safe as best I could.
    Paul shook his head and shrugged.
    I wasn't much more than a babe, sorry sir. D'you want to come in and eat? Lunch will be ready shortly, you're more than welcome.
    Noah nodded and Paul welcomed him to the home, sat him at the table and offered a drink. Noah took a little glass of water all he needed and asked about his mother. Paul sipped a glass of whiskey and poured a second and sat opposite the guest. Two young girls not older than seven came and hugged their pa and sat on his lap and held him close.

The Ferryman Upon The Plains

She lived with us for a while, until I was ten, then she did what she always wanted to do and took off. Left me with Aunt Sissy. She met a man in Oregon, they had themselves a life up there, he had kids already lost their mom and she seemed happy taking the role of wife and mother out among nature, best of all worlds. Ma passed on a couple years back, lived a good, long, happy life. I miss her, sure, but I got my girls, and Aunt Sissy's more my mother than she ever could be.

Noah smiled at the image of the man and his family surrounding in warmth and love and happiness and ate with them, Paul's wife and Aunt Sissy who didn't recall him from their adventures either. They hugged him each warmly as he left and thanked him for all he did, he shuffled away from the house and took one last look back at the family still going strong all these years and walked on.

Noah Wright sat on the beach looking out to the setting sun over the eternal water, the orange of the last of day reflecting and shimmering on the waves cresting across the infinite horizon, and in the dark of night encroaching behind he felt the starry sky of many souls eternal and forever looking down, and felt the weight and burning of the coins in his pocket. He laid on the sand, his right side to the ocean listening to the waves crashing nearby and closed his eyes and put the two coins on his lids, no more light breaking through the skin and dancing despite. He listened to the water coming closer, and felt the cooling air of the evening and in the total darkness saw them all once more. The coins were light. The tide lapped onto Noah's body. His soul already left

Acknowledgements

Johnny – The long-suffering friend and confidante, through worst and sometimes not-worst, you've kept me going, kept me from the edge, and somehow not ghosted me in the process. I'm a lucky person to have you by my side, even from a country away.

Carla & Brian – My found-sister and quiz compadres, kind souls giving time and love and offering positivity and an ear when things spiralled (and if you've read this far, you can be certain when things spiralled). Bless you both, my next one might not be so daunting, maybe even fun.

Carl – The writer's writer, a man who knows so much about the process, the act and the reasons we put ourselves deep in the woods to plot our way out. You've raised my game through conversations and discoveries and got me back on the reading kick, you made this happen, this book wouldn't be a book without you.

Jamie – A visionary, a friend and a true artist. You threw me some bones in the deepest and darkest, I delivered little but it got me back to where I needed to go, and our mutual love of genre was the push to build this beast.

Mother & Father, The Brother, Sister-In-Law and The Boys– The backbone, the shelter, the mess sometimes but the hope and connection as the world isolated before, during and after. Three generations together, seeing everything as a unit. I hope I can achieve to be the best uncle, if not the best brother and son. One out of three isn't too bad.

Ivan & Aileen, Janis & David, Eoin, Jonathan O, Mark H, Darren, Team Endgame (Ben, Edan, Kinte, Mike, Mark, Tom), Ben, Kayleigh & Jackie, Tara, Becky, Christa, Hannah, David B, Odd, Julie, Lars, Ted, Jonathan S, Jake, Clive, Robert, Paul, George, The TMOA Team, Sarah O'C, Simon, Marc P, Ian M, Richard S, Bradley P, Nile, Nick, Alessandro, Ian, Marc & Becky, Will & Kevin & The Best Bits Discord. At different times over the years you've been there, in person or on the screen, in the daytime or the bleakest of insomnias, for laughs or distractions, or spending hours at events, or hanging out watching weird media, or just putting out material for our edification.

And of course, the most wonderful podcaster himself **Paul Giamatti**. Maybe adding this might make our worlds collide.

About The Author

Andrew Jones is a writer. This book proves that. Get off his back, he achieved something. He has been a journalist in the film and TV realm around the time that streaming services took over and access to artists became harder, and money too sparse.

He moved over to editing trailers for a year that involved getting thumbs up from the likes of Marty S, Sir Ian McKellen & Sir Kenneth Branagh and spent 6 months with Dreamworks' Trolls, yet still enjoys that Timberlake song. It is a bop.

As a screenwriter he has one short film produced (credit not on screen but payment was given), an award-winning screenplay that cannot seem to get its foot into the door of anyone with money and many ideas half-finished.

For now he'll turn anything he can into a book, I guess, it's easier to do that alone than make a movie, turns out you need more than one person who care to make one of those.

Printed in Great Britain
by Amazon